ACKNOWLEDGEMENTS

Deep thanks must go to my beta readers and biggest fans,
Nic Page and Rachel Cass.
Their generosity in being my first readers for The People's Princess
and their enthusiasm for my words are inspirational. Thanks also to
these ladies for their critical feedback during cover creation.

To Duncan Carling-Rodgers for his assistance during the edits of
The People's Princess and for the formatting.

To Dar Albert for her stunning cover.

To my husband, Michael, my sons, and their ladies for their
unending love and support and for sharing in the disappointments
and triumphs of a writing life.

Titles by Bernadette Rowley

(in suggested reading order)

Princess Avenger - Queenmakers Saga I

The Lady's Choice - Queenmakers Saga II

Princess in Exile - Queenmakers Saga III

The Lord and the Mermaid - Queenmakers Saga IV

The Elf King's Lady - Queenmakers Saga V

The Lady and the Pirate - Queenmakers Saga VI

The Master and the Sorceress - Queenmakers Saga VII

Elf Princess Warrior - Queenmakers Saga VIII

The People's Princess - Queenmakers Saga IX

THE PEOPLE'S PRINCESS
QUEENMAKERS SAGA IX

BY
BERNADETTE ROWLEY

Table of Contents

CHAPTER 1

ALECIA came awake, a ragged scream tearing at her ears. She was in bed, the room in darkness, and, as the echoes of the scream died, her panting breaths grew louder. Where was she? Iona! She had dreamed of Iona in the clutches of a wolf's teeth. *Vard.* It was Vard!

She sobbed as she pulled at the covers and pushed herself out of bed. Her feet hit the softness of an expensive rug, and her brain froze. Where was she? And Iona? Alecia halted, trying to calm her breathing and still her mind which rang from the scream.

Deep breath! Calm... She closed her eyes and took in several slow, deep breaths, then opened them. There was the faintest light in the room. It was dawn. The outlined window was large, much more so than the farmhouse she was used to. *Think!* A snuffle came from her right, and she looked that way, finally seeing the vague outline of a crib.

Iona was alive and with her. In Brightcastle! It all flooded back—the long journey from the western farm of her exile, and her arrival yesterday, cloaked to disguise her disgrace. She had no notion how the single mother, daughter of the late Prince Jiseve Zialni, would be seen by the populace—her people. Would they judge her? *Probably.*

She took a deep breath and walked over to the crib. It was growing light enough to see her daughter's face. Now five months old, Iona's dark hair was long enough to rest on her pillow. She touched the baby's soft cheek, and her daughter's eyes opened to reveal the deep blue irises and gilt flecks. The child was almost certainly a Defender, just like her father, destined to protect the weak, and with the ability to shift into animal form.

Iona squawked and beat her little fists on the mattress, a sure sign she was hungry.

"Come on then!" Alecia lifted her from the crib and carried her to the rocking chair in the corner of the room. Soon Iona's noisy slurps filled the chamber and Alecia released a long sigh. Feeding Iona never failed to bring peace to her soul.

But the peace was soon replaced by memories of the nightmare. Flashes of it returned. The terrible dark wolf, its fangs in her daughter's neck; so much blood and the beast's golden eyes staring at her without recognition. She knew it was Vard, but why? Why would she dream such a thing? Or was it a *true* dream, destined to become reality?

Since Vard left her when Iona was a month old, she hadn't dreamed of him at all. Prior to that, the dreams had come when he was in animal form—but now? Perhaps it was just a result of the stress of arriving in Brightcastle yesterday and her reflections on Vard and his search for mastery of the bear. But why the wolf form, then?

She looked down at Iona. "We'll be fine, Daughter. No one will hurt you, I promise."

Iona smiled around her breast, an action which always made Alecia overflow with love and protectiveness. Her baby didn't have a care in the world beyond her next feed and a dry bottom. She smiled again and went back to her meal with renewed vigor.

There was a knock at the door, and Alecia groaned. It was too early for the maid. She detached Iona from the breast and fixed her dress, then crossed to the outer door.

Ramón Zorba, Guardian of Brightcastle, stood in the hallway, fist raised, ready to knock again. Had he heard her screams? Or did he just have more questions than their brief discussion of yesterday had answered?

"What happened?" he demanded, blue eyes wide, blond locks fighting their way from their restraint at his nape. "There were reports of screaming. Was it you?"

"I'm quite alright," Alecia snapped, feeling a blush creeping up her neck. "I had a dream."

He stepped into the room, and she pressed her lips to stop a groan of protest. It was too early for this, surely?

"While I'm here," he said, "I wanted to speak to you about my wife. Please don't be hard on her. Benae's had it tough for months, what with the pregnancy and then her babe being sickly. She needs a friend, not another enemy."

"What do you mean, 'another enemy'?"

Ramón frowned. "Nothing, it was just a slip of the tongue."

"You expect me to be friendly with the woman who married my father and watched him die? I think you ask too much!"

Iona squawked and she hushed her. Ramón reached for the child, and she let him take her. Iona gurgled at him and tried to grab the strands of long blond hair that had escaped from his band.

"She looks just like her father," he said. "Where is he, by the way?"

She huffed out a breath, then met his troubled gaze. "He left four months ago."

Alecia had awoken one morning to find Vard with Iona clutched to his chest. He was saying "goodbye". Something must have scared him, made him fear harming his daughter. Tears returned at the memory, and she brushed them away.

Ramón shook his head. "It's not right. You shouldn't be on your own."

"He believes we're better off without him."

"And what do *you* believe?"

She gulped down a sob. "I don't know what to think anymore. I've given him so many chances. But I still love him. I hope that, one day, we can be together and safe."

"You have no pride!"

Alecia straightened her shoulders and met his angry gaze. "What's pride when your family is threatened? If you had a child, you might better understand!"

He flinched at her words, which she took to mean she'd struck her target. How dare he attack her for making the best of a horrible situation? He knew what she'd been through this last year.

He handed Iona back. "I understand better than you think, and I still believe you're giving him more credit than he deserves. I saw the *man* he was when I brought him back to you last summer—against my better judgment. You deserve much more!"

"I don't wish to discuss this with you." she said. "Please have breakfast sent up. Then I want to meet your wife."

She turned to the bedroom and heard the door close as Ramón left. How dare he condemn her? *How dare he?*

Once she finished breakfast, Alecia put Iona into her crib and gave instructions to the nursemaid who had been allocated to her. She dressed in the only black gown she could find amongst her old gowns and brushed her long blonde hair until it shone. The dark of the gown made a startling contrast to the lilac of her eyes.

As she wandered through the castle, memories returned of happy family events, as well as sad times like the death of her mother, but the place felt foreign after more than a year away.

She heard voices and followed them, coming across a petite brunette, who she realized must be Benae Zorba, giving instructions to a stout woman with a large ring of keys on her belt.

Alecia paused on the threshold of the modest reception room, observing the woman who had won her father's heart. Benae appeared to be only a couple of years older than Alecia herself, perhaps only twenty-seven?

She was beautiful, with vibrant green eyes and a musical voice. As she conversed with the housekeeper, her hands moved gracefully. She had a ready smile. And then Benae's gaze found Alecia, and her face transformed. She stopped mid-sentence; her eyes narrowed as she studied the newcomer.

"That will be all, Mistress Elison."

The servant bowed and left, nodding to Alecia as she exited. Alecia stepped across the threshold and closed the door behind her. She had anticipated this meeting for months, had played it over in her mind more times than she could count.

"Lady Benae, I presume," Alecia said.

Benae nodded. "Although I go by 'Princess' now. I'm pleased to meet you, Alecia."

"I wish I could say the same, Benae."

The woman frowned. "There's no need for us to be enemies, Your Highness. We must make the most of a difficult situation."

"That will be hard, to say the least," Alecia said. "Imagine how startled I was to discover my father had married a stranger."

Benae stepped closer, her hands outstretched. "It must have been tough."

"My father married to a woman barely older than myself? It's a scandal. How did you win his heart? What did you promise? My father loved my mother and would never have betrayed her memory!"

Alecia turned and strode to the window, but her attention wasn't on the view. Her mind played the scenes of betrayal, and her anger grew.

"I know it's hard to accept," Benae said, "but Jiseve was lonely. He needed someone to share his life, and he wanted a son to carry on the Zialni line. I could supply both. We could've been good together."

"And now you're with Ramón. When did that start?"

"After your father died, of course. What do you think I am? And Ramón! He's too honorable to have betrayed the prince."

Alecia faced her stepmother and shook her head. "I struggle to believe you. Tell me how you came to marry my father!"

Benae invited her to sit and offered tea.

Alecia refused. "Just tell me what happened."

"The call went out for eligible women to present themselves in Brightcastle as potential wives of the prince. I was in a bind. My parents and brother were dead, and my estate poverty-stricken. I didn't know where my next penny would come from. The dark elves threatened not only my estate but those around us. I had few choices, so I traveled to Brightcastle.

"Jiseve was instantly attracted to me, even though I was last to arrive. The other women appeared unsuited to him. In only days, he proposed, and we became betrothed."

"So romantic," Alecia offered, sarcastically. "And I suppose the marriage was equally rushed?"

"Jiseve couldn't wait to start his new life."

Benae appeared uncomfortable, but was her discomfort natural or did it hide some untruth? She couldn't imagine her father with this woman. He surely possessed more self-esteem than to announce a competition to win a bride. Didn't he?

"What went wrong?" Alecia asked.

"Nothing went wrong!" Benae protested. "The king and queen attended the wedding. We had their blessing. It was a wonderful event."

"Then you set to fulfilling your obligation as a wife? To give the kingdom another heir?"

"It was my duty."

"Did you love my father?"

Silence filled the room. As the seconds ticked by, Alecia had her answer. Of course, Benae hadn't loved him. He was a means to an end. A way to save her estate and gain power she would never have otherwise. And now the woman was Guardian of Brightcastle and a princess. It made Alecia sick to the toes.

"You don't need to answer," she said. "I can see how it was. How long after the wedding did my father die?"

"It was less than three weeks." Benae wrung her hands. "He was taking drugs for fertility, and they weakened his heart. I had no idea. If you only knew what I went through!"

"*How* did he die?" Alecia was like a boulder rolling downhill.

Benae's fingers bunched in her skirts, and her cheeks flamed. "He died in the act! His heart gave out, and he collapsed on me. There was nothing I could do to save him! *Nothing*!"

"What's going on in here?" Ramón's voice sliced through the room. "I can hear you both all over the castle." Benae rose as he approached, and he placed his arm around her waist.

"I'm getting to the heart of what happened in my absence." Alecia stood with her hands on her hips. "*I'm* mourning my father, which is more than I can say for his widow. For all I know, she drove him into an early grave. Where is *her* mourning black?"

Ramón shook his head. "Princess, trust me. There's nothing untoward. You're upsetting Benae and I won't tolerate it. She's been through a lot."

Alecia couldn't believe her ears. "*She's* been through a lot? She didn't love him! I've lost my father. I've lost my home and my people. And I'd like to know what you plan to do about it."

Ramón released Benae and took a step toward Alecia. "There's nothing to be done. Your uncle, King Beniel, declared us Brightcastle's guardians. We'll continue in those positions until he says otherwise. And we will raise the new heir to the throne—Benae's son."

Alecia froze, unable to take all the information in. Benae had a *son*. He would inherit the kingdom, and Alecia's dreams of being a warrior queen would be ashes.

"I want to see my... brother."

She stood before the infant boy, now three months old, and tried to resist the emotion that fought its way from deep within her. *Love.*

She hadn't expected to feel this for a child she had never met. Considering her feelings for Benae, shouldn't she resent the child, even hate him for the power he had given his mother? But—he was her father's son... her half-brother. They were connected by a blood bond there was no escaping. She'd lay down her life to protect him. How could she dream of making this child pay for his mother's sins?

Alecia wiped a tear from her eye and traced a finger along the boy's downy cheek. Golden hair framed his face like a heavenly halo. She wondered what color his eyes were—blue... or green like his mother?

Her heart thumped in her chest. This small, fragile life carried the hopes of the kingdom—this tiny mite and the king's other nephew, Piotr.

Alecia was not an heir at all because she was female. And Iona wouldn't be considered either, female and illegitimate as she was. One day it would not be so, but, for now, her daughter was not wanted; not needed.

"What's his name?" she whispered.

"Solomon Daire Zialni," Ramón said. "He is to be a king, so Benae wanted something grand."

"It certainly is that." Alecia wondered if the child could live up to the name. "He will need to keep the peace and produce many children, or he'll be a laughing-stock."

Ramón snorted softly. "I hardly think the populace will expect that. It was more the sound of the name than the meaning Benae was aiming for."

She drew Ramón away from the crib. "He's beautiful, but you must be on guard. His life is under threat from many quarters."

Ramón bristled. "You've been back all of ten minutes, and already you think you know more than I how to care for this child. We know the risks. That's why King Beniel named Benae and me joint guardians. He trusts we'll care for his heir and for the principality."

Alecia drew herself up. "Then what guards do you have stationed around Solomon? I noticed none when I entered."

He swallowed. "No one gets in here without me or Benae knowing about it. I assure you, your brother is safe."

"I'm not so sure, but I intend to see that he is protected."

And that my people know who has their best interests at heart…

She returned to her chambers to discover Iona awake and fussing; the nanny was having trouble settling her. Alecia dismissed the woman and sat down to nurse the child. She settled quickly once suckling, as did Alecia. However, as much as the baby calmed her, nothing could stop her mind from churning through the next steps she must take.

Brightcastle was unprepared. The region needed more vigilant leadership. She would see Hetty and assess what needed to be done.

CHAPTER 2

IT felt like old times. Alecia disguised herself as a man—her long golden locks concealed by a woolen hood, wearing breeches and a shirt, with the lot covered by her serviceable forest green cloak. Leaving Iona with her nanny, she took the servants' stairs to the kitchen. She exited the castle grounds via the side gate and headed into town.

Periodically, Alecia touched the knives concealed about her person. It calmed her to know she had weapons at hand if accosted. She must be ready for anything. There was an air of brooding watchfulness in the town, as if the people waited for something. She didn't understand what caused it. Perhaps Hetty would have light to shed on Brightcastle's mood.

Using backstreets and alleys, Alecia made her way to Hetty's home. The old woman was a witch, but had been Alecia's nanny and governess. That ended when her father accused Hetty of witchcraft.

Her heart raced at the memory of her friend tied to a stake in the center of town, flames lapping at her feet. Alecia had disguised herself then and rescued Hetty, but not before the woman sustained serious burns.

But today was not that day, and Hetty was safe. Alecia entered Firedrake Alley and turned right into the lane that ran past Hetty's front door. Nothing had changed in the months since Alecia had fled Brightcastle, yet everything had. She raised her hand to knock, but hesitated. Would Hetty judge her for being an unwed mother? Would she scold her for returning? Might she have information regarding her father that Alecia would rather not hear?

Never mind. She knocked and waited. The door swung inward, revealing her old friend, unchanged from the woman who had helped her escape from the mercenary called "The Devil". She pulled Alecia inside and slammed the door behind her.

"Hetty!" Alecia cried, and hurled herself into her friend's bony arms. "It's so good to see you. I thought this day would never come!"

"You're a sight for sore eyes, girl." Hetty wrapped her arms around Alecia and patted her back. "You look well."

"I'm better for seeing you." Alecia drew away and held Hetty at arm's length. On second examination, she saw Hetty *had* aged in her absence. Her wild and wispy hair was almost white, and her wrinkles had deepened. But the dark eyes still held intelligence and sharpness.

"How is your babe?" asked Hetty. "I'd love to see her."

Alecia froze. "How did you know about her?"

"Don't be dense, child! I scried her, of course. I knew as soon as you set foot in Brightcastle."

Alecia huffed out the trapped breath. Of course Hetty could see what she was doing if she wanted to. "I'd bring her to visit, but I can't see how to do that in secret. It's not as easy as it once was."

"No girl. You must think of her now. What did you call her?"

Alecia smiled. "Iona… Iona Izebel… Zialni."

"So, he's gone then?"

Alecia hardened her heart to the reality. "Several months ago. I don't know what happened, but one day he up and left with no warning." She squeezed her eyes shut, trying to guard against the pain of that time. "When I was pregnant, Vard almost lost himself to the wolf. Ramón went in search of him and found him a raging animal. He was able to bring Vard back to humanity just in time for him to deliver his daughter. We both nearly died."

Hetty clutched her throat, dark eyes wide. "I always knew it was a risk," she said. "What if it happens again?"

"I hoped he'd been back to see you."

"I've not seen the captain since the second enchantment of the amulet." The old woman referred to Vard's previous rank in the Brightcastle Army, and to his amber talisman, which she had enchanted to aid his control over the bear. "I've been so worried. Occasionally, I could scry and see you. But him… all I saw were claws and feathers. He hurt you."

Alecia shook her head. "That's water under the bridge. I have a beautiful daughter and she has her father's talent."

Hetty's eyes narrowed. "A Defender?"

Alecia nodded. "Neither of us knows exactly what it means, but I'm excited by her future."

"As long as her father learns enough to train her," Hetty said, her brows drawn together. "I'm too old to go through all that again." Her sharp gaze fixed on Alecia's own. "What beasts do you think she'll transform into?"

Alecia laughed. "I really hope the bear isn't one of them. I've had enough encounters with that particular animal to last a lifetime."

Hetty nodded and a far-off look entered her gaze. "I wonder where he is."

"I can't dwell on that, either. I must keep moving forward. And that means securing Brightcastle. Which is why I'm here. I wanted any information you can give about Benae and her marriage to my father."

Hetty turned and headed up the hallway. "Let me prepare the tea first. Then we can have a proper chat." She stopped at the kitchen doorway as a coughing fit seized her. It continued for too long.

Alecia grasped her friend's shoulders from behind and ushered her to a chair at the table. She fetched a mug of water and bade Hetty drink. The water seemed to help; the coughing settled. Alecia's rapid heartbeats slowed too.

"What's the matter, Hetty? How long have you had that cough?"

"It's nothing, girl. I had a cold a few weeks ago and the cough never settled."

"It sounds serious. Have you made a tonic?"

"I've done everything I can think of to rid myself of the cursed affliction. Nothing shifts it." Her breathing settled and her color returned. "But I don't want you to concern yourself with me."

"Hetty," Alecia said, fixing her friend with a stern look, "you must take care of yourself. This town needs you... I need you."

"Hush. I'll make the tea."

Hetty set the kitchen table and poured water into a teapot. She cut thick slabs of fresh bread and spread them with butter and honey.

Alecia watched closely for signs of serious illness, noting Hetty's breathing was more labored than it was last time she saw her friend.

She was brought back to the present when Hetty placed a plate in front of her. "I've dreamt about this bread over the last year." She took her first bite. "Mmm, so much better than I remembered. Spending time on the road really makes you appreciate the simple things in life."

Hetty grinned. "Your mother would be proud of you—as I am."

"That's one of the nicest things you've ever said to me. I wonder if father would be proud of me too?"

"Don't spend your time worrying about that. I hate to speak ill of the dead, but things are better without him."

"Hetty! I know he caused trouble for you, but he was my father." She studied the woman. "Tell me of this sham marriage."

"It was no sham, Alecia. The prince called for eligible noblewomen to present themselves to him. Benae Branasar was one of those who came. She won his hand fair and square, from what I heard."

Alecia pushed her chair from the table and paced across to the window. "But he *loved* Mama. How could he betray her that way?"

"The kingdom waits for no man or woman. You were absent, and he was desperate to secure the throne. When his plan to marry you off to Finus failed, what else was he to do?"

Alecia shuddered. "Just the thought of that man..." She recalled her evil betrothed and his untimely death at Vard's hands after he found Finus about to rape her. "What then? Once my father and Benae married, how did they seem? What did the populace think?"

"You know, girl, the people don't worry much about the goings on in the castle. Your disappearance distressed some, though. Many's the chat I had with my neighbors about that. I can't wait to see how they react when they know you've returned."

Alecia waved a hand, frustrated at the change of topic. "Tell me of the weeks after their marriage. What was the talk?"

"It was quiet. They weren't seen in public together after the wedding, though Princess Benae ventured out with her lady guards. She had to exercise that horse of hers. The prince was conspicuous by his absence."

"Doesn't that seem strange to you? Why wouldn't they be out and about?"

Hetty cackled. "Too busy performing their 'duties', I expect."

Alecia gasped. "That's my father you're talking about. Just the thought of him with that woman and what they did to produce Solomon makes me blush."

"Solomon's a fine name."

Alecia softened. "He's a beautiful child. I love him already, and I never expected to."

"Who does he look like?"

She considered. "He has golden hair and a fair complexion. I've yet to see his eyes as he was asleep. He's like an angel come down from heaven."

"Golden hair, you say? That's unusual when both parents are dark."

Alecia frowned. "It's the same color as mine and look at Iona; she has raven-dark hair even though her mama is fair. There's no accounting for who a child will resemble. I think Solomon must look like me as a baby."

Hetty smiled. "When I see him, I'll be able to tell you. After all, I was there when you were born."

"You detected nothing amiss in their relationship, Hetty? I'd love to have some ammunition to use against Benae. She's far too smug in her new role. She may have won over Ramón and Uncle Beniel, but she'll find me a much tougher nut to crack."

Hetty cleared her throat. "All is well, Alecia. The kingdom has its heir, and we have Benae and your father to thank for that. He did his duty in the end, and I, for one, am glad. Better that than your cousin Piotr getting his grubby hands on the throne."

"I know that, but what I can't stand is having my rightful place stolen. I should be Guardian of Brightcastle, not Benae and Ramón. I think I'll visit my uncle and tell him so."

"You do that, child. In the meantime, keep your eyes open. There are dark elves about, and they may have an eye on Brightcastle."

"Ramón's soldiers mentioned the elven civil war. One faction wants peace while the other aims to take back the kingdom lands for themselves. I also heard the general of the Wildecoast army has been dismissed after it was revealed he's the son of a past elven king."

Hetty nodded, frowning. "There's plenty to be worried about. We could use Kain Jazara's experience right at this moment."

"I spent time with the elves in Amitania while I was in exile. I thought there was something suspicious, but I never realized they'd come this far. Vard was right to be concerned."

"I'd suggest you get the lie of the land before you go charging off to Wildecoast, Princess, or you might find yourself in a lot of trouble. That daughter of yours is too young to be left without a mama."

Hetty's words struck a chill through Alecia. She was right. Her cavalier days of roaming the streets at night, exacting revenge on men who would harm her or her people, were at an end. She must be smarter than that—more cunning—if she was to defeat her enemies and take the first steps toward her ultimate goal.

Alecia had gone to Hetty for answers, but came away with more questions. Not only was she uncertain about who should hold the power in Brightcastle, but now the safety of the kingdom was threatened. With the future of her family and the throne in question, the elven infiltration into the kingdom couldn't have come at a worse time.

But, before she could tackle the elven incursion, Alecia knew she must discover the events that led to her father's death. She began by interviewing the servants, high and low. The high, such as the chief steward, had little to say. The maids and serving staff spoke in hushed tones of a period of great household tension immediately prior to and after her father's marriage to Benae.

Alecia learned that, on the way to Wildecoast for a wedding gown fitting, Benae and an escort of twenty soldiers led by Ramón, were attacked by elves. Only Benae and Ramón survived.

Within days of their return to Brightcastle, tension in the castle had run high, and all who worked there were on tenterhooks. Prince Zialni had flown into a rage directed at Ramón and Benae. Soon after, the prince and his fiancé married, but the staff reported no joy around the occasion. Princess Benae appeared ill, and there were whispers of bruising on her arms and legs.

After only a few short weeks of marriage, Alecia's father died amid rumors he had succumbed during the act itself, and that there had been a suspicious fire. Ramón was involved, and also Jacques Vorasava, Brightcastle lieutenant at the time. Vorasava was now married to an elven princess and lived in Amitania.

It was almost too much for Alecia to believe. The information the servants imparted amazed her. Even if half was false, there was enough suspicion to make her question what really happened around the time of her father's marriage to Benae.

Alecia rode her gray mare, Silver, toward the archery field north of Brightcastle. She had been delighted to find her beloved horse in the palace stables. Ramón had looked after Silver, certain that Alecia would eventually return. The beautiful creature pranced under the trees, skidding on the remnants of old paving stones, and sparking an answering excitement in her rider.

It was liberating to have a horse under her again—to know that she rode a creature with a mind of its own, that she could be seconds from disaster. Of course, Silver was generally too well-behaved to rear or bolt, but she had been confined to the stable for over a week during a blizzard. One couldn't blame her for being frisky.

"Princess, I wish you'd reconsider," Ramón called from behind. "I'm concerned your mare may be too much for you today. It can't be that important to practice the longbow."

"The world's a dangerous place, Ramón. My archery skills need sharpening. I must be prepared."

"Prepared for what?"

"The dark elven threat, for one thing." She reined Silver in and waited for him to join her.

Her companion's eyes roamed the immediate area, reminding her of the time she and Vard had ridden this way. Vard, too, had been on alert for danger.

"One may hope you won't be called upon to defend yourself or the castle, Princess," he said, his earnest blue eyes meeting hers.

"Stop calling me 'Princess'!" she said. "I'm Alecia to you, especially since your elevation to Guardian of Brightcastle." She frowned at the thought.

"Someone had to help Benae, and you were gone. Don't expect me to apologize for doing what had to be done."

She raised her brows at him. The old Ramón would never have used that tone or those words with her. He really had changed—grown a backbone—and now seemed older than his twenty-five years. She studied him for the hundredth time since returning, hardly recognizing the man he had become. What was he now capable of?

She rode ahead once more.

She had dismounted and strung her bow by the time Ramón arrived. He tied his black gelding beside hers and came to stand with her, his bow slung casually over his shoulder.

Alecia drew an arrow from her quiver and nocked it, drawing the string to her ear, and sighting down the length of the arrow. She let her breath out and released. The arrow hit the target at 100 paces but in the outer ring. Still, not bad when she hadn't fired an arrow for months.

Ramón folded his arms and watched as she shot four more arrows, each closer to the bullseye. Finally, on the sixth shot, she hit center.

"Ha!" she said. "Your turn."

He nocked an arrow, and it slammed into the bullseye on the first try. The second split the first. The third hit the next target, 50 paces further on, and the fourth the 200-pace target. Finally, Ramón's fifth arrow slammed dead center into the 250-pace target.

Alecia stared. The feat was one to rival Vard. Ramón had been practicing. There would be few who could challenge him. But there was no way he could hit the 300-pace target; not with mere human vision.

As if he read her mind, Ramón turned, nocked an arrow, sighted, and released it into the target at 300 paces. It appeared to have hit inside the inner circle, though not the dead center. That would truly have been inhuman.

He turned to her, his gaze challenging.

"Very good," she said. "I wouldn't have believed it if I hadn't seen you do that."

"Now perhaps you'll respect me," he said. "These skills I developed were all to bring you home. To prove I was worthy of your hand in marriage. And it almost worked. Prince Zialni was about to send me in search of you. Instead, he sent me to Wildecoast with Benae and elves ambushed us. Nothing has been the same since."

Alecia wondered if she'd finally learn the truth. "What happened on that trip? I heard they killed all except for you and Benae. There are rumors of indiscretion between you. It's said that my father was furious with both of you on your return to Brightcastle. There's only one reason I can think of for that anger."

Ramón remained silent for a long time. "Danger pushes people together as nothing else does. But I have nothing to tell you." He appeared to choose his words carefully—or was she imagining it?

"I *will* get to the truth," she said. "This entire episode has a rotten smell about it. Perhaps it would be better for our friendship if you told me the facts."

He looked at her, his clear blue eyes troubled. "I don't wish to fight with you. I've risked my life for you and your family. That should be enough to win your trust. Haven't I always been true? Perhaps if you hadn't been so eager to leave Brightcastle with Anton, you'd now be in a position of power."

The breath caught in Alecia's throat. "I didn't have a choice! It was leave or face a future with Finus. A fate worse than death."

"It left your father with few options. Consider that before you throw more accusations of wrongdoing around." He paused and studied her. "Benae is a good woman and has done her best for Brightcastle. You and she would make a formidable team."

Alecia started walking toward the targets, intent on collecting her arrows. "You're blinded by your love for her. When I said there was a better woman out there for you, I didn't mean a fortune-seeking opportunist like Benae."

Ramón caught up to her and grabbed her by the arm. She spun to face him.

"You're wrong about my wife." His fingers dug into her flesh. "I just hope you don't ruin all our futures with your vendetta."

Alecia tore her arm from his grasp and continued toward the targets. Ramón was a fool, and the sooner she found out the truth of her father's death, the sooner she could convince him of that.

Alecia paced her room, gut churning with frustration at the lack of progress she had made into the investigation of her father's death. Iona cried.

She fetched her daughter from the crib and continued pacing, the babe in her arms. Usually the child calmed her, reminded her that nothing else was as important as the life she and Vard had created. But Iona's future depended on unearthing incriminating evidence on Benae and, perhaps, on Ramón. She had to concede he might be complicit in her father's death. At the very least, he knew something he wasn't telling.

Iona let out a squeal, and she realized she clutched the baby too tightly.

"I'm sorry, my love," she said, kissing the little girl's soft cheek. "How about we have a feed and a cuddle?" She settled in the sitting room before the fire, and soon Iona was sucking contentedly.

"What should I do next, Daughter?"

Iona smiled as she suckled, her gilt-speckled eyes meeting her mother's. It lightened Alecia's dark mood. A fierce protective love rose in her breast, and she renewed her vow to discover the truth of her father's death.

Doctor Monive, the castle physician, hadn't been helpful when she had spoken to him. He had declared Prince Zialni dead of natural causes. It would make him look a fool if he said anything now to contradict that verdict. He said her father was taking herbs to increase virility and fertility and had taken too many. His heart failed.

She snorted quietly, not wanting to disturb Iona. As if her father ever had a weak heart! But the evidence had been there, Monive said. The organ had failed.

Were the herbs the reason, or was there a more sinister cause of death? Such as poison…

Ramón would never be party to that, but Benae could have orchestrated it herself. She was said to have skills in healing. Indeed, she had nursed Ramón from death's door following his shooting by an assassin at her father's funeral. Surely, she had knowledge of poisons.

It was said also that Alecia's cousin Piotr was in Brightcastle at the time of the funeral. She didn't remember him well, but he was next in line to the throne after Solomon. Alecia shivered. Her baby brother would need to be guarded carefully.

She realized her mind was whirling out of control and laid her head back, closing her eyes. Someone out there must know what happened and be prepared to tell her. Despite the wrong he had done, she had loved her father. Brightcastle wasn't the same without his strong leadership. Benae Branasar couldn't be allowed to benefit from Prince Zialni's death. Alecia would see that the people of Brightcastle didn't suffer under a woman who was prepared to murder her husband to gain control of the throne.

* * *

Benae's mind churned with agitation. She hadn't known a moment of peace since Alecia returned. And Ramón wasn't helping. He'd let her down when she needed his support most. She was so enraged, she thought steam should be coming from her ears.

"You *must* convince her she's wrong, Ramón!" she said. "You know her best. Assure her I had nothing to do with Jiseve's death."

Ramón pulled her into his arms. He rested his chin on her dark hair. "You *weren't* responsible for his death, Benae. She'll see that in time."

"Doctor Monive told me she quizzed him about the inquiry. She won't stop until she finds something."

Ramón looked down at her. "There's nothing *to* find, my love," he told her.

He tried to smile, but she could tell he was as worried as she was; perhaps more. After all, he had sought help from the witch in rescuing Benae from her abusive marriage to Jiseve.

Though the man's death was pronounced natural, Benae could never be sure that black magic hadn't been responsible. But she wouldn't allow her suspicions to undermine her marriage to Ramón. She loved him deeply and completely. She had forgiven him for seeking magical help; to do anything else would poison their love.

"Alecia is being unfair, Benae. You won the prince's hand in a competition of his own choosing. And you tried to be a good wife. You even produced an heir. How can she be critical of you?"

"How indeed," she said. "At least she's not questioning Solomon's parentage. I couldn't deal with that as well."

Benae closed her eyes and pulled him tight against her, drawing comfort from his presence.

"We must hope she doesn't question it. But there's no reason she should," Ramón said. "No one knows the truth of it except for us. And we'll never tell…"

CHAPTER 3

VARD Anton rode his horse through the woods north of Wildecoast, a patrol of twenty rangers behind him. The King's Rangers were an elite fighting and tracking group, recently formed by Vard and under his control. Only the best and bravest were selected and Vard had personally trained each of the men.

Some days he had to pinch himself in order to believe this life was real. He had dwelled so long fearing the bear—more than half his thirty-one years of existence—it was difficult to let his guard down. But now, thanks to the elven lord, Melandrach Arenil, Vard had mastered his bear. He had the chance to relax for a small moment in time; to settle into his role as Defender... and as the King's Blade.

He shook his head. It was a new role, created on the advice of the queen, Adriana Zialni. Her Majesty was rather entranced by his Defender traits, but Vard had done nothing to encourage her. He merely fascinated the beautiful monarch. And, instead of being suspicious, King Beniel embraced the queen's will and her advice.

After all, the king could hardly trust his general, Josef Formosa. The man was too full of himself with little reason to be so. The power vacuum left by the removal of former general Kain Jazara, due to his being half-elven, allowed the advancement of men who weren't ready for more challenging roles. Formosa was one of those men.

Vard was now answerable only to the king and queen, which gave him more power than anyone else... and more enemies. The men below him admired him, but they didn't understand his origins, and they never would. They had heard only rumors of his past connection to Princess Alecia Zialni.

He smiled at the thought of Alecia and of their daughter, Iona. But laced with the happiness was deep sorrow that he'd left Alecia once again. This time, perhaps, she wouldn't take him back. She'd be mad to trust him again, especially after hearing nothing from him for over four months. But he had needed that time to fully settle into his Defender powers and to gain a position that would allow him to care for his family.

He halted the patrol and dismounted, telling the men to stand down. He tied Trax, his black and white stallion, to a branch and stalked into the forest.

Once he had gone twenty paces, he built the picture of the huge black wolf in his mind—hair by hair, claw by claw, and tooth by tooth. In seconds, a great hulking wolf, tongue lolling to the side of his mouth, replaced the man. He set off into the forest and padded up the hill that lay within this patch of woodland.

In no time, he reached the summit and gazed out over the trees, sharp eyes peeled for anything unusual, nose twitching with the scents of the forest. Off to the west, he smelled elf. Vard morphed directly into the hawk and launched himself for a better look at the intruders. The elves weren't known for their longbow skills, but he stayed high anyway, out of range of any but the best marksman.

The hawk spied the elves, three of them, likely an advance scouting party. He turned on the wing, heading back to his men. Landing in a low tree, Vard transformed back into a man before joining his patrol.

"Elven scouting party of three to the west. Leave the horses here, but weapon up. Only kill if you must. We need information."

He collected his bow, sword, and knives, and re-entered the forest.

They detained two of the three elves. The third thought he could best twenty men in a fight. None of Vard's Rangers were injured. That was just how he liked it. Men like the rangers were few, so he couldn't afford to lose them. As the patrol returned to Wildecoast, Vard's thoughts turned to building his force and perhaps recruiting more Defenders. But he must find them first.

Defenders were an ancient order of shapeshifters, sworn to guard the innocent. It was part of their being—the drive to protect the most vulnerable. And that meant killing. But it wasn't easy to control the animal within.

He'd spent years trying to understand and control his animal urges, especially the bear—the form that had almost killed Alecia. If not for Melandrach, he'd still be wandering the kingdom and beyond, searching for a mentor who could help him come properly into his gift.

At least he could recognize it as a gift now. It was still a risk if he stayed too long in animal form, especially the wolf. Last winter, only intervention by Ramón Zorba saved him. He had a lot to thank that man for—not that Zorba would give him the time of day.

The second-in-command took the elves for interrogation, and Vard entered the palace. His thoughts were with Alecia and Iona this morning. Would they be in Brightcastle yet? He knew how Alecia had agonized about returning.

Part of her wanted to stay on that remote farm and pretend the world didn't exist. But Thorius needed her. He wondered how big their daughter was now, and a desperate longing to see her swept over him.

Vard stepped into the small reception hall and was announced. Queen Adriana, a woman only a few years older than himself, was in attendance. Her undeniably luscious form was draped in scarlet, her dark hair arranged in an elaborate twist. She had just poured tea.

"You're back from patrol early, Vard," she said. "Can I offer you refreshment?"

He waved it away and bowed. "Good morning, Your Majesty. I came to tell you we have *Lenweri* prisoners. They deny it, but I believe they are of the *Sis Lenweri* faction. I suspect they were scouting as part of a plan to free Faenwelar's son from our prison."

The rebel elven group wanted the return of kingdom lands they said belonged to them. Their prince, Niel Gorin, had been a guest of

Wildecoast since his capture after a battle in Amitania four months ago.

Adriana's slanted emerald eyes narrowed. "How far out were they and how many?" she asked.

"They were a scouting party of three within less than a day's march to the northwest of here. One resisted and was killed. We brought in two with no losses of our own."

She nodded. "Well done. I will inform the king. Continue the patrols. And increase the guard, especially around the prison."

"Already done, Your Majesty." Vard hesitated. "I wondered if you had news… of Alecia?"

Adriana smiled. "I do not, but when I do, you will be first to hear."

Of course, the queen didn't know of their child, and Vard wouldn't volunteer that information. She and the king also didn't know of his shifter abilities. Some things he just wouldn't share.

He could control it and wasn't a risk to anyone except their enemies. Many in the kingdom, including the king, were suspicious of anything magical. No, he wouldn't be sharing his special talents any time soon.

But he must get news of Alecia and his daughter. The nagging ache in his gut had him in its grip. He hated being apart from them, and, now he enjoyed the prestige of his new position, he had no real reason to stay away… except for a deep fear of rejection.

After leaving her twice, he knew she likely didn't wish to see him ever again, no matter the reason for their estrangement. His failure to master the bear had led to danger for his love, and when Iona was born, the danger doubled. He couldn't risk an innocent child or the woman who meant more to him than life itself.

The wolf had lurked close to the surface last autumn after he'd existed in that form for many months, and culminated in Zorba having to save him.

The urge to return to the body of the wolf had overwhelmed him, and he succumbed on more than one occasion. Even though he stayed far from the farmhouse at these times, it took little to imagine his fangs sunk into Iona's throat… or Alecia's. And the bear had actually killed his cousin. He wouldn't allow his weakness to destroy his family.

A gently cleared throat brought him back to the present. His gaze met that of the queen's.

"I'm sorry, Your Majesty." He took a moment to recall their conversation. "Please let me know if you receive news of the princess. Also, I wondered if you would consider recruiting more rangers. Two units of twenty won't be enough to cover the territory. And it wouldn't hurt to extend our program to Brightcastle."

Adriana nodded. "I'll speak to the king this evening. Perhaps you can spend today recruiting the men you need. Do you know who we should approach in Brightcastle?"

"Guardian Zorba would do an admirable job, but perhaps he can't be spared?"

"A good suggestion, but he will need help. I'll have Jacques Vorasava recalled from Amitania to oversee the recruitment and training. Once done, he can return to the lost city, leaving Zorba to command the rangers."

Vard wondered if he dared voice his next suggestion—Kain Jazara.

He'd been general of the King's Army until a mere nine months ago, when it was discovered that he was the son of the past elven king, Orionkael Arenil. Vard still couldn't believe the tale, but it appeared to be the truth.

Kain now commanded the peaceful *Lenweri*, proving a formidable opponent for the rebel *Sis Lenweri* who were commanded by High Prince Elvor Faenwelar, father to Prince Gorin. Faenwelar was a slippery character and had retreated to the vast forests north of Amitania after his last battle defeat.

Vard had only met Kain fleetingly, but his leadership and weapons skills were legendary. Add to that his familiarity with the elven race, and he would be an asset to the Kingdom. Vard decided to venture his name.

"I also thought of Kain Jazara."

The queen's eyes hardened. "I hardly think the *Lenweri* high prince would be willing to help train our rangers. And he goes by the name of Kain Arenil now. He has taken his real father's name."

"We won't know if we don't ask," Vard said. "I could finish my recruitment here and take a small group of rangers to Selinore for extra training—if Jazara should agree. At the least, it would be wise to keep in touch with our allies."

The queen frowned and turned away from him, facing a tapestry of the battle queen, Izebel, leading her soldiers into an attack against a dragon. It was a magnificent work of art and reminded Vard of Alecia. His love worshipped Izebel and she wanted to be like her. She had also given Iona the battle queen's name as her middle name. But queens didn't rule as primary sovereign anymore. Not since Queen Daphne, Izebel's daughter, whose madness ruined the kingdom.

Vard waited patiently for Queen Adriana to consider his suggestion. Finally, she faced him once more.

"I will discuss this matter with the king also," she said. "You may be right. It would be advisable to meet with Kain Arenil and discover his plans for his people. But Beniel will wish to go in your stead." A cloud swept across her face and was quickly gone. "I do not think his mind is in the right place for such negotiation at present," she admitted. "He has still not recovered from losing Jiseve and his judgement… His passions run high."

"I understand, Your Majesty," Vard said. "Losing family is never easy. I imagine he too is eager to hear news of Alecia. When last I saw her, she planned to return to Brightcastle before winter set in. She should be there by now."

Adriana frowned. "Perhaps when we receive news of her return, the king will wish to journey to Brightcastle, and you and he can go on to Selinore together to meet with High Prince Arenil." She sighed. "Things have become so complicated. And, to add to it all, my nephew, Piotr Zialni, is out there, waiting to strike when we least expect it. What would be your council on that matter?"

Vard had already considered the matter of the king's nephew long and hard. He was a threat they must neutralize. He couldn't be allowed to ascend to the throne, especially not if he was responsible for the attempted assassination of King Beniel at his brother's funeral.

"We must find evidence of his part in the attack on the king—or give him a position from which we can observe him. We must know what he's doing."

"I suspect my nephew would decline a position. However, your suggestion is sound. He once offered marriage to Lady Esta Aranati. Perhaps if I can create an event to draw him out again, I can tempt him into marriage to one of my ladies. *She* can inform us of his activities."

Vard grinned. "You're as devious as you are beautiful, Your Majesty. I would hate to have you as an enemy."

She smiled. "And yet you have turned me down on more than one occasion. Is that not playing with fire, King's Blade?"

Vard shook his head. "I hope you understand it's no insult, Your Majesty. My heart belongs to your niece, and I would never betray her."

Not so in the past. Vard would've done whatever was needed to advance his cause of protecting the innocent then, but that was before Alecia. She was good personified, and he had vowed to protect her above all others and, if possible, deserve her love. The woman before him would never tempt him to stray, as enticing as her flashing green eyes and welcoming body were to other men.

Adriana smirked. "All is fair in love and war, Vard. The invitation is always there, should you change your mind."

He bowed and left the queen. As he closed the door behind him, he wondered at her audacity. If Alecia ever found out about her invitation, it would drive a wedge between the two women—one which would be difficult to remove. He just hoped she never discovered her aunt's outrageous behavior.

It was certainly never dull in Wildecoast.

* * *

Alecia laid Iona in the cradle and opened the door of her wardrobe.

Her gut bubbled with a fine tension as she contemplated the day ahead. Yesterday, as she practiced the sword with the weapons master, she had overheard the soldiers discussing Jacques Vorasava. The joint ruler in Amitania was due to arrive in Brightcastle. Today.

No one seemed to know the purpose of his visit, but Alecia had determined she would arrange a meeting with him. Captain Vorasava, then a lieutenant, had presided over the arrangements when her father died. If anyone could shed light on those tragic hours and days, it was him.

She decided something somber would give her more credibility with the captain. Her deep blue velvet gown fitted to the hips, then flared out into a full skirt. Maroon collar, cuffs, and skirt inserts brightened the dark outfit and, though it exposed her collar bones, it was modest. She'd wear her maroon velvet choker with the sapphire feature.

Alecia slipped on the gown and called her maid, Patrice, to help with the back ties, which were nigh on impossible for her to secure herself. Patrice had served one of the Brightcastle noblewomen until Alecia took her into service. She had to have trustworthy people around her, not servants who could be spies for Benae.

She had also chosen her own nanny for Iona, a woman Hetty had recommended. Of course, Alecia wished she could have Hetty here to look after her daughter, but it wasn't possible. Not yet. One day she hoped to bring her friend to the castle, to live her last days in comfort.

She tried to do as much for herself as possible. But occasionally, she had to admit defeat. That was why she preferred simple gowns or men's attire—it was easier to dress oneself.

She gasped as Patrice laced her up tightly. Uncomfortable it might be, but the effect was worth it.

"Has Jacques Vorasava arrived yet?" Alecia asked Patrice, moving to sit at her dressing table.

"Lord Vorasava's entourage has just been shown their rooms, Princess," Patrice said as she fixed Alecia's hair. That too was a simple affair, her long golden locks pulled into a low bun at the base of her skull. "He's very striking with those blue eyes and dark hair. It's a pity he married an elven woman."

Privately, Alecia thought the allegiance might come in handy. And she noted that Patrice had called him "lord" so Vorasava must have gained a new title with his marriage. No matter, he was not yet her equal and that gave her an advantage.

"Do you have any knowledge of his agenda in Brightcastle?" she asked, casually. "I assume he'll be meeting with Princess Benae and Lord Zorba?" Alecia gritted her teeth at having to give Benae that title. She dampened her anger and smoothed her face. It wouldn't do to show her emotions, though she had never found it easy to hide her feelings.

"Lord Vorasava is freshening up in his rooms and will meet with the lord and his lady within the hour, Your Highness."

Alecia retrieved a sheet of parchment from her bedside table and wrote on it, then folded it and gave it to Patrice. "Please deliver this to Lord Vorasava. Tell him you'll wait for a reply. Do it now."

"But Your Highness, I've not finished your face!"

"I'll do it myself, Patrice. And have the nanny attend me as soon as she can."

The maid bobbed a curtsy and left. Alecia completed her lip color and blush and surveyed the effect in her mirror.

She wondered what changes others saw in her since her time in exile and the birth of her daughter. It was difficult to judge oneself. Hours spent outdoors had tanned her skin, but that would fade as she spent more time indoors. She examined her penetrating lilac eyes and huffed at the insecurity she saw in them.

Now I'm a mother, my appearance isn't important!

In truth, appearance never mattered to her anyway. What she wished to be judged for was her determination, her leadership, and her weapons skills. But attractiveness could be an advantage, and motherhood too, especially when it led to a woman being underestimated. The rumors which must swirl about her would also be an advantage.

Her enemies wouldn't know what to believe.

Alecia had asked that Lord Vorasava be shown to the library after his visit with Ramón and Benae. There was no telling how long *that* meeting would take. One thing was certain—*they* wouldn't be asking him the same questions as she.

She sat before a cozy fire, ostensibly reading, but finding it difficult to concentrate. It was a book of poetry written by Queen Izebel, her personal heroine. The library held a comprehensive array of books from all the kingdoms on many subjects.

She had spent several hours in the room each day this week and had learned things not taught to her by those who had schooled her, such as how a woman might reduce her disadvantages when she fought, and what weapons were easiest for females to master. For she didn't just want to study Izebel, she wished to emulate her. What she had learned so far had convinced her that Izebel was the greatest monarch of them all.

A footman cleared his throat. "Princess—Lord Vorasava to see you."

Alecia stood and turned toward the door. Vorasava entered and stood just inside the room. He reminded her of her father, with his slender, muscled frame, dark hair and beard and deep blue eyes. The man before her had come far in his thirty years, even for one of noble birth. She wondered if his family had welcomed Gwaethe Arenil, the *Lenweri* princess Jacques had married.

Vorasava bowed then continued toward her, taking her hand and placing a kiss on her fingers. "It's marvelous good fortune that I can speak with you, Your Highness," he said.

His enthusiasm surprised Alecia. She looked at the footman. "Have wine, cheese and bread brought here. I'm sure Lord Vorasava is hungry."

Her guest smiled as the footman left. "Indeed, I am, Princess. It's been a long journey and difficult, though we only encountered two small groups of *Sis Lenweri*."

"And what occurred?"

"They killed two of my men, one each on two separate occasions; no outright attack, just shot an arrow through their throats and took off. We didn't see much, but, on investigation, it was clear elves were involved."

"That's concerning news. What have you done with the bodies of your men?"

"One we buried on the trail and the other lies waiting a burial this evening. Lord Zorba has agreed he must have a hero's service."

"Of course!" She contemplated the men the kingdom had lost. They deserved a few moments of silence. And she'd attend the funeral. "I hear congratulations are in order. Your marriage has seen you elevated to Earl."

"To tell the truth, Your Highness, I don't hold much by titles anymore. The elven people ignore my existence much of the time. I'm a problem they don't wish to acknowledge."

"I can see how you would be. I'm impressed you saw fit to fall in love with an elven woman. Your life can't be easy."

He tilted his head to the side and frowned. "You fell in love with a commoner, Princess. Surely my life would be a picnic compared to what you've endured over the last year or so."

She raised her chin. "I don't wish to speak of it, but you're correct— it has been difficult." She allowed the silence to lengthen. "I wanted to ask you about the events that surrounded the death of my father."

"Ah, I wondered if you would wish to discuss that."

Faced with the moment of truth, Alecia suddenly didn't want to have her fears confirmed. She'd rather believe the fantasy that Benae and Ramón painted for her; that her father had died of natural causes. But Vorasava must not see her fear.

She drew a deep breath and met his eyes.

"I believe you were involved in the investigation; that you personally supervised the removal of my father's body after he died."

He nodded and stepped closer. "It was a most distressing time, but I conducted matters to the best of my ability."

"How did Princess Benae behave?"

"She was distraught when I spoke to her, which was the next day."

"Surely you should have questioned her sooner?" Alecia asked

"Lord Zorba guarded her like she was a precious jewel. Granted, there had been a fire in the prince's chambers. She could have died."

"I heard rumors of a fire. What started it?"

Vorasava lowered his voice. "A lantern was knocked off the bedside table. Zorba said he was doing a last patrol of the hallways and smelled smoke. He investigated and put out the fire, discovering the prince dead at the same time."

"Where was Lady Benae?"

He cleared his throat, and a flush climbed up his neck. "She was trapped under the body of her husband. It must have been quite terrible for her."

Alecia's mind drew pictures she didn't wish to see. She closed her eyes, but still the scene of Benae desperate to escape from the dead weight of her husband played itself out in her mind's eye. But no—Benae was petite, but surely she was strong enough to roll him off and escape?

"We're missing something, Lord Vorasava. It doesn't make sense, neither the fire, nor the fact that Benae needed help to escape. Do you believe Lord Zorba knew more than he told at the time?"

Vorasava frowned. "Possibly." He hesitated. "Princess, I assume you wish me to be frank."

Alecia's heart stuttered. Would she finally learn something explosive? Something she could use against Benae, and possibly, Ramón?

She steadied her leaping thoughts and nodded.

"He was cautious with his answers," Vorasava said." I thought he and Princess Benae were closer than was proper, but I saw no actions that would prove infidelity. When Lady Benae and Zorba returned from Wildecoast after the elven ambush, there was trouble. Prince Zialni no longer treated either of them as he had before. There was no joy. But the wedding went ahead."

"And Doctor Monive declared death by natural causes?"

"It appears the prince was taking medicines and other substances to increase his fertility and virility. They affected his heart over time and the organ failed during the act of —"

She threw her hand up. "I get the picture, My Lord." Alecia walked across to the window and stared out. Benae was just leaving for a ride with Ramón. The two were laughing, their heads close as they rode through the gate together. It was touching, but were they guilty of killing her father?

"This entire series of events is sordid in the extreme," she said, turning to her guest. "Do you think they had an affair before my father died?"

"I can't say, Your Highness."

"But you suspect." She fixed him with all her attention.

"It's one theory I had. But the king presided over the entire investigation and was content there was no foul play. He even made Lord Zorba joint guardian with Lady Benae and granted her the title of "Princess" in her own right. Would he do that if he had any suspicion they killed his brother?"

"I fear you've raised more questions than you've answered, Lord Vorasava."

"I'm sorry for your loss and that you were unable to say goodbye to your father."

She nodded. "Thank you. You're excused."

He went to leave but hesitated and turned back.

"Yes, Lord Vorasava?"

"Lady Benae and I don't really see eye-to-eye, though she saved my life a while back. She forced my retirement from military service on health grounds. I wanted to offer you my support, should you need it. You have only to ask, and I'll be here to help you… whatever you need."

She stared. That was quite a statement. "Thank you. I'll keep that in mind."

He bowed and left the library, but Alecia hardly noticed. She found the bread and wine which had been delivered, untouched, and sat before the fire, imagining all the ways she might need Jacques Vorasava in the future.

Over the ensuing days, a pressure built within Alecia; a yearning to be productive. The problem was she had no idea what to do. Brightcastle was starting to feel like a prison, and she wasn't getting anywhere with her investigation. Jacques Vorasava had raised more questions, and he had been cautious; careful not to say anything that could be construed as outright criticism.

It made her blood boil. All she wanted was the truth, and it seemed to be the only thing she couldn't attain. Certainly, her father had been no saint. He had arranged a marriage between herself and that cruel old lord, Finus. Vard had dealt with the vile man, praise the Goddess. It was said Finus had taken a month to die after the sword wound to his gut.

She felt a cold smile upon her lips and pinched her mouth. What was happening to her that she took such pleasure in another's suffering? True, queens had to be cold and calculating on occasion, but she must guard against allowing her heart to grow too hard. Surely, she could defeat their enemies while maintaining her platform of justice and decency?

She nodded to herself and returned to the problem at hand. Who could supply the answers she sought? Would a trip to Wildecoast and an audience with her uncle, the king, bring clarity? She could appeal to him to make her heir as well. It only made sense that she should succeed her father as next in line to the throne. But had anything changed? Her last discussion with Uncle Beniel had shown he cared more for the heirs she might produce than for the talents she could bring to the kingdom.

She grabbed her cloak from the wardrobe and left her chambers, intent on taking a turn around the castle grounds. As she stepped out of the front door, Ramón was coming up the steps. He frowned at her.

"Good afternoon, Ramón. I was about to take a walk. Care to join me?"

He frowned harder. "I should really get back to the reports. You have no idea how they pile up when left for a few hours." He looked around the forecourt. "But I did need to tell you something."

"Oh?"

He took her arm and led her toward the castle garden. It was more a small forest but contained within the high wall of the castle premises. With the heightened risk of dark elves, guards patrolled outside and inside. They walked to the stone seat at the base of a huge old oak.

"Please sit, Princess."

"I came out here for exercise, not to sit," she said. "Speak your news, please."

He walked away a few steps and then back to her. "I have word of Vard Anton. The king has enlisted his help, and the scoundrel is on his way here as I speak."

Alecia's heart gave a great leap at the mention of his name. *Vard!* "I don't understand. What help is he giving my uncle?"

"I received a message by pigeon this morning. Anton is based in Wildecoast and has formed, for the king, an elite military group called the Rangers. He's hoping to enlist more talent and is travelling to Brightcastle on a recruitment exercise. He'll be here within three days."

Alecia couldn't process the information for all the thoughts zapping around in her head. She couldn't meet Vard—not yet. Not until she had settled herself and Iona. The memory of the dream came back to her and her palms grew sweaty. She couldn't see Vard if he was a risk to her daughter. But at the mere mention of his name, her first instinct had been overwhelming joy that he was alive. Her body yearned for his, and her heart concealed a gaping hole that only he could fill.

"Princess, are you listening?" Ramón stood in front of her, hands on hips, blue eyes boring into hers.

"What? No," she said. "What did you say?"

He rolled his eyes, which sent a sharp spike of anger to her gut.

"I asked you if you would see him. I can protect you if you don't. He doesn't need to know you've returned."

Her heart's frantic beating stilled. Perhaps Vard didn't know she was here. But then she thought it through and realized it would take no time for him to discover her presence in Brightcastle. And then he would confront her. Better to control the moment, but how to ensure that Iona was safe?

She shook her head. "Thank you for trying to protect me, Ramón, but I need to see him sometime."

Ramón flicked his blond fringe off his forehead. "Every time you think of him, there's despair in your eyes. He put it there. If you allow him back in, he'll ruin you."

She drew a deep breath. "It's my decision. I must face him. I must take the first step."

He sighed. "I hate to see you do this. I feel responsible as it was I who brought him back last time. I should have left him in his insanity."

Alecia stepped closer and grasped Ramón above the elbows. "Don't ever say that! He saved Iona and he saved me. The Goddess only knows what would have become of us if Vard hadn't intervened in the birth." She gave him a little shake as his eyes slid away. "*You* saved us by your actions. I'll never forget what you did."

She allowed her hands to fall, and he nodded. "Perhaps you're right. Perhaps I should stop regretting my actions."

"You've always been a friend, Ramón. I hope that never changes, despite your marriage to Benae."

"It seems we're at an impasse. You can't accept Benae, and I loathe Vard Anton. We must somehow deal with the conflict this will bring."

She raised her chin. "I can't see how the future will unfold, but I hope I'll always remember your kindness and sacrifice last summer. Even if you *are* hiding the truth of my father's death."

He drew himself up. "I'm hiding nothing from you."

As he said the words, she saw a flicker in his eyes that certainly confirmed the falsehood of his words.

"It doesn't matter, Ramón. I understand you want to protect your wife. I admire your loyalty." She held his gaze for a moment longer, trying to impress upon him her determination to get to the truth. Then she turned and headed back to the castle.

CHAPTER 4

VARD'S heart was light as they neared Brightcastle. His rangers rode behind him—ten men hand-picked for the recruitment drive. It had been an excellent journey, and the only cloud on the horizon was the king's refusal to allow him to approach Kain Arenil. It grated that he must obey his monarch, used to following his own whims as he was.

Over the last five days, he had morphed into all three of his animal forms, enjoying the freedom each of them gave. The hawk he used to scout the surrounding land. He had seen nothing of the dark elven menace. Perhaps the increased patrols were working.

The black wolf form he used for hunting, and when he wanted to run. As the wolf, he was one with the forest and the fields he traveled through. The bear he used for sheer joy. Once the animal he had most dreaded, he could now control this mighty beast. The pure power of the bear transported him to a high without equal.

For the first time in decades, Vard lived without fear that he'd harm others. Full control of his gift had freed him, and sometimes it was difficult to contain his joy. But then he'd remember his family and the elation would dissipate like smoke on the wind. He could never hold on to his happiness without them in his life.

He wondered where Alecia was and what she was doing. Would she return to Brightcastle soon? He knew one thing. He wouldn't seek her out. If she forgave him for abandoning her, it would be on her terms; that was the only way they would ever be together. But for now, he'd enjoy his freedom from fear, and he would hope that, eventually, his love would give him another chance.

* * *

Alecia dressed carefully for her luncheon with Ramón and Benae. She had dithered over what to wear and how to present herself to face Benae—and Vard, who should arrive later today.

Her hands trembled at the thought of seeing him again.

In the end, she had chosen her new black mourning gown, relieved by silver at the neck and cuffs. It would serve two purposes: it made her appear regal and would remind Benae of the treachery that had brought Jiseve Zialni's death.

She was more certain than ever that her father's bride had his blood on her hands. She must find the clues. Perhaps she might journey with Vard when he returned to Wildecoast? The thought sent a shiver of anticipation through her. But what would she do with Iona? And when she had yet to speak with Vard, she shouldn't be contemplating spending time with him—certainly not on a long journey.

Upon completing her preparations, she went downstairs to the formal dining room, dreading being in the same room as Benae. When she entered, Benae was already there, dressed in a fetching gown of deep blood-red velvet with black piping. Solomon was with her. Alecia approached and held out her arms for the baby.

"Good afternoon, Benae," Alecia said, receiving Solomon from his mother.

She drew the babe to her chest and love for him brought tears. She closed her eyes and breathed in the soft infant scent. Solomon should be a reminder of everything she had lost, and yet she loved him as a sister should.

"Hello, Alecia," Benae said, her eyes fixed on her son. She breathed deeply and continued. "How is Iona?"

Alecia smiled as Solomon's little fists tried to grasp the tendrils of hair beside her ears. "She's well, but I worry she misses the Andras. They own the farm where she was born and have been like grandparents to her."

"Perhaps you can visit them on the farm or have them come here."

"They're too busy to travel to Brightcastle, and it will be some time before I can visit." She knew her voice was frosty. She must not warm to this woman, no matter how charming she was.

"Please don't blame me for what happened to Jiseve, Alecia. We could be friends. I miss the company of a woman, especially since the elves killed Merel." Tears sprang into her eyes. "I never knew how much I loved her until she was gone."

"Yes, I heard about her. How brave she must have been to defend you like that against the *Sis Lenweri.*"

Benae retrieved Solomon and held him to her breast. Perhaps she needed the comfort of her babe. "Brave, and loyal to a fault. She didn't deserve to die. But she received a hero's burial in Wildecoast."

"I'm sure it was fitting." She hesitated in the face of Benae's distress, but forced herself to ask the question. "What happened between you and Ramón? I hear you were alone with him for days after the ambush by the elves."

Benae's eyes narrowed. "You know Ramón. He'd never be disloyal to his prince, my betrothed at the time. He was a complete gentleman."

Alecia searched for any sign that the words were a falsehood and found none. "And what of the beach incident? I believe you and he spent the night together again. Was he a gentleman on that occasion, too?"

"We had both almost drowned! A storm forced us to seek refuge in a deserted hut. The last thing on our minds was… oh, never mind! You won't believe anything I say."

"That's convenient. You refuse to explain because I won't believe you. Now that you and Ramón are husband and wife, I find it unlikely the two of you weren't intimate on that occasion. I'm sure my father found it equally difficult to believe. Is that true? Was he harsh with you and Ramón on your return? Do you contend he was merely grateful his betrothed was returned to him unscathed? Surely there were rumors; in fact, I know there were."

"That's enough, Princess," Ramón said, as he entered the dining room. Solomon startled at the raised voice and began crying. A maid swooped in and carried the infant from the room. "I must insist you treat my wife with respect."

Alecia tipped her head to the side. "Or you'll do what? Throw me out of the palace?"

He sucked in a deep breath. "For the sake of our children and the memory of your father, you and Benae must find a way to get along. The way you treat her is unfair. She was a good wife to Prince Jiseve and is a wonderful mother."

Alecia smirked. "I'll do that, if it's appropriate, when I learn the truth. Until then, I reserve the right to withhold my approval of both your choice of bride and my father's. Let us eat!" She pulled out the nearest chair and sat at the table.

They followed her lead, Ramón grim faced at the head of the table and Benae to his right, jaw tight and eyes downcast. A maid laid napkins on their laps, and another served the soup.

For several moments, there was no conversation.

Alecia's gut churned, and the thought of filling it with food made her sick. But she wouldn't allow the others to see how the disharmony had affected her. If she held her nerve, eventually she'd get to the truth of her father's brief marriage and his death.

Surprisingly, they managed polite conversation during the meal. Two large goblets of red wine did wonders for her appetite, and she ate a little of every course. Ramón and Benae also imbibed more than usual.

At the end of the meal, Ramón cleared his throat.

"I'd like to propose a truce between our families, though we are really one and the same," he said. "War with the *Sis Lenweri* looms. We can hardly afford to be fighting amongst ourselves when we're going to need to pull together to survive." He stood. "Princess Alecia, I request that you and Benae spend time together with me each day to make plans for the defense of Brightcastle. Vard Anton's arrival and his search for new rangers gives us a good starting point. Perhaps you could aid him in his search for men—and even women—to fill his ranks."

Alecia stared. "You expect me to work with Benae *and* Vard?" She stood. "Can I see you outside, please?" She left the dining room and awaited him in the hallway.

As he joined her, she spun to him. "How can you place me in such a position? Only three days ago, you asked if I wished to see Vard at all!"

Ramón stepped closer. "I'm sorry. I was thinking on the run. Of course, your involvement with Anton should be your choice. However, I need you to work with Benae, otherwise Thorius doesn't stand a chance against the elves. Would you put your feud with my wife above your people?"

Alecia opened her mouth to argue—then realized he was right. *Damn him!*

Someone cleared their throat nearby, and Alecia looked into the eyes of the chief steward.

"Excuse me, Princess, Lord Zorba," Master Goselin said, "I have news that Lord Anton's entourage has requested an escort to the keep. I thought you would like to know?"

Ramón drew himself up. "Thank you. Send soldiers immediately and let me know when Anton arrives."

The man nodded and hurried out. Ramón faced Alecia.

"You have about twenty minutes. Unless you've changed your mind and wish to hide, that is…"

Ramón stalked back into the dining room. Alecia drew a deep breath. She just had time to feed her daughter and tidy herself up. But she wouldn't expose Iona to her father until she could ensure her safety.

* * *

Vard rode through the streets of Brightcastle, conscious that he had been a wanted man the last time he showed his face here. The suspicious and hostile looks cast his way had him watching the rooftops. He had stolen their princess from under their noses, and Prince Zialni had defamed his character.

And now the prince was dead. King Beniel Zialni had few heirs and a fragile grip on the throne of Thorius. Still, the weak grip of a benevolent monarch was better than the uncertainty of a strange king. His mind turned to those who might have a claim to the throne. Of the few who popped into his head, Alecia was the least likely to succeed. Female monarchs had been outlawed in the kingdom for hundreds of years. But he knew of her dreams and of her admiration for Queen Izebel. Alecia fancied herself on the throne of Thorius—and she would make a fair and courageous monarch.

He shook his head as his gaze slid across the rooftops. In these times, who would accept a woman on the throne? But his love was tolerant and brave and true. She respected her people, and that was a good start. He recalled what she had endured under her father's rule. She had never lacked courage, just experience in knowing the right time to push ahead.

Throngs of people now lined the streets, and Vard heard a little of their conversation. There was speculation that he was being brought in to answer for his crimes. When his rangers heard that, they gathered closer. He cast his eyes to the heights again and spied a man in black, an arrow nocked and pointed *at him.*

"Assassin!" he shouted, and spurred his horse forward, ducking at the same time. Several of his men took off in the direction of the attacker while the rest closed ranks around him but kept moving.

A woman screamed, and he glanced in that direction. The arrow intended for him had lodged in the neck of a child who was sitting on a wall at the back of the crowd. He slid off his horse amid the protests of his men and pushed his way through to the woman, who clutched the girl to her chest. The child's eyes were closed, but his senses detected the tiny movement of air through her nostrils.

"She lives. Give her to me. I'll get her help."

The mother was clearly reluctant to hand her daughter over, but Vard gave her no choice. He held the child to his chest and ran to his horse, climbing on and urging Trax toward the castle.

"Bring the woman!" he shouted.

Time was critical. Even now, he heard the gurgle as she struggled to breathe. This mad dash could kill her. The gates loomed ahead, and they were opened for him. He dashed through and up to the steps, where a group awaited his arrival. Shock froze their faces as they saw him and the child, both covered with her blood.

"Get help for the child!" He dismounted and laid her down on the cobbles. Someone handed him a cloak, and he made a pillow for her head. He took off his tunic and laid it over her.

A diminutive brunette threw herself down beside him and laid her hands on the chest and forehead of the child. The woman closed her eyes, and Vard took the time to focus on the girl; to see if she still lived. Even with his eyes closed, he could hear nothing.

"She lives," the lady hissed, "but only by the barest thread. Fetch my medicines!"

A maid scurried off and Vard sat on his haunches. He watched as the lady laid her hands around the arrow wound and closed her eyes once again. This must be Benae, joint Guardian of Brightcastle. He raised his gaze and looked straight into the burning lilac eyes of the only woman he would ever love. Alecia Zialni.

The sight of her punched his gut and stole the breath from his lungs. If he'd been able to look away, he wouldn't have. He drank in the sight of her after all these months of yearning. They had a chance because of those months. But it appeared she was furious with him and for good reason. He had left her alone and with their child. He had left without saying a proper goodbye.

Until this moment, he hadn't known where she was or if she was well.

She was beautiful, regal in a black and silver dress. Once the shock of seeing her had worn off, he allowed his eyes to inspect her. She had lost none of her presence. Her long blonde hair was restrained at the nape, with tendrils escaping at the sides of her face. She was more beautiful than when they first met. He risked a smile, and her frown deepened. She probably thought he was responsible for the child's injury.

He glanced down and observed the girl's color had improved.

"Thank the Goddess," he said. "Will she live?"

The question was directed at Benae, who turned her head to face him. "She may. I'll need to remove the arrow, a precarious operation. What do you have to do with this injury, Sir?"

"I am Vard Anton, and the arrow was meant for me."

* * *

Alecia was unprepared for the wallop Vard's arrival gave her senses. Her stomach still resided at the base of her gut and her heart was trying to batter its way out of her chest. It seemed the blood in her body had shifted south, and she swayed. A firm hand gripped her elbow and a voice whispered in her ear.

"You mustn't faint, Princess."

The voice belonged to Jacques Vorasava. Apparently, he really did wish to support her and was doing so literally. She took deep breaths and felt her heart slow its racing. Her head cleared and the black at the edges of her vision disappeared.

"Thank you, Jacques." His grip on her elbow was welcome. As much as she knew it would be difficult seeing Vard again, she hadn't imagined the physical impact it would have. And the manner of his arrival was shocking in the extreme. The child! Her eyes searched the crowd, and she spotted a woman trying to push her way past the guards.

"Jacques, have that woman brought to the child," she said. He moved to do her bidding.

The mother was escorted to her daughter's side and collapsed, sobbing. Benae patted her shoulder. "She's alive, Mistress. I'll do my best to save her." She looked at soldiers standing close by. "Bring a shield to use as a stretcher and have her conveyed to a guest chamber." Her orders were carried out, and soon Benae, the child, and her mother entered the palace. Ramón followed close on their heels.

Alecia remained with Vard. She studied the man before her, or rather the Defender; the man who could become a hawk, wolf, or bear. The shadows that had haunted his sea green eyes were gone, but the golden flecks were not. She allowed herself the indulgence of falling into his gaze for just a few moments. The magnetism he exuded was greater than before. He held his head high, shoulders back. His dark shoulder length hair was restrained at his nape, and he wore a black leather headband worked in silver.

"You found your mentor," she said. It wasn't a question.

"I did."

His voice sent a shiver up her spine. It caressed her ears and rippled like a gentle breeze across her skin. He appeared to be waiting for her to do or say something.

"You look good, Vard. I'm glad to see you well."

He took a step toward her. "You're as beautiful as ever, Alecia." His eyes devoured her as if taking inventory. "How is our daughter?"

"She's well. Growing fast and so like you."

"Can I see her?"

Alecia hesitated, still unsure of the threat he might pose. But Vard had found his mentor and so must have come fully into his gift. He should no longer be a threat to Iona, or to any innocent person.

Then what had the dream been about?

"You may see her. But we must speak first." She stepped closer and placed her hand on his forearm. "I'll wait for you in the small audience chamber. See to your men and get cleaned up."

He stared into her eyes for a second, and she felt the connection like a caress to her soul. Then he turned away, and Alecia gulped down the emotion that rose to engulf her. She would do no one any good if she succumbed.

On entering the audience chamber, she ordered tea and refreshments be brought, and tried to compose herself. Why had she thought this would be anything but impossible?

Vard was a part of her, and, despite her anger at his leaving, and her fear of his return, she had missed him every moment of every day. Iona had been a continual reminder of the man who had created her, the man who had made Alecia a woman.

She walked up and down before the fireplace, trying to breathe away her nerves. It didn't help. Closing her eyes, she sucked in a full breath that filled her lungs to bursting. She held it until she saw spots and slowly let it out. When she opened her eyes, Vard was before her.

He took her hands and raised them to his lips, kissing first one, then the other. She held her breath again.

"I never deserved you," he said.

The words struck fear into her heart. She shook her head. "Don't be silly. It's not about deserving."

"Isn't it? I did my best to live up to you and protect you. Without success. Now I might finally be worthy of you and it's too late."

She didn't understand his words, but feared the worst. She pulled her hands from his and went to pour tea. The warm liquid helped to calm her nerves. Vard sipped from his cup, his eyes studying her.

"Vard, I can't go back to the way we were before. I couldn't stand losing you again. And Iona shouldn't have to face that either. But she's a Defender and needs you—that's if you're no longer a threat."

The gold flecks in his green eyes flared. "I've come fully into my gift. I'm not a threat to anyone, including Iona."

Hope burned bright in her heart. She gasped and tears filled her eyes. Her dream must have been the result of stress and her fears. Still, there were problems to be worked out.

"Even so," Alecia said, "how are we to move past all that has led to this moment?"

"I want you back," Vard said, a fine tension straining his face. "The king has employed me as head of his new rangers and also as the King's Blade, a position he created for me." His voice took on an edge of excitement she had never heard in it. She examined his uniform; green and brown in a complicated pattern that would give camouflage in most environments. A silver hawk adorned each shoulder.

"It sounds like my uncle trusts you, if he's creating new roles."

"It seems he does, though I'm not sure why. Perhaps I have the queen to thank. She's a persuasive woman and, once she knew you were safe in exile, she convinced the king that my actions were in your best interests."

Alecia sighed. Word of her being locked in the dungeon by her father must have reached Uncle Beniel. That was why he had forgiven Vard and brought him into the fold. She wilted a little at the shame of her uncle knowing the details leading to her exile.

"I suppose it has nothing to do with your effect on the fairer sex?" she asked.

"I can't help that," he said, grinning. They both knew Defenders attracted women like moths to a flame. Even the queen wasn't immune, as had been obvious to Alecia when her aunt had first met Vard.

"It's wonderful news that Uncle Beniel has embraced you," she said. "I'm glad you're in such a happy circumstance, but I can't forget your abandonment, even when it was for good reason."

He put down his cup and stepped closer, taking her cup and placing it beside his.

"Can I just hold you?" he asked. She allowed him to fold her into his arms.

She breathed in his scent, a mixture of musk and outdoors and the forest. Her heart quieted its thrumming as she held him tight, feeling their bodies join as one. This was where she belonged, but could her heart convince her head of that? Should she let it?

CHAPTER 5

AS Vard held Alecia, he knew he had come home. Was it truly possible that, after all their trials, they might come together as one forever? He longed for that; wanted her and their daughter more than life itself. Many a time since discovering his Defender heritage, he had wondered if this life was worth living. The death of his cousin, the disappearance of his father, and the constant threat of the bear had sapped his energy and optimism until all that remained was doubt and fear.

But Alecia had shown him light and love in the darkness. Until he presented an even more present danger—that of the risk to her if he lost control.

However, with full control of the bear and the wolf, he could return to Alecia and Iona and never fear for their safety again—at least not from him. If Alecia allowed him to be with her again, he could protect the most precious part of his world.

When he pulled away and looked down into her eyes, he saw the shadows of doubt remained in them. Despite the love, there was the vestige of anger and mistrust. That niggling uncertainty would erode the essence of their love, and he wouldn't have that happen. If they became one again, it must be with no doubts, no reservations.

"I don't blame you for mistrusting me," he said. "I hope, in time, you can forgive."

"Tell me what has transpired all these months since you left?"

He drew breath and prayed for the words that would convince her.

"I traveled across the land and finally heard of an elf, brother of the old king, who lived as a recluse. I hadn't considered an elven mentor, but the fact that he shunned his society made me wonder if he might help." He picked up his cup and sipped the strong brew.

"At first Melandrach Arenil was hostile to me, but he exuded the same power that I had seen in Lord Leth, and so I was even more convinced of his Defender status."

He saw Alecia shudder at the mention of the wizard who had once lived in the ancient ruins of Amitania and manipulated him into helping the *Sis Lenweri* cause. In the end, he and Alecia had barely escaped with their lives.

It was a dark chapter of their relationship, and what Vard endured at Leth's hands only weakened his control of his animal forms. He didn't regret killing the sorcerer.

"How did you convince him to help?" she asked, taking a seat at the tea table.

Vard sat, feeling awkward in the dainty chair. "I hung around his campsite and wouldn't take no for an answer. After a week, he agreed to speak with me just to be rid of me. I stayed for a month after that." He grinned. "The old elf is feisty but gentle. He was generous with his lessons. I found it easy to learn from him."

"What are his animal forms?"

"He swore me to secrecy, and I owe him so much. I won't betray him."

Alecia stiffened before him. "You ask that I trust you and yet you desire to keep secrets from me?"

"Only those that have no bearing on us or our future. It should be enough that I have full control over all my animal shapes. I no longer need the amber talisman, nor do I fear becoming trapped in animal form. I only wish I had found Melandrach sooner."

"He could have spared us much heartache," she said. "I still don't like secrets."

"They are Melandrach's secrets, not mine."

She frowned, and he held his breath. He had created this distrust and must endure it until she learned to trust again.

"I'll respect that for now. I'm grateful to him for teaching what you needed to learn. He has given us a chance to be together again, not to mention giving you the happiness you now enjoy. It shines from you, Vard."

He smiled. "Perhaps it was how I was always meant to be. But only one thing will complete me, and that's when you say you'll take me back."

She opened her mouth, but he held up his hand.

"You don't need to say anything, my love. There's no rush. We have all the time in the world."

"Perhaps not. These are uncertain times, Vard. But thank you for giving me the chance to consider." She placed her cup on the table and stood. "I'll take you to Iona."

Vard struggled to contain his excitement as Alecia escorted him to the chamber she shared with Iona. They entered, and a maid curtsied and left them alone in the drawing room. He heard a squawk from the adjoining bedroom and shared a smile with Alecia. Her joy at the sound of their daughter was obvious.

They entered the bedroom, and Alecia crossed to the crib and lifted Iona for Vard to inspect. The infant looked at him with serious blue eyes. Flecks of gold danced in her irises.

"Hello, Daughter." He reached for her, and she came willingly into his arms, her mother watching on as though absorbing every moment of the reunion. The baby's scent enclosed him, reaching into his heart, and squeezing it. He closed his eyes and swallowed down the love that threatened to overwhelm him. But he couldn't stop the tears that escaped.

"I've imagined this moment so many times," he said, his voice hoarse. "I didn't want to, in case it never happened, but I couldn't help it."

Iona reached up a fist and grabbed his nose.

"Ow," he cried. She laughed and squeezed harder.

Alecia giggled and pried her daughter's tiny fist from his nose. Iona promptly grabbed his ear.

"She has a firm grip," he said.

"Tell me about it," Alecia said. "I'm usually the one on the receiving end. Let me feed her and perhaps she'll be ready for a cuddle then."

He watched as Alecia retrieved their daughter, sat, and unpinned her dress. Iona promptly latched on, and the sound of noisy slurps filled the bedchamber. A feeling of calm descended as he watched his daughter nurse, and it took him back to the days after her birth. He recalled the fear he harbored then—the fear of hurting her he didn't think would ever leave. He closed his eyes and listened to Iona, the birds outside, and the small sounds of the surrounding castle.

* * *

As Alecia fed Iona, she watched Vard. She had never seen him happy, let alone this carefree. Perhaps she might have something permanent with *this* Vard. But, at the thought, her heart lurched, and she recalled the moments on the farm after realizing he had left her—again. She shuddered at the memory of the animal scream that had ripped from her. Iona had wailed, and Dana Andra came running as though there was a wolf in the cottage.

She couldn't go through that again, but was there any guarantee that all would be well this time? *No, guard your heart.* There would be no rush to take the father of her daughter back.

His face relaxed and she wondered if he was asleep. He rarely let his guard down to this extent, seeming to be moments from action, even when at rest. But seated on her lady's chair in her bedchamber, Vard appeared almost tame. She smiled and allowed herself to imagine them as a family together; perhaps having more children… Would they all be Defenders?

Stop it, Alecia! Keep your hands to yourself and wait this out.

When Iona was satisfied, Alecia stood and carried her to Vard. She placed the child against his chest, and he awoke, his arms instinctively curling around his daughter. He beamed down at Iona and then up at Alecia.

"She's asleep. Now perhaps I can hold her without losing any of my features."

Alecia laughed softly. "She'll be a fierce warrior. Perhaps a rival to her father."

"I have no doubt." He smiled at her again, and it was all she could do to stop from falling at his feet. It was unfair the power he had over her.

She cleared her throat. "I feel it only fair to warn you that I've made no decision regarding your position in our lives. I intend to take my time."

He stood with the baby, his face closed to her. This was more the old Vard, who kept his soft inner core hidden, protected.

Finally, he faced her. "I understand. I wish it were not the case, but I'm willing to wait."

"I'm sorry, Vard. You can't expect me to fall into your arms at the merest suggestion that you've changed." She stood with her arms around her chest, as if protecting a deep wound. "I need time to see that you really have. And I think you need time too."

He stood before her, his head high, Iona cradled against his chest. "I love you. I worship the ground you walk on. And the fact that you gave me this child? I can never repay the sacrifice you made bringing her into this world. It kills me when I remember how you've suffered; that I caused much of it. But if you think a few harsh words from you will keep me away, you're wrong. I'm yours, forever."

She took a step backward, shocked he had exposed so much of himself. This man was intensely private, and he had made a declaration of his love that would last a lifetime; or so he thought. He could be wrong. *She* could be wrong if she followed her heart and forgot her head.

All she could do was nod. Vard handed Iona to her and left her chambers.

* * *

Benae sat by the bed of the innocent victim of the attack on Vard Anton. She shivered. The man had only been in Brightcastle moments and already he had caused chaos. She shook her head. It wasn't his fault. The watch should have been more vigilant. Thank the Goddess the child, Gracie, would live. She looked across at the mother who had fallen asleep, her head on the bed beside her daughter.

She heaved a sigh, exhausted from her overnight bedside vigil, which had included having to feed Solomon twice. Laying her hands again on Gracie's chest, Benae closed her eyes, sending a thread of spirit through the wound and into the damaged tissues. She knitted some vessels together and watched the blood start to move through them. Before leaving, she inspected the wound again to make sure there was no infection.

Removing her hands from the little chest, she looked up into the worried eyes of the mother.

"All is well, Mistress," Benae said. "Your daughter will make a full recovery. I'll have a pallet made up so you can stay with her and rest. Do you have other children?"

She shook her head. "My husband died several years ago. Gracie and I are on our own. I don't know what I would've done if I lost her."

"How do you make ends meet?" Benae asked.

"I live in my sister's house and help wherever I can with her children and their business. They have a bakery so at least there's always plenty of bread." She smiled tiredly. Benae knew how she felt.

"Well, you're welcome here while Gracie heals. I'm sorry the arrival of the King's Rangers caused such a threat to your daughter."

"It's not your fault, Princess. You've been more than kind." She dropped her eyes for a moment and then raised them again. "I've long been an admirer of Princess Alecia. I hope I can catch sight of her while I'm here."

Benae struggled to keep the smile on her face. Alecia was beloved by the people of Brightcastle while she, Benae, was still an outsider.

No matter what she did, she struggled to convince the populace of her worth. Even when they believed she had produced a son to carry the Zialni name.

"Princess Alecia was at the entrance when Gracie was brought in. I'll see if she can spare a moment to visit when she is well enough."

Gracie's mother clutched Benae's hands, but then released them as if burned. "Sorry Princess, I presume too much to touch you. When do you think my daughter will awake?"

Benae bit her lip and swiped a stray lock of hair from her forehead. "I hope today, Mistress. I'll check her when I've seen my son."

Benae left without waiting for an answer and returned to her room where Solomon slept. She wished to collapse on her bed and sleep for a week, but, as a Guardian of Brightcastle, she couldn't allow herself the luxury. Turning from her sleeping son, Benae found a table laid for two by the window. She took a step toward the table, torn between sleep and food.

There was a noise at the door to her chamber, and Ramón entered. He smiled at her, and she took a moment to admire him. The past year had transformed her husband into a stunning example of male perfection. She was the envy of all the noblewomen, but it wasn't only his looks that set Ramón apart. His sword skills were the equal of anyone, and she trusted his advice on all matters. He was her rock and without him, she'd struggle to cope with the myriad of duties her role encompassed.

He approached and wrapped his arms around her.

"My love," he said. "The night has been long."

She smiled up at him. "But it's over and I rejoice I have you to come home to."

"Sit and eat. Then you must rest."

Benae warmed inside at his words. He never made her feel frail or tired; never questioned her ability to deal with all she was presented with. He had unshakeable faith in her, so much more than she had in herself. It had always been the case—well almost always. At the start of their friendship, Ramón was angry with her for lowering herself to sacrifice love for security with Prince Zialni. He had been right as usual, and it wasn't long before that was clear.

But if Benae hadn't sought a liaison with the prince, she wouldn't have met this man who was spreading her bread with marmalade and pouring her tea. She wouldn't have it any other way, even if the populace still treated her as an interloper.

It didn't help that she was from the neighboring kingdom of Tylevia. One day she hoped that would be forgotten, and that her family would herald a new line of Zialnis to command Thorius.

As long as no one discovered the secret she shared with her husband. No one must know that… ever.

"Do you wish to be present when I speak with Vard Anton?" Ramón asked. "I scheduled the meeting for later this morning, so you could snatch an hour of sleep now."

"As long as Solomon allows it." She smiled at Ramón and took his hand. "I'd like to be present to read his intent. This mission of his could be a ruse to gain information. I don't trust him. He's getting too close to the king."

"Anton's acceptance by King Beniel will delight Alecia," Ramón said. "I'm not sure she's wrong."

"You said he was insane," Benae said, drawing her hand from his.

"That was some time ago. At present, he appears as whole as any man I know. And it wouldn't be easy to convince the queen if that weren't the case. If the king approves of Anton, then it's because the queen approves of him."

"It seems Alecia isn't the only woman Anton has cast his spell upon," Benae said. "I wonder what it means for us." Her eyes snapped to her husband's. "You must be on your guard. He can't know the truth of Solomon."

"Don't worry, my darling. I know how to hold my tongue." He rose and kissed her on the top of her head. "I'll expect you in the great hall in two hours."

At her raised eyebrows, Ramón continued. "I think formality will be in our best interests this time, Benae. It will keep him on the back foot—if anything can."

Ramón left.

Benae sat, sipping her tea and musing on what the future might bring.

CHAPTER 6

VARD strode into the great hall after being announced by the chamberlain's attendant. His eyes swept the large space and settled on the three figures seated on the dais. Ramón Zorba met his gaze squarely and without the flinch which was present at their last encounter. He wasn't proud of the circumstances of the previous meeting. Having to be dragged from the mind of a wolf and return to the world of human reality wasn't something he wished to dwell on. And to have a man who hated him perform the favor was maddening.

He owed Zorba so much, including the lives of Alecia and his daughter. Without his efforts, Iona would've died and most likely Alecia too. Vard would've been condemned to the life of an animal. He shuddered and shook off the memories of insanity that had so nearly been his fate. One day, he'd repay Zorba for the risks he took. It had been a favor for Alecia, but Vard would never forget.

As he walked toward the three assembled, he made a brief study of the small, dark-haired woman in the center of the trio. She was a beauty and highly intelligent if her eyes were anything to go by. There was a fire in her gaze that would have attracted Vard in the past, before Alecia. The woman regarded him with veiled hostility, and he wondered what part of his past caused her resentment.

And then there was Alecia, who grew more beautiful each time he saw her. This morning, she wore another of her ebony gowns. It was a slim design with a high collar and black lace sleeves. The dark fabric looked wonderful with her blonde hair cascading over her shoulders.

But he must focus. He stopped before the trio at the foot of the dais.

Ramón stood. "Welcome, Ranger. I hope you find your accommodations to your liking. Please let me introduce Princess Benae Zorba, my wife and joint Guardian of Brightcastle."

Vard bowed over Benae's hand. It trembled in his grasp, but only just enough for him to detect. He didn't smell fear from her, only prickly irritation and wariness.

"I'm pleased to make your acquaintance, Princess."

She smiled, showing perfectly shaped teeth. "I bid you welcome, Lord Anton. I've heard much about you."

Vard glanced at Ramón. "I can imagine. I'll try to dispel some of the rumors while I'm here."

And then he met Alecia's gaze and nodded. "Good morning, Alecia."

"Vard." His name was a whisper of sound that swirled around him and stopped his breath. How was it that she affected him so with just one whispered word? He fell into the mesmerizing lilac pools of her eyes and would've happily stayed there had not Ramón cleared his throat.

"If you don't mind, Anton," Ramón said, "we all have things to be getting on with this morning."

If Vard could've blushed, he would have. Luckily, embarrassment was one emotion he never allowed to touch him. "Of course." He dragged his gaze from Alecia and engaged Ramón. "I'm here to expand the numbers of my rangers. The king hoped you'd help."

Ramón scowled. "I'll aid the king in whatever way he requests. How will you go about your search?"

"I thought you might have suggestions of those who could be suitable," Vard said. "And also hoped you and Princess Benae might make soldiers available to aid in the search."

"Will you take female candidates, Lord Anton?" Benae asked.

Vard met her gaze and again detected the flutter of unease from the lady. "I can't see why not," he said, "assuming they're suitable. They'd have to have hunting, tracking, and fighting skills."

"There's no reason females couldn't show those abilities," Benae said. "I have several amongst my female guards who would be keen to apply."

Ramón grasped her hand. "Do you think it wise to offer your guards, my dear?"

Benae pursed her lips. "I have plenty of guards and more ready to graduate. I believe female rangers would be an asset to Lord Anton and the king."

Vard nodded, beginning to see why this woman had risen to the position she now occupied. Not only was she intelligent, but thoughtful and generous. It was an unusual and powerful combination. Throw in the rumors about her being a formidable healer and she was a woman to respect.

"I'd be happy to assess those you put forward, Princess." He looked at Ramón. "And you, My Lord? Do you have any suggestions; men you think could be of use?"

"I'm loath to leave our defenses depleted, Anton; however, there are one or two who might make good rangers. Jacques Vorasava is in the city and may help you further. I believe you know him?"

"Of course."

Vard remembered Vorasava from his short time as a captain in Brightcastle and later had helped that same man when he was injured in a mudslide. Vorasava was a competent soldier and a member of the aristocracy. Personally, Vard preferred men who had ascended through the fighting ranks, not officers. Still, the man might prove to be a valuable ally. When previously in Brightcastle, Vard had kept to himself, shunning the company of others for several reasons. Perhaps that had limited his assessment of those around him.

"I'll make the training ground available for you to assess your candidates during the next few days. If you need anything else, please ask." Ramón paused, then continued. "Princess Alecia? You wished to offer your help?"

Vard froze, but tried not to reveal his shock. Why would Alecia agree to help him?

"I grow bored, Vard," Alecia said, "and thought this might be a way to fill my spare hours."

"That would be welcome, of course." His mind shuffled through the countless tasks he could assign her. "Thank you."

Ramón and Benae rose, and Vard bowed.

"I'll have any guardswomen who are interested—and can be spared—meet you at the training ground in one hour, Lord Anton," Benae said. "Good day." She left without further ceremony.

Ramón stepped closer to Vard, and, though the blond man didn't intimidate him, his size and presence impressed. This man was a far cry from the one he had left on the night he fled with Alecia; someone to be reckoned with.

"One thing you mustn't forget, Anton," he said, a determined glint in his eye. "Alecia is under my protection. If you hurt her or Iona again, you'll have me to answer to."

He stalked out to Alecia's outraged gasp. His love stood with fists clenched and delightfully rosy cheeks. Her eyes snapped sparks.

"That man makes my blood boil!" she said, watching him leave the hall. "I'm not under his protection. I'm my own woman. You'd think his wife and her child, not to mention Brightcastle, would be enough to keep him occupied without lumping me in."

Vard stepped closer and grasped her elbow. She trembled and her gaze sought his.

"Don't fear, beloved," he said. "I know you can look after yourself. I can hardly have missed the fact."

She pulled her arm from his grasp. "I'd rather you not use terms of endearment in public, Vard. It might give the wrong impression. I want us on a business-only footing while you're here." She stepped back a pace and heaved a sigh. "I'll meet you in the practice yard in an hour."

She turned and left.

Word spread and there were a dozen women waiting for Vard when he arrived in the practice yard. He paused a moment and opened his senses to his surroundings, stopping here and there when a thorny scent drew his attention. He detected no threat and turned his consideration to the women. They eyed him with varying degrees of curiosity. He took some time to size them up and immediately dismissed two from his list. They stood with barely disguised insolence and wholly obvious arrogance.

He approached and waited until he had their complete attention. He fixed them with his gaze, allowing it to settle on each woman for a full thirty seconds and watching their reactions.

Some squirmed but held his stare; others immediately dropped their eyes; one held his gaze without fidgeting—though she had to scowl to do so. He kept his amusement at her determination hidden. It was exactly what Alecia would've done had she been in the same position.

The mood of the women bubbled with frustration and no little anxiety. *Good.* He needed to know how they conducted themselves when discomforted. He grinned at them and several shivered.

"Good morning, ladies," he said. "My name is Vard Anton, and I'm here in Brightcastle to find more rangers for the king's service. This is an elite force, the purpose of which is to protect the kingdom. Rangers must be brave, intelligent, and competent fighters with high standards of forest craft. They must know how to move with stealth and to track in the toughest conditions." He paused again to glance around the group. "If any of you believe you don't have these attributes, you may leave."

A few of the women shuffled their feet, and there were whispered discussions. Vard waited patiently, knowing a little time now would save more later. He walked to the fence closest to the stable, and leaned against the rail. Alecia, clad in breeches and a cream shirt and green tunic, joined him.

"I see you're just as good at putting people at ease as you were when we first met," she said, her voice sarcastic.

He smiled. "It's not my job to put these people at ease, but to discover those who can serve the kingdom." He continued to watch the women. "At least two of these ladies will decide the life of a ranger isn't for them, saving me valuable time in assessing them."

"That's a little harsh, isn't it?" Alecia asked. "Many women undervalue their talents."

"That's *their* problem."

She huffed out a breath but remained silent.

Two of the candidates approached and bowed to Vard and Alecia.

"We have decided to withdraw, Ranger," the taller of the two said. "Thank you for the opportunity."

"You're excused, ladies," Vard said.

They bowed and left, and Alecia turned to face him. "Can you really afford to lose valuable candidates? I'm sure I've seen those two in Benae's guard. They would've been excellent."

"Not if their hearts aren't in the job. If you're going to fight me in every decision, this is going to take too long." He fixed her with the stare that usually made the strongest man crumble. Alecia only folded her arms under her breasts.

"You win for now as you're in charge," she said. "Tell me what you need me to do."

"Thank you so much," he said, sarcastically. "You can help me assess their fighting skills."

* * *

It wasn't really Vard's tactic that had Alecia on edge and angry. She was intuitive enough to recognize what irritated her. And that made her want to jab at him; try to annoy him and set him on the back foot. It wasn't working, and it was childish of her to attempt it. But it was so difficult being with him and having their relationship on a wholly professional footing. The joke was very much on her. If there was one thing they would never be to one another, it was professional colleagues.

But that was exactly how they needed to conduct themselves if they were to survive this duty. She stalked to the weapons rack and selected a wooden practice sword. It was still dangerous enough to inflict serious injury, but she'd be careful. The sword wasn't her favored weapon. She preferred knives and the longbow. But she was good enough to test these women—she hoped.

She approached the group as Vard was giving his instructions. He introduced her and selected a candidate to pair with Alecia. The rest chose their own partners, except for a tall, dark-haired woman whom Vard fought.

Alecia was soon too consumed to think about anything but keeping one step ahead of her auburn-haired partner. The lass was short, but what she lacked in height and reach, she made up for in speed. In her mind, Alecia dubbed the woman "Red", and she was good. Easily good enough to be selected. Red launched an aggressive flurry of sword strokes at Alecia, then moved in and swept her foot out from under her. Alecia went down, just barely getting her sword up in time to prevent her opponent's blade reaching her neck. The two glared at each other, breathing hard. A slow hand clap began, and Red reached down and helped Alecia to her feet.

Vard stood watching from across the compound, not even a faint sheen of sweat on his brow. "Very good, ladies. I enjoyed that last move. Where did you learn it?"

"I have four brothers, Ranger. I learnt it fighting as a child."

"What's your name?" Vard asked.

"Maerwyn Paige, Ranger."

Not "Red" then, Alecia thought.

"Maerwyn, you may choose three other candidates to battle," Vard said. "Your goal is to defeat all of them."

Red did as ordered, and Alecia stood with her arms folded, watching as the woman defeated all her opponents in quick time. From what Alecia could judge, Maerwyn was the best sword fighter in the group.

The morning passed quickly, and Alecia fought most of the others, only being challenged by the tall woman whom Vard first fought. The mood in the group was combative, but fair. No one was hurt apart from superficial bruising. It was soon time for luncheon, and Alecia's stomach grumbled. She needed to find her child and feed her as well.

Vard dismissed the women and asked them to return for archery and knife skills in the afternoon. He walked Alecia to the castle entrance.

"What do you think of them?" she asked.

He raised his brows. "I'm impressed. I hadn't thought to find this many women trained to the sword." He considered her. "You held your own exceedingly well. I'd offer you a place in my rangers tomorrow if you wanted it. Of course, the idea is silly, but I thought you'd enjoy hearing my assessment." His green gaze bored into her.

What did he expect her to say? Thank you so much for approving?

"I surprised myself. However, I assure you I don't need your approval to feel good. And if I wanted to join the rangers, I would. It just so happens I have other priorities."

"As I said, Alecia. I wasn't trying to insult you."

"Oh, I know you weren't *trying*. You can't help it." She started up the stairs, but turned back to him. "I'll meet you after luncheon. I'm looking forward to the rest of the skills tests."

She entered the castle, smiling to herself that she had succeeded in having the last word in their verbal sparring match.

The following morning, Alecia dined in the formal breakfast room, having fed her daughter and assigned Millie to her. The maid had tended to Alecia before she left with Vard, and she had finally found her in the laundry. Though annoyingly talkative at times, her skills were too developed to waste washing linens. Alecia's blood still boiled over the slight on her old hand maiden.

She shook her head as she helped herself to toast, bacon, and eggs. That was something that must change in the palace. There were too many unfamiliar faces amongst the staff. It was as if the keep had been cleansed, and she wanted to know why. Perhaps Ramón or Benae would tell her.

She looked forward to the day. Vard had chosen eight women from the ten who trialed yesterday, and Alecia was keen to put them through their paces. It was really the weapons master's job to do this.

But she'd report to Vard and take part in the training. The fighting of yesterday had made her feel alive and tempted her to take a job that would further develop her skills.

But she could not. Iona needed her, especially now when she was at the breast. The child could be weaned, but Alecia had vowed to feed her until she no longer wanted to. Even should she stop feeding her from the breast, there was more to mothering than feeding. Her priorities needed to be her daughter, finding the truth of her father's death, and convincing her uncle to name her heir.

The trouble was Uncle Beniel resided in Wildecoast, and she couldn't travel there with Iona. It was too dangerous. Would the king come to her? Perhaps she might invite him to meet her daughter. And Solomon would have his naming day soon. Surely Uncle Beniel would travel here for that?

She smiled as she remembered the humble ceremony where Iona had received her name. At least Vard had been present, along with the Andras and the local priest.

Ramón entered the room and paused when he saw Alecia at the sideboard.

"Good morning, Princess," he said, inclining his head. It wasn't really a bow, but it still irritated her when he stood on ceremony like that.

"Would you stop calling me 'Princess'?" she said. "At least in private, 'Alecia' should suffice."

"As you wish." He pulled a chair out for her and helped her sit. "How are you this morning? That was quite a workout you had yesterday."

She flinched as she sat. "I'm fine. A little stiff, but that's only to be expected. I was pleased my skills had developed so far." Truth be told, she was sore in more places than she could count, but she wouldn't complain to Ramón.

"You fought well," he said, helping himself to food and pouring them both teas. "However, it wasn't quite what I foresaw when I asked you to help Anton. You don't need to be so physically involved. I don't want you hurt."

She raised her brows at him as he sat opposite. "Surely you knew I could never sit idly by and do paperwork? Where's the fun in that?"

He leaned across the table. "You always were your own worst enemy," he said. "And impulsive with it! You have a daughter to think of and those practice swords can kill almost as easily as a real sword, especially when wielded by the inexperienced. I'm stunned Anton allowed it."

She tilted her head at him. "Can you please hush? I don't want to fight with you. I'll save my energy for the women today." She paused. "Instead, I want to know when and why Millie was banished to the laundry."

His head snapped up. "What the devil are you talking about?"

"My old maid? The one who served me before I left with Vard." She fixed him with a steely gaze, the one guaranteed to fluster him once upon a time. All she got in return was a narrowing of the eyes.

"Oh, yes. Now I recall." He thought for a while. "I believe your father had her banished to the laundry when you left. He suspected she had helped you escape."

"That's poppycock!" she said. "If he had suspected that, he would have executed her, or at least dismissed her. What really happened?"

Benae chose that moment to enter, and Alecia ground her teeth.

"Good morning, Alecia," she said breezily. "How goes the ranger assessment?"

Ramón appeared relieved. But she'd get the truth out of him eventually, and there would be no blaming her father.

"I'm well, Benae. We recruited eight women yesterday and I'm to help again today. It was wonderful to swing a sword against them. You should try it."

The dark-haired beauty frowned. "I believe I have enough to keep me busy."

"Ah yes, there's Brightcastle to run, and Solomon, of course. How is he this morning?"

"Fussy. It's why I'm late. He had me up all night."

"Sorry to hear. Iona is a good sleeper."

Ramón shook his head at her, but Alecia ignored him. This woman knew more about her father's death than she was telling, and she would not be kind to her!

"You know, Benae, being a new mother is difficult. I would be happy to help since you don't have your own mother to give advice."

"That won't be necessary, Alecia," Benae said, showing her teeth in what Alecia took for a smile. She turned to Ramón. "I believe I'll break my fast in my room, dearest." With those words, Benae left.

Alecia looked at her friend wide-eyed. "What did I say?"

He scowled. "You know very well what you said, but, in case you don't: Benae lost her mother and father to an illness. She nursed them and couldn't save them. She has never forgiven herself. Now, if you'll excuse me…"

He left the room abruptly, no doubt to follow Benae. Alecia tried to harden her heart to the other woman's suffering. but failed. She hadn't known the details of Benae's parents' demise. If she had, she would never have said what she just had.

Alecia tried to put the encounter with Benae out of her head, but it dogged her all morning. A heavy cloud of guilt sat upon her as she fought the women, and she channeled the feelings into her battles until her opponents asked for mercy. Even Red held up her hands in surrender.

"Excuse me, Princess," Maerwyn said, hand up and breathing hard, "but your face wears a scowl as though you fight an enemy instead of your kinswoman. I need a break."

"There will be no break when you're fighting an actual enemy," the weapons master said.

Alecia stood with her hands on her hips, sword dangling from her fingers. "She's right. I'm in a mood this morning and I'm taking it out on the recruits. I'm sorry… Maerwyn." She had almost called her "Red". "I'll take a break and return after luncheon."

She threw her sword down and marched from the training ground. She wouldn't be coming back this afternoon unless she was in a better mood. Nothing was as it should be, but one thing she could fix was to apologize to Benae.

Alecia returned to her room and changed into a fresh tunic and breeches after giving herself a sponge bath. Iona wasn't present, but she often spent time with Solomon, so Alecia went in search of her daughter. *Kill two birds with one stone.* Her gut churned as she imagined saying the words she must to Benae.

She tapped on Benae's door and was bid enter. Benae, Solomon, and Iona were with Millie in the sitting room. Iona gave a squeal of delight when she saw her, but Benae fixed Alecia with an angry green gaze and tilted her nose in the air.

Into the lion's den. She walked over and picked up her daughter, then dismissed Millie. Once the woman had left, Alecia turned to Benae.

"I'm sorry for my words at breakfast, Benae. They were thoughtless and hurtful, and I deeply regret them."

Benae's eyes widened briefly before she smoothed the surprise from her face. "Apology accepted. Ramón told me he informed you of my parents' history. But I didn't know if I should expect an apology."

The frank admission had Alecia's attention. It was a pity they could never be friends, because this woman was interesting and intelligent. But she had secrets.

No matter what happened, Alecia had to remember that.

She sat and placed Iona to the breast to stop her fussing.

"You know, I'm not such a bad person," Alecia said. "I'm happy to admit when I'm wrong."

"You're mistaken about me having had a hand in your father's death, but you won't admit that."

"The entire episode feels wrong. I can't place my finger on it, but something happened between you, my father, and Ramón. There's too much silence on the matter, and you and he get a hunted look each time it's mentioned. And, when I returned, I found Millie in the laundry. She was my maid. Why was she banished?"

"It's not unusual for a lady to choose new staff when she takes over a household."

Alecia brushed the downy black hair on her daughter's head with a finger. "Then you did banish her?"

Benae made an indelicate sound. "I arrived a month after you departed. I brought my own maid. Millie was already absent from the position of lady's maid by then. I'd seen her around the castle, but I didn't know she was your maid until now."

Alecia looked at Benae with narrowed eyes. Was she telling the truth? It was easy enough to check by asking Millie, but one didn't just come out and ask the servants some things. Nonetheless, perhaps she would have to.

She pursed her lips then sat Iona up and swapped sides. Once the baby was slurping again, Alecia tackled the next question.

"Did you and Ramón betray my father?"

Benae gasped at the abrupt change of subject, her hand flying to her throat. "I was a loyal wife to your father. No one could have tried harder to make him happy. I gave him an heir, for the sake of the Goddess!"

The necessity of feeding Iona kept Alecia seated when she wanted to surge to her feet. "That doesn't answer my question," she said in clipped words. "Were you unfaithful to my father?"

Benae stood, dignity wrapped around her like a cloak. "You've made your apology. I think you should leave. Now."

Alecia stood, cradling Iona against her chest, and left without another word, closing the door with a sharp click. *Damn it! Her apology had been sincere and now she had ruined it with her questions!* Her stomach rumbled, and she remembered it was time for the midday meal. She went in search of food and of Millie.

CHAPTER 7

VARD had been in Brightcastle for five days and had barely seen Alecia or his daughter. He suspected Alecia was avoiding him. She frequented the practice yard only when he was absent. Apart from the first full day of his visit here, he hadn't spoken to her.

However, his visit had been fruitful, and he had another thirty ranger recruits, plus the eight women. He also had an idea where he could find one or two potential Defenders. An informant didn't come right out and tell you they thought a shapeshifter dwelled amongst them. Rather, the pattern of activity of some people suggested it. Defenders were solitary, usually men, who were often mercenaries, assassins, or soldiers. They kept on the move and had an air of mystery about them. He should know… he had lived like that for long enough.

The time drew near when he must return to Wildecoast. On the return journey, he could investigate a few of the Defender leads he had gathered. That task was one best done alone, so he'd send his rangers and the recruits ahead of him.

Currently, he lay in wait for Alecia, tucked out of sight behind a tree trunk beside the practice yard. The female ranger recruits were just finishing their luncheon, and his love would be along soon—unless she got wind of his presence. He wanted to test her fighting skills—to satisfy himself that she could take care of herself and Iona. He hoped it wouldn't be necessary.

His senses went on alert as she approached the yard, her gaze darting around as she crossed the parade ground. Her shoulders relaxed, and she smiled a greeting to the women who awaited her. Vard grinned. He never tired of watching her move, her long legs eating up the ground as she appeared to glide over it.

Everything about Alecia was long and lean, and the last few days in the sun had dusted freckles across the bridge of her nose. She reached for a practice sword and laughed at something one of her companions said. It was a shame to interrupt such grace and carefree focus.

He stepped from the cover of the tree and waited, pleased to observe the immediate attention of the women. He would've been disappointed if the trainee rangers hadn't noticed him immediately. Alecia spun, her sword before her, gaze narrowed. The force of her glare struck him in his core and seemed to try to force him back. No one had ever had this effect upon him, but, from the first day, Alecia had gotten under his skin—and there she had stayed.

"Good afternoon, Princess," he said. "Ladies. I want to congratulate you on your attention. You've passed the last test of your admission to the Rangers. You'll all leave for Wildecoast and the next stage of your training within two days. I suggest you spend time with your families while you can. Whatever ties you once had to work in Brightcastle, I relieve you from. Put up your practice blades and prepare for your journey."

He had their full attention. "Questions?"

"Nay, My Lord. Thank you, My Lord."

"Then leave us."

The women departed with hurried bows. The woman called Maerwyn stopped by Alecia.

"I've enjoyed our association, Princess. I wish you well in the future."

Alecia nodded. "Go in peace, and may the Goddess protect you." Alecia watched her go and then turned to Vard.

"You had them eating from the palm of your hand. Nothing changes."

"You sound jealous."

She shook her head. "I don't know what to be around you."

"You've been avoiding me." He fetched a practice blade and came to stand before her. "Now let's see what you've learned this week."

She brought her sword up. "I'm not one of your trainees, Vard. This isn't necessary."

"You're the love of my life and the mother of my child." Emotion gripped his throat, and he struggled with the words. He took a deep breath and let it out. "Of course, it's necessary. Sword up!"

He lunged at her. She barely blocked his strike before sliding away. He chased her as she spun and swept her sword at his waist. But he avoided the blow and whacked his weapon across her calf. The blow was light, but enough to unbalance her. She went down on her back, barely bringing her sword up in time to stop his weapon from taking her in the throat.

He stepped away. "Good, very good. Now let's get to work on your weaknesses, and perhaps I can leave with a little peace of mind."

Vard struggled for concentration as Ramón Zorba raised his practice sword. Alecia hovered in the background, the cause of his distraction. She should be resting after her four-hour training session, yet she had stayed to watch. She wasn't the only one.

He kept on the move, sword raised, as he observed the former squire. Theirs was a complicated relationship. On Zorba's side, it consisted of hate and revulsion. On Vard's, he didn't feel much for the man at all, besides gratitude for bringing him back from the wolf.

As he had once before, Zorba had appeared in the training ring and challenged Vard. It meant naught to Vard whether he won or lost, but clearly Zorba had longed for this duel for months.

Zorba's blue eyes narrowed a split second before he launched a blistering series of strikes aimed at Vard's body. Vard fended them away, dancing around his opponent's blade with practiced ease. Even tired, his performance was little impacted.

Blowing a bit, Zorba paused to recover his wind and attacked again.

This time, Vard's defense got through Ramón's attack, and he struck the blond man a glancing blow on the skull. Vard's mind zapped back over a year ago to the last time he had fought Ramón and put him in bed for a day. But this time, Zorba wiped away the blood and redoubled his attack, jaw clenched and bringing all his strength to bear.

He forced Vard back, and only his extreme agility and fitness enabled him to stay ahead of the attack.

Finally, Zorba succeeded in trapping Vard against the wooden fence of the practice ground, their swords crossed between them, points to the sky. Zorba's face stopped mere inches from Vard's.

"I've waited months for this," Zorba ground out, eyes blazing with determination. "Consider this your punishment for everything you've done to Alecia. You don't know the meaning of love."

Vard pushed back, but the heavier man was an immovable block. He slid to the side instead and swapped positions with Zorba, swords still trapped between them.

"You need to get over this competition you think we share," Vard sneered. "That's unless your marriage to Benae is a convenient farce."

At Vard's words, Zorba roared and shoved Vard backward. Vard tried to dance out of the way, but lost his balance and landed on his back, the wind knocked out of him. He forced the air into his lungs and rolled to the side just as Zorba's blade speared into the dirt of the yard.

Vard leapt to his feet and danced away, on full alert for the first time in this fight. That last blow would have been a killing strike, even with a practice blade.

Zorba turned to him, eyes cold.

"What's the deal?" Vard asked. "Is this now a fight to the death?"

"I wouldn't waste my time on you." Zorba threw his sword at Vard. He caught it a moment before it would have speared his throat. He didn't take his gaze from the man until he had left the yard.

Alecia joined him. "Are you alright?" Her eyes slid over him, taking inventory, but she must have been satisfied he had sustained no serious injuries.

"The young pup has grown some teeth," Vard said, sending his wolf senses out to ensure Zorba was at a safe distance. Fury and frustration swirled in the man's wake.

"I don't know what got into him," Alecia said, "but I'll be having words with him about his behavior."

"Don't bother," Vard said. "I can fight my own battles, and you have more important matters to attend to."

He tore his focus from Zorba's scent trail and looked down at Alecia. Her lilac eyes were wide with fright. His heart jumped in his chest.

"I'm fine, Alecia. I'll see you later." With that, he replaced both swords in the racks and left the ground.

* * *

Alecia groaned as she slipped under the hot water of her bath. Long forgotten muscles protested every movement. At this rate, she'd be unable to get out of the tub without Millie's help. The maid hummed as she fetched a bucket of warm water and gently poured it over her head. Strong fingers massaged soap through her hair, and eased away the dirt and sweat from hours of sword practice.

It was her own fault. Vard had wanted to quit after two hours, but she insisted on another two, wanting to make the most of his training. He had never devoted this length of time to her weapons instruction. Perhaps before, when the bear had threatened his control, it had been too dangerous.

No matter the reason, he was generous with his time, and she had taken full advantage. A crowd had gathered to watch, but she'd been mostly oblivious to the attention.

And that crowd had been rewarded with Ramón and Vard's fight. What had begun as a professional challenge had deteriorated into a grudge match. She huffed out a breath at not being able to take Ramón to task over his behavior. Vard was right, though, it was best she stay out of this. Best to focus on the night ahead.

"Do you think it wise to host Lord Anton in your chambers, Princess?" Millie asked. Already the maids were setting the table in the sitting room, and a cozy fire crackled in the grate.

"Millie, I appreciate you're only looking out for me, but he's the father of my child. I have nothing to fear from him." Millie overstepped at times, but Alecia had few female friends, so if the maid wanted to assume the role of older sister, she would allow it.

As her hair was rinsed and back scrubbed, she mused on Vard. *Did she have nothing to fear?* Her traitorous heart thumped like a drum every time she was close to him. It was why she had avoided him for the last four days. But she was no closer to deciding if her future lay with him. Vard assumed it did, and she loved him enough to forget their past problems. But was that the right course of action? Did she need her life complicated by this man?

Most of the time, the answer to that question was "no". But she must think of Iona. Her daughter needed a father and a mentor. Every time she contemplated her future and Vard, her thoughts circled round, and nothing was ever decided. Well, tonight she would speak to him and decide on a course of action.

The dining table was set and Millie had departed. Iona would spend the night with Solomon and his nanny, at least until after dinner. Alecia peered at herself in the mirror. Since returning to Brightcastle, she had sought her looking glass more frequently. Her appearance mattered more here than it ever had on the Andras' farm. Tonight, she wanted to remind Vard of what he had walked away from.

She had cast aside the black and wore a deep purple satin gown with a plunging neckline and full sleeves. It was trimmed with silver thread, her hair piled up and restrained with a silver tiara. Nerves tingled in her stomach. She took herself in hand. This night, she would enjoy to the fullest, whatever it brought.

There was a knock at the door, and she went to open it. Vard stood without, breathtakingly handsome in black. His lips curved in a smile as he gave her a leisurely inspection. She heated under his gaze.

"Good evening, Alecia," he said. "You're magnificent."

She smiled. "Come in." She stood back to allow him to enter and closed the door. "I was just thinking the same thing about you."

He took her hand and kissed it, then drew her close and kissed her on each cheek. He stood looking down upon her as if absorbing each tiny detail. The golden chips of his eyes drew her in, and time ceased to have any significance.

Alecia didn't know how long they stood like that, but, finally, Vard cleared his throat.

"I apologize for staring," he said. "I hope you don't mind, but I have a surprise for you." He walked to the door and opened it, beckoning for someone to enter.

It was several someones as it happened—three men carrying lutes. Before she knew it, Vard had swept her into his arms. They danced to the soft strains of a waltz, and she tilted her head back and giggled. It was frivolous and so delicious she could hardly believe her ferocious Defender had thought of it.

"You astonish me, Vard," she said. "I would never have expected this from you, but I love it. Thank you."

He grinned and drew her closer until she could feel the beat of his heart. She drew a deep breath and rested her head on his chest, closing her eyes and allowing him to guide her around the room. That song flowed into another, and they swayed in each other's arms, oblivious to anything but the beat of their hearts and the movement of their bodies.

When the song ended, Vard asked the musicians to leave and seated her at the dining table. A maid served them and left quietly. Now it was her turn to bask in Vard's delight as he sampled cheese, meats, loaves and flatbread, followed by beef and potatoes. Alecia had raided the cellar and found a heavy red wine to accompany the meal.

As they ate, Vard told her of his search for ranger candidates and a little of his learning with Melandrach, his mentor. Slowly, she realized this was a different man from the one she had fallen in love with. This Vard was more hypnotic, more endearing than the haunted Defender whose care she had been placed into so long ago.

She relaxed and opened her heart to him, telling him of the months he had missed with Iona. Her heart broke at the sadness in his eyes. Slowly, the pain which had long constricted her heart, lifted.

At the end of the meal, Alecia reclined in her chair and sipped the wine, her gaze drifting over Vard as he talked. Finally, he ran out of words and relaxed into his chair.

"We could have this every night," he said.

And just like that, the spell broke. His words reminded her this was an illusion, a temporary respite from the loneliness she had become used to. This night had shown her that Vard had changed. He was no longer the dangerous man who had captured her heart, but a confident leader with a place in the world. It was a place she lacked.

She stood and walked to the fire, staring into the flames as though they could give her answers. Vard joined her.

"Tell me what to do and I'll do it, Alecia."

She turned to him. "That's just it, Vard. You're master of your own destiny, as you never were before. It's not my place to order you. That's not how our relationship has ever functioned. Before, I depended upon you for everything, although I was unprepared to admit that."

He shook his head. "You're too hard on yourself. You've faced more hardship and loss in the last year or so than most people do in a lifetime. Of course, you depended upon me. And I let you down. You should be proud of what you've achieved—on your own."

She shook her head. "I ran away when I should have faced my father and Finus. I had so many chances to make different decisions. Instead, I acted impulsively. Hetty tried to warn me that taking matters into my own hands would lead to grief. I should've listened, and perhaps my father would be alive today."

"Forgive me Alecia, but how would that be better than the situation which now exists? You'd have your father, but would the kingdom be better off?"

Pain blazed through her. "At least I'd know I hadn't caused his death."

He gripped her upper arms, and his heat warmed a core suddenly cold at her admission. She had indirectly caused her father's death. That's what this anger at Benae was really about!

"Alecia, listen to me." He seemed to choose his words with care. "Your father made many poor decisions which you tried to rectify. But you're not responsible for his decisions or his death."

She tried to absorb what he said, but couldn't. "You're wrong. I know he wasn't perfect, far from it. But he would've listened, eventually. I could have asked Uncle Beniel for help. When I think of my arrogance!"

"All the young are arrogant. But, at your core, you're good, only wanting the best for everyone in your life. I won't have you berate yourself for your choices." He paused, studying her. "What do you want, Alecia? You must decide and then go after it."

"I know what I want, but not how to get it. It's insane that a woman can't rule in Thorius. I'm the logical successor to the throne being my father's oldest child. I know I can rule after Uncle Beniel. If only I could speak to him, I'm sure I could make him understand."

Vard's eyes widened at her admission. "Alecia, please don't set yourself up to fail. Your uncle has already named Solomon. He'll never make you heir."

"I love that baby," Alecia said, "but I won't accept him over me as heir. Admit it. I could govern the kingdom, be a wonderful queen. There's no reason we can't return to the days of kings *and* queens. All I must do is convince Uncle Beniel."

"And how will you do that?"

"I'll travel to see him. I can go with you when you leave, and I'll take Iona."

He shook his head. "It's not safe, Alecia. I forbid you to travel with our daughter."

She drew her shoulders back and speared him with her frostiest glare. "What makes you think you have a say?"

He jerked, the gold flecks in his irises flaring and dying. "I'd like to think I have some say regarding our daughter. And even accompanying me, I couldn't guarantee her safety. I'm sorry Alecia, but I don't want you to travel east with her."

"We were perfectly fine travelling here from the Andras."

"That also was foolhardy. I'm not sure what Zorba was thinking when he allowed it."

"Never mind. I'll take your words into consideration, but I can't promise anything."

"I leave the day after tomorrow, but I go alone. I plan to search for a couple of these reported Defenders on the way back to Wildecoast. So you see, I won't be able to protect you."

"Then the king must come here. Somehow, I'll speak to him, face to face."

Vard laid his palm along her cheek, and she closed her eyes as the tender gesture flooded her with desire. When she opened them, Vard's lips hovered close to hers.

"Keep yourself and our daughter safe." His mouth covered hers and swept her away on a cloud of desperate wanting. Too soon, the moment was over. "Iona must be your priority." He brushed her lips once more, then turned and left.

She stared after him, unsure what to make of the dinner and their time together. He wanted her and she him, but they had both changed in the past year. Could they still create a life together? Would she endanger her battered heart yet again if she allowed him in? Or should she share their child, but nothing else?

She shook her head, more confused than ever. Once she had thought they were destined to be together, but now she was uncertain.

Perhaps her destiny lay with the people and service. But if she became queen, she must have more children to secure the succession. Iona wouldn't be enough. And that meant marriage, perhaps to a man she didn't love.

Her heart skipped a beat. Would she condemn herself to exactly the life her father had mapped out for her? Deep inside, she knew her spirit would wither if she denied her passion and freedom.

She sat before the fire, watching the flames long into the night, but was no closer to a solution when she sought her rest.

CHAPTER 8

VARD took the road east from Brightcastle, his mood low. It had been much easier when Alecia was but a memory, when Iona's little face was only imagined. Now he had spent time in their company again, he longed to be with them. True, he had purpose and a confidence he had long sought. But what was that worth without his family?

He distracted himself with plans for the next week. He would set his rangers and their charges on the road to Wildecoast then strike south.

Reports of two men with strange behaviors had come to him during his time at Brightcastle.

One young man was said to vanish when the moon was full, and when he reappeared, he was wild and unhinged. Another older man had disturbing eyes and lived alone in a cabin in the woods. Both reports filled Vard with hope that he might discover others of his kind.

Around midday, he bid his men farewell and struck off to the south. They weren't comfortable with him traveling solo. He had used compulsion in the end to convince them to continue without him. He hated doing it, preferring to allow others their free will. It was a skill easily abused, and he was determined only to use it when necessary. But it was a slippery slope. In the wrong hands, it could be disastrous.

He had come close to using it on Alecia last night—so close. But he had sworn never to do so. She didn't know he had the power to compel someone to act a certain way, and he wouldn't abuse her.

When it came to Iona's safety, however, he'd been tempted. But how could he ever face Alecia again if he succumbed to forcing her against her will? Even if she didn't know, *he* would know what a low act he'd performed.

There were so many ways he could use the gift for ill. He could force a woman to lie with him, could convince anyone to walk over a cliff or off a wall, could coerce a man to stab his neighbor. He shook his head as he rode along, senses tuned to his surroundings, a stone of fear in his gut at the thought that one day he might step over that line.

He rode south all day, morphing into the hawk at regular intervals to scout the terrain ahead. By dusk, he was nearing the place where one of his targets lived. At least, the patch of woods was as close as Vard could narrow the location down to. The older man with the strange eyes was reported to live alone in a cabin, hunting and selling skins to make a living. He was keen to find him and judge for himself.

Vard's stallion snorted as the path entered a thick patch of woods. The black and white beast threw his head up, ears twitching in all directions. The hairs on Vard's neck stood up, a warning he couldn't ignore. He stopped his horse and dismounted, leading him into the woods a way and tying him to a tree.

He patted Trax on the neck. "Easy boy, nothing to be worried about."

Vard left his mount and returned to the path, continuing until he came to a game trail which headed west. He crept along it, everything in him screaming that the next few moments would be crucial. His movements slowed, and he slipped from shadow to shadow.

He was about to transform into the wolf when he spied a cabin through the trees. He sent his senses out. A heart beat on the edge of his hearing—it was slow and strong. It was human.

Vard was uncertain if he should transform or not. He had no desire to scare the man in the cabin—it would be a poor way to convince him to come with him if he turned out to be a Defender. The lure of the wolf form tempted him, and he almost succumbed, but forced the canine away. Let the man come at him if that was what he wished.

He was equal to the threat.

He circled around to the rear of the cabin, examining the structure from every angle. It looked deserted, but had been made to appear that way. His heart kicked up a notch at the thought of finding someone like him, but he breathed the excitement away—it would only make him careless.

As he crouched in the shadows, an arm looped around his neck, and he felt the sharp metal of a knife against his ribs.

"Don't think about fighting, laddie," a gruff voice warned from beside his ear. "This knife is long enough to reach your heart."

"I mean you no harm." Vard kept his voice calm, however, on the inside, he was anything but. Sweat broke out under his leather head band as he tested the strength of the man who had ambushed him. *Damn him!*

"You're in a pickle, laddie." He gave the knife a shove and Vard grunted. "I'm in a similar plight though. I don't doubt you can best me in a fight. This is my only chance to be victor, while I have this knife against your ribs."

"I'm not here to hurt you," Vard said. "Put the knife down and we can talk. You can trust me."

"I can't see your face. How should I trust you?"

"I won't harm you. Can't you feel my sincerity?"

There was a moment of silence in which Vard sent out a thread of reassurance. It wasn't compulsion, just enough encouragement to convince the man to trust him.

Finally, he loosened his hold, and the knife moved from Vard's ribs. He stepped back, and Vard raised his hands in the air. "Can I turn around?"

Again, there was silence. Vard sent another trickle of comfort to his companion.

"You may turn but keep your hands where I can see them."

Slowly, step by step, Vard turned until he faced the man. He was seeing things, surely! "It can't be!" he said, his hands falling to his sides.

The man before him wore a full beard and stood as tall and lean as Vard. But he had changed since Vard had last seen him. Vibrant golden flecks sparkled in his hazel eyes.

Vard grasped the older man and pulled him close. "Father..."

Slowly, the older man wrapped his arms around his son. "I thought never to see you again."

Lyam Anton had come back to him as Alecia said he would. Vard's heart ached in powerful bursts, as though it wished to escape his chest. His father, his only remaining link to his childhood, the only man who had ever understood him.

They stood, arms around each other, for long moments as the sun set. It was almost dark when Lyam stepped away. "You're a sight for sore eyes, lad. I'm equally surprised to find you hale and well. Will you stay the night?" Vard wiped a tear from his cheek. "I'd love to. Let me get my horse."

By the time Vard had retrieved Trax and made him comfortable in a small lean-to, his father had dished up two bowls of rabbit stew and cut thick wedges of crusty bread. He poured wine and set the fare before the fire. Vard gave the cabin a brief inspection as he entered, then joined his father at the hearth. He picked up the goblet of wine and drank half of it, though it wasn't his custom to imbibe much alcohol. A pleasant warmth spread from his stomach.

"What brought you here, Father?" he asked. "You disappeared. and I thought you dead—or worse." All this time, he had locked away the grief of losing his father, thinking he had dealt with the pain. Now it rose to stab at him.

"Worse, lad," he said. "I've been to hell and back." He looked everywhere but at Vard, and when finally he met his eyes, he flinched.

"Tell me," Vard said. "I won't judge you. I'm glad to have my father back. You should know there'll be no reproach from me, considering my past."

"Think of the worst you ever did and multiply it many times over."

"What happened?"

"I didn't mean to abandon you, Vard. I tried my best to support you, but I had no real idea of how to help. It was more and more difficult to cope with… everything. In the end, I ran away rather than face what you had become."

Vard reached for his father's hand, but the older man didn't touch him.

He continued. "It was a kind of insanity, lad. I'm not proud of how I reacted. I found a cave and lived off the land, trying to block out your existence. For a time, I succeeded, but then the dreams started—nightmares. I dreamt I was roaming the woods in the body of a bear. Only they weren't dreams."

Vard recalled the time he woke in a clearing to find the battered body of his cousin, killed during his uncontrolled transformation. More hidden pain leaked out. "Please, just tell me."

"Soon I started waking up to the remnants of my meals." His father sobbed and took a large gulp of wine. "Men and women—even children. Each morning, there was a fresh horror to face. I didn't know how to stop it."

Vard sat frozen, reliving his father's pain as no one else ever could. "What did you do?"

"I was halfway to being an animal by then. The part of me that was still a man knew I had to flee. I had to go into the wilderness and break the cycle or kill myself; anything to stop the slaughter." He looked at Vard, eyes red, and Vard witnessed the desperation he still felt. "I've been hoping to find you for the last year, yet afraid of doing so in case I killed you."

Vard put out his hand and grasped his father's shoulder. "You have nothing to fear. I've mastered my gift, finally. I can help you a little, but then you must go to the Defender who trained me. An elf called Melandrach. He lives deep in the mountains to the northwest, and he's powerful."

A hopeful light had entered his father's eyes. Vard undid the amber talisman from his neck, the gift his father had given him when he first manifested the talent, and held it out. "I'll teach you what I can, then you must seek the elf."

Lyam extended his hand to receive the stone.

"You still have it." The older man's throat bobbed with emotion. "You don't know how many times I've thought of this amulet over the years and wished I held it. For a time, it was all I thought of."

"How did you survive, Father?"

"I travelled as far north as I could into remote country where few humans lived. I avoided meat of all kinds and lived on berries and plants. Gradually, the bear left me, and I became only the hawk. The bird was a form I hadn't become until the bear left me."

Vard nodded. "The hawk is one of my greatest joys, but it's also vulnerable. Are you sure you weren't trying to kill yourself?"

"Better that than kill any more people." He paused, eyes closed, then met Vard's eyes once more. "I don't deserve to live, lad. I should ask you to kill me and be done with it."

Vard stood. "No! I won't lose you now that I've found you. Please promise me you'll study and gain control of your transformations, just as I have."

Lyam gave a deep sigh. "I'm tired, Vard. I've spent the better part of fifteen years fighting myself, hating myself. It wears a man down. I don't know if I have the strength to carry on."

"You have a granddaughter."

His father's eyes went wide. "You have a child?"

Vard nodded. "She's like us. You can't turn your back on your family again. You must fight."

He stood, running the fingers of one hand through his long greying hair. "I'm not sane, not whole. I'm not truly certain how I'll react in any situation, Vard. Best I stay away from people, especially my family. I have nothing to contribute to society except grief."

Vard pulled his father against his chest, distressed that the man who had made him had so little hope. The older man trembled like a child. He was right; his father was broken.

"You can remake yourself, Father. I thought I was lost, but there were kind souls who wouldn't give up on me. More than one person saw a kernel of humanity worth fighting for. I have purpose and control I could never have dreamt of a year ago. Hell, even six months ago." He paused and looked his father in the eye. "You must try. Tomorrow, we start your training, and once I'm happy you're safe, then you'll go to Melandrach."

* * *

Alecia paced back and forth in Hetty's upstairs bedroom. She blamed herself for her friend's illness. Thank the Goddess she'd had the dream last night and come to visit. She had known it was a true dream, one she should heed. After a hasty breakfast, she donned her customary disguise and hurried to Hetty's house. And found her friend unconscious.

She had only woken twice during the day, and both times it was a coughing fit that had roused her. Alecia had fed her watery broth all day when she could get Hetty to swallow some, but she withered before her eyes. One thing Alecia knew for sure—Hetty was dying.

She knew a panic deeper than any she had felt, including when she was in labor with Iona. Back then, she was almost beyond knowing what was occurring. Now she was responsible for a rescue mission, but was totally unequipped. Healing was beyond her skill set; Hetty had always provided those talents. And now her friend needed them more than ever. Was there another wise woman in Brightcastle who could fix potions?

In the meantime, Alecia raided the jars on the kitchen shelves and rifled through the books and parchments in the sitting room. As far as she could tell, the one recipe she found for a cough required magic to work. But perhaps if she mixed the ingredients together, Hetty could say the spell.

She spent half a day searching for and measuring ingredients in between racing up and down the stairs to check on Hetty. Her patient grew less responsive with each visit.

After lunch, she trudged up the stairs with her potion and placed it on the bedside table. She sat on the bed and shook Hetty's shoulder gently.

"Hetty, wake up." She shook her a little harder and Hetty moaned, then started coughing.

Alecia sat her up and rubbed her back, speaking soothing nonsense. When Hetty would have slumped against the pillows, Alecia gripped her shoulders.

"Hetty! Wake up!"

Her eyes flickered open and for the first time that day, there was an awareness in her friend's dark orbs. "What is it? Can't you see I'm dying?"

"I can quite easily see that. What I can't see is any fight from you." She picked up the potion and showed Hetty the spell she had found. "Say this spell and perhaps I'll believe you wish to live."

A flash of defiance lit the old woman's eyes, and she muttered strange words in a guttural tongue. Alecia shivered as the hairs stood up on her arms. She offered the potion and Hetty drank it down and shuddered.

"That's worse than the ones I make, girl." She lay against the pillows, took a deep breath, and fell asleep.

Alecia peered at her patient, trying to see if she was better. Apart from that one deep, untroubled breath, she appeared the same. As much as she wanted Hetty to be better, it was a lot to hope for. She needed more. Perhaps Ramón could offer some advice.

She made Hetty as comfortable as she could and left the humble residence in search of answers.

When Alecia reached the castle, she entered via the servant's quarters and went to find her daughter. She must never forget she was a mother with responsibility for her child. Iona was screaming, Millie unable to console her.

"Oh, Princess! I'm glad you're here. She wouldn't take the goat's milk. I'm sorry, but I think she needs you."

Alecia's heart cracked in two at the sight of her distraught daughter. She hastily changed her clothes and washed her hands and arms before gathering her sobbing child against her chest. Seating herself in the feeding chair, she placed Iona to her breast. The next several minutes were full of the gentle slurping and sniffling of her daughter. Her contentment went a little way to calming Alecia's racing heart. How could she help Hetty if Iona couldn't cope without her for a few hours?

"What am I to do, Millie? I have a sick friend with no one to look after her? But Iona needs me, and she has to be my priority."

"Oh, your poor friend. Is there naught Princess Benae can do? I've heard miraculous things about her healing."

Alecia wanted to remind Millie that Benae had allowed her husband to die, but thought better of it. Could Benae really help—and would she?

She would finish feeding Iona and take her for a visit to Solomon. Perhaps she would ask Benae about Hetty. No—she would certainly ask. With Hetty's life at stake, she couldn't afford to allow her prejudice and ill feelings for Benae to hamper her helping her friend.

When Alecia knocked on Benae's door, her maid answered. She was admitted and found Benae eating her evening meal. Solomon was on the rug in front of her, kicking his legs in the air.

"Good evening, Benae," she said. "I brought Iona for a visit." She lay Iona down beside Solomon and caressed his cheek. "He's growing so quickly."

"Yes," Benae said. "Are you well? You look distracted."

How perceptive! "I am well, but I have a friend who isn't. I've spent all day with her and fear for her life."

Benae's hands clutched her throat. "You've exposed yourself to a sick woman and then returned to Iona and Solomon?" She stood abruptly and hauled Alecia away from the children. "Have you changed your clothes? Washed your hands?"

Alecia pulled her arms from Benae's tight grip. "Of course I changed my clothes and cleaned up! I know about disease and its spread. And I'd never place Iona at risk."

"That's good!" Benae said, eyes wide and bosom heaving.

"What has you so flustered?" Alecia asked.

Benae frowned and glared at her. She pointed to Solomon. "That child is everything to me! And he hasn't had the best of starts. My pregnancy was difficult. I almost lost him on two occasions. You might say I'm sensitive when it comes to protecting him."

Alecia drew a deep breath. Overprotectiveness she could understand, but Solomon appeared healthy, and Benae was a healer. "I'm sure you have nothing to be concerned about. My friend is an old woman and has been sick for weeks. Hetty never does look after herself."

"Hetty?" Benae's voice had gone up an octave. "Your sick friend is Hetty?"

Alecia placed her hands on her hips. "Yes. Do you know her?"

"Only by reputation. She's a witch."

A shudder raced up Alecia's spine. "How do you know that?"

"Ramón told me." Benae chewed on her bottom lip.

Something about Hetty caused Benae discomfort, but it shouldn't, considering Benae's magical healing ability. "Why does she upset you so?"

Benae shook her head. "She doesn't. I just don't want you seeing her then risking the children. Send one of the kitchen staff to care for her and perhaps enlist the services of a healer."

Alecia's eyes popped. "Do you hear what you're saying? For a start, Hetty is dear to me, and I'll nurse her myself. And second, I came here to ask *you* for your help."

Benae folded her arms across her chest. "Alecia, use your common sense! If you don't care for Solomon, at least Iona's health should matter to you."

Alecia paused to take a breath and get her anger under control. "Please, you must help Hetty."

Benae drew herself up, emerald eyes flashing. "I'm not leaving this castle to attend a witch and place my son at risk. No matter what you say, there's at least a slight chance that something harmful could spread to the children. I won't make an exception."

Alecia glared at Benae through narrowed eyes, but it didn't intimidate her. She turned, collected Iona from the floor and stalked with her to the door of the chamber. Iona shrieked at being taken from her playmate, but Alecia hardly noticed. At the door, she turned and faced Benae.

"I won't leave my friend to die. But don't worry, I won't visit Solomon again until her illness has passed." She stepped through the door and closed it behind her, her daughter's shrieks filling the hallway and continuing all the way back to their chamber.

By the time she reached her bedroom, tears streamed down her face; tears of worry for Hetty. How would she ever help her? She lay down on her bed, Iona by her side, and cuddled her until they both fell asleep.

Alecia spent the next several days with Hetty, trying all she could to keep the old woman alive. She even sought the help of a local wise woman, who declared Hetty would die before the week was out. The woman left a tonic, which Alecia faithfully gave to Hetty three times a day. She also mixed more potions from the spell book in the kitchen, but now her friend was too ill to mumble a spell over the medicine.

On the third day, Alecia was flicking through the spell book as she sat by Hetty's bed, which she had moved into the kitchen, when the old woman mumbled words that caught her ear. It was something about Ramón and a ring. She drew closer and strained her ears to hear the words. *A ring for the prince.* It made little sense. Did she mean her father, Prince Zialni? Or Solomon? The baby was too young for a ring. *Impotent.* Her ears pricked up at that. Her father was taking herbs to enhance his fertility. What if he really was impotent? But why was she mumbling about a ring?

One thing was sure. Ramón knew something. Had he visited Hetty, possibly, and asked her for help? Had she given the prince something to assist in the goal of an heir? Or was it more sinister? Her gut told her there was evidence to be uncovered, but was it a true feeling or just prejudice toward Benae? Ramón wouldn't do anything to hurt her father, would he? And Hetty? Would she help or hurt Jiseve Zialni? The man had tried to have her executed, burned at the stake. If anyone harbored ill feelings toward her late father, it was the old woman who lay before her, battling for each breath.

Alecia shook her head. If she didn't discover the truth soon, she felt like she would go mad. It was time to confront Ramón and ask if he had approached Hetty for help. She made the old woman comfortable and left the house.

Alecia received good news when she returned home. Iona had finally accepted the goat's milk. She entered her suite to find Millie with Iona on her lap, the child sipping from a silver goblet. Her little arms and legs flew up and down at the sight of her mother. Alecia drew a deep breath at the love that washed over her.

"Finally, Millie!" she said, crossing to place a kiss on her daughter's forehead. But Iona wouldn't let her get away and grasped her thick ponytail. "Ouch! You little minx!" She gently lifted the baby and hugged her, Iona squealing with delight.

"I knew you'd be pleased, Your Highness." Millie said. "She just had to get a taste for it." The maid grinned broadly as she watched Alecia with her daughter, much like a grandmother would. Alecia knew a sharp pang of grief that her mother would never know her granddaughter. But Iona wouldn't be short of grandmotherly influences. Perhaps it was time to move Hetty into the castle, where she could have a relationship with Iona.

"I couldn't be happier, Millie. However, I can't stop now. I must find Lord Zorba. Do you know if he's in the castle?"

Ramón could be anywhere; indeed, he had seemed to avoid her lately. It was even more reason to suspect he hid something. He had never been one to avoid her in the past. But that was before Benae.

"Lord Zorba and the princess went riding together and should be back by now, Your Highness. I'll give Iona her bath while you're gone, and you can play with her when you return." She took the baby from Alecia amid howls of protest.

Alecia laughed. "She certainly makes her feelings known."

"That she does," Millie said, "but she's a good baby, all in all."

Alecia smiled and patted her child on the head before leaving her with Millie. Time to ask a few hard questions of her friend.

She found Ramón in the kitchen, checking details for an upcoming banquet. Ramón and Benae were hosting the guild masters to ensure that Brightcastle craftsmen continued to support their guardianship. That's what Alecia thought, anyway.

"Hello, Ramón," she said. "I need to talk to you."

He turned from the squire he'd been talking to. "Certainly, Princess. What can I help with?"

Alecia swore there was extra tension in his shoulders. "Can we speak in private?"

He frowned, but led her to the office which served as the hub for the downstairs servants.

He opened the door for her and closed it once they were inside. A candle burned on the desk, casting more shadows than light.

"I saw Hetty today."

Ramón nodded. "How is she? Benae told me you asked her to attend."

Alecia turned and rested her hands on the desk. She drew a deep breath. "She's dying. I can't help her; no one can."

His hands gripped her shoulders from behind and squeezed. "I'm sorry. I know how much she means to you."

She turned to face him. "Hetty said something in her sleep which I want to ask you about." She looked down at her hands, clasped before her. "Did you visit her while I was gone? Around the time of my father's marriage."

He tried to school his features, but a narrowing of his eyes answered her question.

"You did! Hetty muttered something about a ring."

He looked everywhere but at her. "What do you have to do with Hetty and a ring, Ramón? And impotence! She muttered that as well."

He sighed. "I didn't wish to tell you this, Alecia, but your father abused Benae. I couldn't stand to watch it day after day. Benae begged me to help."

She gasped and choked, spit going down her windpipe. As she struggled to get air, her mind shut down on the picture of her loving father, the man she had known as a child. He couldn't stoop so low!

Ramón thumped her back, and eventually she drew a shuddery breath.

"You can't be serious!" she gasped.

"I was desperate to help. Your father tortured her, tied her to the bed. It was monstrous. I saw the bruises and made her tell me what had caused them."

She was shaking her head. "It can't be true. Father wouldn't hurt his wife. He never hurt Mama. Why would he hurt Benae?" She paused, trying to remember what the servants had said. "Things were tense before the wedding and after. Why?"

Darkness hovered behind his eyes, but at least he met her gaze. "Who told you that?"

"Tell me, Ramón!"

"All I will say, I have said. Your father abused Benae, and I went to Hetty for help. I feared for Benae's life. So I bought the prince a signet ring for his birthday, and Hetty enchanted it. She said it would make him unable to accomplish the act."

Alecia staggered backward into the desk. "And he died… in the act." Moths of panic battered her brain. Two people she trusted had betrayed her father… betrayed her! She looked at him. "You and Hetty killed my father."

He threw his hands up, palms facing her. "You must understand, Alecia. I never meant to hurt him. All I wanted was to save Benae more pain. This wasn't supposed to happen."

She walked past him to the door. He grabbed her arm as she passed.

"What will you do?"

Alecia looked down at his hand and pulled her arm from his grasp. "I don't know." If only she could talk to Hetty, get her version of the story. Ramón couldn't be trusted, and neither could Benae. "I need to think before I do anything or…" Tears of anger and grief filled her eyes.

Ramón reached out a hand but she stepped away.

"Don't touch me!" She left the office, shutting the door behind her. The servants in the kitchen averted their gazes as she passed, acting as if she wasn't there at all.

She returned to her chamber to find her daughter asleep, and Millie mending a stocking.

"Leave us, please," she said. "I'll call for you when I need you."

Millie stood. "As you wish, Princess. Your meal is by the fire." She curtseyed and left.

Alecia crossed to the fire and poured herself a goblet of mulled wine. She sat in the rocking chair and sipped the drink, her gaze on the flames. Her world had turned upside down with that one admission from Ramón. He might be responsible for her father's death. And if he was, so was Hetty. But would Hetty do such a thing? Would she act to hurt Alecia's father when she knew what it would do to his daughter? Surely not! Despite the bad blood that lay between the prince and the witch, she wouldn't seek her revenge on him in this way. Would she?

Alecia shook her head. Perhaps there wouldn't be more answers if Hetty died. But that was unacceptable. She'd do her best to save her friend, and now she had another reason to succeed.

CHAPTER 9

ALECIA was fixing lunch for Hetty the next day when there was a knock at the door. A wary prickle slid up her neck. She froze, certain no visitors should be expected. Wiping her hands on the tablecloth, she tip-toed to the front door. As she peered through a crack in the old wood, she saw a young woman, a pack over her shoulder.

She cracked the door open a little. "Who are you?"

The visitor drew herself up, vibrant blue eyes flashing. Did she have gold specks in them? Like Vard?

"Katrine Aranati. And your name is?"

"Alecia Zialni." She grasped Katrine's arm and pulled her into the house, closing the door and leaning against it. "Hetty muttered your name in her sleep."

"How is Hetty?"

Alecia looked away, and she swallowed hard. "She's very ill." She lowered her voice further. "I've known Hetty for years. She's never sick, and now nothing seems to make her better."

The dark-haired beauty, who looked similar in age to herself, turned and headed for the stairs which led to the bedrooms. How dare she take such liberties in Hetty's home when she hadn't told her what she was doing here?

Alecia called after her. "I've made a pallet in the kitchen where it's warmer—"

Katrine stopped in the doorway to the kitchen, her eyes drawn to the bed in the corner where Hetty lay, her breath rasping in and out of her body.

"Don't just stand there, girl," Hetty said to Katrine. "Since you ignored my order to stay away, you'd best come closer. I won't bite."

Alecia gasped. Thank the Goddess! She was awake. Now perhaps she could reveal her part in the ring story. It was clear she knew Katrine Aranati well. As she watched, Katrine advanced on the pallet and knelt beside it, letting her bag drop to the floor.

"Hetty!" Katrine reached for the frail body, drawing her close, and Hetty's skeletal arms latched onto her. Who was this woman?

When Katrine drew back and settled Hetty against the pillows, a hacking cough wracked the old woman's fragile body. She turned to Alecia. "What have you been doing for her?"

Alecia wrung her hands but schooled her voice before she replied. "I've kept her warm and fed her twice a day with chicken broth. It's the only thing she can swallow." She drew closer. "The local wise woman has attended, and I tried to make a potion which Hetty said a spell over. Her magic has failed, or she'd be better."

Katrine shivered, then reached out and squeezed her hand. "I'm here to care for her now. I'll see all is done to help her recover."

"Who are you?"

"I'm Hetty's apprentice of sorts. I've traveled here from the coast."

Alecia nodded and closed her eyes, a tear escaping. "I... I need her, Katrine. She's all I have left of my childhood. Please don't fail her."

"I'll do everything I can." Katrine turned to the kitchen shelves with an assurance that Alecia found encouraging. Perhaps she really could save Hetty.

Alecia barely recalled her return to the castle, so preoccupied was she with thoughts of Katrine Aranati. Judging by her bearing, Katrine was a noblewoman. What was a member of the nobility doing apprenticed to a witch? Hetty obviously knew Katrine well, and there was a genuine tenderness between them. But Alecia didn't know her, and that made her uneasy. She should feel happy there was someone else to care for her; perhaps Katrine could make a real difference to Hetty's recovery.

This was another thing that had changed during her absence from Brightcastle. Hetty had befriended a noblewoman who had no place being in this town. And what was with the silver sparkles in Katrine's eyes? The woman reminded her of Vard, but she couldn't be a Defender—could she?

She berated herself for not finding out more, but, truthfully, she was a little intimidated by Katrine. She was so self-assured and completely gorgeous, even attired in men's breeches and tunic. There was a story behind her, but all could be revealed in time. For tonight, it was enough that she was no longer alone in her care for Hetty.

The next morning, Alecia presented herself to Hetty's house and rapped on her front door. When Katrine answered, Alecia pushed past her and went straight to the kitchen. She lay her bag of food and medicines on the table and stood looking down at her friend. Did she breathe easier?

Katrine came up behind her. "I should have come sooner."

Alecia turned to her. "What do you mean? Did you know she was ill?"

"I scried her in the fire and came as soon as I could get here—against her orders." She ran her fingers through her dark hair.

"You scried her? Then you're a witch? When you said you were Hetty's apprentice, I thought maybe herb lore."

Katrine's eyes widened and she frowned. "I must be tired to forget myself so, but if you're Hetty's friend, you must know and approve of her witchcraft." She waited as Alecia nodded. "Yes, I'm a witch. Hetty is honing my magic, or she was. I love her dearly, despite how cranky she gets occasionally. I don't know what I'd do if she died."

Alecia blew out a deep breath. "Then you know exactly how I feel. She was my nanny and is vital to me." She bit her tongue to stop from revealing more. She didn't know Katrine, and must be cautious until she could determine all her intentions.

Katrine looked down at her patient. "I'm not skilled in healing, but I have a little knowledge and will do what I can. Thank you for the medication and food."

Alecia felt the woman was trying to get rid of her. "You said you were from the coast?"

Katrine stiffened. "My family has an estate south of Wildecoast. My sister is the head of the family, and I'm something of a black sheep. You know, the younger sister with a talent for magic. I've traveled here to study with Hetty in the past." A shadow crossed her face. "The last two weeks have been… interesting. But I intend to stay with Hetty until she recovers. Anything else wouldn't be tolerable."

Alecia grabbed her hands. "Thank you for coming. I know you love her but thank you." She walked out to the front door. "I'll return tomorrow and hope for better news. I can see she's in excellent hands."

She squeezed Katrine's shoulder and closed the door quietly behind her.

The following day, Alecia returned to Hetty's house, only to find the old woman's condition virtually unchanged. She breathed a little easier, possibly, but Katrine looked horrid. Alecia felt a pang of guilt that she had left Hetty's care completely to the beautiful witch.

"How is she?" Alecia lingered by Hetty's pallet in the kitchen, hoping her summary of her condition was incorrect.

"Perhaps a little better."

"You look dreadful." She studied Katrine. "Are you sure you haven't caught what Hetty has?

Katrine pushed her hands through hair that looked as though it hadn't seen a brush in over a day. "I'm tired, that's all."

Alecia frowned and turned to Hetty. "What else can be done?"

She shrugged her shoulders. "I can't think of anything. I've exhausted my potions, spells, and charms for only this slight improvement. Are you sure you don't know of another wise woman we could call on?"

Alecia snorted. "Wise woman, indeed. If *you* can't help, then such a person will be useless. There's only one who might aid us, and she has refused."

Katrine's mouth dropped open. "Why? Who is she?"

"She's the woman who married my father!"

"Princess Benae?"

Alecia cut her gaze to Katrine. "She's no princess!"

Katrine placed her hands on her hips. "Regardless, why did she refuse to aid you?"

Alecia again wondered how much to reveal. "There's bad blood between Benae and Hetty. I've recently learned a little of what occurred, but have yet to speak to Hetty about it. She has been too ill. Ramón Zorba told me something unsettling two days ago."

"He's Guardian of Brightcastle and Benae's husband, is he not?" Katrine asked.

Again, Alecia snorted. "Guardian of Brightcastle! My uncle the king needs his head read to place those two in charge of such an important region. I'm preparing to petition him. He must give this principality to me. *I* am the rightful heir. Let him tell me himself that being female means I can't inherit the throne."

Katrine looked confused, and Alecia realized she'd said more than was wise. That was what one did when they had no one but a young baby to talk to.

"Princess, what about Hetty? Can't you ask Benae again? Perhaps she has a potion she can prepare for us. She need not even see Hetty."

Alecia scowled, and Katrine glared back, appearing totally unaffected by her ire. The witch went up further in Alecia's estimation. Perhaps she really was worthy to study under Hetty.

"Her healing isn't through potions," Alecia said, "though she uses them to disguise what she is really doing. She must lay hands on her patient, but she won't leave the castle. She says she won't place her babe at risk." Alecia's heart melted at the mere thought of her half-brother. "He's such a tiny mite and not robust."

"That's the reason she won't help? Fear for her child?"

"It's one of them. She seems to dislike Hetty, however, or perhaps hate is closer to the mark."

"This is getting us nowhere!" Katrine strode across the parlor and back again. "I can't stand this waiting."

Alecia stood watching her. "I thought I was the only one who cared for Hetty."

Katrine stopped, hands on hips. "I care very much. The whole time I traveled here, I was terrified I'd be too late."

"And you traveled unaccompanied?"

Katrine's peaches and cream complexion turned a rosy red. "No, I had an escort. I traveled with James Tomel, a respected citizen of Costa." She paused as if uncertain and then continued. "We met Vard Anton two days out from Brightcastle."

Alecia swallowed an instinctive gasp. What was that man doing? Then she remembered Vard's plan to search for Defenders. "You *did?*"

"Do you wish to hear how he is?"

Alecia's eyes dropped to her hands, which she was dismayed to find clenched in front of her. "He and I recently spoke. He's on his own path, and I'm on mine. I can't let him back into our lives until I'm sure it will be forever."

"Then you still love him?"

How dare this stranger question her about Vard? "It's none of your concern. Iona and I are fine just as we are and need no man to play with our hearts."

She watched as Katrine gulped, her eyes wide.

"Vard helped us on the road," Katrine said, "then left us when we reached Brightcastle. He said he was on a mission from the king."

Alecia nodded. "He's a different man to the one I knew before." She knelt beside Hetty's cot and held the old woman's hand. "Dear Hetty, you must fight and get well."

"I've decided," Katrine announced. "I'll take her to the castle, and Benae will have no choice but to help. I've heard she's unable to resist the sick, so I'll force her to look upon Hetty's wasted countenance."

Alecia snorted yet again. Katrine would think she was part sow at this rate. "I wish you good luck, but I think the rumors you've heard exaggerate Benae's compassion."

Katrine shook her head. "Regardless, we must decide how to get Hetty there without the journey killing her."

The next morning, Alecia fed Iona and breakfasted before dressing carefully. Today, Katrine Aranati would bring Hetty to the palace, and they would see if an appeal by a third party could sway Benae. She chose a new green velvet gown and five strands of creamy pearls. Millie arranged her hair in looped plaits. Giving Iona a kiss on the forehead, she sought Benae. It wouldn't hurt to be present when Katrine made her appeal.

As she crossed the castle entry, Alecia noticed a nondescript carriage in the forecourt and Katrine pacing back and forth before it. Alecia descended the stairs and hurried over to her.

"Did Benae agree to see her?"

Katrine stopped pacing, her body tense and the sheen of tears in her eyes. "The footman was rude to me and asked us to move. Can you please do something?"

Alecia squared her shoulders and nodded. "Wait right here."

She returned inside and heard voices coming from the small audience chamber. Benae was there with a man, Master Tomel she called him, and she was refusing to aid "the sick woman in the carriage". But why was this man involved? She entered without announcement, and they both turned. Benae appeared angry, but Master Tomel merely raised his eyebrows and studied her. Finally, he bowed.

She speared him with her gaze. "Excuse me, Sir, but I must interrupt." Her eyes snapped from him to Benae. "*Stepmother*," she said, "you *must* help Hetty. She's close to death."

From the corner of her eye, she saw Master Tomel step aside. Wise man to avoid getting between them.

"Hetty?" Benae said. "The sick woman is the witch known as Hetty?" Her hands bunched into fists at her sides. "I'll *not* do as you say."

Alecia took a step toward her. "Keep your voice down. Some would kill Hetty on the strength of those words." She glared at Tomel as though daring him to repeat what he had heard.

He raised his hands. "I have no interest in this woman you speak of."

"That's good, Sir," Alecia said. "Unlike my *stepmother*, I'll defend my friends unto death."

He inclined his head. "I'm sure you're most loyal, Princess."

Alecia narrowed her eyes. "Benae, you can't allow Hetty to die. She's important to me. I don't know what you hold against her—perhaps if you told me, I'd understand—but you can't stand by and allow her to die. Please help."

"I can't place my son at risk."

"I've been nursing her and am as hale and hearty as the day I began," Alecia countered. "Iona is well too, and she isn't much older than Solomon. Please. Don't let her die!"

Benae crossed to the window, her shoulders hunched, hands opening and closing at her sides. Perhaps her conscience wouldn't allow her to walk away from Hetty either. Alecia held her breath as she waited.

"I'll attend her, but she must remain outside." She turned to her maid. "Fetch my medicine box."

Benae, her maid, and Master Tomel left the chamber while Alecia took a seat before the fireplace. She closed her eyes and said a heartfelt prayer to the Goddess for Hetty's full recovery. She hadn't prayed so hard since her mother lay dying. And she said another plea that Solomon should remain well. Despite his mother, Alecia loved the little boy with all her heart.

She remained in the chamber, hoping to speak with Benae after her visit with Hetty, but she didn't return. She wandered outside and stood in a sheltered spot, watching as Katrine and Master Tomel spoke beside the wagon Hetty lay in. There was no sign of Benae. The conversation between the two appeared sometimes tender and, at others, tense. In the end, Katrine turned abruptly and entered the coach.

Master Tomel watched the coach move off and then spoke to the footman who hovered near him. He saw Alecia watching and so she approached.

"You're James Tomel?"

He swept a low bow. "It's a pleasure to meet you, Your Highness."

Alecia inclined her head. "You met Vard Anton on your way here."

He nodded. "He was of assistance to us when we ran into trouble. I'm in his debt and would like to repay him. Can you tell me where he is?"

She shook her head. "I cannot. I simply wished to ask how he fared."

"He was well when last I saw him, and that was entering Brightcastle several days ago. He implied he wished to see you."

"I've already seen Vard. He must have met you on his journey back to Wildecoast. I doubt he would've entered Brightcastle a second time." The first good-bye was hard enough.

Master Tomel exhaled. "He also said he had been pardoned for your abduction. Is that true? Anton is now an operative of the king?"

A spike of anger stabbed her. "It's true he is pardoned. But it was rescue, not abduction." She turned the topic from Vard to him. "They say you're a spy master. Are you?"

He frowned. "You're blunt, Princess. If you needed to know that information, you wouldn't have to ask the question."

"And you, Master Tomel, are rude. I'm your princess, and you'll answer my question."

"I've already said as much as I intend." He bowed to her and turned to leave.

"Consider, Sir, there may come a day when you'll need my friendship, and that day may be sooner than you think."

He nodded and turned toward the stables, leaving Alecia staring after him. She realized she was gawping at his retreating back, and turned and walked with what dignity she could muster inside the castle.

At breakfast, four days later, Alecia decided she would visit Hetty and ask her about the signet ring Ramón had given her father.

Katrine had sent her a note the morning after Benae saw Hetty, advising the old woman was making a miraculous recovery. But it had been too soon for Alecia to confront Hetty. With Katrine in attendance, there was no need for Alecia's daily visits. Now it was time to get answers.

She had a leisurely breakfast, fed Iona, and dressed in her usual disguise of breeches and tunic. She drew her forest green cloak around her shoulders and exited the castle, slipping out the service entrance in the side wall. As she walked the streets, Alecia tried to sense the mood of the city. It was still subdued, as if the citizens waited for something.

She arrived at Hetty's via the back alley and knocked. To her surprise, Hetty answered her own door. Alecia slipped inside and turned to hug her friend.

"Hetty! You look wonderful!"

The witch held onto her for a little longer than usual, and her eyes were moist when Alecia drew away.

"I *feel* wonderful, at least compared to four days ago."

Alecia shook her head. "Benae is a marvel. Thank the Goddess she agreed to see you."

"Her healing is strong. I must thank her."

Alecia walked through to the kitchen, laying her cloak over a chair. "Good luck with that. I can't imagine she would accept anything."

Hetty followed and started making tea. Her breathing was much better, and she had gained weight. Alecia watched as Hetty moved around the room, taking the kettle off the hook, and filling the teapot then cutting bread. She wondered how to broach the subject of the ring. Hetty had previously had the opportunity to tell Alecia everything, and had not.

Finally, she drew breath and began. "While you were sick, you muttered something that caught my attention."

Hetty didn't look at her, but her body stiffened a little, and she dropped the knife on the floor. "What did I say?"

"Something about a ring for the prince and 'impotent.'" She watched Hetty closely as the witch met her gaze.

"I wonder what I meant by those words?"

Alecia's insides crumbled. "I asked Ramón, as you mentioned his name, and you were too sick to ask. You know how I feel about my father's death. Ramón said he brought you a signet ring to enchant, and that he gave it to my father for a birthday gift. He said my father was abusing Benae, and he asked for your help to stop it."

Hetty drew herself up. Alecia swore she heard her joints creak. "Then why ask me when you have all the answers?"

"I needed to hear those words from your mouth, Hetty! Tell me, is it true?"

Hetty's shoulders drooped, and the fire faded from her. Alecia felt sorry for her, but she had to know.

Hetty's dark eyes met hers. "Zorba came to me in desperation. The prince was abusing his wife in the marital bed, and your friend was determined to stop it."

"You have proof of this?"

"I took him at his word," Hetty said. "I know when a person is telling me the truth."

"What if Benae manipulated Ramón? Made him think she was being harmed in order to secure his help to kill my father?"

"That's possible, but not likely. You forget what your father is capable of, Alecia."

"*Was* capable of," Alecia said. "How could you act without checking the facts?"

It felt wrong to censure Hetty, the woman she had always respected, but anger burned within her, along with loss and pain. She had been let down by her friends. People who should have at least been honest.

"Hetty, what did you do?"

"I suggested the boy get a present, and I would enchant it to make the prince impotent. As he was abusing the princess within the marital bed, if he couldn't complete the act, perhaps he would leave her alone."

Alecia shook her head. "Or it could push him over the edge! Hetty, what if it caused him to fly into a rage?"

"At least he wouldn't be able to pound into her night after night. And Zorba was there to help. He said he'd watch out for her."

"And now my father is dead! What went wrong?"

"I don't know that the enchantment had anything to do with your father's death." Hetty's black eyes glittered, and Alecia shivered. Her friend could be a ruthless enemy and she *had* acted against the prince.

"But it could have been a factor? If he was taking other substances to aid his performance in the marital chamber, could the enchantment have backfired?"

Hetty shook her head. "I don't think that's what happened."

"But you can't be sure! No one will ever know." Alecia paced back and forth across the kitchen, tugging on her braid. She wanted to hit something. Iona would never know her grandfather. Jiseve could never be redeemed. Solomon would never know his father. It was wrong, and perhaps evil.

She turned to Hetty. "I won't return for some time. I must come to terms with what you and Ramón have done. If you need me, send a messenger to the palace."

She turned and strode from the house, Hetty's pleas following her. But nothing could stop her flight from the woman she had trusted like a parent.

CHAPTER 10

L ADY Merielle Cosara stood on the cliffs overlooking the ocean south of Wildecoast and breathed in the fresh air—not a whiff of sheep dung to be smelt. The salty tang swooped into her nostrils, and she smiled, pushing her brilliant red hair from her eyes. She loved the country where she and her husband Nikolas had their estate, but there was nothing like the days they spent each month in their little cottage by the sea—the place they first met.

She walked into the house and stood recalling the weeks she had first spent there, when she was a very different being, a creature born of the sea. Humanity had come to her, but she wasn't quite human either. The fear and desperation of those early days were far from her mind now, but they were all too ready to assail her in a weak moment. There was no point in doing that. She and Nikolas led a dream life, and it was best to dwell in the present rather than in the past. Occasionally, she thought about the bargain she and Nikolas had made with her sister over their first-born daughter. They had pledged that daughter to her sibling, but as she and Nikolas would never have children, they had nothing to fear.

Strong arms enveloped her from behind and scratchy-bearded lips made her shiver with delicious anticipation.

"Do you remember how it used to be between us at the start, wife?" Nikolas growled.

His voice sent shivers up her spine. She had loved him from the first time she had met him that day on the beach. The feeling had not been mutual. Back then, he had been angry, not so much with her, but with mermaids in general. And later he was furious with her secrecy. But time and patience had seen her win through, and it would this time too.

"I remember, of course I do. You hated me."

He chuckled. "I never *hated* you. I allowed you to stay with me, didn't I? Is that the action of a man who hates?"

She turned to face him, laying her arms around his neck and playing with his tangled blond locks. "You had so much anger in you, my love. You didn't know what to do with it." She lay her hand gently along his jaw and kissed his lips. His mouth had always been the part that she loved best. His lips were plump and soft, and his beard stimulated her skin oh so seductively. And when he moved down there… her nipples grew tight just thinking about it.

Nikolas noticed and pulled her close, so she felt his arousal. "I was drawn to you despite my prejudices. I'm glad I acted despite my feelings, gave you a place to stay. I'm sorry for what I put you through."

She laid her finger on his lips. "Hush, there's no going back, only forward." She kissed him again, and he tightened his arms until it seemed they had become one beating heart.

"Come to bed, love," Nikolas murmured against her lips. "I have plans for you this day, and they don't involve talking." He kissed along her jawbone and on to the leaping pulse in her neck. "We can talk when we return home."

* * *

Lady Alique Jazara pushed a strand of blonde hair from her face and shielded her eyes from the early morning sun. A spikey disquiet nagged her. The elven tree city of Selinore was beautiful, but it was also foreign. She and Julli were the only Thorian women present, and, though she knew it shouldn't trouble her, it did. She had been in Selinore six months, and had celebrated her twenty-third birthday there. It was long enough to settle in and be happy, however with each day, her disquiet grew.

What she observed this morning was the building of her hospital. She wondered how her infirmary outside of Wildecoast fared under the care of her old mentor, Doctor Mosard. Still, it was better than no doctor in attendance. She longed for the quiet rural aspect of her own home. Having been raised on a mixed farm south of Wildecoast, it was no wonder she was a country girl at heart.

Her new hospital grew rapidly. Last week, it had been foundations only, and now the roof was going on. At last, she could stay on the ground, not sleep in one of the great trees that were the elves' homes. She was ungrateful, but there was no escaping her feelings.

She observed Julli, her maid and attendant, discussing a wall with an elf who was part of the building team. Luckily, Julli knew enough about building from her father to speak with authority on the subject. Alique's husband, Kain, whose stepfather was a carpenter, had also been invaluable, though no one expected the High Prince of the *Lenweri* to be involved in such menial chores.

She sighed. How had their lives become this complicated again? And things wouldn't settle any time soon with war looming.

"What is the matter?" Her friend, Isiloe, appeared at her shoulder. "The hospital looks good for a human dwelling. I thought you would be happy they have built it so quickly."

She turned to the diminutive elven woman. "I *am* happy, Isiloe. I just miss home, and I was wondering when our lives would return to normal."

"What is this normal you speak of? Wouldn't that be rather dull?"

She smiled. "It would be for you, but for me, I had enough excitement in that first battle with the *Sis Lenweri*. I have no desire for more; nor yearning for more death."

Isiloe ran her hand through her cropped white hair and frowned. "You are tired."

"It's not that. I'm perfectly well. I'm just out of place here."

"Out of place where?" Kain Arenil appeared on her other side. "The hospital is almost done. I have the beds arriving at the end of the week.

You can move in next week, Alique." He kissed her on the cheek, and Isiloe looked away.

"I will go and …" she muttered as she stalked off.

Isiloe's relationship with Kain was still uneasy. She blamed him for taking her place in her cousin Gwaethe's affections. It was silly, of course. Gwaethe Arenil had room in her life for her cousin *and* her half- brother, but no one would be game to tell Isiloe that.

"What's the matter, darling?" Kain asked.

He could always tell when she was out of sorts; which was all the time lately.

Alique shook her head. "I want to go home to Wildecoast. I want things to be the way they were before you accepted all of this. I want you to myself." She laid her head against his chest and closed her eyes. His arms enveloped her, and she breathed in his manly scent. She inhaled deeply until her heart slowed.

"Better?" he asked.

"Yes, but nothing has really changed, has it? You have this place, a new sister, and a new people. What do I have?" She stopped and tried to bring her voice to a quieter level. "I want to return to the way we were before, when you were just Kain Jazara, and I was nothing more than your wife."

He raised her hand and kissed her fingers. "You'll never be 'just my wife'. You're my partner in all things and a wonderful healer. Never forget that."

His words melted her heart, and the warmth in his dark eyes caused a flare of desire in her belly. But his dark good looks and pretty words didn't change her predicament. "Your distractions won't work. I yearn for those days when we could please ourselves."

"You know we can't turn back time. This role is what I was born for."

"Do you really believe that?"

"I didn't at first, but have come to see the truth. I've also come to know the type of king my father was. Orionkael would've wished for me to take up his mantle. And I'm beginning to love my people."

"You have two people. And I think you should remember that."

He laid his hands on her shoulders. "I'll never forget I'm half-human. I'll never forget my family or yours. This isn't an either-or situation, Alique."

"The community that raised you must mean more than this! For thirty years, you thought you were the son of a kingdom man. He's a good man, a great man. I won't stand by and watch you trash your family."

Kain put his arm around her shoulders and guided her to their home tree. When they were in their chamber, he led her to their bed and sat her down.

"None of this is easy for you, I see that. But it will get better as you become accustomed to the elves and their exotic ways. You can do great things here, my love."

"I can do those things at home too." She folded her arms, knowing she sounded unreasonable. Her husband was doing what was right. The elves needed him, and he might be the difference between war and peace between Thorius and the *Lenweri*.

"Give this a chance, Ali. Things won't always be tense like this. We'll get the *Sis Lenweri* defeated, unite the elves, and then we'll be able to move around more freely. Perhaps we can spend half our year here and half in Wildecoast. You might even decide you like it here."

Alique breathed in deeply and held it, then breathed out slowly. She nodded. "You're right. It's just that sometimes I have to pinch myself at the changes that have occurred. I can't believe any of it."

"You know, I need you to keep me grounded, to remind me of my human half. We can both accomplish great things, though the elves won't call you queen."

"I don't wish to be their queen. I wish they would believe that. Perhaps then more of them would accept me."

"Isiloe accepts you."

"And that's the strangest thing of all. She and I are friends. If it weren't for her, the last six months would've been bleak."

"I'm sure Julli and myself are pleased to hear you say that!"

She punched him lightly on the arm. "You know what I mean. It has been difficult to get the elven people to accept me. I fear they never will."

"They will in time." He kissed her cheek and nuzzled down to her lips. As usual, Alique turned into the kiss, the worries of a moment ago forgotten.

He laid her down on the bed and deepened the kiss, their lips melding in a burst of passion she had only known in Kain's arms.

"I love you, High Prince," she said, kissing along his jaw.

A shiver ran through his body, and she delighted in his response. While they had this, they had all they needed. She just had to remember that.

* * *

Princess Gwaethe Arenil stood naked at the arched window in her chamber and stretched her fingers to the ceiling. A pair of strong masculine arms reached around her and pulled her against a naked chest. She laughed.

"Come back to bed, wife. I haven't finished with you yet."

Gwaethe turned in Jacques's arms, still entranced by the way their bodies fit together.

"Oh, and what would you do with me?"

"Well, for a start, I don't wish for the entire city to see you naked. You can't stand thus at the window."

"It's early. Few would be about, and my skin is dark enough to blend into the shadows. Besides, are you not proud of my body? Do you not rejoice that you and only you get to be naked with me, join with me?"

"Oh, Gwaethe! You don't know how proud of you I am. I'm proud of everything about you." He kissed each part as he listed them. "And most of all, I'm in love with the part of you that lives in here." He tapped her on the head. "The last six months have been all I've ever wanted and more."

She leaned back and studied his face. He looked good; blue eyes bright, olive skin healthy and dark wavy hair glowing. Yes, he was finally healed from the terrible effects of the landslide that had buried him.

"Do you not wish to see your parents again? Perhaps we can bring them here to live. Then you can care for your father as he needs to be cared for."

Jacques's father was paralyzed from the waist down and had never coped with his handicap. Add to that his dreams that his only son would lead the Kingdom Army and marry a noblewoman, and Jacques's father was an unhappy man.

Jacques sighed. "You saw how they were with you on our first and last visit. Stiffly polite would be a generous way of describing it. Especially Father. I won't put you through that again." He pushed his fingers through his dark beard. "No, correspondence by letter will have to suffice. I'll let them make the next move."

She kissed him, desperate to erase the sadness that had entered his eyes as he talked about his parents. As she concentrated on wiping the thoughts from Jacques's mind, the hard rod that poked her belly told her she had succeeded.

"Come to bed and show me how much you love me, dearest," he whispered, picking her up and cradling her against him as though she were a fragile crystal figurine. That was what she loved most about her human husband. This was the only place she could be feminine, felt as though she had value other than as an elven princess. If you had told her she would feel like that last year, she would have laughed at the idea.

But the elven woman she was with Jacques was the essence of her, her very inside most private self. She didn't have to hide anything from him. If she tried, he knew and would gently pry the grain of truth from her until she lay bared before him. She enjoyed sharing all of herself with him; loved it. She hoped her brother Kain had just such a relationship with his wife, Alique.

She smiled at the thought that her dreams of the last year were coming true. Her life wasn't perfect, and there was strife to come when they dealt with Faenwelar, but she could see how the future might look. It was rosy indeed.

Gwaethe was drawn to the present as Jacques nipped her on the side of the neck.

"Ouch! That hurt!"

"Your thoughts had strayed, and I won't have you distracted when I'm trying to make a baby."

She placed her finger on his lips. "I've told you that may not be in the cards for us. It's incredibly rare for elves and humans to procreate."

He grinned. "I don't care how rare it is. I intend to give it my best shot, literally. If your father and Kain's mother can do it, so can we. Orionkael deserves many grandchildren if we can accomplish the feat."

Jacques pushed into her, his hands under her buttocks, and she arched her body, desperate to be as close to him as possible. At times like this, she almost believed in miracles. When she and Jacques melded their bodies like this, she knew they were always destined to be together. And if that were the case, then perhaps children were in their future. She didn't remind Jacques that six months of trying had produced nothing but great delight.

She surrendered to that pleasure.

Gwaethe walked with her second in command, Ruven Magbalar, down the cleared main street of Amitania. The ruined city was retaking shape. Already half of the city walls were restored thanks to a joint effort between Brightcastle and the elves. They had used much of the larger rubble from within the city in the reconstruction of the outer wall. Her heart burst with pride at the results.

But there was more to be done, and no one knew how much time they had before the *Sis Lenweri* struck again. The recent news that Gorin had mysteriously escaped from his prison in Wildecoast had sent Gwaethe and her people into a fury of preparation for war. Sooner rather than later, Faenwelar would emerge from his hideout in the northern forests and return to claim the kingdom.

She burned to teach him a lesson, ached to take his life in retribution for the death of her father. Then she would kill his son, Gorin, the elven prince who had almost caused her own death, who had humiliated her before the *Sis Lenweri*. He had almost defeated her. But she was an elven princess of Orionkael's line, and she would not be broken.

They left the main street and approached one of the training grounds. It now had a fully functioning forge which worked night and day. Elven and human soldiers trained together, teaching each other the skills each possessed. Squads of soldiers trained around the clock with the sword, the bow and arrow, and in hand-to-hand combat. The commander studied strategy with Jacques and several other leaders. Gwaethe was proud of what they had achieved in such a short time.

"Will it be enough, Ruven?" she asked. "I can't help but fear the aftermath of outright war with Faenwelar."

"He needs to be stopped, Princess. You've taught me the truth of that. And I will do whatever it takes to bring his reign of terror to an end."

She turned to face him, and, in his steadfast gaze, she could almost believe those words might come true. "Then I shall have to trust you are right." She smiled, and he led her out of the training ground.

"I have a surprise for you, Princess," Ruven said, leading the way to the center of the city. That way lay the largest square, the site of many atrocities when Faenwelar had occupied it six months ago.

Gwaethe had only been back once and had no desire to return.

"Oh? What would that be?"

Ruven grinned, a twinkle in his eye. "You'll just have to wait and see."

They continued and soon Gwaethe suspected they were heading straight for the center of the city. She held her tongue, believing Ruven would not hurt her. Unfortunately, he led her to the archway that opened into the cursed place.

She stopped stock still. "I don't wish to revisit that place yet."

He turned to face her and bowed low. "I would never do you harm, Highness, but this is the site of a special surprise, and I believe you should enter. Your refusal would upset Jacques Vorasava, as it is his project."

Despite her discomfort, Gwaethe was intrigued. But the last visit had resulted in nightmares for weeks. The worst ones were those where she watched her friends' bodies being paraded around the square after their deaths. They died because of her.

She took herself in hand. *You are an elven princess, daughter of Orionkael. You will not baulk at this!* "Lead on, Ruven."

With slow steps, Gwaethe followed her commander under the arch, through a short tunnel and out the other side. What she saw astounded her. Her heart kicked up and her spirit soared.

The square where her people were murdered was not recognizable. Trees grew through the space with areas of more dense foliage made to replicate small forests. Benches sat beneath the trees and fountains sprayed water in cleared spaces. The fountains were magical, and each appeared to be a tribute statue to an elf who had perished the day she had been tortured.

Seven beautiful fountains dotted the square, and she stopped to read the plaque at the foot of each statue. The words brought tears to her eyes.

"This is so unexpected!"

"You are happy, Princess?" Ruven asked.

She smiled at him. "What was once ugly and stained is returned to beauty. More than that, it is a tribute to those elves who died that day." She looked around. Quartz steppingstones led the way around the gardens, and there were lawns where children could play.

"Jacques Vorasava had the bodies of the seven bound and interred within their statues, Princess. I know this is not a ritual that our people recognize, but I thought it might be appropriate. Their families agreed."

She shook her head. "Who am I to disagree if the families of the dead allow it?"

She turned at a footstep behind them and Jacques was there, an uncertain smile on his face.

"What do you think? A fitting tribute to brave soldiers?" He stood still as a statue, his chest barely moving.

Gwaethe tossed reserve to the winds and launched herself at him. "I love it. You have taken a place of horrible memories and created a beautiful memorial. Thank you." She kissed him and soon forgot where she was. When she came up for air, Ruven had left them.

"I'm glad," Jacques said. "I knew how it affected you to be in this place; that it was a stain on the entire city. And I wanted to create a fitting tribute for your people who died; something that can help us heal."

She kissed him again. "It is times like this that I know I've done exactly the right thing in marrying you, Jacques Vorasava."

CHAPTER 11

VARD rode his horse through a little used western gate and into the forecourt of the keep at Wildecoast. He dismounted and handed his reins to a stable boy, who led his horse away. He stood against the wall and closed his eyes, tuning his senses into the surroundings, the sounds, smells, and mood of the place.

All was calm—on the surface—but there was a simmering tension in the air. He wondered what that was about. He opened his eyes and studied those around him, mostly servants and soldiers, going about mundane chores. Nothing seemed amiss and indeed, it may not be. He sighed and approached the servant's entrance. Better to keep a low profile until he got the lay of the land. Old habits died hard, but Vard had learned that the keep could hide as many threats as the forest could.

His wariness was at odds with the contentment with which he had approached Wildecoast. Indeed, he'd been happy for almost his entire journey from Brightcastle.

Finally, his life was beginning to make sense. The pieces of the puzzle were clicking into place. First his time with Alecia and reuniting with Iona—she was a complete joy to him. He harbored a spark of hope— more a strong flame if he was honest— that they could be together as a family. Alecia still loved him and might take him back if he was careful.

Finding his father was totally unexpected, and discovering he was a late blossoming Defender was a miracle. Thank the Goddess he had come into his powers fully and could help his beloved Papa. Melandrach would complete the training, and he and his father could be a team, a family, once more. The other man Vard had sought had proven to be further along in his gift, and he gave him directions to Melandrach as well. The advent of two new Defenders gave Vard hope he could raise an elite squad of shapeshifters who could restore the kingdom to peace and keep it so.

He smiled as he traversed the halls where servants quickly stepped out of his way. All knew who he was, but none knew *what* he was. Still, most were intimidated, and those who weren't had fallen under his spell—including Queen Adriana, Alecia's aunt.

He sighed more heavily as he contemplated the monarch. Of late, she'd been more aggressive in her advances, and there would come a time when Vard must openly rebuff her, instead of the polite avoidance he had used to date. He looked forward to their next meeting with trepidation and sought to delay the moment, if possible.

Vard reached his chamber on the eastern side of the keep, unlocked the door, and stepped inside. He again closed his eyes and sent his senses, including the sixth, into the rooms, searching for anything out of place. *Nothing*. The window attracted his attention. The cover was rolled up and he could see the ocean. An occasional sailing boat danced over the waves, and gulls swooped and squawked.

Though a child of the forest, Vard loved this part of Wildecoast. Perched high on a coastal cliff, the lower reaches of the keep were carved from the land it stood upon. Vard loved waking to the sound of the waves each morning and falling asleep to them at night.

As he watched the waves lap the shore, he mused on the things he wished to teach Iona. Not only Defender skills, but the sharing of other experiences like swimming, riding, and hunting.

His heart cracked a little at the thought that she'd grow up quickly, and they would miss too much. He shivered as an icy blast tore through the window and turned to throw more wood on the fire. Someone had started the blaze and aired the rooms which told him he hadn't hidden his return nearly well enough.

It wouldn't be long before he was summoned.

But first he wished to find the new rangers he had sent from Brightcastle and see how their training fared. Vard placed his belongings in the bedchamber and returned to the sitting room. On the table, there was a covered half loaf of bread and a block of cheese, as well as a jug of watered wine. He made himself a hasty sandwich and gulped down a goblet of wine.

Throwing his cloak around his shoulders, he strode to the door, food in hand. He opened the door to find a footman with hand raised, about to knock.

The man bowed. Vard would never get used to that!

"Lord Anton, the queen wishes to see you in the blue audience chamber immediately." The man stepped aside to give Vard room to exit.

His stomach tightened on the food he had just swallowed. This was a quick summons, even for Queen Adriana.

"Tell her I'll be there presently," he said.

The footman bowed and hurried off. Vard stared at the retreating man until he turned a corner. *Dammit!* He wasn't in the mood for the queen and her games, though it could be a serious interview. Queen Adriana was his 'handler', for want of a better word. It was she who gave him his instructions, and she to whom he reported. This was likely only a request for information from his latest mission. She could have given him a chance to draw breath, though.

He closed his chamber door and walked up the hallway, munching on his meal as he went. His mind worked furiously to decipher how much he should tell Adriana. He liked to keep information in reserve, though it became exhausting remembering what she knew and what she was ignorant of. Did she know Alecia had returned to Brightcastle? Likely yes. The new rangers would've been excited to report that nugget of gossip, even though his team of experienced scouts would've kept the news to themselves. They knew Vard by now.

As he stalked the corridors, servants hustled out of his way until he reached the door to the blue audience hall. This was Adriana's favorite room for discussions with her cronies. Vard smiled. He was calling himself the queen's friend. Perhaps that wasn't strictly true, but he had a good relationship with her—when she wasn't trying to seduce him.

He paused and the attending footman knocked on the door, stuck his head within, and announced him. "You may go through, My Lord."

Vard almost growled at the title. He was no lord, though Adriana had offered him an estate and a title. He nodded and entered, his gaze traveling to the queen, resplendent in an emerald green gown that matched her eyes exactly. She was seated at a small table, set for tea.

Vard bowed low and stayed down for just a little longer than required. When he rose, he caught the queen studying him, a predatory gleam in her eyes.

She offered her hand, and Vard moved forward to take it. He placed a kiss on the huge emerald stone that adorned her right ring finger.

"Vard!" she breathed. "It's so good to have you back in Wildecoast. I trust you had a successful mission?"

He released her hand and sat on the other chair when she gestured to do so.

"I did, Your Majesty. How are things here?"

"Not so quickly, Vard. First, we must discuss your mission. I hear my niece has returned."

He inclined his head. "She has. Her daughter is with her."

"You mean *your* daughter. How are they?"

"They're both well." The last thing he wished was to discuss his relationship with Alecia and Iona. He kept his tongue in his head, though pride in his child was trying to burst from him.

"And?" Adriana said, a frown on her brow. "You spent time with my niece, I assume? How do things stand between you?"

He let out a frustrated sigh. "I spent less time with Alecia than you might expect. This was no social visit, and I have the new rangers recruits to prove that. As to how things stand, I'm on good terms with Iona's mother. Let's leave it at that."

"Then you haven't rekindled your romance?"

"Your Majesty, I have no desire to be rude—"

"Then don't be, Vard." Her tone was hard, reminding him she wasn't only a queen in name. "My husband and I need to know what Alecia's return means to the kingdom, and to the guardianship of Brightcastle. Your relationship with my niece is critical to that. Do you have an understanding with her?"

Vard raised his teacup to his lips and sipped as he mused on his answer. "Not yet. She's wary of me after I left her again. But one day, who knows? I *will* raise my daughter, that's certain."

Adriana appeared satisfied with his answer, as a smile graced her lips. "I have a surprise for you. As the position of King's Blade is a new one, it required a meeting of lords to ratify. This was completed in your absence. Congratulations. As the king's closest advisor, that places you above the admiral and General Formosa."

Vard was glad he was seated. "I had hoped we could keep my position low key. I've been in Wildecoast for only a short time. It will cause resentment amongst the nobles and officers."

Adriana beamed. "That is exactly why Beniel wants you. You care nothing for yourself, and everything for the kingdom. But though it makes you uncomfortable, the position also gives you the power to make your rangers more important than they otherwise could be. And I trust you to look after Beniel if there's a war with the dark elves."

There was no laughter in the queen's eyes this time, not when the king's life was at stake.

Vard nodded his acceptance of this most solemn duty. The queen stood and Vard followed suit.

"Oh," she said, "the lords have attached a title, estate and household to the position of King's Blade, *Lord* Anton."

Vard stiffened, kept his eyes straight ahead, though he wanted to swear. She had outsmarted him again. *Dammit!* "I'll accept the position and the estate." At least he could move out of the castle and out from under the queen's royal gaze.

She beamed then clasped his upper arms and pulled him down to kiss his left cheek; highly inappropriate behavior considering their relationship. "Use the baths. You need a shave," she said, and waved him from her presence.

Vard was out the door and in the anteroom before he realized. He shook his head as he took himself to the baths for a long-needed wash. Adriana had bamboozled him yet again. She was a tough woman to stay ahead of, but he vowed next time he'd gain the upper hand.

Refreshed and relaxed, Vard headed out to the practice yards to see if any of his rangers were there. As he walked through the keep's outer wall and toward the barracks, a feather swept past on a swirling breeze. Ordinarily, that would have been insignificant, but this feather was different.

He stopped to pick up the plume from the cobblestones and examined it. Then he cast his eyes to the heavens. Almost beyond seeing, a banded hawk floated on the air currents, merely a speck to mortal eyes. But Vard detected the golden and black plumage of the magnificent bird. It was no ordinary hawk, but a human in disguise. Was this a challenge? It seemed too much of a coincidence.

He sprinted around the side of the barracks, ignoring the calls of greeting from those who had noticed his approach. Once in the cover of a small, wild garden, he morphed into the hawk and shot into the sky.

As the hawk's powerful wings carried him skyward, it searched above for the rival bird. This was his territory, and there could be no invasion. If the presence was a challenge, then he accepted it. A small part of its mind retained the essence of Vard. His heart pumped and wings flapped, conscious this was a precarious situation. Anything could happen in his most vulnerable of forms. But it was vital he discover the identity of the threat. The banded hawk was his own creation. It didn't exist in nature. Therefore, this bird had to be the figment of a shifter's creation.

There! A little higher and to the right! The hawk angled toward the invader, fury lending his wings extra speed and power. He slammed into the rival hawk before it was aware of his approach and feathers burst in a spray of black and gold. The bird tumbled toward the ground for a few seconds before halting its uncontrolled descent. Sunlight glinted off its eye as it rolled in Vard's direction. He prepared for a counterattack.

The rival hawk flew at Vard but swept away before making contact, climbing before turning and swooping at him from above. Vard dropped and his enemy flapped overhead. Vard's anger was tempered by thoughts of strategy and how he could best the invader. He climbed higher, wing muscles screaming in protest. The enemy flew after him and was gaining.

As the other bird reached him, Vard spun and presented his talons, latching onto the hawk where its right wing joined its body. The enemy shrieked in pain before rolling and tearing his flesh from Vard's talons.

Their battle had now descended to a level where the humans below could watch, and Vard saw more than one with raised bows. If he wasn't careful, they could take his life with one well-placed arrow.

The other bird must have seen it too, for it shot off in a spray of feathers, headed toward the ocean. Vard gave chase as an arrow sliced below him. He needed to get clear before they corrected their aim. He zigzagged across the sky to avoid the darts, and the next time he looked for the rival hawk, it had vanished. Reaching the cliff edge, he flew along it, sweeping east and west up the coast, but the hawk was gone.

He flew toward the keep, his eye studying the outer wall to pinpoint his chamber window. There! Vard landed on the ledge and popped his head into the chamber. It was his, and no one was in attendance. The vestige of humanity that remained sentient grew, and Vard morphed back into his human form as a knock sounded at his chamber door. As he completed his transformation, he looked up into the startled gaze of Admiral Nikolas Cosara.

Vard climbed slowly to his feet, trying not to appear distressed. He looked down at his clothes and flicked a feather off his tunic. His boots were stained with a substance suspiciously like blood, and a bloodied feather stuck to the leather of the right one. He slowly raised his eyes to the admiral, whom he had met on a handful of occasions.

"Well met, Lord Cosara," he said, bowing.

The admiral had still said nothing, and his turquoise eyes were wide.

Dammit, what had he seen? "Lord Cosara?"

The man shook his head. "Ah, yes, hello Ranger." He lapsed into silence, still frozen in the doorway.

"Can I help you?" Perhaps he could be convinced he'd imagined it all. *Dammit, dammit, dammit!* This couldn't be happening! Anything magic was taboo in the kingdom, and here he had shown this virtual stranger his transformation. Cosara was arguably the third most powerful being in the kingdom, after the king and queen. And he was Adriana's cousin!

Cosara took a deep breath and squared his massive shoulders. "What did I just witness?"

Vard frowned at him. Looked like there was no getting out of this one. "I'm sorry if I scared you."

"What did I see?!"

"I don't suppose I could convince you to forget it all?"

The man's eyes turned ice cold. "No."

Several scenarios played through Vard's mind. He could kill the admiral and end the problem; or compel him to turn around and keep walking until he died of exhaustion and hunger. He could tell Cosara the truth. How would the admiral react? What if he killed Nikolas Cosara? What would that do to his future and that of the kingdom of Thorius?

The admiral cleared his throat and placed his hand on his sword. Vard was unarmed, but that didn't matter. As the bear, he could kill Cosara in seconds. And yet the admiral stood before Vard with no scent of fear. He couldn't eradicate an ally just because his identity was threatened. Luckily for the admiral, his Defender heritage meant more to him than his own life. Sometimes he really wished it didn't.

Vard straightened his tunic and his shoulders and faced the leader of the King's Navy.

"What would it take for you to forget this?" he asked, fixing his gaze on Cosara.

"What are you?" Cosara's low voice held no fear. "Tell me or face the consequences."

"I could kill you before you knew what had happened, Cosara. I have that power in my hand." He held out his hand palm up and closed his fingers as though squeezing a heart.

Cosara raised one eyebrow. "I've been watching you since you came to Wildecoast." He closed the door behind him and moved further into the chamber. "I knew you held secrets beyond where you'd been for the last year or more. And now I find you like this." He picked a feather off Vard's shoulder.

"You need to back off. We're on the same side," Vard growled.

"Tell me what you are."

The gravelly whisper echoed around the room, and Vard was suddenly afraid of what would happen when he stepped over this line. But there was nothing for it. He had to trust Nikolas Cosara to keep his secret.

"I'm a Defender."

Cosara's eyes widened as if, up to that moment, he hadn't been sure he had witnessed anything untoward. Perhaps he could've talked the man around?

"A shape-shifter?"

"If you know that much, you'll know Defenders are named because they aid the weak and defenseless," Vard said.

Nikolas Cosara crossed his heavily muscled arms. "Is that what you were doing when you kidnapped Alecia Zialni? How have you gotten into the king's good graces, by the way? I remember when the princess vanished. He was furious."

Vard shrugged. "The queen can be a persuasive woman. I bring much to the table, including my rangers."

"You place me in a difficult position."

Vard bent his will to the other man and was surprised by what he found. The admiral wouldn't be easy to compel. Perhaps he had fewer options than he thought.

"Much the same as the position I was in a moment ago, and yet I decided to trust you. Perhaps you could make that same choice. We could be a formidable force."

Cosara narrowed his gaze and frowned. He crossed to the window, but Vard noted he kept his body partially turned toward his potential enemy.

"I should report this to the queen at the very least. Magic is forbidden in this kingdom. It wouldn't take much for my cousin to lose her faith in you. Your death would be swift."

"Perhaps," Vard said, his mind running through his options and opportunities. "Or perhaps there's no force that can stop me, and I'm on your side."

"So you say, but how can I trust that's really the case? I've heard that Defenders can compel the mind. Have you ensorcelled my cousin? Is that why she's supporting this elite force you've gathered and the title you hold? There's too much at risk, and now I find I can't even trust the judgement of the queen."

"You can trust her," Vard said. "I've not used anything on her. I spend most of my time just trying to stay one step ahead of her when we meet."

Cosara raised one eyebrow and his rigid stance relaxed. "I know what you mean." He fell silent and turned to stare at the ocean. The quiet stretched, and Vard used the time to plan.

He must ascertain if he could trust the admiral. He reviewed what he knew. Nikolas Cosara wasn't of noble birth, though the queen had granted him an estate. He was first and foremost a sailor who had risen through the ranks to the highest position. He had no close family, having lost his parents and brother, the latter at sea. There was controversy in his past with the loss of a ship and most of its crew while Cosara was captain. That had almost ended his naval career.

Doubtless being the queen's cousin had been instrumental in his return to the navy, not to mention his position as admiral. Vard had heard many things of Nikolas Cosara, not all of them good. But the man was respected where it counted, amongst naval and military leaders.

He had a wife, Merielle, whose exotic manner intrigued Vard. Her background was murky, to say the least. No one was sure where she hailed from, and she had several curious habits. Her hair was a brilliant and unnatural shade of red, and she appeared to enjoy eating raw seafood.

Nikolas Cosara had tragedy in his past and mystery in his present. Perhaps he harbored secrets that Vard could exploit. One thing was sure, he couldn't be allowed to expose Vard's secret.

Cosara turned to him. "You said you were motivated, even driven, to help the weak. What purpose do you have in Wildecoast?"

It was an excellent question. He wasn't yet certain if he had the answer and certainly didn't want to answer to Nikolas Cosara.

He sighed. "I'm not sure, myself. The last year has been rather chaotic. I've traveled a lot and searched the land far and wide for someone who could help me master my gift. I finally found that mentor recently. During my travels, I saw much, and it was then I came across the *Sis Lenweri*. In my experience, the elves have always been a peace-loving people, but this branch of them seems to covet that which is ours. I want to help us reach a peaceful solution."

Cosara narrowed his eyes. "You want nothing for yourself?"

"I have all I need, as long as I can return the kingdom to safety. Indeed, I recently found my father, whom I had thought dead for decades. I have even more reason to fight for peace."

"And, of course, Princess Alecia is a large part of that world, is she not? Is it true you have a child together?"

Vard froze. "Alecia is her own woman. She will accept me in her life or not—it's her choice."

Cosara held up his hands in apology. "I understand. We all have parts of our lives we wish to keep private. However, we aren't all in love with the king's niece, or accused of her abduction."

Vard growled, the wolf close to the surface. "The king has cleared me of all charges. If he can see sense, then you should be able to."

Cosara's eyes hardened. "You admitted you can compel. Even if the ability is recent, you could've influenced the king and the queen to trust you or forget things. Swear you haven't used your powers on them."

"I have not!" Vard swallowed hard. He couldn't say he wouldn't do so in the future and hoped the admiral didn't make him swear not to. "I only wish to keep the populace safe and make a home for my family."

"You have no ambition for yourself? No desire to run Thorius? Seems to me you're making a mighty cozy niche here."

Vard faced him square on. "If you knew me, you'd know I have no need for that sort of power. My only drive has been to master the ability I have within. If you reveal me, it puts everything I've built at risk."

Cosara still hesitated, and Vard saw the questions in his eyes.

"If you don't believe me, spend time with me. You can help train the rangers. They grow bored with their current teachers."

Nikolas Cosara nodded. "That's a good suggestion. Can I bring a friend?"

"Certainly. Meet me at the barracks training grounds at dawn tomorrow." They shook hands, and Cosara turned to leave.

"Oh, Admiral?"

Cosara paused, eyebrow raised.

"Be on the lookout for a man with a bandaged bicep. Report any arm injuries to me."

Cosara frowned, but nodded and left without another word.

Vard blew out a breath and sagged against the wall. He had to be more careful. That couldn't happen again!

CHAPTER 12

VARD met Nikolas Cosara the following morning in the training yard. The admiral brought with him a man who looked much like him. He turned out to be Samael Delacost, Nikolas's half-brother. Delacost was leaner than Cosara, with short brown hair and a scruffy beard. He might have been a little older than the admiral, perhaps in his mid-thirties.

There was something that hung between the brothers, like trouble lurking in the shadows. It put Vard on edge. He got these feelings from time to time, even before he had fully accepted his gift. It wasn't prophecy, just a finely tuned radar for trouble. These two had plenty of conflict between them. They stood before him, hands on hips, on edge and on alert. Time to get on with it.

He turned to the assembled rangers.

"We have a treat today. I've arranged for Admiral Nikolas Cosara and Samael Delacost to assist with your training."

There was a low murmur from the rangers. The women all crossed their arms over their breasts as though erecting a shield. It was a curious response. Perhaps his training was working better than expected. He swore some would try to seduce the two men during the morning, but perhaps he was wrong. He hoped so. Some had already tried it with him and failed.

The brothers were enigmatic. He supposed they would be attractive to women, and yet these female rangers eyed them with distrust. He shook his head to clear his thoughts.

"First," he said, spinning to face Cosara and Delacost, "I'd like you to show these students what you can do with a sword. Fight each other."

The two collected practice swords and moved away from the assembled rangers. They both moved with grace, but with the rolling gait of sailors. They faced up, bowed to each other, and then the clash of swords rang in the yard.

Delacost soon found himself at the mercy of a swift strike at his throat, bringing his sword up in time to block the thrust before sliding away. Cosara chased him, but Delacost spun and intercepted another strike, this one aimed at his calves.

Cosara, the bigger man, had more power and used it to his advantage, but Delacost was the nimbler. His quick-stepping feet got him out of scrapes. Both were excellent swordsmen. In fact, Vard was hard pressed to decide who was the better. The brothers fought back and forth across the yard, scoring the occasional blow which made the students flinch. There were few flaws in their techniques. He wondered what other weapons they excelled at.

The fight ended when Delacost tripped Cosara, who fell on his back, sword at his throat. Delacost laughed before stooping to help his brother to his feet. Both men were blowing hard.

Cosara cast Delacost a hard look. It was clear he disliked being beaten, especially by his kin.

Vard clapped and the watching rangers joined him.

"A splendid display, gentlemen," he said. "I wonder if you could stay for a while and teach these students?"

Both men studied the rangers, especially Cosara, who allowed his gaze to rest on each individual for a few seconds as if measuring them. He nodded.

"I'd be glad to help for a few hours, Anton. How would you like the group arranged?"

"I'd like to watch you train them this morning," Vard said. "I'm looking for gaps in their technique. I'll take notes, and, this afternoon, I'll pair them so they can work on their deficiencies."

Several of the women groaned. His sharp eye found them, and he marked those who were uneasy with his plan. They fell silent.

"Split into two groups. Lord Cosara will take one group for an hour, and Delacost, you take the other. Then we can swap leaders for the second hour."

They did as instructed; the students collected their practice swords, and the leaders spent time with each ranger. As they worked their way through their students, Vard watched closely, scratching on his parchment when something occurred to him. At the end of an hour, they swapped groups.

He was pleased; more than pleased. The ranger students were highly motivated; the men trying to impress their teachers, and the women striving to show the men they could compete. A few of the women *could* compete. Which was excellent considering their smaller size.

He watched Delacost closely. The man could prove an excellent instructor for the women and shorter men. He wasn't small by any means, but he had learned to use speed, not brute strength.

Vard nodded to himself as a plan shaped. Perhaps it was providence that Cosara had stuck his nose into his chambers unannounced. If not for that, Vard wouldn't have asked him to be involved, would never have thought the admiral had time to help, let alone the inclination.

As he watched Cosara, he gained new respect for the admiral. Though his brother was the victor in their display, Vard judged them evenly matched. The admiral had several genius techniques that made up for his slightly reduced speed, and he used his strength well. Vard would match him with his larger and slower students. That was if the brothers agreed to be involved.

At the end of the session, the trainers drew to one side and the students to the other.

Vard showed them a rare smile. "An excellent session, Rangers. Take yourself off to the hall and eat. We'll meet in an hour, outside the north wall, for tracking practice, then finish the day back here."

Once the students had moved off, he faced the brothers.

"Thanks for your help. It has given me a few ideas moving ahead."

He met Cosara's gaze. "Perhaps we should meet to discuss making your involvement with the students official?"

Cosara frowned. "I don't have time for that."

"Well, perhaps Delacost would help?"

"Where he goes, I go," Cosara said.

Vard studied the two men. Delacost smirked and then shrugged.

"This morning was enjoyable, Nik," Delacost said. "It will sharpen our skills for the coming conflict. I say we help out." He looked at Vard. "What time commitment would you require?"

Vard considered. "Two to three sessions a week? Would that be possible?"

Cosara grunted. "Two sessions of two hours each and no more." He looked at Vard, suspicion in his gaze. "And you'll work around the times I give you. I'll have the first month's sessions for you on the morrow."

He turned and stalked off.

Delacost shook Vard's hand. "Don't mind him. Working with me makes him grumpy." He grinned. "I look forward to our sessions."

Delacost trotted after his brother, leaving Vard uncertain if he should've involved the crusty admiral. Had he allayed the man's concerns? He'd find out soon enough.

Vard spent the next month training his recruits in sword skills and tracking while those rangers already trained scoured the countryside for any sign of the *Sis Lenweri*. While the enemy elven high prince's son was their prisoner, there was the risk of an incursion. It was a relief for him to delegate a few of his tasks to others. Some of the rangers had proven to be gifted trackers—perhaps good enough to rival Vard. He asked them to be on the lookout for anyone with a bandaged upper arm. He had a bad feeling about that other hawk.

Nikolas Cosara continued his brooding approach to Vard, but Samael Delacost was a breath of fresh air. Vard was drawn to him, as were many of the students. The man was full of the joy of life, despite being tied to his cranky brother. He appeared to be a man who made the best of a situation. He clearly enjoyed teaching the recruits his skills.

A month after Vard's return to Wildecoast, the queen held a ball. She had invited the nobles and heads of guilds and their wives, as well as Vard and Samael. Vard ground his teeth at having to appear at court and dress up. However, he needed the queen's support so it wouldn't do him any good to turn down the invitation.

As he dressed, he mulled over the night ahead. Occasions like this reminded him of the ball at which Alecia had been betrothed to the old letch, Finus. That night had changed everything. An assassin had shot Vard in the Brightcastle palace garden, and he had morphed into the bear. He had almost attacked Alecia, but something had stopped him. Thank the Goddess!

He shook the black thoughts from his head. No sense dwelling on the past when he had this night to get through. It was always a chance to learn something important when people mixed and drank. It was also an opportunity for assassins to strike. He'd have to be on his guard. Several of his rangers, disguised as servants, would help with surveillance.

He checked his appearance in the mirror and tied the headband around his forehead. The talisman was freshly cleaned and oiled, the silver glinting in the light of the candles. He had swapped his leather tunic for a white shirt and forest green vest, but kept the dark grey leather breeches with their hidden knife pockets.

Vard slid his six knives into their slots on his person. His rangers had been allowed to carry only one knife each, by order of the queen. She clearly didn't trust them, and that meant she didn't fully trust Vard to select and train his men and women. He shook his head. There was a point at which you had to have faith in others; had to believe you had made the right choices.

He left his chamber, a fire crackling in the grate which would be attended by his man servant during the evening. That was another thing Vard couldn't get used to. A servant clipped his wings, so to speak. It was a needless complication, but the queen had again insisted. The man had to be a spy for Her Majesty, reporting Vard's movements to her. He sighed. Trust was in short supply in this palace.

He avoided the official entry and slid into the ballroom via one of the servant hallways. No need to announce his presence or watch the chamberlain struggle with his status in the kingdom. He was early so he could watch the guests arrive.

He picked up a goblet of wine and sniffed its contents. It was of high quality and clean of poison. He took a mouthful and added crushed ice from the table display. The queen had the ice brought weekly from the mountains inland. It was untainted, unlike much of the local water. Vard could safely use it to dilute his wine and keep his head during the night.

He chose a slab of cheese and leaned against the wall in the shadows, watching the door. As he waited, he picked out his disguised rangers who worked around the room, delivering food to the table and wine to early guests. To his eyes, they blended in well. None returned his gaze, a fact which pleased him.

The first arrival he witnessed was the master goldsmith, Reid Vetta. He had on his arm an elegant blond woman who was a stranger to Vard. She was clad in a deep grey ballgown, almost black. He wondered if she was a young widow, as it was a strange color for a woman to wear to a ball. Reid appeared entranced by her, but Vard would be surprised if he rushed into marriage again. He had virtually been left at the altar by Esta Aranati when she chose to marry Samael Delacost.

That made Vard wonder if there would be trouble tonight. Sam had said he would attend with his wife, Esta, whom Vard hadn't met. One of the trainee rangers had told Vard the story of Lady Aranati and her pirate lover. It was one thing he hated about Wildecoast—the gossip that plagued the castle and town. Personally, he thought it stemmed from the queen. Her eyes sparkled with life when on the trail of a good scandal.

His thoughts returned to Reid Vetta and the lady on his arm. Other guild leaders greeted the couple, and all were soon chatting and laughing. Next announced were two minor lords, followed by Nikolas Cosara and his wife. Merielle was attired in a sparkling aqua sheath that showed off her body and drew the eye. Her hair was piled up and cascaded over her left ear in a luxuriant spray of crimson curls. Pearls, seemingly her favored jewel, were scattered through her hair, and adorned her wrists, neck, and ears.

The admiral's eyes gleamed with pride as he guided his lady with a protective arm about her waist. They made a splendid couple and were clearly very much in love.

Vard watched as they traversed the room, making small talk with the guild leaders, and their wives and companions. But as they moved on, some of those who had spoken to them watched them go with thinly veiled dislike.

It put Vard's nerves on edge to witness such antipathy. Did it stem from ill-feeling over the loss of Captain Cosara's ship in years past? Was there still resentment that he had survived while most of his men had died?

And what of Merielle Cosara? Had she been accepted into the community her husband inhabited? Such beauty often provoked jealousy from other women.

Merielle possessed an ethereal beauty not shared by the other ladies. Everything about her screamed exotic, so it wouldn't surprise him if she didn't fit into this conservative community of nobles. She spent most of her time on their country estate where, no doubt, she felt more at home. He had also heard the Cosaras were in the habit of spending days at a time in their beach shack, which lay on the coast north of the city.

Samael Delacost and his heavily pregnant wife arrived close on the heels of the admiral and Merielle. Vard pushed off from the wall and went to meet them.

He bowed to Lady Aranati and shook Samael's hand.

"My Lady," Vard said, "I don't believe we've met. Vard Anton at your service." By Esta Aranati's wide caramel eyes, his reputation had preceded him.

"Pleased to meet you, Sir," Lady Aranati said, her hand smoothing her rich chestnut hair. "How do you like it in Wildecoast? I'm told you only arrived a few months ago."

Vard smiled, something he wasn't in the habit of doing often. Lady Aranati's lyrical voice and her beauty set him at ease. "I find I like the ocean very much," he said, "though court can be wearying. Luckily, I spend little time with nobles."

Samael laughed. "You won't hear me disagree with you on that, Anton. If it weren't for Esta, I wouldn't be here tonight. She loves to dance, you see."

"Yes, Lord Anton," she said. "I'll save you a dance later."

"I look forward to it, Lady Aranati. And please, call me Vard."

"As you wish, Vard." She wrote his name on her dance card, and he bowed as the couple moved on. Suddenly, he wished Alecia were on his arm, and he was able to dance with her and show her off. The few times they had danced were etched in his memory, and he longed for more. His mood turned maudlin, and he mentally shook himself. It was best to push thoughts of his alluring princess from his mind for tonight. He'd stick to the matter at hand, which was observing the guests for signs of trouble and making sure his rangers were up to the task.

Last to arrive were the king and queen, Beniel and Adriana Zialni. The stocky blond king looked tired. Many said he hadn't been the same man since his brother Jiseve died. The queen was resplendent in an emerald and silver gown that showed off her bosom. She wore her favorite imitation silver chain mail necklace, designed by master jeweler James Tomel, whom Vard had recently met in the forest east of Brightcastle.

He vaguely wondered what had become of Tomel after arriving in Brightcastle, and if he and his companions were safe from the night hounds that had plagued them.

The appearance of the beasts after half a century of dormancy was a mystery Vard was yet to solve. He shook the matters from his head and concentrated on the royal couple. All appeared in order. The king and queen moved into the ballroom, and immediately the musicians began the first dance of the night.

Vard stepped out of the crowd and found a secluded alcove from which he could observe the guests and stay one step ahead of the queen. He could feel her seeking him, but he knew better than to be caught off guard.

Samael joined him. "Good idea, Anton. Staying out of the press. How are the recruits coming along?"

"Very well, thanks in part to you and the admiral. I'm pleased with your training techniques."

Samael laughed. "I'm enjoying my involvement. They learn quickly, and it gives me something useful to do. Otherwise, I'd just be hanging around with Nik, and he's been like a bear with a sore head lately."

"I've heard he's your jailer, so to speak."

A frown marred the amiable man's face. "I have a checkered past, Anton. You may have heard of my pirating. The king wanted to make an example of me, but then my kinship to Nik was revealed. Well, he couldn't hang a nobleman's brother, so decided I could become Nik's ball and chain, instead."

Vard considered. "That can't be easy for either of you."

He shrugged. "There are worse fates. And Nik is becoming used to me. We've been in a few tight spots together on the ocean and that builds trust quicker than anything."

"I'd like to continue my association with you both. Is that possible, do you think?"

Samael smirked. "That will be up to Nik. I'll do what I can, but he can be temperamental. Something's eating at him, and he won't tell me what it is."

"Perhaps his wife can help?" Vard suggested.

"Merielle… she and Esta are friends. Perhaps she *can* shed light on my brother's troubles." He grinned at Vard. "Thanks, Anton. It's been good to chat, but I need to get back to my wife. Don't forget you have your name down on her card. Make sure she can find you when it's your turn."

Vard watched Sam stride off. He couldn't help liking the affable pirate and could see them becoming friends. His heart lifted at the thought of having someone he could talk to, confide in. He hadn't had that since his cousin Frel when he was a teenager.

Except for his too brief moments with Alecia, Vard had been alone so long, he'd come to see it as normal. While keeping people at a distance, he'd forgotten how good it was to have a simple friendship. No longer was he a risk to others since his transformations were under control. Perhaps it was time to relax the tight hold over his interactions with others and re-enter normal society.

"Vard! There you are!" Queen Adriana tapped him on the shoulder, and he turned to her and bowed, bringing her fingers to his lips. "I swear you've been avoiding me."

"Good evening, Your Majesty. This is a splendid gathering. I trust you've been enjoying it?"

"Even more, now I've found you." She raised her arms. "I demand a dance."

He kept his features schooled to politeness and whisked Adriana onto the dance floor. She was an exceptional dancer, light in his arms and letting him lead her between the other couples.

Unfortunately, it was a waltz which called for closer contact than he would have liked.

"What have you been up to?" she asked, looking up at him.

He steered her around an old lord and his wife. "Training the new ranger recruits, Your Majesty. It's coming along rather well. Though I'd like to make another trip to find more. Perhaps I'll head south this time." He'd also like to find more Defenders, but that was a far more difficult proposition.

"Perhaps I might find funds for such a trip," she said, her voice lowered conspiratorially. He heard her heart rate climb as though the idea excited her. "We should meet and discuss it." She inched closer, her body pressed against his. "Have dinner with me tomorrow."

Vard considered, aware he had only moments to give her an answer. He needed her support. What he didn't need was her romantic attention.

"I'd be glad to dine with you tomorrow, Your Majesty. What time?"

Triumph lit her eyes. "At dusk, Vard." The music finished; the dancers separated. "I shall look forward to it."

He led her to her ladies-in-waiting and bowed. "Until tomorrow, Your Majesty."

Vard turned to retreat to his quiet spot next to the wall, but Esta Aranati appeared before him. "My dance, Vard," she said. "I'm a poor substitute for the queen, especially in this condition," she lay her hand on her expanding waist, "but there you go."

He drew her into his arms. "I wouldn't say that at all, Lady Aranati."

They danced together, this time a slow but stately dance with steps that brought them together and moments when they were apart. Esta was clearly an accomplished dancer, and she appeared to truly enjoy it.

"You're a marvelous dancer, Vard," she said when the song ended. "How did you become so skilled?"

"Ah, My Lady, that would be telling." He led her to the refreshment table. "Are you hungry?"

"Starving. You know, out of all the men here tonight, you're the most fascinating—except for Sam, of course." She looked up at him, her gaze open and assessing. "I can't work you out, and I'm usually good at judging people."

He handed her a plate with a selection of small morsels. "I assure you, Lady Aranati, I'm just a simple man trying to serve the kingdom as well as I can. Your husband has been a big help, and I hope will continue to be."

"You've fired him up, and for that I'm thankful." She chewed her bottom lip. "He's a good man, but he needs to be kept busy. He's enjoying working with your rangers."

"I'll be sure and keep your husband in mind when I require help. But for now, I foresee no change to the training schedule."

She sighed. "The elven threat hangs over us all. How do you see that being resolved?"

Vard felt like sighing, too. He didn't want to discuss matters of war with Esta Aranati.

"As we've already faced many battles with the *Sis Lenweri,* resolution has to be through war. I just hope we don't lose too many good people." He placed his plate on the table. "And now I must leave you, My Lady. I hope you enjoy the rest of the night."

He bowed and walked off, conscious that those around him moved out of his way. He knew that rumors swirled around him, many of them at least partly true. The eyes of the party goers caused an itch between his shoulder blades. Perhaps tonight was a good night for a run through the northern forests?

CHAPTER 13

SOMETIMES Alecia longed for the peace and simplicity of the farm on which she had spent her year in exile. Today was one of those times. In fact, each day lately she had yearned for those serene days, especially since learning about Hetty's involvement in the events surrounding her father's death.

Restless energy zapped within her, an energy that no amount of meditation could calm. The only things that helped were Iona's cuddles and her weapons training. When she thought back to the time she had sought revenge against Jorge's killers, she almost laughed. She had been naïve, thinking she was hard and skilled enough to take the life of another human being without risk to her body and soul.

In those days, Vard was her savior more than once, his steady presence rescuing her when she overstepped. It was how they had met—in the street beside the body of a mercenary she had attacked. Her heart gave a great lurch as she imagined never having that connection again. She hugged Iona to her chest and her daughter gave an indignant squeak.

"Sorry, love," she said. "I was thinking of your daddy. He has been my rock, and I wish he were here to talk to. But he has his life now and we have ours."

She kissed Iona's forehead and breathed in the scent of her skin and hair. Her racing heart settled. Things were different now. She had a child to protect, and that placed shackles on her she hadn't known before. It was all very well to want to be queen, but another thing to take the steps toward that day. She had no one on her side, and she couldn't travel with Iona. She couldn't take the risk of an elven attack. How would she gather her supporters together? How could she find them?

She placed Iona in her crib and patted her chest to rock her off to sleep. It was almost time for her weapons training. That at least was one thing she could work toward. If she was to be a battle queen, she must know how to fight, to hold her own against the foes who would challenge her. And in future, her enemies might be men.

Vard had assessed her as able to defend herself, and she trusted his opinion, but he had not assessed her for battle. She could just imagine his face if he knew she was preparing to fight in a war.

The weapons master was training her and had agreed she could fight the men under his leadership. The man was skeptical in the extreme, especially since she was a royal and any harm that came to her could see him disciplined. He had imposed strict safety rules upon her and the men she practiced with, which made Alecia grind her teeth. How was she to know if she was good enough when the men tried not to hurt her?

She couldn't blame the men, but she had to have a way of improving and assessing her readiness for battle. The weapons master humored her, and she suspected he wasn't putting his all into her training. It was time to speak with Ramón.

Once Iona was asleep, she went looking for her friend, if he was still that; if he could be her friend *and* Benae's husband; and if she could count him her friend after what she had learned regarding her father's death.

She found Ramón in his office, signing papers. She paused to observe him. He had grown into his role in the time since her father's death. It suited him, but her heart ached at the empty place her beloved father should have occupied.

She knocked and he looked up. Wariness leaped into his gaze.

"Good morning, Princess," he said, standing. "Come in."

"I wanted to talk to you."

"I've been expecting you since we last talked. Did you speak with Hetty?"

"Yes." She entered and crossed to the window, which overlooked the forecourt. Benae's guards were training down there. "She confirmed everything you said. She enchanted the signet ring you gave my father, and he died."

"That didn't kill him, Alecia!"

She spun to face him. "You don't know that! The spell could've contributed, but we'll never know. You and Hetty betrayed me and my father."

Ramón looked down his nose at her. It did nothing to improve her mood.

"You *do* remember what the prince did to Hetty? How can you accuse her of betraying your father? She had no cause for loyalty to him."

Alecia frowned. "But you did, and you both have reason to care for me."

Ramón approached her, hands outstretched. "You weren't here. You didn't have to live through those times. Benae wasn't lying when she told me she was being abused. I saw the bruises."

That was another thing Alecia didn't understand. "My father didn't abuse women. He adored my mother and treated her like a precious vase. What happened that tipped him over the edge?"

Ramón puffed out a sharp breath. "It's time you accept that your father could be a bastard, Alecia! He abused Benae because he could."

"What made him so angry? Something happened, and I'm going to get to the bottom of this if it's the last thing I do." She drew a deep breath and pushed the matter of her father and Benae to the side. "I have a request."

Ramón stiffened and her temper shoved at her. She forced it away again, counting to ten and finding her calm center once more.

"What request?" he asked.

"Master Jenkin is doing his best, but he's too cautious with my weapons training. Can you help?"

"Of course, he's cautious. You must be protected!"

Alecia snorted. "For what? So that I might have a son who can take his place in the queue for the throne?"

Ramón stepped closer. "Sometimes I feel I don't know you anymore. This bitter and angry woman isn't you."

Alecia placed her hands on her hips. "Humph! I know how you feel. Once I believed you and Hetty were my friends. And yes, that makes me angry as does returning to find you and Benae cozied up together and running my principality!"

"Alecia, I haven't changed. I'm still your friend. I have your best interests at heart."

She threw her hands in the air. "I don't wish to discuss this now. And if you're my friend, you'll ensure I can train to the level I need to improve."

"You have soldiers and guards. I don't want you putting yourself at risk."

"What you want isn't my concern. Do you have any ideas?"

Ramón folded his arms. "First I need you to explain to me why this is important to you."

The truth wasn't an option. To tell Ramón that her aim was to be the first modern battle queen of Thorius would first make him laugh and second warn him of her goal. She needed him and Benae to believe Brightcastle was theirs, that she had accepted their guardianship. Unfortunately, her outburst earlier hadn't helped with that. But, dammit, the thought of them in that position, conniving to wrest power from her while she was absent… It didn't matter that her impotence wasn't their fault. They were taking advantage.

She thought of Solomon and her anger settled. He was a precious babe, and she'd do everything she could to protect him.

"I wish to be prepared for every eventuality. Iona needs a mother who can protect her, and Solomon spends time with us. If we should be threatened, I want to be competent to fight off any threats. At the least, I could buy time until the guards arrived."

Ramón studied her, his clear blue eyes still those of the man she had depended on not so long ago. They were the eyes of a friend who had never given up looking for her; eyes of one who had loved her. But now he was *more*, and it was reflected in his gaze. She was no longer his only priority. Clouds marred his once carefree attitude, and Alecia suspected they hid more than one secret. She wished she knew what those secrets were.

Finally, he spoke. "I can see that would be an advantage. The children need all the protection we can give them. Also, I have no wish for you to be defenseless should that dark day come when we join battle with the *Sis Lenweri*." He paused again, and Alecia saw regret in his gaze. Perhaps this antipathy between them hurt him as much as it did her.

"I'll speak to Master Jenkin about placing you in the training program for Benae's female guards. Once you graduate that, if you feel the need, we shall speak about the next step."

Alecia drew a deep breath. "Thank you." She wished to say more; to express her regret for the gulf that had opened between them. But it was a gulf that would ever be present while Benae was his wife. She turned and left the office.

* * *

The night after the ball, Vard presented himself to the footman outside Queen Adriana's private dining room. As he waited for the man to announce him, he wondered how many other men had been in his position. One thing certain, most of them would've welcomed the queen's attention more than he.

"You may enter, Lord Anton." The footman waved him in and Vard swept past.

He pulled up short at the sight of Adriana, clothed in what resembled night attire. He tried to hide his surprise, but feared he had failed dismally.

Adriana beamed. "What do you think, Vard?" She stood with her arms outstretched, the light from dozens of candles silhouetting her curves through the flimsy material of the gown.

He felt his neck grow warm and determinedly pushed down his discomfort. The footman would have to be dense not to realize what the queen had planned. Unless the man was discreet, news of Adriana's tryst with the King's Blade would be the talk of Wildecoast by morning.

He drew a deep breath. "As always, you're the greatest beauty in the land, Your Majesty." He approached and bowed over her outstretched hand. As he rose, the predatory gleam in her eyes tightened his gut.

"And do you like what you see?" Her voice struck his nerves and calmed them, as though she had some power of her own. But that was insane. She was just a mortal woman, even if she was the most powerful in the kingdom. "I mean, the candles are a pleasant touch," she continued, "don't you think?"

She was playing with him as a cat would a mouse. But he was more than a match for her.

He tilted his head and spread his arms. "All this can't be on my behalf, Majesty. If it is, I worry about your reputation."

Anger stormed her gaze. "My reputation is my business; besides, no one would dare spread evil about me."

Vard swallowed, and she followed the movements of his throat. This wasn't going as he had planned.

"Majesty, I caution you to be discreet. No one is above the harm of gossip. *I* know I'm here merely to discuss my plans for another scouting foray, but I wouldn't wish the wrong message to be sent."

Adriana smiled. "And the wrong message would be what, Vard? That the queen had a handsome and virile man in her private dining room?" She stepped closer. "That she dressed for a night of passion? That the delicacies served were chosen to enhance the sexual experience?"

She smiled again, wider this time, and took another step toward him. "You must know I'm attracted to you, My Lord. And I can have any man I desire."

He cleared his throat. "I suggest we sit and discuss how you see our relationship progressing." He must delay her. Adriana wouldn't take "no" for an answer in this mood.

Vard took her hand, led her to the table, and seated her, shaking the napkin out and laying it over her lap. Then he poured Adriana a goblet of the rich red wine from the decanter. He turned away and her fingers slid down his buttock. Best to ignore that move from the monarch.

He took his seat and poured himself wine, taking a deep sniff to check it for foreign elements.

It was clear Adriana had full confidence in her seduction skills. He doubted she'd ever been denied. When he raised his gaze to hers, she was watching him as if his movements hypnotized her. Perhaps that was all it was; his Defender attraction exerting its power. He should feel sorry for the queen—except he knew it wasn't just him. Plenty of women met him and could control their baser instincts.

A footman delivered their first course, and Vard let the queen do the talking. At first, the silence stretched out, then Adriana smiled and began commenting on the weather and the gossip she had gleaned from her ball. Vard was careful to make only enough replies to be polite and keep her talking.

Once they had finished the first course, Adriana dabbed her lips with her napkin and laid it down beside the plate. She clapped her hands and three musicians entered. As she rose from her seat and stalked toward Vard, they played a slow song. She stopped by his chair and drew him to his feet.

Mind scrambling to stay ahead of her game, he clasped her hand and pulled her into his arms. She melted against him as if they were lovers. He recalled the last time he had Alecia in his arms, but avoided thinking of the things he had wanted to do with her on his last visit to Brightcastle. Instead, he bent his will to controlling his heartbeat. The queen could not know how agitated she made him. She would misinterpret and redouble her efforts.

"Mmmm," she purred. "You dance like a courtier, Vard. I would swear you've spent your life wooing queens and ladies. Except no courtier has muscles like you do. I can feel your hard strength against me—and I want us to be closer."

So saying, she pressed against him and laid her head upon his chest.

Vard cleared his throat. "You flatter me, Majesty. I assure you I'm no courtier, though I suspect you're trying to round off a few of my edges, are you not?"

She looked up at him, eyes wide. "I make no secret of the fact that I want you in my court—for many reasons. I'm drawn to you. Sometimes I wonder if you have cast a spell upon me."

"I assure you I have not, Majesty. I am, forever, your humble servant." The song stopped, and he led her to her seat.

She held onto his hand when he would've drawn away. "Must you stay at arm's length, Vard? I know we could be wonderful together. Must I command you?"

It appeared she would push the issue. If she did, he'd have no choice.

"Adriana, I beg you to remember your niece. Alecia has my heart."

The queen closed her eyes. "I love it when you say my name." Her bright emerald gaze speared him. "For the rest, I shall forget you said it. Have a seat and let us continue our meal."

Vard sat, and the meal continued. He wouldn't betray Alecia; had no desire to do so. His family meant everything to him, and it should mean something to Adriana. He argued back and forth in his mind about whether to use compulsion. He had no wish to force his hand, but if Adriana gave him no choice, he would.

After dessert, Adriana rang for port and tea. The footman poured the wine, but Adriana insisted on pouring the tea herself.

"Can I offer you tea, Vard?" At his nod, she reached for the pot and let out a sharp cry, clutching at her right shoulder.

Vard was out of his chair and beside her in an instant. "What's amiss, Majesty?"

She pushed him away. "Don't fuss, it's nothing a little time won't cure. But I might get you to pour."

Vard complied, wondering how the queen had hurt herself. Or was it just a recurrence of an old injury?

"Care to tell me why you're so sore you can't pour tea?" he asked.

"I told you," she said. "I will heal in time. Drink up."

Vard frowned, wondering why she didn't wish to discuss it. Was it embarrassment? Perhaps she'd had a fall and didn't wish to be reminded of her clumsiness.

They fell into an uneasy silence, but there was a reason for this meeting, and Vard wouldn't leave without canvassing the queen for his southern trip.

"Majesty," he said. "I wonder if you've thought any more about my journey south to gather more rangers?"

She waved her left hand. "Oh yes. Beniel thinks it a splendid idea. You are to organize it with all haste. And take Samael Delacost with you."

"Delacost? I thought he was tied to Nikolas Cosara's apron strings."

"He is, but I am sure you will keep him under control." She gazed over his shoulder, tapping her lips with a finely painted fingernail. "Mmmm. It's such a pity Delacost has a shady past. He would have made a fine addition to the naval leaders."

And no doubt the queen would have pursued him, too.

The monarch's gaze flicked to Vard. "Now we have that settled, I suggest you escort me to my chambers. I find myself in need of rest."

He left his port and tea unfinished, glad to escape the night earlier than he had feared. They traversed the keep, their way lit by far spaced candles. Only the occasional servant was still about. Any who saw them kept their faces down.

At the queen's chamber door, Vard stepped away from Adriana and bowed over her hand.

She smiled. "I had every intention of seducing you this night, Vard, but I find I can't concentrate on anything. I will go to my bed and look forward to our next meeting. You may not get away so easily then." She smirked and turned, entering her chamber and closing the door.

Vard drew a deep breath… and grinned into the dark. If that was all he ever had to use compulsion for in future, he'd be a happy man.

CHAPTER 14

VARD and Samael Delacost dined in a shabby inn in the town of Costa, two days ride south of Wildecoast. They'd been in the area for the better part of two weeks and had found another thirty men and women to add to the ranger ranks. King Beniel had asked Vard to contact one of his spies while in the town. Imagine his surprise when the man turned out to be James Tomel, Master Jeweler. Tomel was having a hard time accepting Vard's sudden rise to popularity after his apparent "kidnapping" of Alecia the previous year.

The three were seated at a corner table in a tense meeting regarding the future of the kingdom. Vard ground his teeth. The only thing that made this meeting easier to bear was the fact that Master Tomel appeared to be enjoying it as little as he. Discontent also radiated off Samael, who smelled like a flighty horse ready to bolt. He had told Vard that Esta had broken her betrothal to Tomel's friend when she fell in love with Sam.

"I don't care how much you resent me, Tomel," Vard growled, "the king himself has asked me to speak with you; who are you to judge me?"

Tomel sneered. "You may have hoodwinked the king and queen, but I'm not so easily fooled. And your association with this pirate doesn't add one jot to your credibility, *Lord* Anton."

Vard felt Sam's emotion harden, his body tense despite the grin he hid behind. "I've risen in this world, Master Tomel," Sam said. "Perhaps the king now wishes to have *real* men in his employ."

Vard almost smiled at Sam's taunt, but he must keep his focus. "Tell me what news you have, or I'll have no other choice but to report your intransigence to His Majesty. The fight against the enemies of Thorius leaves no room for petty squabbles."

Tomel sighed and stared hard at the tabletop. "I see I have little choice in the matter. But let it be known that I'll voice my displeasure to His Majesty at the earliest opportunity." He paused again and Vard ground his teeth. They had to be on the road soon, or it would be too dark to safely find the next camp.

"It has been quiet on the *Sis Lenweri* front. All my contacts report is a general unease in the towns and cities of Thorius, but there's one thing you should know. I had a bird from Wildecoast this morning." Tomel took a mouthful of his ale. "Prince Gorin has escaped from the prison. It appears he has also escaped the city."

"Damn!" Samael leapt to his feet and paced to the fireplace. Vard waved him back to his seat, but he understood his companion's agitation. Gorin's loss could be a blow Thorius wouldn't recover from. He was High Prince Faenwelar's son and general of his forces. Not only that, but the kingdom had lost its bargaining tool.

"You're sure?" Vard asked.

"As sure as I can be. The birds have never been false before. The seal was unbroken."

"It's fell news," Vard said. "We'll return to the city immediately. Alert your spy networks. The king must know of any elven movements, particularly *Sis Lenweri*. Now that he has retrieved his son, there's nothing to stop Faenwelar from launching his next attack."

Tomel studied Vard with a narrowed gaze. "It will be as you say, and I'll send birds to Wildecoast to advise you're on your way home. May the Goddess guide your path."

Vard stood and shook Tomel's hand. "Thank you."

Samael also shook Tomel's hand, though the spy made contact only briefly, and followed Vard out of the inn.

"With allies like him," Sam said, "who needs enemies?"

"He seems rather diminished since last I saw him. I wonder what ails him?"

"Luckily, that's none of our concern," Sam said, mounting his horse.

"It will be if he fails to do his job."

Vard shook off his niggling concerns about the master jeweler and urged his horse out into the street. Their thirty new rangers and twenty old converged on them from nearby streets, where they'd been waiting. He smiled and nodded, well pleased at the discipline of his team.

"We ride for Wildecoast, Rangers! Form up." Vard set off, heading north at a fast trot.

They made camp several hours out of Costa in a clearing just off the road. Previous campers had stacked the fire pit with wood, and a stream gurgled nearby.

Sam tended his and Vard's horses while Vard organized the rangers and set the watch. Vard smiled as his companion gave the mounts a last pat on their noses and joined him before the fire.

"You have great affection for horses," Vard said.

Sam sat on a log and stretched his legs out in front. "I had little experience with them until recently; until Esta. Oh, I rode, but never formed a bond with anything but my ship. Since I've spent more time with them, I've grown to understand and admire the humble steed."

Vard grinned. "Where would we be without them?"

"Agreed." They fell into a companionable silence as the fire crackled and the men and women made camp and dinner.

"I wonder what we'll find in the city?" Sam pondered. "And how the hell did that bastard Gorin escape? There'll be hell to pay!"

Vard shook his head. "There will indeed. I find the timing curious, it happening while I was absent. I'm certain I could have foiled the attempt had I been present."

Sam grinned. "Confident, aren't you?"

"No point being otherwise. As you well know, I'm responsible for tracking and surveillance. Although I left most of my rangers in the city, I took the more experienced trackers with me. It makes me wonder if the *Sis Lenweri* had knowledge of my trip and timed the raid accordingly."

"I guess it makes sense to wait until your enemy is at his weakest."

Vard nodded. "It certainly does. No matter how small the advantage may seem, it's better than none. Elves are brilliant at leaving little trace of their passing. Only myself and a couple of other trackers could have found their trail after the rescue attempt."

"You seem to have a sixth sense about these things."

Vard smiled to himself. Sixth sense and all the others, too. "We shall soon discover the truth of how the escape was accomplished. I hope the trail isn't too cold."

They ate dinner, and most of the rangers and recruits sought their beds or sentry posts. Soon, only Vard and Sam were left at the fire.

Sam cleared his throat. "Do you find it hard being in Wildecoast after your past adventures? I mean, I know what it's like to have my wings clipped."

Vard studied him. "You're in the same boat, so to speak. You've exchanged the freedom of being master of your ship and your destiny to depend on another's whims."

Sam nodded. "It's been tough, I don't mind admitting. I'd never tell Esta, but some days I feel so trapped." He swallowed hard, his shoulders tense.

Vard nodded. "I know that feeling. When I get it, I go for a run in the forest." He left out the bit about that run being in wolf form. "Wildecoast is stifling on occasion, but the ocean is my savior. Just watching the waves and the sea birds dipping and calling… I breathe in the salty air, close my eyes and imagine I'm speeding over the waves like a gull, splashed by the briny water."

Sam was staring at him, and he realized he had gone a little too far with his description. He cleared his throat. "Sorry, I got carried away."

His companion clasped his hands between his knees, head down, and Vard patted his shoulder. "What do you do when you feel trapped, Sam?"

He shook his head. "I have no proper solution yet. Sometimes I practice the sword or go for a ride. What I really need at those times is to feel the rock and bounce of a ship beneath my feet. It's where I'm happiest, and I never fully realized that, until I lost it. I'm not cut out for this landlubber life."

"What will you do?"

Sam pursed his lips and dragged his hands through his hair. "I owe so much to Esta and Niko, even the king. I must atone for my time as a pirate, and if that means I'm unhappy some days, well, I can endure that. I just wondered if you had any strategies for coping. We're cut from a similar cloth."

Vard didn't think they were similar at all, but he did like Sam and would help him if he could. He had few friends, so to count Sam amongst them was a surprising pleasure. "How about we practice the sword before turning in?"

Sam's eyes lit up, and he jumped to his feet. "I'd like that!"

Controlled chaos reigned as Vard entered the western gate into Wildecoast. Soldiers in the Zialni colors patrolled the walls and the streets, and a large contingent questioned those entering or leaving Wildecoast. Carts and wagons were being searched, and the angry cries of farmers and merchants protested the interruption of their day. Everywhere Vard looked, columns of soldiers marched or rode on their way to the Goddess knew where.

"Looks like no one's in charge," Sam muttered.

Vard had to agree. He grabbed the attention of a passing soldier. The man approached and saluted.

"Lord Anton, Sir!"

"Where's General Formosa, soldier?" Vard asked.

"Leading a scouting mission, Sir! He left for the north two days ago, on the tail of those scumbag elves and their prince."

"So, who's in charge?"

"Besides the king, the general's second, Vignier, Sir!"

"On your way, soldier," Vard said, frustration boiling in his gut. He turned to one of the junior rangers. "Peat, take the new recruits and find them accommodation. See that they're fitted out with uniforms. Find horses for any that don't have mounts."

Peat was young, but had a good head on his shoulders. Time to see if he could work things out for himself. He bowed and ushered the wide-eyed recruits away.

Vard turned to the experienced rangers he had taken with him to Costa and gave them their orders, basically that of information gathering. He needed to know the details of what had passed and how things stood.

"Come with me, Sam, we're going to see Her Majesty." He mounted his horse, and they rode through the crowds to the keep. Their way led past the prison, which was ringed with even more guards than usual.

"Talk about closing the stable door after the horse has bolted," Sam said, shaking his head.

"Indeed!" Vard turned his attention to the keep and spurred his horse into a canter, Sam close on his heels.

The chamberlain took one look at Vard's face as he dismounted in the forecourt and ushered him into the blue audience chamber. The man didn't even try to stop Sam from accompanying him, which he usually would've tried to do. Things were bad.

"Your Majesty," Vard said, bowing to Adriana, who wore a burnt orange gown that left her shoulders bare. "I came as soon as I heard."

Adriana drew her shoulders back and nodded, then turned to her ladies. "Ask His Majesty if he will attend me here and then prepare my rooms. I shall take tea there."

"Lord Anton," she said, "I know of no reason that Master Delacost should be in this chamber. Please have him wait outside." She averted her eyes from his companion and that angered Vard.

Sam made to leave, but Vard stopped him. "Your Majesty, I hesitate to question your order, but Samael Delacost has accompanied me on my southern mission and has proved himself a capable and valued advisor during that time. The tasks of my office are many and varied, and I need an aide. I've made him my second."

Adriana's eyes widened, and her mouth dropped open for a short time before she snapped it shut. Her assessing gaze swept Sam from head to toe. She had never welcomed him, and Vard knew he would hear more about this. "Master Delacost, you may take a position near the window."

Vard speared the queen with his glare, but she let it roll off her with a shrug. Sam moved to the window, all the while staring at Vard.

The queen took a deep breath, squared her shoulders, and seated herself, then looked up at Vard. "The investigation into the escape of the elven prince is progressing. Four days ago, the prisoner's attendant took Gorin his breakfast, only to find him missing. The bars on his external window had been removed, but were not recovered."

"Was there any sign of an explosion?" Vard asked.

"None. It was as if they were pulled out with a chain or rope. Of course, there's no evidence to say which. I suppose someone could have chipped down to the bars within the stone and weakened the window edges, but there was no evidence of this. And that would have taken a deal of time and attracted attention."

Vard looked at Sam, who shrugged his shoulders and shook his head. Seemed he couldn't fathom how the escape was accomplished either. He turned back to Adriana.

"What then? Are you suggesting Gorin climbed out the window and scaled the outside wall of the tower? That's six stories! Even an elf would have trouble doing that. There are no footholds they could use."

"Regardless, we believe that is what occurred. Once down, he evaded the patrols and left the city. From there, we have been unable to find his trail."

Vard stared at the monarch, unable to believe what he was hearing. "Nothing?"

"His Majesty, the king!"

King Beniel entered at the footman's declaration, dark circles under his eyes. Had he lost more weight?

Vard bowed, but Beniel approached him and placed his hand on his shoulder. "We've lost our advantage, Lord Anton. I was counting on Gorin to keep the devils at bay. Now they have him back, they will come for us, and we are not ready." His eyes fell on Sam. "Delacost! We would appreciate it if you left the chamber."

Sam bowed and left, winking at Vard as he passed. Considering the king's agitated state, it was best the news of Sam's promotion was delivered at a later time.

"Your Majesty, take heart," Vard said. "It's a blow to lose the prince, but we must try to retrieve him. If that proves impossible, then prepare for war."

The king's shoulders slumped further. "It seems nothing has gone right since Jiseve died. With him alive, I always had strength in Brightcastle; now… who knows?"

"You still have that strength. Don't forget we have won all our previous battles against the *Sis Lenweri,* and we have the *Lenweri* to call upon as well." Vard itched to mention Alecia's leadership capability, should it be needed, but remained silent. The monarch appeared determined to sideline his niece in favor of his infant nephew and the Guardians.

The king paced back and forth across the chamber. "The *Lenweri* could turn on us and join their traitorous cousins. But perhaps we must have a meeting with Kain Jazara and make the details of our alliance formal."

Vard frowned. "I can travel to Selinore on your behalf, Your Majesty. Have you sent a bird to the *Lenweri* prince in Selinore?"

The king scowled. "I have not. We have no birds trained to achieve that feat. However, I dispatched a squad of scouts as soon as Gorin escaped. I hope Kain Jazara will soon hear this fell news. Another group travels to Amitania."

"And General Formosa is in the field in the search for Gorin?" Vard asked.

"Yes, I thought I should send him, but now wish I could rely on his council. And there is no telling when he will return."

"Your Majesty," Vard said, "I can have Formosa recalled, and send one of the senior rangers to replace him. That way we have your general here if he is needed."

The king nodded. "Yes, yes, do that. I want him here should there be an attack."

Vard ground his teeth, both at the king's lack of forward thinking and at his dependence on Formosa, who was at best an average leader.

"Is there anything else I should know, Majesty?" Vard asked.

The king had drifted to the window overlooking the parade ground, his eyes focused northward. "No, I think you have all of the diabolical tale. Have Formosa recalled and find Gorin. I must know how he escaped. Also, set up a parley with Kain Jazara. He may be part elven, but he was always a brilliant commander." The king squared his shoulders. "Perhaps if we can count on Jazara's aid, we still have hope of victory."

Vard nodded and bowed, then bowed to Queen Adriana before taking his leave.

CHAPTER 15

THE days dragged by, and Alecia felt like a caged lion. Not that she'd ever seen the large wild cat, but she had read books and seen an artist's impression of one. They lived across the seas in a barren land of deserts and plains. One day she might take Iona there, but for now, she had other priorities. She only wished her plans were leading somewhere. The machinations of government in Brightcastle went on without her input.

Iona was nine months old and could sit by herself. She happily drank goat's milk, which meant Alecia could leave her. She'd survive just fine, but would she cope without her mama? And, in addition, would Alecia cope without Iona? Since her birth, there hadn't been a day they'd been separated. But that must change eventually.

The thought of leaving her child for an extended period set her heart to aching, but that was exactly what Alecia was contemplating. She must move forward with her plan to rule Thorius, and to do that she had to leave her cozy nest in Brightcastle and start building her own squad. But first she must speak to her uncle. That would happen at the end of the week.

She heaved a sigh of relief that her separation from Iona would be delayed at least until after Solomon's naming ceremony. Her Uncle Beniel was due to arrive in Brightcastle on the morrow. She knew a flutter of unease at the thought of confronting him.

At midmorning the next day, Alecia took her place among the household of Brightcastle Keep as King Beniel of Thorius arrived with his entourage. It reminded her of another time when the royal couple came to celebrate her betrothal. The thought sent a sour flux through her stomach. On that occasion, her uncle hadn't been the slightest bit supportive of her desires; had advised she get used to being married to an old and lecherous lord; it was her duty to have a son who would be heir to Thorius. She had no reason to believe his view of her future would be any different now. But she had to try.

Ramón and Benae headed the line, Benae with Solomon in her arms. Alecia was next with Iona, who had chosen that morning to fuss over everything. After Alecia came the chief steward, the housekeeper, and the rest of the staff. Opposite the family were the army heads. The new captain looked dashing in his black uniform, his golden locks tied in a ponytail, pale blue eyes sparkling. His eyes met hers, and he nodded, his lips tipping into a smile.

Alecia nodded back and made a note to find out more about him. She turned her gaze to the royal party alighting from the carriage, and again wondered where her uncle got the white horses for his mounted guard. They looked splendid. Beniel's head of guard shook hands with the Brightcastle captain, who formally accepted the parchment with his orders. The responsibility for the king's safety now passed to the local army leader.

Of course, that was only for show. Beniel's captain would lay down his life before he'd allow the king to be harmed.

Meantime, Beniel approached Ramón and Benae.

"Guardians, Lord and Lady Zorba, it is long since I have enjoyed your hospitality," Beniel said. "Who is this delightful child?"

Benae laughed as she rose from her curtsy. "This is Solomon, your nephew, Sire."

Solomon reached toward the king, and Beniel took him into his arms.

"Something tells me this one is special, Benae." Beniel's eyes sparkled with moisture. "He has Jiseve's eyes. It's like my brother is still with us." The king's words were strained with emotion as he handed the baby back to Benae.

Watching, Alecia's heart ached at the touching scene, but her hopes plummeted. Emotion clogged her throat as the king turned to her.

"Niece," he said, drawing her into his embrace. "I thought never to see you again. And here you are with a babe of your own." His blue eyes smiled down upon her, but they didn't warm her as they once had. "Are you well?"

Alecia drew back and held Iona up for inspection. "I'm well, and this is Iona." Of course, Iona, in her fussiness, chose that moment to wail. Her little face puckered in brick red folds and tears streamed from her eyes. Alecia clutched the babe to her chest and sent a quick prayer to the Goddess for some peace.

"Never fear, Alecia," Beniel said. "Babies fuss. We will have the chance to get reacquainted later in private."

Beniel moved on, receiving bows and curtseys from the staff as he entered the keep. Alecia stood in the forecourt in her finery and had rarely felt more lost, even when in exile.

Ramón stopped beside her. "What's the matter with Iona? She's usually such a happy girl."

Alecia shook her head. "She's teething, so perhaps that's it. More likely she knows I wanted her to make a good impression and was determined to embarrass me."

He laughed. "I highly doubt that." He stared into Iona's eyes, which Alecia knew would sparkle in the mid-morning sun. "Alecia, her eyes are exactly like Anton's. I hope that doesn't mean she's prone to the same madness he is?"

"Vard isn't mad," she snapped, "and Iona's eyes don't signal an affliction. I expect you to support her, not cast doubts on her sanity."

"Alecia! I didn't mean to give offence!"

She ignored his urgent words and cradled her daughter to her chest, stalking into the castle, Millie on her heels.

She continued to her room, where she fed Iona and settled her for a nap. Millie had laid Alecia's betrothal gown on her bed. Fury swept through her as she gazed upon it, and she hurled the cream dress into a corner. She would *not* be wearing that gown ever again. Damn her father for ruining her memories of the gown from earlier times. Damn Finus!

Millie entered, and her eyes soon found the dress on the floor. "Princess! What are you doing?"

Alecia fixed her maid with a look that had the woman standing ramrod straight. "Take that gown and give it to someone who needs it. I will not wear it again." When Millie didn't immediately move, Alecia snapped. "Now!"

The maid bundled up the gown and hurried from the room, leaving Alecia feeling terrible. Nothing was going right, and now she had been short with Millie.

She'd apologize when she returned. In the meantime, Alecia was stuck in her rooms when all she wished for was escape. She'd find a few of Benae's lady guards and have a weapons session with them. There was still time before the naming ceremony. She began changing into breeches.

Alecia rode with four of the female guards to a large clearing in the nearby forest. She had used it in the past and had sworn the ladies to secrecy regarding its location. Out of the corner of her eye, she spied the women glance at each other as they rode, perhaps wondering why Alecia had asked for so many companions.

Since beginning training with Benae's lady guards, she'd been drawn to these four. They had fallen into an easy friendship, and she instinctively knew she could trust each of them. If she was to be the next queen of Thorius, who better to help her than these women? Benae's initiative to train women to guard her had been a stroke of brilliance in many ways.

She found the clearing and dismounted, tying Silver amongst the trees. The others did the same. When the five of them were ready, she gave her instructions.

"I wish to practice with multiple opponents. Arelle, you come at me first, then, Cretia, when you think I'm being pushed to my limit, you join Arelle. Linnet, you can warm up with Kenna and join in when you think it appropriate. Arelle, take up your practice sword."

And so it began, Alecia pitting herself against Arelle, and then, when she was at a disadvantage, Cretia. She extricated herself from Arelle just in time to block Cretia's sword from her skull. It wouldn't have been a hard blow, but hard enough to hurt. When she had recovered and fully engaged with Cretia, Arelle launched an attack on them both, and then Linnet and Kenna joined Arelle.

Now Alecia and Cretia battled the other three, and it was all Alecia could do to remember this wasn't an actual battle. She tried to pull her swings but, by the blows she sustained, the other ladies were having just as hard a time remembering this was practice.

Suddenly, Alecia was flat on her back with Linnet standing over her, sword against her throat.

"Halt!" Linnet cried.

The other three battled on, their blood running hot. Before Linnet could stop them, Arelle took a blow to her forearm, Cretia was knocked to her knees and blood poured from Kenna's nose.

Linnet helped Alecia to her feet, and she looked around at the toll the practice session had taken on them. Alecia had a bloody scratch across her neck and one above her left eye. Arelle cradled her arm as if it were broken, and Cretia limped to a stump on her injured ankle. Besides her suspected broken nose, Kenna's ripped sleeve revealed a nasty bruise to her upper sword arm. Linnet was the only one not obviously wounded.

Alecia laughed as she imagined Ramón's face when he saw them in this state. Soon they were giggling and slapping each other on the back. Despite her injuries and sore bits, Alecia had forgotten her troubles for a time. Linnet approached her.

"Princess, I believe you're ready to face the men."

"I didn't best you!" Alecia gasped.

"I'm coming with you!" Linnet slapped Alecia on the shoulder and laughed. "By your leave, I shall be your fighting partner, and we'll see what the men make of that!"

They were a sorry sight as they returned to the keep. Alecia had aches and pains in more places than she could count, and the other ladies had fallen silent except for the odd groan when the ground became rough. The idea of weapons practice had been a good one at the time, but she felt in no state to take part in a naming ceremony. They had lost track of time and Alecia was running late.

Linnet rode up beside her. "That was the most fun I've had for a long time, Princess. The rest of the girls will be so jealous."

Alecia clutched her arm. "Can we just keep this between the five of us? I chose you all to be my guard, and I need you to be discreet." She stopped her horse and turned to the other women. "That clearing is our secret for now. If we add others to our group, it will be myself or Linnet who decide to do so. Agreed?"

The other three nodded vigorously without a shred of suspicion in their eyes.

"I regret your injuries, ladies. I'll see that you're given everything necessary for healing."

Kenna shook her head. "That won't be necessary, Your Highness. Princess Benae sees to our injuries personally. We'll just report to her after her son's ceremony, or perhaps tomorrow."

Alecia drew her shoulders back. "Please don't tell her I was with you when you sustained those wounds. I'll let her know I've selected you as my guard, but at a later time." *Oh yes, I can just see how that discussion will play out! Benae will be so happy!*

They walked their horses into the stable and dismounted. The grooms took the animals away and Alecia parted company with the female guards, who had rooms in a separate barracks.

She took the servant's entrance into the castle. Inside was a hive of activity, the halls full of servants hurrying to complete tasks before the festivities.

Alecia chewed her lip as she returned to her chambers. She hadn't thought this through very well, or she would've used her secret passage. Too many servants' eyes had widened when they saw her, before their gazes fell and they hurried on. She must look a fright.

She let herself into her chamber and was crossing her sitting room on the way to her bedroom when Millie screamed.

"Princess! What happened?" She hurried forward and put her arm around Alecia's waist. A wail issued from the bedchamber, followed by another.

"Don't fuss, Millie. I'm fine. How is Iona?"

"But your neck and face!"

Alecia stopped in front of her looking glass and gulped. Her hair was disheveled, her clothes muddy and torn in places, but what shocked her most was the severity of the damage to her neck and brow. She touched the wounds and hissed. The skin had swollen and her eye was half-closed.

Millie tutted. "Step out of those filthy clothes and into the bath, Highness."

By that stage, Iona was screaming for her mother, so Alecia ignored Millie and picked her up. The infant's face was red and puffy as Alecia put her to her breast. She relaxed in her feeding chair, glad of the peace that had descended.

A loud banging sounded on the outer door. Millie went to answer.

"You can't enter, My Lord. The princess is feeding her daughter."

"It's fine, Millie, I'm covered."

Ramón appeared in the doorway to the bedroom, and his face flushed when he saw her.

"What the devil have you been doing, Alecia? You look like you've been dragged behind a horse!"

She closed her eyes and let his ire wash over her. "I've been practicing."

"Yes, but *what* have you been practicing? We were getting concerned for your whereabouts, and you return looking like something the cat dragged in."

"Thank you so much!"

"Your uncle has been beside himself. He thought you had vanished again."

"I'm sorry, but I thought I was free to come and go as I pleased?"

"And look at your neck and face. I'll have the doctor attend you as soon as I can find him."

"There's no need, Ramón. I'll just clean up and put a little of Hetty's cream on. I'll be good as new in no time."

"I wish you'd behave like other ladies. You'll cause another scandal!"

Now he had gone too far. "I think you've said enough. I'll see you at the naming ceremony."

He scowled, opened his mouth, then closed it again. He turned and left the room, the outer door closing with a firm click.

Millie appeared at the doorway.

She pointed at her maid. "Don't say a word. I know I'm a mess, but I assure you all will be well."

In the end, Alecia arrived at the ceremony late, amid deep frowns from the special guests. She had tried to settle Iona, but had failed and left her with Millie rather than interrupt the service. Millie had finally chosen a deep blue gown for her, which looked wonderful. It was a pity her battered face hadn't quite scrubbed up as well as she'd hoped. Hetty's ointment had helped with the swelling, but hadn't worked wonders. She added a blue net veil to her ensemble to avoid drawing attention. After all, this day was for Solomon and his family.

It was a beautiful service. She couldn't help the tears that escaped as she watched Ramón hold her little brother. He was so devoted to the infant, but nothing could replace Solomon's real father—*her* father; the man who had comforted her in times of sadness and raised her in joy. And now she had no one to lean on.

Alecia had never felt so shut out—from her family, from her city, and from her dreams of a happy family with Vard and a kingdom in which she could be ruler. She knew she could be a better leader than whomever her uncle chose to succeed him. Frustration and impotence ate her up. The high she had experienced after her session with the lady guards evaporated, leaving her flatter than ever.

The service ended, and the guests and dignitaries moved to the ballroom for a meal and music. There were toasts and good wishes for Solomon, and many expressed regrets that his father was missing out. Alecia drifted among the guests, smiling here and nodding there, not entering any conversations. If she kept moving, perhaps she wouldn't crack into a thousand pieces.

The king caught up to her as she took a sip from her second glass of wine.

"At last I can speak with you, Niece. Where is my great niece?"

"She has been fussy lately and today was no different. I left her with the nanny." She smiled up at her uncle, wishing she still felt about him the way she had when she was younger.

"Ahhh." Beniel nodded. "I remember you were cranky at the same age."

"Some would say I still am."

"How have you been? Did I express how happy I am that you have returned?"

"Not in so many words, but I imagine you're pleased to have family to support you."

Beniel frowned. "It's not just your support I want, but your happiness. I want everything for you that Jiseve would have wished for."

"I'm sorry, Uncle, I can't tell you I'm happy right at this moment. But this isn't the place for this discussion. Perhaps we can talk tomorrow?"

Beniel drew in a deep breath and nodded. "Tomorrow it is, then."

Benae joined them. "Your Majesty, my husband requested your input on a matter he is discussing with the guild masters. Do you mind?"

The king beamed. "Of course. Ladies…" He swept away.

Benae watched him go and then turned to her. "I'm concerned for you, Alecia."

Of all the things she expected Benae to say, that wasn't on the list. "Oh? What concerns you so?"

She drew Alecia to a more private alcove. "The wounds on your neck and face; our guests are whispering about them. Can I help heal them?"

Alecia glared at her. "I know you're trying to be kind, but no thank you. I'm sorry to have embarrassed you, but I wouldn't have missed Solomon's naming for anything."

"That's not what I meant! Why must you think the worst of me? I promise I just want the best for you and Iona."

Alecia stared at Benae, examining her face for any sign of artifice. She was either a talented actress or she was being sincere. She sighed. Sometimes she tired of fighting.

She drew herself up and looked Benae in the eye. "Thank you for your offer. I'll heal just fine."

"Alecia, I want you to know that if you need someone to confide in, I can be that person. I too am lonely here at times."

Alecia bristled. That Benae should assume she was lonely. And she was nothing like Benae! "Thank you, but I'll manage. Now I must see if Iona is ready for a feed."

She turned and left, Benae's sigh chasing her from the room. She didn't know why the Guardian bothered trying to befriend her. Was it a guilty conscience? She was about to mount the staircase to the upper floors when Ramón caught up with her.

She tried to brush past him, but he stopped her.

"Alecia, this recklessness has to stop."

She turned to him on a higher step, so their eyes were at the same level. She liked it that way. "Oh? What recklessness? I'm simply going about my business the best way I know how. I told you I wanted to improve my fighting skills. That involves risk."

His lips tightened. "I can't have you parading around with great slashes across your neck and eye. People will talk, and pretty soon rumors will spread. It's my responsibility to manage the image of the royals."

"Oh. And I'm not helping? I don't care what people think of me, especially stuffy lords and merchants. I'm a princess of the people, and they know they can depend on me to be their champion."

"You've been gone for more than a year. Don't you think you need to re-establish yourself? If you want to perform good works and help the community, I'm happy to give you a staff to help. You only have to say the word. But please, no more injuries!"

She placed her hand on his shoulder and squeezed. He really cared for her and wanted the best. As far as Benae was concerned, she wasn't sure. "Thank you for your suggestion and offer. Good works are rather a splendid idea. I'll give it some thought." She smiled and continued up the staircase.

Iona was her fussy self when Alecia arrived in the chamber. As she fed her daughter, she pulled out a parchment and wrote a list of the ways she could help her people.

One thing was for sure. Her father would never have supported this endeavor. Ramón, on the other hand, was happy to divert her from what he considered destructive pursuits. She was grateful for the distraction, but it didn't mean she'd stop her fight training. No. That would go ahead as planned, and now she had a ready group of women she could build on for the future.

Alecia stood before the window of the small audience chamber. From here, she could just see the heads of soldiers as they practiced at arms. She longed to be out with them, but this was more important. Her meeting with the king was long overdue.

She had dressed in her most conservative gown. It was dark blue with a white lace collar and cuffs, hiding most of her scrapes and bruises. Her eye she couldn't disguise, but she had done her best with powders and kohl. Even Benae would admit she was presentable.

Her gut churned with fear that this audience wouldn't deliver the outcome she longed for. Somehow, she must convince her uncle that she should be his heir. At least she should be regent until Solomon came of age. Surely, he would see that was sensible. She took a deep breath, held it, and then slowly let it out. Her heart settled a notch.

She crossed to the tea table and poured herself a cup, adding lemon but not milk. The citrus scent in the steam swirled up her nostrils. She inhaled deeply, closing her eyes and concentrating on the delightful aroma.

She could do this. All she must remember was to have faith in herself and her plan. She might be alone at this moment, but the people would support her if Uncle Beniel did.

The door opened and a footman announced the king. Uncle Beniel swept through, and she put her cup down and went to meet him, sweeping a deep curtsey.

"Your Majesty," she said. "Good morning and thank you for meeting with me."

Beniel pulled her upright. "Such formality is not required, Niece. We are and always will be family. In private, you need not be so rigid."

"Uncle, I wish you to know that I respect you, even if we don't always agree."

"Alecia, I have always loved you like my child. I know you respect me, and I regret it upset you that I didn't support your betrothal objections. Sometimes, we must do distasteful things if they are in the best interests of the kingdom."

Alecia lowered her gaze, recalling those horrible days when Lord Finus was her future. His hands on her body still gave her nightmares, but she had learned to distract herself and replace them with memories of Vard's hands and lips. It helped.

"My mother always instilled in me a love and commitment to my people. That's why I wished to speak with you." She paused and filled her lungs with air to steady her nerves. She breathed out and faced him. "I wish to be your heir, next in line to the throne."

His face blanched, and lines appeared beside his lips. "You know that's not possible. You are female. My heirs *must* be male."

"I beg to differ, Uncle. As king, *you* can decide who will be your heir. You can make me heir if you choose. All you must do is choose me."

She fell silent, as did the king. He walked to the window and stared out, but she suspected he didn't see a thing. Alecia dared hope his consideration and focus was on her request. *He must see sense!*

"Benae and Ramón can help me for a time, perhaps quite a long time. They could stay here in Brightcastle, and I will study under you in Wildecoast."

Yes, that would work well and keep the Guardians happy. Solomon could still be heir to the throne, though he may never ascend. I know I can do this!

Beniel turned to her. "I can't do it, Alecia. The people would never agree to a queen."

Even though she had expected his objection, Alecia's heart constricted, and her breath quickened. "You can't give me an answer so quickly, Uncle. It seems to me the perfect solution to your lack of an heir who is of age."

"That's where you're wrong, my dear niece. This kingdom has not had a queen for centuries. I cannot see any circumstance where the people will agree to one."

"And so Thorius will be permanently without a ruling queen? That's ludicrous! I don't like to blow my own trumpet, but I'd make a good ruler. My father taught me about governing, and so did Mama. In fact, Mama taught me most. I'd make a better heir than my father ever would have."

Beniel studied her. "I suspect you are right about Jiseve. There were disturbing reports of his behavior before he died."

Alecia pounced on his words. "Do you mean stories of his abuse of Benae?"

The king turned to the window, his shoulders tense, his hands gripping the sill. "I am told that is the case, though I can't reconcile my brother abusing his wife. And yet, I saw the evidence. Jiseve abused Benae repeatedly after they married."

Alecia approached him and stood just behind. "Why would my father hurt Benae? Did she give you a reason?"

Beniel shook his head. "Does there have to be a reason for cruelty? To think of Benae being harmed makes me sick to the stomach. She is such a little thing… you should have seen the bruises!"

Alecia didn't want to ask the question, but she had to. "Uncle, is there a chance that Ramón and Benae had an affair, and that was why my father hurt his new bride?"

Beniel's shoulders rose further. "The queen suspected they had been intimate, but Benae swore she was nothing but faithful. Ramón also assured me he had acted in all propriety. But they spent a night together in a beach shack during a storm. Anything could have happened." He turned to face Alecia. "They denied all accusations of impropriety. And even if they did what you allege, that is no excuse for Jiseve to act as he did. If he was aware of some indiscretion, he could have put Benae aside or, if he chose to persist with the marriage, forgive her and put it in the past."

Alecia folded her arms across her chest. "Could you, Uncle? Forgive such an indiscretion?"

His serious blue gaze bored into hers. "I have been in such a position many times, my dear. My marriage to your aunt was arranged, but our friendship grew into love. However, Adriana has strayed from my bed in the past and will do so again in the future, I suspect."

"Uncle! That *can't* be true! Why would you accept such behavior?"

"Adriana is a free spirit, and I wish for her to be happy. If the occasional discreet lover can keep her that way, then I can turn a blind eye. So, you see, I can't accept Jiseve's behavior if that is the reason for it. There is no excuse for harming a woman."

Alecia stood, mouth open, not knowing how to respond. She stepped close and wrapped her arms around his waist. "You're a good man, Uncle; a gentle man."

Beniel returned the hug, and they stood like that for long moments until Alecia broke the contact. "Thank you for being honest with me. I *will* get to the bottom of this 'affair'."

"Alecia, leave Benae in peace. She doesn't deserve your anger and accusations. She is trying to do her best as joint guardian. I placed her in that position. You need to have more respect."

"But she shouldn't be in that position. If you need a regent, appoint me. If you can't make me heir, appoint me instead of Benae and

Ramón. I'll oversee Brightcastle until Solomon comes of age. It makes so much more sense. Please, I'm begging you to give me this chance." Begging should have been beneath her, but she didn't care.

Beniel frowned. "This behavior must end, Alecia. And I mean your aspirations to the throne and your weapons practice. Have some dignity. If you wish for a project, raise Iona to be a good citizen as your mother taught you. Perhaps Adriana could find you a position as lady-in-waiting if you really feel you don't have a place here. However, I am sure the Guardians would have you if you could work cooperatively."

She stared at her uncle, her mouth open. The way he spoke to her, anyone would think she was a child. And yet she had killed more than once; had birthed a baby. She told herself it was just that the king didn't know what she was capable of. But the cold realization hit. He didn't *care* what she could do. He had relegated her to the sidelines where she'd be safe; where she could have only a minimal influence on Thorius and its people.

"Lady-in-waiting? Is that all you think me worthy of, Uncle? You don't want to marry me off to an old lord to beget more heirs?" Her voice rose, and she fought to bring it under control.

He scowled at her. "That is enough, Alecia. You forget yourself. I don't wish to hear any more on the subject. Bring me my great niece. I wish to meet her properly."

She drew herself up. "Before I do that, what do you plan for Vard?" He frowned. "I wondered when you would ask that question." Again, he walked to the window. It seemed to be the thing to do when you were king and needed to collect your thoughts. "Your aunt has seen talent in the man, and you know how I depend on her judgement. Recently, I made him a lord and granted him property with the title. As the King's Blade and leader of the Rangers, he has been doing a rather fine job, if reports are to be believed."

Lord Vard Anton. It had a nice ring to it. "He's climbing the ranks and has become your advisor while I'm nothing to you?"

Beniel strode across to her. "You are family, girl. But I won't be accused of insanity by putting you forward as my heir. You must accept what you have."

"*I* deserve to rule here," she said, "not the woman who presided over my father's death. The sooner you see that, the better."

Alecia spun and strode from the audience chamber, the startled footman jumping out of the way as she flung the door back. She battled tears of fury as she took the stairs to her chamber. Why had she been born a woman? Why couldn't she have been the son Jiseve had always yearned for? Perhaps then all would have been settled long ago in Thorius.

Instead, she must accept the scraps from Benae and Ramón's table. Well, it wasn't fair or just, and if the king expected her to agree like a timid mouse, he'd be disappointed. Stopping before her chamber door, she dried her cheeks and took a deep breath. From now on, no one would see her anger or her desire. She'd plan and deliberate coldly, keeping her secret schemes close to her chest. No one would suspect her of any aspirations… until it was too late!

She entered and prepared Iona to meet her great uncle, the King of Thorius.

CHAPTER 16

ERIELLE Cosara was back on her estate, having had a glorious three days at the coastal cottage and a week in Wildecoast. As she saddled Storm, she mused on the events of the last year, and how far she had come. A year ago, she was a mermaid, beached and alone, the victim of a vicious plan by her family to turn her into a monster. Now she was a respected lady, wife of the admiral, and no one suspected she hadn't always been human.

Life was, if not perfect, good. She did crave more female friends. Why was it so difficult to form friendships? Her only one was Lady Esta Aranati. She had seen Esta too little of late, her pregnancy keeping her close to home much of the time. Meanwhile, the ladies at court kept Merielle at arm's length, possibly because her husband was a powerful man—or was it her mysterious past or even something else? Meri had to admit she could be a little strange at times.

And on the estate, though she had tried to befriend the staff, they gave her odd looks and kept their distance. Nikolas said they were only being proper, that it was not commonplace for a lady to befriend her staff. However, it left Meri bored and lonely.

To fill the hours, she had determined to learn as much as she could about the farm and the ways of humans. Her mermaid roots, though now latent, still bestowed her a strength greater than normal women.

She had to be careful not to display that power too overtly, but it meant she was handy at manual tasks. And she had learned to ride most proficiently. Storm, Nikolas's dapple gray stallion, was now hers.

They had bonded after she used him to escape the cottage and go looking for Nikolas in the early days after her transformation.

Back then, she could not ride, and was so fearful of Storm her daring adventure still amazed her. It had been foolhardy to ride in search of her beloved, not knowing where he was and having little knowledge of the countryside or its people. A woman on her own was vulnerable, as had been shown to her since then. However, she had succeeded, and Storm had looked after her.

She rode Storm every chance she got. The manager gave her lessons when he had time, and Nikolas had given her pointers on how to avoid an attack when on horseback. He thought he was just being careful and keeping her safe. Little did he know her secret plan. And it was all coming together. When Nikolas was at sea or elsewhere, Meri took lessons with the sword and the bow and arrow. She had hired Vard Anton to teach her, and if Vard could not attend he sent one of his senior rangers.

Vard was a man she trusted to be discreet. Word of her training would never escape to worry Nikolas or cause gossip. Vard understood women had value not just as pretty decorations but as partners in strategy and battle. She was looking forward to meeting Alecia Zialni, whom Vard had fallen in love with. From what Meri had heard, Alecia was a woman to be reckoned with; not one to sit idly by while the menfolk did the fighting.

Vard did not say much, but she scrutinized him. He was devoted to Alecia. In brief moments of vulnerability, she had seen a flash of longing in Vard's gaze and believed Alecia was the cause. And she had heard there was a child involved as well. She could not imagine how difficult it was for Vard to be apart from his daughter. Of course, she could never ask about it. She knew enough to realize that was not a topic she should discuss with her tutor.

Vard would be here shortly. He was a mysterious man who arrived and departed with almost no notice. She had no idea how he traveled or why he was so secretive, but sooner or later, she would know more. She was learning patience, not naturally a trait of hers or her sisters. Especially not her sisters.

Storm was unsettled this morning, but she had long ago learned his vices and quirks. For a stallion, he was gentle, and she no longer feared him as she had at the start. How Nikolas must have laughed at her! She saddled Nabby, a spirited charcoal grey mare from the Zorba stables. Nabby suited Vard's nature, though she never settled well under him. Vard appeared not to mind her fussing and shying. He was a superb horseman, but then most military men were.

Meri led the two horses out to the stable yard and mounted Storm, smiling at the difficulty this used to give her. Back then, she was still learning how to walk, let alone climb on a horse. She clucked to Storm and trotted out of the yard, Nabby in tow. The far meadow was her destination, and Vard would meet her there.

In fact, he was waiting for her when she arrived. He pushed off from a gigantic oak that gave shelter to the sheep on the hot days.

"Morning, Lord Anton," Meri said. "I hear congratulations are in order."

He shrugged. "The queen is a tough woman to refuse. Whatever assists me to safeguard the kingdom and help the people must be borne."

She frowned at him from Storm's back. "You sound as though having lands and a title is a chore."

He quirked a brow at her. "Isn't it? Titles and lands come with irritations and responsibilities. I'd rather decide my own fate."

"Now you sound just like Nikolas."

"Then I have something in common with your husband, lady."

"I have told you to call me Merielle, Vard."

He nodded. "Merielle." He reached for Nabby's reins and vaulted into the saddle. "Today we take to the forest. It's all very well to practice weapons in an open field, but the elves are masters of warfare amidst trees. We all must prepare for that."

He turned Nabby and they cantered into the forest. All morning, they practiced galloping through the narrow trails. At first, Vard chased her on horseback, and she had to avoid him. She didn't do well for the first half hour, but, after a rest and more tuition, she learned to change direction just when she thought he was close. She avoided him on two occasions, which made her heart race madly. It was arduous work, but she loved it. This was the excitement she had dreamed of when imagining life as a human woman.

At lunch, they sat in the shade under the big oak and ate berries from the forest, as well as the cheese and bread she had brought.

"Why are you doing this, Vard?"

"Because you asked, and there was no reason I should refuse. You would've asked someone else if I had said 'no'."

She laughed. "You are right in thinking that. I can be determined."

"I'd rather teach you than have an inferior man mess it up."

She smiled. "You have a high opinion of yourself, I see."

"I know my strengths and weaknesses. I can teach you better than anyone."

He said it without bragging, and Meri knew he was right. Nikolas certainly would not have been able to teach her. He would worry about her getting hurt. If he found out what Vard was doing, though, he would be furious with both of them.

"What has you concerned, Merielle?"

* * *

Merielle Cosara was a mystery that Vard would eventually solve. Not much escaped him, but this lady was unlike any woman he'd ever known. Not to say he really knew her. To start with, her bright red hair appeared natural, yet he had traveled extensively and seen no one with hair like it.

And she was strong, with powerful muscles that could match the strength of a man, especially after the training she had undergone. It was clear she was comfortable in the breeches and tunic she wore when many women would've felt self-conscious, exposing their legs and backside to scrutiny. Alecia was an exception, but she had worn men's attire for many years. The thought of his love sent an unwelcome pang of pain through his heart.

Merielle's question about why he had agreed to train her had caught him by surprise. He didn't have the time to spend a day out here each week, but was moved to say 'yes. He always followed these hunches. It was his Defender instinct that called to him on these occasions, and he wouldn't ignore it. Sometime in the future, Vard knew instinctively that Merielle would need these skills.

Besides, she was good company and often said things that a lady would not. In many ways, being in her company was like being with a man. They discussed weapons, horses, strategy, and fighting techniques. Perhaps she'd been deprived of female company, or grew up with brothers. He wasn't complaining. He enjoyed their lessons, and the horse Nabby was a challenge.

"Why do you think I'm worried?" she asked.

"That frown tells me. Care to let me in on your secret?"

She jumped and sucked in a deep breath. Now he was sure she was hiding something.

"Secret?" She stood and brushed the grass from her breeches. "My only secret is these practice sessions. I was just thinking about Nikolas's reaction should he find out."

"Then why not tell him?"

"He wouldn't approve. I don't know how he would react, and I don't care to find out."

"He'd put a stop to them would be my guess."

She spun to him. "That can't happen. I need this. A force drives me to learn all of it. I don't fit in on the estate or at court, and, for the first time, I feel I'm growing. Nikolas is a wonderful man and husband, but he is comfortable in his skin despite the troubles in his past. He doesn't understand how I need to be. He tries to protect me and it is stifling. I'm used to being free. I feel that again, since these lessons, and even before when I was learning to ride."

"Well, we'll just have to be careful. There's much to learn, though you're a quick study. This afternoon we'll practice hand-to-hand combat, as the horses are tired."

Merielle laughed. "*They* are tired! I'm exhausted, but I have the feeling a battle doesn't stop for rest."

"You're right, My Lady. The most exhausted I've ever been is during battle. Luckily, battle lust takes over and gives you strength and endurance. Afterwards, you could sleep for a week."

"Let us give the horses a rest and test each other. Do not hold back, My Lord."

Vard grinned and fetched the weapons, hobbling the horses before leaving them to graze in the field.

* * *

Nikolas Cosara trotted his bay mare into the forecourt of his estate and allowed her to drink from the ornate fountain. He dismounted as the horse slurped her fill, then led her to the stables which lay to the rear of the manor house. Though he'd been reluctant to accept this estate from the queen, he'd grown to love the place. He hoped it wouldn't be threatened in the coming war with the elves.

Merielle was coming out of the stone stables as he approached. Her eyes widened as she saw him.

"Nikolas! You're home a day early!"

He took a moment to drink in the view of his love—emerald eyes ablaze, wisps of crimson hair escaping her plait, and men's breeches revealing the delights of her long legs. Of all the events which had occurred in the past year and a half, the advent of this woman into his life was the most treasured. And then he noticed the tension around her eyes.

"Indeed, I am. I thought to have a quiet drink with my love." He folded her into his arms and his body stirred. "What have you been doing today?"

He didn't miss the slight stiffening of her spine.

"Oh, Storm and I have had a big day of riding. I decided that if I wanted to be safe on a horse, I needed to practice in all environments. We have been charging through the woods all day." She pulled back to look up into his face. "I must make sure Cook knows you're here."

He framed her face with his hands and kissed her. "I missed you."

Again, the vague alarm rippled across her features. "I always miss you, beloved. You are my sun and moon. I have never regretted a day of my life since we met."

He studied her face and allowed the words to settle in his mind. She was sincere, so perhaps there was no cause for alarm. But lately, he'd been disturbed by the niggling worry that Merielle was keeping something from him. His mind had listed the secrets that she could be hiding, and he hated the way his thoughts had turned. He needed to confront her, but how? He didn't wish to damage their relationship.

"What's the matter, Meri?" he asked. "Lately you've been…" He sought the right words. "*Distracted*. If there's something worrying you, I wish you'd tell me."

She laughed, but it sounded forced. "Nothing is wrong, Nikolas. I worry about you and the elves and losing you, but, apart from that, I am happy. Now put your mare to bed and we will have that drink."

She kissed his cheek and turned for the house. He watched her graceful movements as she entered the building. Perhaps all was well. A shiver ran through his body. He couldn't lose her like he had lost everyone else in his life; he *wouldn't* lose her! He led his mare into the stables and unsaddled her, giving her a thorough rub down, though he wanted to simply cast her into a stall and join Meri.

As he went to fetch a feed of oats for his mare, he ran his eye over Storm. The stallion was munching happily on his dinner and his recently brushed coat contained rivulets of sweat. Merielle certainly *had* worked him hard, but he didn't look the worse for wear. He fetched the oats and was on his way back to his horse when he saw Nabby. The mare also looked as if she had worked hard. But who had ridden her? Merielle wouldn't need both horses, and she wouldn't ride Nabby.

He ran his hand across the horse's forehead as she fed. Yes, she was still warm. Dammit, Merielle *would* tell him what was going on! No more speculating about phantom ideas that gnawed at his gut.

He threw the oats into his mare's bin, topped up her water, and strode from the stables. His manager would cover the horses with blankets before turning in. Mind on exposing the mystery, he entered the house and walked directly to the chambers he shared with his wife.

Merielle was in the bath, singing a song she had learned when growing up. It made him wonder if she regretted her decision more than she let on. He walked to where he could observe her. Her eyes were closed, and her hands moved over her body, washing off the grit and grime of the day. He breathed deeply of her soap's perfume and felt himself grow hard. He had missed her.

Entering the bedroom, he fetched a cloth then used it to wash her body.

"You spoil me, Nikolas," she said. "But I do love to feel your hands upon me. Why don't you join me?"

He didn't need to be invited twice and had his clothes off in seconds. He slid into the bath, facing her, his feet beside her hips.

"This is just what I need after today. It was another grueling session with Anton's students. But they learn fast. Unfortunately, so does Sam. You know, I think he may be a better swordsman than I am?"

Merielle sat up and ran the cloth over his body. It did wild things to his heart. Would he ever tire of the drug that was his wife? He didn't think so. She leaned forward and kissed his mouth before trailing kisses down his neck. He was so hard it was painful.

"It appears you need a little attention, husband," she said, wrapping her hand around his member. He gasped and threw his head back, glorying in the feel of her fingers against him.

"You could say that," he growled, eyes closed as she pleasured him.

Her fingers left him, and she kissed him again before settling on his lap, her sex close to his manhood. Luckily, the bath was just large enough to accommodate them. She taunted him with her proximity, rubbing her heated flesh against him. When he couldn't take much more, she lowered herself and he slid home.

He groaned again as her tightness encapsulated him. This feeling of being inside her was like no other. She was made for him. Her flesh fit him like a glove. When she rode him, he saw stars. She picked up the pace, her hands on his shoulders, head thrown back and uttering throaty moans that threatened to push him over the edge. He drew closer to his climax, and Meri spasmed around him, shuddering as she cried his name.

Nikolas crashed over with her, emptying himself, his hands around her bottom, pulling himself deeper into her body. In that moment, they were one, and he never wanted it to end.

But end it did. They came back to awareness together, and her eyes met his.

"You're an angel to welcome me so… completely," he said, kissing her breasts and extracting a violent shiver.

"And you are a devil, husband. I have much to do tonight, and now all I wish for is to make love with you. Ohhh!" She shuddered again as his lips worked their way up to her earlobe.

"Surely you have time for your husband? There can be nothing that can't wait until tomorrow." He extracted himself from her long limbs and luscious body and stepped from the bath, wrapping her in a soft towel as she rose to join him.

"I'm sure something can be arranged," she said, as he pulled her to him. "Dress up, Nikolas, I've arranged a special dinner to welcome you home. It will be ready within the hour."

He didn't let her go. "Plenty of time for me to show you just how much I've missed you then," he said, drawing her to their bed. He pushed her down beneath him and spent the next hour reminding Meri just how good they were together.

Nik could almost forget the nagging doubts he had experienced earlier as he lay before the fire, Meri's head in his lap. After a superlative dinner, their conversation had ranged wide, including Gorin's escape and its consequences, local court gossip, farming topics, and estate concerns. Now they had fallen into a companionable silence. It was a shame to spoil the evening. But he must. Perhaps there was an innocent explanation for Meri's odd behavior?

He cleared his throat. "I must ask you a question, beloved."

She sounded half asleep, and he knew a pang of guilt at disturbing her. "Mmm?"

"Lately you've been distracted. I wondered if there was anything bothering you."

"I am perfectly content, Nikolas. After an evening like the one we have just had, how could you doubt it?"

"I'm certain you have a secret, and I'd like to know what it is."

She pushed herself up from his lap and turned to face him. "There is nothing you need to know, Nikolas."

"There is. You're behaving just as you did before I found out about Jon and the details of his death. You knew more than you were telling then, and it's the same now. I wondered what was giving me this uncomfortable feeling—a feeling that took me back to the days in the cottage when we first met. Now I know it's because you're holding a secret; something I won't be pleased about."

She dropped her gaze to the rug, and he watched as her eyes traced the swirling patterns of the weave. "You will be angry, and I don't want you to be angry. Tonight has been so magical. Can we not speak of this tomorrow?"

"Let me start. There were two tired horses in the stables tonight. Why?"

Fear danced across her eyes. "Someone is helping me learn to ride and fight."

Nikolas bolted to his feet, hands in fists. "Who?"

"He comes once a week and teaches me to ride and to fight with sword, knife, and bow. I knew you wouldn't allow it, so I organized it myself. You can't stop me, Nikolas. I'm doing this for us, so I will be safe and I can protect myself and my staff."

"Who is it who dares spend time alone with my wife?" He clenched his teeth, fury warring with jealousy. He was dead, whomever he was.

Merielle's shoulders drooped, her gaze glued to the rug. "Lord Anton."

"Vard Anton? I knew I didn't trust that man. I'm helping him train his rangers, and he's out here messing with my wife!"

She stood and went to him, but he stepped away. "How can you doubt me? It is innocent. Tell me you would have allowed the lessons if I had asked you."

"Of course, I would have said 'no'. It's totally inappropriate. And it stops now. Anton will be lucky if he survives this."

She heaved a deep breath. "You have no cause for jealousy. I love you and only you. But I need to learn how to defend myself. And I am strong; as strong as a man. It's only right that I fight like a man." She placed her palms on his chest. "You know it's true. If I have skills with weapons and hand-to-hand combat, I will be safer to be around. Otherwise, if I get frightened, I could hurt someone. You remember what happened at the inn. I can't risk that again."

"But you're willing to risk gossip about the admiral's wife who spends time with another man? Already there might be gossip at court. I can't stand another scandal. Your association with Vard Anton will end."

"Please, beloved. I have nothing else of my own. I can be a warrior; can be of help to the kingdom." She squared her shoulders. "And I will be, no matter what you say."

Fear struck his gut. Had he already lost her? No matter what she said, she was a beautiful woman, and Vard Anton would be a stone not to be drawn to her.

"If that's what you have your heart set upon, then I can't stop you short of locking you up—which I would never do. I leave for Wildecoast in the morning." He turned and left the room.

CHAPTER 17

MERI lay in her bed, gut churning. Nikolas was already on his way to Wildecoast, and she had no way of warning Vard about his imminent arrival. It was all happening as she had feared. Her love was a jealous man. She had begged him to leave Vard alone, but he would not be swayed from the confrontation. Hopefully Vard could look after himself. What was she thinking? Of course, he could look after himself. Perhaps she should fear for her husband? Blind with rage as he was, he would go charging into this without caution.

They should not be fighting amongst themselves when they must prepare for war with the elven aggressors. All she had wanted was to learn and be useful. Now she had caused this trouble between Vard and Nikolas. Well, she would not lie abed and do nothing.

She threw off the covers and leapt out of bed, drawing on a new set of breeches and tunic, along with her light cloak. She had a footman saddle Storm while she ate breakfast and gathered a pack of necessities. Her housekeeper followed her around, wringing her hands and begging her to reconsider. The coach could be readied, and she could travel as a proper lady should.

Meri ignored most of what she said, and the woman gave up. Her maid was almost as bad. In desperation, Meri invited her to travel with her to shut her up. Of course, the girl was not a proficient rider, and she could never have kept up or mastered any of the horses in the stable except, perhaps, Storm. At that suggestion, the girl's eyes widened, and she fell silent, enabling Meri to leave alone.

She was ready in a half hour and was soon charging along the road toward Wildecoast. She rode like a madwoman, taking only the briefest stops for watering her horse and to allow him rest. Vard had impressed upon her the proper way to ride swiftly without breaking your horse, and she would never wish to harm Storm.

Still, he was blowing hard when she finally arrived in the city around midday. Now what? Meri had thought little about what she would do on her arrival, except find the men and see they didn't cause each other damage. Vard would be with his rangers. She rode sedately through the city, heading to the keep and the barracks just outside it. The building was a hive of activity, with soldiers coming and going on foot and horseback. Sentries and scouts hustled back and forth, and she thought she saw several rangers.

Meri approached a woman ranger and asked for Vard.

"He took a group out for a scouting lesson, My Lady." The woman said. "I believe they headed to the northern forests."

"Thank you. Have you seen Samael Delacost?"

Perhaps Sam could help her stop Nikolas from doing something stupid, though he didn't listen to Sam often.

"I believe he said he was heading to the Dragon for lunch, My Lady. I can escort you there if you care to wait."

Meri didn't wish to delay, but if she didn't get help now it could cost her time later. She nodded and waited as the woman fetched a mount. In quick time, they pulled up at the inn, and the ranger went inside to find Sam.

He appeared outside, chewing on a chicken leg, and bowed. "Lady Cosara, this is a pleasant surprise. How can I help?"

Meri dismounted. "Perhaps we should talk inside?" She turned to the woman. "Thank you. I will mention your help to Lord Anton."

The woman bowed and left them. She tied Storm to the rail and went inside, joining Sam at a table in the corner. It seemed fighting men always sat with their backs to the wall.

"I need to find Nikolas," she said.

Sam's brows rose. "I thought he was at the estate with you?"

"He was, but he left early this morning. We had an argument last night, and I'm afraid he may do something silly if I don't find him."

Sam leaned back in his chair, a dancing light in his eyes. "What happened?"

Meri folded her arms. This was not funny! "I've been having riding and fighting lessons, and Nikolas found out."

He tilted his head to the side. "Not much of an issue on the face of it. Though Nikolas can be stubborn. What's the problem?"

"My teacher was Lord Anton. He has been coming out to the estate, and Nikolas found out. He thinks it was inappropriate and is concerned about gossip."

"He doesn't like being lied to. But surely you explained there was nothing untoward?"

"I tried, but he was furious with me, and with Vard. My husband has no reason to be jealous, Sam. I adore him and would do nothing to hurt him."

Sam pushed his hands through his hair as if he would rather be anywhere but dealing with her. "I don't know what you expect of *me*. He never listens to me. I could make things worse merely with my presence."

"Please, Sam. Help me find him and talk him out of confronting Vard. No good will come of it."

Sam pushed his chair back and stood. "Come on. I have a few ideas about where we might find my brother. If he hasn't already gone in search of Vard, we might have a chance."

They mounted their horses and made their way to the keep, checking in the places Sam thought Nikolas might be. No one had seen him. Perhaps he had gone in search of the scouting party after all?

"There's nothing for it," Meri said, after they had searched for an hour. "We must head into the forest and see if he is there."

"Or we could wait here and pick up the pieces when they arrive. I'm in favor of the second option."

She glared at him. "I see what annoys Nikolas so much about you. Don't you care that your brother could be making a big mistake?"

"My brother was making mistakes long before I came along. He won't appreciate my interference."

Meri would not be deterred. She would fix this if it was the last thing she did. "I was told Vard had taken a group of rangers to the northern forests. Nikolas could have gotten that information as easily as I did. I am going to ride north and see what I can find."

With those words, Meri mounted Storm and trotted toward the northern gates of the city. She was tired and thirsty, but it didn't matter. And Sam could follow or not as he saw fit.

After a few minutes, she heard him cursing behind her and smiled to herself.

"Thank you for keeping me company, brother-in-law." She kicked Storm into a slow canter, and they passed through the city gates and took the road toward the northern forests.

The country ahead was beautiful, and Meri would have enjoyed the experience under different circumstances. They had almost reached the trees when a group of mounted men and women appeared, coming toward them.

Meri kicked Storm into a gallop and pulled him up before the group in a cloud of dust.

To her eyes, they must have been Vard's Rangers, but she didn't see him among them.

"Excuse me, Rangers," she said. "Were you with Lord Anton today?"

One man in front smirked. "Yes, My Lady, we've just left him. It appeared he didn't need us around."

"What do you mean?"

Sam rode up. "Yes, I'd like to know what you meant by that as well."

"Master Delacost," the man nodded in respect. "The admiral is with him, and he dismissed us. Though it would've been entertaining to stay."

Meri's eyes flew to Sam's and back to the group.

"How long ago did you leave them?" Sam asked. "Where are they?"

One woman spoke. "They are only a few minutes into the forest. You can't miss them."

Sam spurred his horse past and Meri followed, calling a "thank you" as she passed. Anything could have happened in the moments since the rangers had left. She only prayed they were in time.

* * *

Nikolas clutched his reins, teeth clenched to control his anger. He had hoped he would have a cooler head by now, but it wasn't to be. Anton sat his horse, eyes cool, but wary.

"I want you to explain what you've been doing with my wife!"

The man's eyebrows raised. "I'm sure Lady Cosara has told you the details."

"I wish to hear them from you."

Anton sighed and Nik's fury burned brighter. *The hide of the man to be annoyed with him!*

"Lady Cosara hired me to teach her horsemanship and weapons skills. She felt vulnerable out on the estate, not knowing how to protect herself. She also wanted to help in the coming war."

"And you were happy to oblige. Is that all you were doing? Nothing else happened when you were together?"

"You don't have much faith in your wife or your marriage if you need to ask me that!"

Nik huffed. "I know how this works. I see how the ladies react when you're around. You even hold the queen in your thrall. Is it anything to do with the 'gifts' you hold? I should have turned you in when I had the chance."

Anton dismounted and stood in front of his horse with his arms crossed. It didn't fool Nik. He knew how quickly the man could move. Did he want a confrontation? Damn right he did. This had been brewing since the day he had walked in on Anton changing back into a man. What sort of creature was he?

Nik dismounted and stood warily a couple of paces from his adversary. "I suggest the victor should be the first to draw blood."

Anton rolled his eyes. "This is ridiculous. I've done nothing to deserve your anger. If you weren't such an ass, *you* could've taught your wife the skills she has learned from me."

The words hurt Nik more than he would've imagined. He was *not* an ass! "Draw your sword, Anton," he ground from between clenched teeth. He drew his own sword and balanced on the balls of his feet. The horses, sensing trouble, backed away from their riders.

Nik attacked as Anton drew his sword from the scabbard. Even taken by surprise, the man was too quick for him and parried, dancing out of the way. Nik spun and attacked hard, putting all his strength into his swings. Anton blocked and danced each time, barely breathing hard.

Nik slid away to regain his breath. Brute force wouldn't work with this fighter. He had to be smarter than that. He attacked hard, but this time stuck his foot out to trip Anton. The man fell, but rolled and came up on his feet, launching an attack that Nik barely defended. Their swords ended up locked above their heads, faces close.

"This is stupid, Admiral," Anton panted.

"It's only stupid if you win, and you won't." Nik pushed the lighter man backward and immediately advanced on him, cutting and slashing in a flurry of death, not caring how great an injury he inflicted. A fury had seized him even as part of his mind screamed at him to stop.

A voice penetrated his frenzy. *Merielle?*

"Stop this at once, Nikolas, before you get hurt!"

It *was* Merielle. The fury of a moment ago dulled, and Anton chose that moment to launch his own assault, attacking in a blinding flurry of strikes that Nik desperately blocked until a last slash struck his arm. Anton kept up his attack, Nikolas backing up until the footing underneath him gave way and he fell.

He peered up into the face of his opponent and saw death. Anton's sword pointed down, but was swept aside by another. *Sam!*

"I wouldn't do that if I were you, Vard." Sam said, "The queen would be upset were you to kill her cousin."

Anton stepped back and sheathed his sword, bowing to Merielle. "My Lady."

Merielle glared at him and fell down beside Nikolas. "Stupid man! What were you thinking?"

"Ah, Meri," Sam said, "I don't think now is the time for remonstrations."

Damn right it wasn't! Nik's chest burned and his arm hurt like a demon. But the thing that hurt most was his pride. He pushed himself to his feet, dusting off his clothes as he stood. He didn't look at any of his companions. Actually, he didn't know what to say to any of them, especially Vard Anton.

Instead, he climbed on his horse and sat staring straight ahead. Something had to be said to Anton, otherwise he'd have to go through the embarrassment of this meeting again.

"You are not to visit my estate again, Anton. And as of now, I'm not available to teach your rangers. Stay out of my way."

He turned his horse and kicked him into a trot toward Wildecoast. Soon, he was cantering, trying to put physical distance between himself—and the shame. It didn't work, and his gut burned worse than his arm.

After a few minutes, he heard hoofbeats pursuing him, and Merielle pulled alongside. With her was Sam.

"Whatever you have to say," Nik said, "I don't wish to hear it. Something had to be done about the situation. It's over, and nothing more needs to be said."

Meri made an indelicate noise, easily heard over the movement of the horses and tack.

"Nothing needed doing, Nikolas. The *situation* was only in your mind. And now I have no one to teach me weapons."

She sounded upset, and, when he turned, there were tears in her eyes.

Sam groaned. "I don't want to be here for this."

Nik fixed his brother with a cranky look. "Well, you should've stayed out of it. I was handling things without you."

"Looked like it," he said sarcastically. "Excuse me, but I was sure Vard had his sword tip pressed to your throat when I stepped in. You didn't look like you had everything under control."

"He wouldn't have killed me. The deal was to first blood."

"He had already drawn first blood," Sam said.

"Stop it!" Meri said. "Stop fighting. I am sick of hearing you snap at each other. I am sick of you not getting along." She lapsed into sulky silence, tears still rolling down her cheeks.

"I hate to remind you," Sam said, "but we are soon to enter Wildecoast, and I don't think the city needs any more gossip. Let's stop and patch your arm, Niko, and Merielle can dry her tears."

Nik nodded, glad one amongst them had the sense to hide the evidence of this disharmonious morning. Sam patched his arm as best he could and wrapped it with a black band which would draw less attention, wiping away the traces of blood. By the time he had ministered to Nik, Meri had regained her composure.

The rest of their return to the city was undertaken in silence, each keeping company with their own thoughts. For Nik, he played the fight with Anton over in his mind, trying to see where he could've gotten the advantage. The conclusion he came to was that the shifter was the superior fighter—which galled him more than he cared to admit. But admit it he must do if he was to move forward. It was a fact of life that he wasn't the best fighter in the kingdom. He was good, but not the best. Even Sam could beat him on a good day.

He may not be a champion fighter, but he could get better. And he could spend the hours he would've given to Anton's Rangers practicing with the sword and getting fitter. He had the power, and he'd use it.

Among the crowds loitering outside the barracks were several of the rangers who'd been with Anton. One man approached him.

"Admiral, how goes it with Lord Anton. Is he well?"

Nik nodded. "He was quite well last I saw him, Ranger. I imagine he'll return soon for afternoon classes. I suggest you be ready."

Sam snickered, though Nik couldn't say why. The man was always full of mirth. He didn't seem to have a serious bone in his body. They entered the keep and stabled their horses, then made their way to their apartments in the castle. Luckily, the queen was nowhere to be seen, and no one accosted them on their way there.

As soon as Meri entered the rooms, she fetched a pitcher of water and a bowl, along with wound ointment, and a needle and thread.

"I assume you wish for me to attend you as I don't imagine you want the doctor knowing what has happened," she said, pointing to a chair.

Nik sat, removing his shirt and tunic. Meri placed a towel under his arm and flushed the area with boiled water. Her attention didn't improve his mood.

"You must speak to me eventually, Nikolas." She wiped the wound edges dry. It appeared to be deep, and he hoped it wouldn't affect the functioning of his arm long term. It would certainly curtail the start of his weapons practice. The thought put him in an even blacker mood.

"This is your own fault," she said. "You didn't need to go haring off and confront Lord Anton."

"*Lord* Anton indeed!" Nik huffed. "Do you know what he really is?" He had kept the man's secrets to himself so far, but no longer. Merielle must know what type of man she had trusted.

"I expect he's ex-army like most of the men the king promotes."

"The king doesn't know who Vard Anton is. I don't think anyone does, perhaps not even Princess Alecia."

"What are you talking about, Nikolas?" she asked. "Please, you are making no sense."

Sam wandered over from the luncheon table where he was fixing himself a snack. "Yes, do tell, brother. Spill your secret."

"Anton is a shifter," Nikolas said. "He can change into at least one animal form. I saw him change from hawk to man."

Sam laughed. "That's a bird, not an animal."

"A bird *is* an animal," Nikolas snapped.

"Well, if that's true, it's silly," Sam said. "Birds should have their own class, since they have feathers and can fly."

Meri had stopped her medical attention to listen but chose that moment to stick the needle into his arm.

"Ow! Dammit woman! Can't you give a man some warning?"

"Stay still! And stop spreading vicious rumors. Honestly, Nikolas, sometimes I swear I don't know you." She resumed her stitching, and Nik ground his teeth to keep his arm still.

"They aren't rumors. I saw it with my own eyes. It was the reason I got involved with him in the first place. He invited me to attend his training so I could get to know him. He was likely already training you at that point." Nik scowled at Meri. "You should've confided in me."

"You would have forbidden it."

Nik opened his mouth to deny the charge, but then thought again. He might have forbidden Meri to train with Vard. Or he might have suggested she train with the rangers.

Then again, did he want his wife's unusual strength being exposed and gossiped about? There were already enough stories circulating about her. If the truth ever came out, they were doomed in Thorius. Even Sam didn't know the truth of Meri's past. And never would if he had any say.

Nik met his brother's riveted gaze. Sam was munching on bread and cheese and looking as if he was enjoying their "discussion". But Anton's secret was all Sam was going to hear.

"Let's just get one thing straight, Niko," Sam said. "You're not joking when you say Vard's a shapeshifter?"

"I'm dead serious, Brother," Nik said. "Now, if you're planning to help with the rangers this afternoon, you had better go."

"I'm free to do that after what you just told me?"

"I hear he's made you his second, so it looks like I'm off the hook when it comes to babysitting you. You're free to do as you please." He stopped short of asking Sam to spy on Anton. That would be out of the question now his brother was in Anton's employ.

Sam bowed to Meri and left them.

Nik sighed. "I hate fighting with you."

Meri kept stitching, her upper teeth biting her lower lip in concentration. It hurt less now she had most of the sutures in place.

"It looks very neat," he said.

"I only hope there is no fouling of the wound. I am told that is common with sword injuries. Though I must say Lord Anton's weapon care is exemplary."

"Can we not speak of him? I've had quite enough of Vard Anton for one day."

Meri finished, wiped off the wound, and bandaged it. It felt good, and he sighed with relief. He lay in the chair and closed his eyes.

"I am sorry I went behind your back to get the training," Meri said quietly.

She didn't sound like her happy, feisty self when she spoke like that.

"No, *I'm* sorry. I don't know what got into me. I miss you, and I don't like to think of him spending time with you when I can't. You can continue your training, but we'll find another way. I wish you to be happy, Merielle."

She approached and sat beside him, pushing his tangled locks from his eyes and looking deeply into them. He felt he was falling into deep pools of ocean green.

"I love you, Nikolas. You are more than enough for me."

"And I love you. I think I went a little mad with jealousy. You're so beautiful, I fear every man who sees you will lose all self-control—even Anton, who seems an iceman."

"I thought we were not to speak of him?"

Nik smirked. "You're right. I have better things to do." He leaned in and placed a kiss on lips so soft he could never believe they were real. "Like this." He slid his mouth to her collarbone, and she moaned, tilting her head.

The pulse at her throat jumped erratically, and her reaction reassured him.

Meri was his, and, if he was fortunate, she'd always love him just as she did in this moment.

CHAPTER 18

MIDNIGHT had arrived, and the castle was dark and quiet. Alecia crept about her chambers, gathering all she would need for her trip. Preparations completed, she paused beside Iona's crib and gazed down at her sleeping child. There was just enough moonlight to see her lips moving in a sucking motion. Alecia's heart cracked open a little. By the time she returned, Iona would be weaned of the breast. Would she remember her mother?

It was almost enough to make her change her plans, but she recalled what was at stake. Her sacrifice would be worth it if she could save the kingdom of Thorius. One day, she would explain to Iona why she abandoned her. She shut her eyes and took a deep breath. *I can do this. Take a step and don't look back.*

She left the bedroom and crossed to the wall with the tapestry, giving thanks to the Goddess that Ramón had housed her in his old room with access to the hidden passage, Alecia triggered the opening mechanism. The wall emitted a low grinding as it opened. Alecia lit a candle and slipped into the hidden passage behind. It closed with a hollow thud. She lifted her candle and swept cobwebs out of the way before setting off toward the outer wall. The passage took her down several flights of stairs until she was below the keep, then along a narrow stone hall to a wooden ladder. It led to the trapdoor outside the walls.

Keep moving. She shoved the trapdoor upward. It barely budged. She tried again, and it lifted a little more. The weapons and satchels she carried weighed her down and restricted her movement. Climbing back down the ladder, she divested herself of her burdens, then ascended the ladder again. Leaning forward so her belly was against the rungs, she pushed with all her strength at the stone above her. It bumped up. She ascended a rung and pushed again until she had cleared enough of a hole to squeeze through.

Alecia descended to fetch her things, then carried them up the ladder and through the exit. She carefully replaced the trapdoor and spread dirt over it, brushing any marks away with a pine branch. Taking deep breaths to calm her racing heart, she entered the forest that lay to the east. She slipped along a narrow path, her passing a mere rustle in the night, hoping her companions were already in place.

She need not have worried. The four women who would accompany her to Amitania were waiting where the trail widened, and they had her horse, Silver, with them.

"I'm glad to see you, ladies," she said. "Did you have any troubles?"

Linnet, a willowy woman with short, curly red hair, grinned. "Nothing we couldn't handle, Princess."

"That must change, Lin. You can't call me 'Princess' on the road. It will be too risky. From this day, we are comrades in a war that I intend to win. I won't ever forget your help. You'll be my generals if I succeed, and, if not, my lifelong friends at the very least."

She studied the women, but it was too dark to judge the effect of her words. A flash of white teeth revealed Kenna's smile.

"We know you're true, My Lady, or we wouldn't be here with you, risking much."

"I'll not allow you to be harmed, Kenna. You have my word." She mounted. "Now, that's enough chatter. We head for Amitania to raise support for my cause. Let's ride, and we'll rest at dawn. I want to put distance between us and Brightcastle before they discover I'm missing."

With those words, Alecia kicked her horse forward to begin the next leg of her adventure.

* * *

An hour after dawn the next morning, Ramón looked up from his desk as the door to his private study opened. Alecia's maid Millie stood there with Iona in her arms. "Yes, Millie?" The woman appeared to have been crying, and the child's face was flushed and wet.

"I'm sorry, My Lord, but I must tell you something. It breaks my heart to be the bearer of bad news, and I hope you don't hold it against me."

Ramón stood and came to her, reaching for Iona. The child went willingly into his arms. "No need to fear, Millie. Just tell me what has upset you."

"It's the princess, My Lord." She wrung her hands, and a shiver ran up Ramón's neck.

"Tell me!" This time he couldn't control his harsh tone.

"Princess Alecia is missing." Millie hid her face in her hands and sobs shook her shoulders.

Ramón placed Iona on the rug and led Millie to an armchair by the fire. He poured a cup of tea and placed it in her hands.

"I'm sorry I snapped," he said. "Please tell me everything you know."

Millie wiped her eyes and took a swallow of the tea. "I checked on Iona in the early hours of the morning as I always do. I noticed nothing amiss. The princess was there, or so I thought. Iona was fussy, so I fed her and put her back to bed. I didn't want to wake the princess, as she seemed to be still asleep. Iona takes the goat's milk well now, My Lord." She looked at him and paused. He tried to school his features to patience, and she continued.

"I returned at dawn to check again, and, this time, I thought it was unusual that the princess was still abed. She's always an early riser." Her voice broke, and she drew another deep breath. "She wasn't in the bed. She had stuffed blankets and pillows under her covers to make me think she was there. I don't know how long she's been gone, My Lord. We must get her back!"

Ramón grasped her hand. "Now Millie, this is no time to go to pieces. Iona needs you. Take the child and see that no harm comes to her. I'll order extra guards to keep you safe, but I need you to keep her in her chambers. Leave everything else to me." He stood and drew Millie to her feet before picking up the child and giving her to the maid. "Go now and let me know if you need me."

Millie sniffed and hugged Iona to her breast, kissing the child on her forehead. "Right you are, My Lord. Oh, I made a quick search of the chamber before I came to you. Some of her clothes are gone, the type she uses for fighting, and I think she took her sword and archery gear."

"Thank you, Millie. Don't worry, we'll find her."

The maid nodded and left with Iona, leaving Ramón more worried than he'd been for months. Damn Alecia! Why couldn't she be a normal woman with feminine pursuits? First her injuries after fighting practice, then her mysterious meeting with the king, and now she had left the castle. What was she up to? And where had she gone? He pulled the bell rope, and a footman appeared. "Princess Alecia is missing. I want an extensive search of the castle and grounds. And have Captain Estevot report to me." Estevot could conduct a discreet search of the city.

"Yes, My Lord." The man left, and Benae took his place.

"What's this about Alecia being missing?"

"It's true. She has abandoned Iona and gone haring off with her sword and bow. The Goddess only knows where she's gone or why. Honestly, Benae, sometimes I wonder about her judgment. Iona needs her, and now she has decided something else is more important."

"Are you sure she left of her own accord?"

"Not completely, but it seems that way. All was quiet, and the bed was made to appear as though she was asleep in it. Millie noticed the ruse at daylight."

Benae nodded. "She wouldn't leave Iona unless she thought she had no choice. I'm a mother, and I know the love a mother feels for her child. Iona is in no danger here, and can drink goat's milk. Indeed, many babies are weaned at this age. Iona will be safe and well. We shall see to that."

He studied her. "You seem to be very much on her side. Why, when she is so confrontational with you?"

"I still hope for us to be friends, even sisters. And I love Iona. Is there anything you need from me?"

Ramón drew her into his arms, needing the steadying comfort of her love. "If you can look in on Iona, I'd appreciate it. Captain Estevot will conduct a search, and then we'll decide on a plan. I'd appreciate your advice at the meeting."

"You shall have it, husband." She kissed him on the lips, slipped from his arms, and left the room.

* * *

After a brief two-hour nap, Alecia and her companions took to the trail once more. Lin was in the lead on her bay mare. Cretia followed on her brown while Alecia had grudgingly accepted her place in the middle of the group. Arelle shadowed her with Kenna bringing up the rear. Every hour, Kenna would scout ahead to check their trail, for there was a high likelihood of dark elves in these woods.

Around midday, they stopped for a meal in a clearing just off the trail. Lin lit a fire to make tea and the other three set about preparing lunch. There was little chat, as they didn't want to alert anyone to their presence. They were seated and munching on their meal, Alecia deep in thought.

After the first thrill of the adventure, she had begun to think of Iona. She missed her daughter already and had wanted to turn back more than once. It was difficult not to when they'd never been separated. She imagined Iona felt even more bereft.

Lin spoke up.

"I know you're missing your daughter, Alecia, but you have to know she'll be fine. She'll miss you, but what you do is for the greater good."

"I know that, but it doesn't help," Alecia said. "I still want to see her. But this was my choice, and it's my mission. I'll see it through with your help. Perhaps you can keep reminding me it's only for a short time?"

Lin nodded. "We can do that. And it will get easier."

Cretia, plaited blonde hair wrapped around her head in a crown, snorted. "Listen to you, Linnet. You don't have a child. Alecia is the only one of us who does. I don't think she needs meaningless platitudes."

Arelle flicked a strand of her black hair out of her eyes and placed a hand on Cretia's arm. "Hush, friend. Lin is only trying to help. We're a team, but still new to each other. The longer we're together, the easier it will be to support one another."

Kenna nodded, her brown eyes studying her companions from behind chestnut curls. "Already I feel a kinship with you. I often heard my brother speak of the friendship amongst warriors. Now I know what he meant. It's pretty special."

Alecia fell silent, humbled by their words. She was fortunate to have stumbled upon them. Still, Arelle was right. It would be some time before they felt the tight bond that marked them as family—the bond she felt with Hetty. Suddenly, she was sorry she hadn't visited her friend before leaving.

She shook her head and tried to concentrate on more immediate matters.

"Thank you all for throwing your lot in with me. You won't be popular with the Guardians, or with my uncle, the king."

"The uncle who turned down your request to be named as heir?" Lin asked. "I think we realize we've dipped our hands into a pit of vipers, don't we, ladies?"

There were nods and a general murmur of agreement.

Arelle spoke up, blue eyes serious. "There were rumors of you having killed mercenaries before you fled Brightcastle, Alecia. Were they true?"

"Why do you ask?"

The raven-haired warrior lifted her chin. "Your example inspired me to better myself. I learned to fight and looked for opportunities to advance the cause of women. I joined Princess Benae's guards because I wanted to make a difference like men do."

Alecia smiled. "I killed some men who had murdered a friend of mine. He was a gentle soul. All he did was stand up for his parents against my father's men. I was naïve back then. I knew Father was a bad ruler, but I blamed the men he sent instead of dealing with him. Perhaps I couldn't have swayed his thinking, but I should've been strong instead of virtually throwing my life away. If not for Vard, there's no telling what would've happened."

"He rescued you then? Not kidnapped?" Kenna asked, sharpening one of her knives on a stone.

"Of course, he didn't kidnap me. But I shouldn't have needed rescuing. If I had made different decisions, enlisted his help earlier…" She shrugged. "I don't know, but going on a rampage of revenge and getting myself almost killed, then allowing my father to discover my actions… I should've had more sense, been less impulsive."

"There will be more killing before this is over, perhaps even on this mission," Lin said. "Are you ready to place yourself in that position again? Are any of you?"

There was silence as they all looked within and asked themselves the question. Alecia knew she could kill, but did she want to do so again? And yet, she wished to be a battle queen, to lead soldiers into war.

"I must be ready to kill," she said, standing. "You know what my future holds if I'm successful. I wouldn't be much of a battle queen if I couldn't kill. And the same goes for all of you. Take this journey to think about what you're willing to do as my supporters. When we return to Brightcastle, I'll ask you again. You must be ready to answer."

Kenna spoke up. "I don't need that time to decide. I've already killed a man. He cornered me in an alley and would've raped me. I slit his throat and I'd do it again if I had to. I was sick of being afraid. That's why I joined the guards."

Alecia nodded. "Women aren't safe on the streets, even in Brightcastle. Perhaps one day, things will be different, but first we must return Thorius to peace. When I'm queen, I'll see that not only men have power."

She didn't know quite how she would accomplish that, but, somehow, she must. Iona needed to grow up in a safe and fair society, not one where she was sold off as someone's wife in order to shore up a succession or gain power. She wouldn't allow that to happen.

"You'll need a plan for all of that," Cretia said, arms folded and baby blue eyes narrowed. "I'll put some thought into it, if that's acceptable."

Alecia nodded, gratified to see the determined faces surrounding her. "I appreciate all help and ideas. You're my first aides. I can see a day when you all have positions of power."

The women stood and bowed to her, pride and approval in their eyes. In these women, she had the core of support she'd need if her plan was to succeed. Now to find out if Jacques Vorasava was true to his word.

With Kenna and Lin taking turns to scout ahead, they avoided the notice of travelers who might reveal their presence to those searching for them. They also avoided two groups of *Sis Lenweri* who had crossed their trail. At least Alecia assumed they were the enemy elven faction, as they appeared not to include female elves. She had heard the *Sis Lenweri* never used females as soldiers.

Alecia had thought they might reach Amitania unscathed when, late on the fourth day, Lin bolted back from her scouting mission, six elves on her tail. The enemy had their short horse bows trained on Lin as they tried to ride her down.

"Form up!" Alecia cried as Lin rushed past them and wheeled her horse around. "Charge!"

The five women drew their swords and rode at the attacking elves, Alecia gratified to see their eyes widen at the sight of five human females charging at them. She kept her eyes on the center elf, who had his bow drawn and arrow nocked. His arrow flew past her ear, and she sucked in a breath. She wanted to check on the others, but didn't. They had agreed it was every man for himself should they be attacked. She kicked Silver hard in the girth, and the mare leaped forward.

Alecia had her sword raised as Silver barreled into the lighter elven mount, her training coming to the fore. She slashed with her sword, clenching her teeth as her blade sliced under the elf's jaw. He crashed down with his mount, and she wheeled to engage the other *Sis Lenweri*. Three of her companions were battling elves from their horses while Arelle stood before a snarling mounted elf, her own mount felled by an arrow.

Alecia spurred Silver forward and smashed the butt of her sword into the back of the elf's head as he menaced Arelle. He toppled to the ground and Silver's dancing hooves trampled him. Arelle sprang up behind Alecia, and they returned to the fray, though they needn't have worried. The other women had slain their elven opponents. The women sat on their horses, panting, eyes wild and weapons bloodied.

"Is everyone unhurt?" Alecia asked.

Lin groaned. "I picked up a sliced arm," she said. "Did we bring a needle and thread?"

"Let's get off this path and regroup." Alecia grabbed the reins of the best-looking elven mount. "Cretia and Kenna, fetch Arelle's saddle and things from her horse, and search the other mounts and the bodies for anything useful."

She trotted up the trail, looking for a good place to rest. A creek crossed their path, and she followed it to the east of the trail, but not so far that she wouldn't see the others when they arrived. Arelle was sobbing against her back.

"Are you well?" Alecia asked, dismounting, and helping Arelle down from Silver.

"My horse…" she sobbed. "Cranky was my pride and joy! I've had him for years; saved up my coin for his purchase. I wanted a decent horse when I tried soldiering. He was battle-trained as well. I didn't even get to kill the bastard elf. I want revenge for his death."

"Arelle, you'll have your revenge. Each elf you kill from now on will have Cranky's name on his scalp. That will give you power you never imagined. I'm sorry you lost him. What happened?"

"He took an arrow in the chest. I was riding behind you, and the first arrow found him."

Alecia's heart leapt. "That arrow was meant for me. It must have been that one. I killed the elf, Arelle, but I don't suppose that will be much comfort."

"You're wrong," she said, wiping her eyes on her sleeve. "Cranky died so you might live. It helps a lot to believe that. And I'll have another horse to love one day."

"Our mounts are part of the battle, just as we are. They'll be targeted as killing them puts us at a significant disadvantage. It's not a pleasant thought, but true none the less."

Arelle nodded, and, when she raised her eyes, she seemed calmer. "Thank you."

Lin joined them. She was pale and blood dripped from her left bicep. "This hurts like a demon. Do we have any liquor?"

Alecia squeezed Arelle's hand and left her. She sat Lin on a log and pulled her aide satchel from Silver's saddle. The slender redhead took off her shirt, and Alecia was relieved to see that, although her arm would need stitches, the cut was superficial.

While she cleaned the wound with water from the stream, the other two ladies arrived. They tied their horses where they wouldn't be seen and pulled the elven mounts over to the same area. Then they began gathering wood for a fire which they set amongst the rocks.

No one spoke as they worked, no doubt reliving their recent skirmish. Alecia replayed the action repeatedly, assessing their performance as she sutured Linnet's arm. Luckily, the needlework practice her mother had insisted upon had finally paid off. The result was quite acceptable.

With one final wipe, she was done and bandaged the arm. "There you go, Lin. Don't have too much whisky or you'll fall off your horse."

"Thank you."

"Lucky it's your left arm and not your right," Kenna chipped in, as she washed her face and tanned forearms in the stream.

"Lucky it wasn't my neck," Lin grumbled. "I should've blocked that elf, not flung my arm up. I still need to work on my defense. It's not good enough to take an injury."

"I thought we did well," Cretia said, blonde plaits in disarray. "We lost a horse and sustained one injury while six elves lie dead. Not bad."

Alecia nodded. "Our first skirmish turned out well. Tonight, we may talk about what went right and what failed. For now, we can rest for an hour, then hit the trail again. Feed your horses and groom them, then saddle up again in case we need to move out quickly." She walked to Silver and unsaddled her, then placed a nosebag on her head. The mare nickered as she found the oats in the bag.

Alecia began rubbing her down with a sack. "Good girl; brave girl," she said. "You kept me safe back there." Privately, she worried about the loss of Arelle's mount. A battle-trained horse was worth twice an untrained mount. It would place the woman at greater risk. Alecia hoped Arelle had selected the right replacement from amongst the elven mounts. It was the largest beast and most like their own horses. With luck, he'd prove strong and brave.

She watched as Arelle approached the nervous elven horse and held out her hand. He blew at her hand and threw his head up. She murmured low and soft, and his ears came forward. She kept it up until she could rub the side of his head and then his silky black neck. Arelle removed the pad the elves used in place of a saddle and rubbed him down, all the while murmuring reassuringly to her new friend. Once finished, she placed her saddle on him. He threw his head and shuffled as she tightened the girth, but he soon settled.

"I'll name him 'Fey'," Arelle said. "I think we'll get on fine."

Kenna laughed. "As long as he doesn't throw you off."

Arelle glared. "There's no reason he should. I'll be good to him, and he already understands me."

Alecia intervened. "I'm sure he'll look after you. He has a kind eye."

Arelle smiled at her and moved to the fire to fetch herself food and tea. Alecia hoped she had moved past her crisis.

They sat around the fire, drinking tea and eating their road fare, lost in their own recollections of the battle.

Alecia wished to get them talking of their experiences and fears. Perhaps if she shared her feelings, it would help the others share theirs?

"Lin, thank you for warning us of the elves. I admit I wasn't expecting you to come galloping at us with them on your tail. My heart was in my mouth as I ordered the charge."

Lin nodded, rubbing her injured arm. "I kept expecting them to put an arrow through me. The back of my neck itched so badly, I could barely stand it. I've never been so glad to reach anyone, but I knew that's where the real trouble would begin."

"Our first skirmish," Arelle said, blue eyes sad, "and my poor horse is our first casualty. I achieved nothing, but I promise that won't be the case next time. I won't let you down."

Alecia smiled. "You have nothing to be sorry for. That's war. Occasionally you're lucky enough not to be in the thick of it. I'm sure you'll pull each of us out of strife in future, perhaps many times."

Arelle nodded.

Cretia cleared her throat. "I don't mind admitting it petrified me when I saw those elves riding down on us." She looked at Alecia. "If you hadn't yelled 'charge', I don't know what I would've done. I might have let them ride over me."

Lin placed her hand on Cretia's shoulder. "You mustn't think like that. There's no point in allowing doubts to grow. Next time, you'll know how to react. This victory will give you confidence."

Alecia nodded. "Lin's right. I don't know what came over me, but somehow I knew what to do. Instinct spurred me to shout the charge."

"You *are* the battle queen," Arelle said. "It's the spirit of Izebel which inhabits and guides you. I'll follow you anywhere, especially after what has just occurred. I too wonder what would've transpired if you hadn't taken charge of us."

Alecia finished her tea and stood. "Let's not wonder what might have been. Just be glad we're alive. It's time to resume our trek." She paused and looked at Cretia. "What did you do with the bodies of our foes?"

"We dragged them into the woods a little way and kicked dirt over the blood on the road. Only experienced trackers will find the bodies in the next day or so. After that, the smell will draw attention. Cranky we could do nothing about. He's too heavy to remove and much too large to bury." She turned sorrowful eyes on Arelle. "I'm sorry, my friend."

Arelle clenched her jaw but then straightened her shoulders. "He is no longer in his body but galloping free across the fields of the Goddess. She'll watch over him."

Alecia placed her hand on Arelle's shoulder. "Let's be on our way." They mounted, each leading a *Lenweri* pony, and were soon cantering toward the mountains and Amitania.

CHAPTER 19

THAT night around the fire, Alecia missed her daughter a little less. The skirmish had boosted their confidence, and she had passed the first test of her leadership. She was beginning to believe in her ability to fulfill her ambition. But it would do no good to get ahead of herself. Though they should celebrate the minor victories, they must not let them go to their heads.

They passed around a skin of red wine, each telling stories of their childhood and how they came to be in the guards.

Except for Alecia, all were from common homes, though some had fathers who were tradesmen. Alecia related a few of her childhood memories, and told of her year in exile and what she had learned. Iona's birth drew gasps from her companions.

"Would you have another baby, Alecia?" Arelle asked. "I can't imagine how painful that was. You might have died."

"Childbirth is one of the most dangerous things a woman can experience," Alecia said, recalling when Mistress Andra had raised her knife, ready to cut Iona from her womb.

"That and giving one's heart to a man." Lin's remark brought giggles from the others. "I know Alecia has lain with a man, but how about the rest of you?"

Cretia piped up. "What about you first, Lin?"

The red-head laughed. "Alright. I gave away my virginity almost five years ago, when I was twenty-one. The baker's boy delivered bread door to door, and I had long admired him. We'd exchange kisses, and eventually he led me to his loft." Her pretty face flushed with color.

"How was it?" Cretia asked. "I'm twenty-one and can't imagine 'doing it'."

"Fumbling and hasty," Lin said, "but I still remember him to this day with fondness."

"I wonder what has happened to your baker's boy?" Arelle mused.

"I hope he's well, with his own baker's shop, a wife, and a hoard of children," Lin said, a faraway light in her eyes.

"How about you, Arelle?" Cretia asked.

"I have yet to lie with a man."

"What about a boy?" Kenna laughed.

Arelle pushed her into the dirt. "And what of *your* past loves?"

"My friend and I loved the same man. He had no objections to taking our virginity on the same occasion. It wasn't as scary when Jorda was there with me. He was much older, of course."

"You had a threesome?" Cretia said, her eyes wide.

Kenna smirked, tugging on her brown plait. "You should try it."

"I could never do that," Cretia gasped. "I'm saving my virginity until my wedding day."

"How noble," Kenna said, "and old-fashioned. Even Alecia didn't do that."

"What do you mean, 'even Alecia'?" Alecia asked.

"Well, you're a princess. Surely you were expected to be pure on your wedding day? And here you have a babe and no husband. I'm not judging you, but isn't that a little unconventional?"

Alecia recalled the moments she had spent locked in the dungeon, waiting for her bruises to disappear so she could marry Lord Finus. He would've taken her virginity long before the nuptials, but Vard had rescued her. She had wanted him to be her first. Nothing else mattered.

"I suppose so, but just because a woman is of noble birth, it doesn't mean she has more power than a commoner. I see no disgrace in what I did, even if my name is still mud amongst the nobility."

Lin stood. "It matters not, Alecia. We shall see if Cretia and Arelle remain intact when they lose their heart to a man for the first time.

It's all very well to believe you'll stay pure, but another thing when the heart is involved."

Alecia laughed. "That's true. Now, let's get some rest."

Seven days later, the five companions arrived in Amitania. The weather was fine but cool through the mountains, and Alecia looked forward to a comfortable bed.

The ride had been difficult, with frequent stops to erase their tracks and avoid elven patrols. They had spied the *Sis Lenweri,* but had avoided engaging the enemy. Alecia had no wish to push their luck.

The borrowed mount, Fey, had performed well. He and Arelle were now firm friends. In fact, he followed her around like a dog. Alecia loved watching them, and Fey had alerted them to enemy elves on two occasions.

They rode around the outside wall of the city, coming to an area where the fallen stones had been cleared to make an entry point. Soldiers were on guard, both human and elves.

A stocky middle-aged sergeant put up his hand. "Halt, who goes there?"

"Princess Alecia Zialni," Lin said, "and I am Linnet Perfore. These others are our companions."

The sergeant studied them as if he hadn't seen women in breeches and tunics before. Perhaps he hadn't.

"What is your purpose in Amitania?"

"We wish an audience with Jacques Vorasava," Lin said. "Please let him know we are here."

"Where have you come from?"

"Brightcastle," Lin said. "It has been a hazardous journey. We are tired and would like to rest."

"Oh, would you? What proof do you have that this is the princess?"

"Does she not look like Alecia Zialni?"

The sergeant's eyes swept up her form and then down again. Alecia folded her arms across her breasts, even though she didn't wish to show she was uncomfortable.

"I wouldn't know the princess if I fell over her," he said gruffly, a deep frown creasing his brow. "Now stop wasting my time and go away." He turned and walked back within the walls, but Lin followed him.

"Sergeant," she said, "do you wish to keep the princess waiting and upset your leaders? I assure you it will displease them greatly if you delay us any longer." She paused and cast him a penetrating look. "I suggest you arrange an escort and convey us with all haste to Jacques Vorasava before he finds out you're a man who can't make a simple decision."

The man's scowl deepened, but his gaze rested upon Alecia and her companions. He appeared to decide at last. "Edit and Bub, find four men and escort these 'ladies' to the palace, if you please." He stood watching them while his orders were carried out.

They formed up with Alecia and Lin in the lead behind two of the men, then another two rode beside their group and the remaining guards brought up the rear behind Kenna, Arelle, and Cretia. They released the elven horses to a small troupe of Lenweri soldiers who appeared happy to receive them.

Alecia found the trip to the palace most interesting. So much had changed since she was last in Amitania. Most of the rubble had been cleared from the streets, and rebuilding work had occurred in many of the smaller houses they passed. The sound of water flowing in fountains was a constant presence. She tuned into the sound and allowed it to soothe her nerves.

"'Convey us with all haste' indeed," Cretia was saying, amid the giggles of the other women. "Anyone would think you were noble, Lin, the way you put on the airs and graces. Even Alecia doesn't speak so."

Lin sniffed. "Sometimes it's necessary to get yourself heard. I can be dignified when I wish to be." She looked to Alecia for support.

"You did well, Lin. I shall make you my spokeswoman from here on in. We'll think of a position for you, and a title, of course." Privately, it pleased Alecia that her friends were showing their mettle and taking their places within her group. Actually, she was more than pleased. Her plans were going rather well. Now if only she could secure Vorasava's support, she would overcome another hurdle.

Lin beamed and sat a little higher in the saddle. Alecia's thoughts returned to the city they were riding through. So much had improved. They rode past a large open space that must have been in the center of Amitania. She couldn't recall how it had looked before, but there weren't any trees or functioning fountains back then.

"What's this, Corporal?" she asked the soldier closest to her.

He followed her outstretched arm. "Jacques Vorasava had the central square made into a monument to those tortured by that scum, Faenwelar. Their bodies are buried here, along with other elven and human dead. Princess Gwaethe is said to be grateful for the gesture. Lord Vorasava had the trees brought in and much of the rubble from the streets was used for the walkways and seating."

Alecia inhaled a deep breath and felt her tight muscles relax. "Instead of being a place of pain, it's now a haven of peace and hope," she said to herself, feeling confident she had come to the right place for help. If Vorasava thought to create this tribute, he was the sort of man she wanted in her camp.

Finally, they came within sight of the grand palace she and Vard had stayed in when last in the city. It looked not much different from the outside, except the gigantic fountain now sprayed water from its statue. Elven and human guards stood at attention at the foot of the steps. They reined in, and a soldier moved forward to speak to the captain of the guards.

Alecia held her head high as the guard looked her over. A slight widening of his eyes suggested he recognized her. He walked down the stairs and stopped before her, bowing low.

"Welcome to Amitania, Your Highness. I'll advise Lord Vorasava of your arrival immediately. In the meantime, please enjoy the hospitality of the city. I'll have you shown into one of the lower chambers so you can refresh yourself from your journey." He bowed again and hurried into the palace.

They dismounted and were shown into a spacious but sparsely decorated chamber. Attendants arrived carrying five jugs of steaming water, which they poured into bowls arranged on a stone shelf. A folded towel lay beside each bowl. Arelle immediately moved to a bowl and washed her hands and face, letting out a long sigh as she dried herself.

"This is heavenly after the dust of the trail," she said.

Alecia followed her lead, then wandered over to a tray of bread and cheese and made herself a sandwich. The others prowled around the room, especially Kenna, who peered into every nook and cranny. Not that there was much that could be hidden. The walls were of stone, and the furniture comprised a modest throne and six overstuffed armchairs. Two tapestries hung on the walls, one of a forest with a wondrous, red leafed tree in the center. The other tapestry appeared to be of the keep at Brightcastle, its quartz walls gleaming in the sun.

Kenna checked behind both hangings and then moved to refresh herself. Finally, they were all seated on chairs, eating, though none had taken the throne. Tea arrived and Arelle poured for them. Alecia sighed as the liquid warmed her insides.

"I could do with something stronger," Kenna said, leaping up and pacing the length of the room. "I never could stand waiting."

Lin smirked. "You'll have to get used to waiting if you want to thrive as a soldier. It's all we do sometimes, as you well know."

Kenna cast her a scowl. "Of course, I know that. It doesn't make it any easier, especially when we don't know what our welcome will be."

"They've been hospitable," Alecia said. "It's a good sign."

A footman entered and started a blaze in the nearby fireplace. Days could still be chilly in Amitania, even in summer. As he left, Jacques Vorasava entered.

"Princess!" he said. "I'm gladdened to see you, though somewhat surprised."

He bowed low to her, and she stood and nodded. "My Lord." Turning to the others, she introduced them. He bowed to each, albeit only small acknowledgements. He seemed bemused about how to treat her ladies.

Jacques turned to her. "I imagine this visit has something to do with your aspirations?"

"You can speak openly, Lord Vorasava. My companions are fully in my confidence. You see before you the core of my support group. And, yes, I do intend to challenge for the throne. I can no longer stand by and allow the kingdom to ignore the plight of women. I should be heir."

Vorasava cleared his throat. "Perhaps you forget Solomon, Your Highness."

"I forget nothing. As the oldest issue of the second son, I should be next in line to the throne. At the very least, I should be Solomon's guardian."

"Don't you think the Guardians are performing their duties admirably?"

"No, I do not. Ramón and Benae Zorba have had an astronomical rise to power. I have to wonder at their motives."

Vorasava studied her, a frown on his brow. "I wonder…"

"You wonder what?" Alecia asked.

"Princess, might we speak in private for a moment?"

Alecia looked at her companions. Lin shrugged. Clearly, Vorasava was reluctant to discuss some topics in front of them. She could share with them later if she chose. She nodded. The lord led her to an intimate audience chamber accessed by a long hallway. When they entered the room, a beautiful elven woman looked up from a book she was reading.

Vorasava went to her bend drew her forward to Alecia. "This is my wife, Princess Gwaethe Arenil. Gwaethe, this is Alecia Zialni, Princess of Brightcastle."

Alecia inclined her head to the elven woman, and she did the same in return. They were on an even footing, though the ethereal beauty of the dark-skinned princess awed Alecia.

"It is my great honor to welcome you to Amitania, Princess Alecia. I hope you will be comfortable here."

Alecia smiled. "It's a far cry from the discomforts of the road. And you've done wonders in the short time you've been here."

Her dark brows rose. "You have visited the city before?"

Alecia nodded. "During my year in exile, I visited this place in search of a mentor for Vard Anton. We found only elves and a dangerous sorcerer. Now I realize the elves were *Sis Lenweri*. At the time, we had no idea of the different factions, though unrest was beginning." She decided not to confide that Vard had trained the elves they found there. Hopefully, his role in helping them wouldn't play a large part in the coming battle.

Gwaethe's eyes widened. "They were here for quite some time then. I recall my father mention an Alen Leth. Is he the sorcerer of whom you speak?"

Alecia nodded. "He pursued us when we fled Amitania. Eventually, he caught up to Vard and was killed when they fought."

Gwaethe nodded. "That is just as well. He was said to be most powerful. What brings you here, Princess?"

"Please, call me Alecia."

Gwaethe nodded.

Alecia drew a breath and spoke. "I have reason to believe your husband would support me if I put myself forward as queen," she said, looking at Jacques for confirmation.

Gwaethe frowned. "Perhaps. We seek peace in the kingdom, though, not unrest. Your quest could be as divisive as the civil war amongst the elves."

"Your husband has offered his support—as recently as his visit to Brightcastle," Alecia said. "I'm here to cement our relationship. There need be no formal agreement. I wish to discuss if he will support me against Benae and Ramón."

"The king supports the Guardians," Gwaethe said, folding her arms under her breasts.

"Something isn't right about that situation," Alecia said. "They swear they behaved with the utmost loyalty to my late father, but I don't believe it." She looked at Jacques. "I asked you if you knew anything about what happened on their arrival back in Brightcastle, after their visit to Wildecoast. There appeared to be discord between Benae and Ramón and my father. Do you still say you have no information?"

Jacques walked away from her and stood before the fire, his hand on the mantle. Alecia waited. At least he hadn't outright denied any knowledge. That meant she might learn something. He walked back and stood with his arm around his wife.

"I know nothing for certain. It's just a feeling… a suspicion, I have. It can't be proven."

"Yes?" Alecia prompted.

He frowned at her. "You must promise not to act upon it if I confide in you."

She shook her head. "You just told me you have no proof, that it's just a hunch. Please, I wasn't there, and I have to know what happened."

He sucked in a deep breath and blew it out. "There was discord for several weeks before Prince Zialni's death. The air was so tense it was like stepping on eggshells in the keep. So, when I was called to investigate the prince's death, I *was* suspicious."

"Of course," she said, "anyone would be."

"I don't doubt the prince's death was by natural causes," he said, "but I believe there's a strong chance that Ramón Zorba and Benae Branasar were conducting an affair while she was engaged to Prince Zialni."

Alecia's heart quickened. "What do you base your suspicions on?"

He shook his head. "I told you, I have nothing certain I can point to. There were rumors after the visit to Wildecoast and the discord on their return. Infidelity could explain it." A muscle tightened in his jaw. "And if that's the case, I have to wonder if Solomon is truly the prince's son."

Alecia swayed as the possibility hit home. Jacques gripped her arm and steered her to a chair. She sat heavily, her heart beating a frantic rhythm in her chest.

"Solomon not my father's son?" It could so easily be true. The timing fit if the two had been intimate in Wildecoast. It would have been easy to pass off the pregnancy as belonging to Jiseve. Benae was capable of it, but would Ramón allow such an untruth? "Why didn't you say anything about your suspicions when last we spoke?"

"I've thought about it since and developed a theory," he said. "But, Princess, you must not act on what we suspect."

"I'll do as I please with this information."

"It's not information. It's only suspicion. An accusation could backfire badly. If Solomon's claim is disallowed, Piotr would become the next in line to the throne. We can't have that."

"But it could remove any threat from Solomon's head." Alecia's mind churned through the repercussions. "If I can relieve him of this burden, I will."

"I urge you to think carefully," Jacques said. "Things as they now stand might be your best chance of seizing the throne. Benae and Ramón are at least friendly to you. Piotr is an unknown entity. If his attention is on Solomon, that leaves you free to plot your ascension."

Gwaethe stepped before her. "I know you are reluctant to place the child at risk, but until Piotr is neutralized, Jacques's advice is sound."

Alecia gazed at the elven woman. "You must support your husband, Gwaethe. You're hardly impartial."

Anger blazed in her dark eyes. "You came here to cement an alliance with my husband. I would think that meant you were open to his advice. What position are you offering him in your administration?"

"I think it's a little too early to speak of administrations," Alecia said.

"It is not," Gwaethe said. "You wish to seize the throne, and you need my husband to help. Those who assist you must be rewarded. What position do you offer?"

Alecia folded her arms across her chest. "As he is skilled in matters of war, I imagine he might be my general." But if he took that position and Vard re-entered her life, as she longed for, *he* would be her general.

"Forgive me, Alecia," Gwaethe said. "but you sound uncertain. You must reflect on my questions and give Jacques an answer before you leave Amitania. At that time, Jacques can commit… or not… as the case may be."

Alecia held Gwaethe's gaze for long moments. She would have liked to disagree with the elven princess, but … dammit… the woman was right. "I'll give it some thought. Can I be shown to our accommodations?"

Jacques nodded. "I imagine they're almost ready. Let's return to the other ladies, and you can complete your meal. Then I'll have you shown to your rooms." He hesitated. "Alecia, we're short on suitable apartments here. You'll have to share with one of your companions."

Alecia raised her chin, ready to be offended, and then thought better of it. The rulers of Amitania had clearly been busy with rebuilding the city. Furnishing rooms would not have been a priority. "We're grateful for whatever shelter you can provide with such short notice. I'll be glad to share with my second-in-command."

Jacques bowed and led her to the others, leaving Gwaethe behind. When Jacques departed to check on their chambers, Alecia frowned. She had made a poor impression on the elven princess. That would have to be remedied. The others clustered around her.

"How did it go?"

"What did he say?"

She sucked in a deep breath. Jacques was correct. She couldn't reveal their suspicions about Solomon's real father. "I met Princess Gwaethe. She was less than impressed with me, I think."

"How dare she not be impressed!" Kenna said. "I've heard elves are haughty. I imagine an elven princess might be even more so."

"At first I was angry, but now I think she has a point," Alecia said, amidst a chorus of denial from her friends. She held up her hands for silence. "I admit I'm impulsive. I must put more thought into my plans if I'm to succeed. Jacques wishes to know what position he'll have in my court, and I haven't given it much thought."

"That's completely understandable," Kenna said. "It's only the start of your campaign."

Alecia shook her head. "No, it's not. Past is the time when I had the luxury of acting without thought. As well-meaning as my actions usually are, I need to plan for the future and act accordingly."

Arelle stepped forward. "As much as I approve of you, Alecia, I think you're right. We can't go blundering into situations. At best, we won't succeed, and at worst—someone will get killed."

Alecia nodded and looked to Lin. "That's why I must formally announce Lin as my second-in-command. Does anyone have any objections?"

They all shook their heads.

"Lin is the natural choice," Cretia said. "She's a little older than the rest of us and has more experience. She is also the best fighter."

"But not for long!" Kenna said. The others laughed.

"Seriously," Kenna said. "Lin has already stepped naturally into that role, and she can have it."

Lin gave Kenna a gentle punch on the arm.

Alecia sobered as she watched her friends. "You must listen to her as you would me. No arguing unless you're invited to give your opinion on a plan. There will be times when you must act without question to survive."

They nodded and assured Lin and Alecia that was understood.

A footman arrived to take them to their chambers, and Alecia and Lin were soon settled in a plain but spacious room that included a steaming bath. Lin immediately turned to her and invited her to use the tub first.

"Really? I could do with a soak after the travel. This is a luxury I didn't expect."

"You think our hosts a little rustic?" Lin asked.

"I didn't want to assume anything. Last time I visited, the buildings were in ruins, and there were no comforts that I ever saw."

"Tell me about it," Lin said. "You got this hunted look in your eye when you mentioned Amitania before. What happened?"

Alecia huffed out a breath as she stripped off her clothes and stepped into the tub. She sank under the water, which was just the temperature she liked it.

"Ah, bliss," she said, closing her eyes. How did she explain the trials of Amitania and Lord Leth? How did she explain the situation she and Vard had found themselves in without mentioning Vard's gifts?

"Vard and I were on the run, and our journey led us here. Father had sent mercenaries out to find us, and each band was larger. We thought perhaps a deserted city might provide a refuge for a time." It sounded feasible to her. Quite good, in fact.

"But when we arrived, the *Lenweri* imprisoned us. We now know they were of the enemy faction, but the true nature of the elven civil war wasn't known then. A sorcerer named Leth oversaw the city and forced Vard to train the elves." She fell silent, thinking of those times and the skills they passed to their enemies. "Please keep that information confidential."

"Of course," Lin said, her gray eyes serious. "You were pregnant?"

She nodded. "Vard didn't know. I feared he'd leave me somewhere safe if he knew. And he would have. Our relationship was severely taxed during that time. I suppose that's one reason for the look you saw. I have few happy memories of our time here or the weeks after."

Lin crouched before the bath. "Do you believe you and Vard can reconcile?"

"I love him, and he loves me," she said, scrubbing her arm with a cloth. "Our daughter needs two parents, and he has already missed so much. But it takes more than love to keep a couple together. We're now on separate paths."

She continued her scrubbing in silence. "When Gwaethe asked me what position Jacques would have, I thought of Vard, and where I'd place him if he was in my life. He'd be prince consort, and the ideal choice to lead my military. He should be the general, but I may have to give the title to Jacques. And I don't know what Vard would think of that. It could be another gulf between us."

"If he loves you truly, he'll support you," Lin declared. "That includes agreeing with your decrees."

Alecia sighed. "I wish it were really that simple. But regardless, I must give Lord Vorasava an answer soon. I think I must offer him the control of my armed forces. He must be General Vorasava."

Lin sat on her heels. "Then he shall be. I've heard he's an ambitious man, and we need his help. I don't think you have a choice."

Alecia chewed her lip. "There are always more choices than you think. I hate making these decisions, not knowing if they are right or wrong. But I appreciate your counsel." She stood up in the bath, and Lin handed her a towel. "I've also been thinking about your title."

Lin held her hands up. "I don't need one. You've named me second-in-command and that's enough."

Alecia wrapped the towel around herself and rang for more hot water. "Others will respect you more if you have a title. I've decided you shall be a countess, and when I'm on the throne, I'll grant you lands."

Lin's eyes widened. She backed away from Alecia. "Oh no! It's too much. And surely it will raise the ire of the nobles."

Alecia dropped the towel and wrapped herself in a woolen gown she found at the end of the bed. "I intend to disrupt the old lines of power… well, perhaps not all of them, but I must place my advisors above those currently in power. It will be tricky, but you are already showing you understand where I may make a misstep. I'm counting on you, Countess!"

She laughed at her play on words, but sobered at a knock on their door. Lin answered, and a maid entered with two pails of hot water which she poured into the bath.

When they were alone again, Lin stood before Alecia. "Please don't give me a title. I don't feel comfortable accepting it."

Alecia huffed. "You agreed to be my advisor, my second-in-command. Do you regret your words? Do you feel you're unable to take that post?"

"I want that post with all my heart."

"Then Countess Linnet you are. From now on, you'll act like a countess. If you desire, you may make up a mysterious past so that no one suspects your humble beginnings. Before long, you'll believe all of it."

Lin frowned at her, arms crossed and an index finger tapping. "You really insist?"

"I do," Alecia said. "Let that be an end to that argument."

And with that, Lin disrobed and jumped into the bath with a long and luxuriant sigh.

Dinner was a grand affair. Along with Alecia and her ladies, Jacques had invited three elven and two human military leaders. All were male, to balance the number of women.

Gwaethe sat at the head of the table and Jacques at the other end, with Alecia placed on Gwaethe's left and her commander Ruven Magbalar on her right. Lin was placed on Jacques's left, and one of his advisors, Captain Dodlan, on his right. The rest were seated around the table randomly. Alecia wondered if it really *was* unplanned.

But she was fascinated when Gwaethe introduced her to Magbalar as a former member of the *Sis Lenweri*. Gwaethe had rescued him from imprisonment in Amitania, and he had sworn himself to her cause—peace between elves and man.

Magbalar was handsome and well-built, but quiet-spoken. He regarded Alecia with intelligent dark eyes.

"These are dangerous times to be on the road, Princess," he said. "I admire your bravery."

The way he said it implied foolishness, not bravery. Alecia raised her chin. "We had a skirmish with the *Sis Lenweri*, Commander. However, we overcame them, and were able to avoid others. They underestimated us, but I had no desire to test them another time."

"I would be happy to provide you an elven escort to Brightcastle when you leave, Princess," Gwaethe said.

Alecia was about to decline, but took a moment to reflect on how that would appear. She was clearly already being judged as foolhardy. Better not to reinforce the impression. "I thank you and accept, Princess Gwaethe. Though I would hate to cause any inconvenience or danger for your men."

Gwaethe smiled. "I believe you are important to the kingdom. I would hate to lose you at this crucial juncture."

"You're kind," Alecia said.

Gwaethe inclined her head. "I have been meaning to enquire as to the wellbeing of your daughter. You must miss her."

Ruven speared her with his dark gaze. "You have a child?"

"I do," she said. "Iona is well, Princess. I miss her very much."

"You must have thought this visit vital to have left your daughter," Ruven said. "I wonder what could be so important?"

Gwaethe frowned. "Ruven, that is none of your concern."

Alecia rethought her first impression of the elven commander. He wasn't quiet-spoken at all. "Iona is quite safe in Brightcastle where she is treated like one of Princess Benae's own children. I miss her, but we'll soon be reunited. It will be good for her independence." She ground her teeth at the need to explain her actions, but it seemed to have put Ruven in his place. She spotted a gleam of respect in his gaze. Hoping to end the uncomfortable conversation, she turned to Gwaethe.

"I admire the work you've done in Amitania, Gwaethe. Perhaps the city can once again be a hub for commerce and enlightenment."

Gwaethe nodded. "Jacques must take much of the credit for the improvements. He has worked tirelessly with Ruven to create spaces which appeal to human and elf alike. Of course, there are always those who find fault." A small frown marred her forehead.

Alecia patted her arm. "Change is always difficult, and you are trying to bring two peoples together. I imagine it will be thornier when Faenwelar is brought to heel."

Gwaethe nodded. "I try not to dwell on that. First, we must defeat him, and I find that enough to contemplate."

Ruven cleared his throat. "Princess Gwaethe is too modest. If anyone can defeat the *Sis Lenweri* high prince, it is she. Her father was a great king. She will avenge King Orionkael's murder and unite our people."

"I hope I can help with the ending of your civil war, Gwaethe," Alecia said. "Our goals are aligned."

Ruven's gaze narrowed. "Exactly how are you able to help, Princess? You have no army, no influence that I can see, and you aren't heir to the Kingdom of Thorius."

Alecia sat up straight in her chair, fixing the elven commander with a glare. He smirked, but his humor was short-lived. Gwaethe stood and everyone at table followed her. She motioned for Ruven to join her and strode from the chamber.

All eyes fell upon Alecia.

"What happened?" Jacques asked as they resumed their seats.

Alecia opened her mouth to reply, but realized she didn't know what to say. Finally, she answered. "Commander Magbalar asked me an awkward question, and I believe Princess Gwaethe is concerned he may have offended me."

Jacques frowned. "And did he?"

Alecia dabbed at her lips with her napkin and then stood. "He only spoke what many will think. I must decide what answer I shall give; what I'll do about those who doubt my ability to achieve my goals."

Alecia pushed her chair in and motioned for her ladies to follow her. "Good night, gentlemen. Thank you, Jacques, for the excellent dinner. We shall retire. Tomorrow will be a long day."

The men stood to farewell the ladies, who made their way to their quarters.

CHAPTER 20

THE king was ill, and the court physician didn't know how to help. Vard paced up and down in the king's sitting room, waiting for Doctor Achan Mosard to emerge. A nagging feeling in his gut told him he wouldn't like what the doctor had to say. The man had been attending to King Beniel for a week, with no change in his condition. What Vard wouldn't give for a gifted healer.

He had heard that Lady Alique Jazara, or whatever her name was now, had studied under Mosard, but was a superior physician. Even Princess Benae seemed to work miracles—she had healed Jacques Vorasava when all thought he would die. However, neither woman was close enough to attend to the king. Alique lived in the elven hub of Selinore, and Benae was in Brightcastle.

Queen Adriana and Mosard emerged from the bedchamber and approached him. Vard had never seen the queen like this. She had lost weight this week and dark circles lay beneath her eyes.

"Well?" Vard asked, when the silence grew long.

Adriana frowned. "That's enough Vard. None of us like this situation."

"Excuse me, Your Majesty, but what situation? The king's illness, or the fact that Doctor Mosard can't help him?"

The doctor drew his boney shoulders back. "Watch your tone, soldier. I still outrank you."

Vard raised one brow. "Actually, you don't. I answer only to their majesties. What have you learned?"

Mosard looked at the queen, who nodded.

"King Beniel continues to deteriorate despite my efforts. He has become increasingly frail since his brother's death, and some foul agent has taken residence in his heart. I've seen it occasionally when grief is great. It can break the heart."

"Are you telling me that the king is dying of a broken heart?" Vard asked.

The doctor drew himself up. "More or less."

"I want a second opinion," Vard ground out. "Your Majesty, surely you agree?"

He fixed Adriana with a hard look but stopped short of compulsion. He wouldn't compel the queen. Not again, anyway.

"I'm afraid my Beniel may indeed be dying, Vard. Perhaps there is nothing we can do. Surely it would hasten his demise to move him?"

"Then you think there could be value in a second opinion?"

Mosard cleared his throat. "My colleague Damald Monive in Brightcastle would be happy to help, I'm sure."

Vard looked at Adriana. "Your Majesty, with your permission, I'll ready an escort to convey the king to Brightcastle. I'll send birds ahead and have Monive ride out from Brightcastle to meet us."

The queen swallowed convulsively and tears filled her eyes. He had never seen her cry. "Go, please—do all you can, Vard. I can't lose him."

Vard headed straight for the training grounds. He needed help to ensure the king's safety and knew just the man to help him. He found Samael Delacost training with one of his best rangers, and they weren't using practice swords. Sam was hard pressed to hold the young ranger off. Vard watched in admiration as the fight progressed. In the end, Sam's speed saved him from losing the round to his student. The two men stood laughing and gasping for breath as Vard approached.

Sam noticed Vard and sent the ranger back to the group. "I don't know if I'll survive this training school of yours."

Vard smirked. "Well, how would you like to help me with another project?"

Sam clapped Vard on the shoulder. "Of course."

"You don't know what it is yet."

"Anything is better than fighting to preserve my expert status. These rangers of yours push me harder each day. I'm feeling the absence of my brother."

"How is he?"

"How would I know? I haven't seen him since you sliced him open. I assume he's still licking his wounds."

Vard rubbed a hand across the nape of his neck. "All the more reason to leave Wildecoast for a time." He drew Sam further away from the rangers. "Listen, the king is sick and needs help. Mosard has run out of answers, so I propose we take him to Brightcastle and see if Monive can help. It's also said Princess Benae is a fair healer. Can I count on you to help me keep Beniel safe?"

Sam sucked in a breath. "The king sick!" he muttered under his breath. "That has to be cause for concern with these damned dark elves slinking around. And you want to take him to Brightcastle? Are you certain that's wise?"

"I'm not certain of anything except that the king's heart is failing, and I won't allow him to die on my watch. Are you in?"

Sam grinned. "Of course. I'll pack at once. I assume we're taking a goodly number of rangers?"

"I'll take thirty, half of them experienced and the rest less so. The queen will provide fifty soldiers. I'd like to take more, but this number will draw enough attention without doubling it. We leave at midnight from the field north of the city."

Vard left Sam to dismiss his students and went to find a plain covered wagon. There was no use announcing the importance of the mission by using a grand coach to transport His Majesty. He made a face at the thought of what the king would have to endure on the trip to Brightcastle. But it had to be done. And the next duty was to send seven birds with messages for Mosard and Princess Benae to meet the convoy as soon as they could. At least he hoped Benae would meet them. She wouldn't want to leave her son, and it would be hazardous being on the road with *Sis Lenweri* stalking the area.

That done, Vard made a list of the rangers he'd take, and sent a message to the queen to ensure the soldiers knew where the departure ground was. Last of all, he returned to his room to pack his gear. As he stuffed the last of his clothes into his saddlebags, his man entered.

"My Lord, I've just heard you're leaving for Brightcastle. I can be ready to accompany you in mere moments."

Vard approached the man. "Master Dunnet, I've told you before. There's no need for you to join me. I'll live rough, as the soldiers do. I've done it before and will again." The man looked positively gloomy, as though he longed for the trials of the road. "I'm sure you have plenty to occupy you here."

When Dunnet didn't brighten, Vard had an idea. "Look, take this time to spend with your good wife. She must have chores for you around the cottage. You haven't had a holiday for some time." He pulled out a gold coin and offered it to Dunnet. "Take this to tide you over until I return, and I'll fix you up for the rest when I get back. If you need anything in the meantime, speak to the queen."

Dunnet paled at the mention of Adriana, and Vard inwardly smirked.

"Oh no, My Lord. I won't trouble Her Majesty. You're most kind. Send a messenger when you're a day out, and I'll have your rooms prepared." Dunnet bowed and left him.

Vard took a deep breath. When would he ever be used to Dunnet's fussing? But at least this trip was a chance to get away from court. And it would bring him close to Alecia and Iona. A warm glow lit inside him at the thought.

The light of a new day caressed the horizon as Vard returned to human form and mounted his horse. He had scouted along the path they would follow east. He galloped west to rejoin the soldiers and found them as they were making camp for breakfast. Most of his rangers were in the field, scouting the forest to the north and south, as well as their back trail.

His stomach grumbled after being out all night, and weariness lay heavy on his bones.

Sam was the first to see him and met him as he dismounted.

"Anything to see up there?" he asked.

"Nothing," Vard said. "It's too quiet. Faenwelar must be planning something."

"He'll wait until we least expect it."

Vard nodded. "I just hope it's not while we're away. I can't trust Formosa to organize a decent defense."

"Niko will see that all is well, and the queen is no slouch with strategy."

"Still, I'd feel better if I knew when the attack was to occur."

Sam clapped him on the shoulder. "Come, get breakfast inside you. We thought we'd have a camp for a couple of hours and then get back on the road."

Vard walked with him to the first campfire and sat with the rangers and soldiers. He was pleased to see the two units getting along. There seemed to be no angst between them, and he hoped his talk with them before leaving had bridged the gap. If neither camp tried to lord it over the others, all might be peaceful.

He visited the king after eating and found the monarch looking worse for wear.

"How are you Your Majesty?"

"Get me out of this blasted wagon, would you? I can't sleep for the blasted rocking, and I can't get comfortable." A fit of coughing laid him low. Vard flinched at the sound. At this rate, the king wouldn't reach Brightcastle alive.

"Your Majesty," Vard pleaded, "stay calm. You'll gain nothing by getting worked up. We're doing our best."

"Blasted Mosard! I should have listened to Lady Alique and replaced him with her. Now I'm stuck with the dunce, and she is halfway across the kingdom."

He lay on his pallet, his face pale and sweating even though it was cool in the wagon. "How many days until we reach Brightcastle? I've lost track of time in this damned contraption."

"Two days, Your Majesty, but we should meet with Doctor Monive tomorrow if the birds arrived in time."

"That, at least, is some consolation."

"Not long now, Your Majesty," Vard said, gripping the king's shoulder. "Just hold on for another day, and we'll have medical help for you."

Vard left the king grumbling to himself about the lack of talented physicians, and couldn't help worrying that help would be too late. This health issue had come at precisely the wrong time for the kingdom. They needed the king, at the very least as a figurehead in battle. Vard rarely felt off kilter, but at present, with extra responsibilities given to him by a monarch in poor health, he had no genuine sense of what the future might hold.

The following morning, the convoy was on the trail for only half an hour when a forward scout rode back to it.

"The doctor from Brightcastle approaches, My Lord," the scout said to Vard. "I've sent two rangers to greet them."

"Are you certain it's the Brightcastle party?" Vard asked, rubbing a hand over the whiskers on his chin.

"Yes, My Lord."

"Stay vigilant, man. This would be a good time for an ambush. Resume your scouting position and take another pair of rangers with you."

The man saluted and wheeled his horse to obey. Vard turned reluctantly toward the wagon where the king lay. He tied his horse to the vehicle, climbed off onto the running board, and poked his head through the canvas.

"Good news, Your Majesty. The doctor's group has been spotted. We should meet him within the hour."

The king barely turned his head, but just waved his hand in the air. "Good news indeed," he croaked.

Vard frowned and climbed right into the wagon, placing his hand on the king's chest to better hear his heart. He should have been able to hear it clearly above the noise of the wagon, but the organ was weakened by His Majesty's ailment. He closed his eyes and his senses leapt to the fore. The sputtering of the monarch's heart cast dread deep into Vard. No doctor could cure what afflicted King Beniel. This had been a fool's mission.

"Hold on, My Liege," he whispered, pushing up from the pallet and exiting the moving wagon. He climbed on Trax and spurred him to the head of the line where Samael rode.

"Guard the king with your life, Sam," he said. "I ride for the Brightcastle party, to urge them to approach with all speed."

With those words, he tore past, shouted words from Sam falling on deaf ears. He considered morphing into the hawk, but he couldn't give his game away to those approaching. He couldn't explain turning up in the middle of nowhere without transport. The time he might save was a minor advantage compared to the significant risk of revealing himself. He had already exposed himself to the admiral and only the Goddess knew if the man had kept his secret.

Casting regret from his heart, Vard rode like a man possessed, judging when his mount was flagging and slowing to a brisk walk until the stallion was restored. He had run through this cycle twice when he spied the mounted group up ahead. Three horses, their riders in fine clothes, trotted in the center of a cluster of soldiers, perhaps thirty.

Vard scanned those in the center and spotted Doctor Monive. With him were two ladies—could it be Princess Benae and her assistant?

The Brightcastle Guardian was a gifted healer. She had saved Jacques Vorasava when all thought he would perish, not to mention her husband and the little girl, Gracie, when both had been shot by crossbow bolts on separate occasions.

Perhaps the king had a chance if Benae had come.

He pulled his exhausted horse to a trot and kept on. He'd take it easy on the way back while the Brightcastle party hurried to the king.

In mere minutes, he approached the group. A soldier, captain by his uniform, rode his horse out in front of the party and held up his hand. Vard slowed to a walk, but kept on. The man drew his sword.

"Captain Estevot," he said, stopping three paces from the soldier. "We've met before. My name is Vard Anton, and I'm here on a mission to save the king. He's in a dire way, and I urge you to hasten to him so that these doctors can bring him healing."

Someone in the group, perhaps Monive, snorted, likely at the word doctor which he had used to include Benae.

"Well met, Lord Anton," Estevot said, ice-blue eyes hard. "How far must we ride to meet your party? Have you had any trouble on the road?"

"If you ride hard, Captain, you'll arrive well within the hour," Vard said. "But you must not delay. The king is close to death."

Monive rode forward. "I'll be the judge of that, Anton." He turned to the ladies. "Princess Benae, you and your maid can follow at a more leisurely pace if you please."

Vard cleared his throat. "His Majesty has asked to see Princess Benae at the earliest opportunity. I'd hate for him to pass before he has that chance." He met Benae's eye and she nodded. "Our journey so far has been a quiet one, but I would urge caution."

Benae rode forward. "My assistant and I will accompany you, Doctor, and we'll keep up. Don't worry." She swept her gaze around her soldiers, ten of whom were women. "Come along! His Majesty needs our help." She kicked her gray stallion forward, and he sprang into a gallop. Her soldiers, including Estevot, hastened to catch her. Doctor Monive glared at Vard and galloped to catch the others.

Vard huffed out a laugh and turned his mount to follow at a more sedate pace.

* * *

Benae delighted in the excitement of their approach to the king's convoy. It was weeks since she had let Flaire have his head, and they both missed the exhilaration of a long gallop. Her soldiers soon caught up, and she pulled back amongst them. It would be foolhardy to allow her wild enjoyment to endanger the mission. But, oh, how she wished she had time for this more often. She felt Flaire's joy through their bond and sent him her love and devotion. He whinnied and pranced in response, and she patted his silky neck.

It was time to return to her duty, and that was ensuring the safety of the king, though Vard Anton had intimated they might be too late. She liked Beniel and would do anything to ensure her monarch and former brother-in-law was safe. But what if his heart had already failed as Jiseve's had?

Her musing was cut short by the appearance of men and wagons moving toward them on the road. Her lady soldiers surrounded her and Tyra, her maid, as they approached. A dashing man with blonde hair and looks that would be difficult to forget trotted his black toward them. Flaire neighed a challenge and stomped his front hoof.

"Easy Flaire," Benae said. "He's a friend." Although Flaire was too well mannered to cause trouble, he was battle trained and so was a weapon in himself.

The man stopped ten paces away as Captain Estevot joined her.

"Samael Delacost at your service, My Lady," the man said, bowing from the saddle. His eyes flicked to the captain.

Estevot cleared his throat. "I'm Captain Jules Estevot, and this is Princess Benae, Guardian of Brightcastle. With me is Doctor Monive, royal physician in Brightcastle."

"If it please you, I'll escort the doctor and Princess Benae to His Majesty."

The doctor rode forward. "I shall attend His Majesty, Delacost. Take me to him." He turned to Benae. "I will call for you if needed, Princess."

Benae knew a flash of pure rage, but tamed it and nodded to the physician. It would do no good to cause a scene. Let it be on the doctor's head if the king died. She followed Monive and Samael Delacost at a distance so she could be close if needed. Her lady soldiers stayed gathered around her, muttering to themselves. They didn't enjoy her dismissal any better than she had.

"Be at peace, friends," she said to them. "Your rancor will achieve nothing." She watched as Monive climbed into the king's wagon with his attendant, who carried the doctor's bag. How self-important he was! But he was a reasonable physician with much experience. She would allow him to examine the king and see what he made of it all.

After several moments of hushed whispers from inside the wagon, a voice from within yelled: "Out!". Benae jumped as Monive and his assistant exited the wagon in a great hurry. Delacost stuck his head in and then strode to Benae.

"The king wishes to see you now, Princess."

Benae dismounted, and she and Tyra approached the wagon. She stopped before Doctor Monive.

"How is the king, Doctor? What can you tell me?"

Monive frowned. "His heart has indeed failed, Princess. Apart from rest and certain restorative herbs, I believe we can do nothing for him."

"How long does he have, Doctor?" Delacost asked.

"That I can't answer. Perhaps only days, and that is if he rests. I believe we must make plans for a transition of power to the Guardians of Brightcastle."

"I will speak with him," Benae said, continuing the last few steps to the wagon. Delacost assisted Benae and her maid into the vehicle. As her eyes adjusted to the low light, Benae locked eyes with King Beniel. She curtsied.

"Your Majesty, I'm most sorry to see you brought low by your illness."

Beniel had gone still, his complete attention focused on Benae. "I've never been so glad to see anyone, my dear. I witnessed what you did for Zorba. Surely you can nurse me back to health?" His hand gripped hers tightly.

"Of course, I'll do all I can, Majesty." She placed her hand on his brow and was assailed by the fear he held within. Next, she laid her fingertips to his throat and noted the fast and thready beat of his heart. She turned to Tyra and requested she prepare the heart tonic.

This had to be convincing, or Beniel would suspect her healing—if she could accomplish anything—had magical properties. *That* she couldn't allow. She took the potion of herbs and honey from Tyra and spooned a little of the medicine into Beniel's mouth.

He coughed and spluttered. "Damn bitter, despite liberal amounts of honey!"

"I'm sorry, Your Majesty." Benae placed her hand over his heart. "Rest, and slow your breath if you can."

He had a last cough and settled against the pillows, his breathing slowing as she had requested.

"We'll say a prayer of healing," Benae said, closing her eyes.

As her attendant said the first words of the prayer, she sent her spirit into the king and down through the layers of his chest, seeking the hurt that dwelt there. His lungs were filling with fluid, which was likely due to improper functioning of his heart.

She cast her attention to the struggling organ and sensed several valves that no longer worked as they should. The muscular wall of the heart had lost its integrity from years of working too hard.

This was one of the most difficult healings she had attempted. She had little experience in helping failing hearts. It was usually too late when she attended them, the organ already having failed.

Benae took a deep breath and travelled back to the damaged valves, using her spirit to reattach the broken strands so that the valves again closed properly. The monarch groaned and clutched his chest.

Have I gone too far? Is this too much for such a weakened organ? She looked at Tyra, whose eyes were wide with fright. The words of the prayer had stalled on her tongue. When Benae returned her gaze to Beniel, his hand still gripped his chest, the fingers like claws. The skin of his face was gray and his fingernails and lips blue.

"King Beniel, can you hear me?" Benae gripped his shoulders and shook gently, but he gave no response.

"Princess!"

Benae hushed Tyra, though she too was frightened the king would pass as they watched on. She might be blamed if that occurred, and it would be just like Jiseve all over again. Only this time, the stakes were higher.

She took a breath and pushed her spirit into Beniel, shuddering at the fluid in his lungs and at the stuttering heart. Her healing had almost been too much for the failing organ to withstand. But perhaps he might still survive. She cursed herself for a fool that she had attempted to fix both valves instead of only one and then the other another day.

Silly woman! What wisdom do you hold? You might have killed him!

Benae and her attendant sat and prayed over the king for a full half hour, with Benae trying to push some of the fluid out of the chest and into the vessels that drained it. She was only partially successful, and Beniel still hovered between life and death. Someone would come to check soon, and she wouldn't be able to answer their questions.

One more try! She sent her spirit into the king again, only this time she concentrated on his brain, and found two places where clots of blood had lodged. Tiny tendrils of spirit broke them up, and she smiled as the blood flowed again into these areas. She returned to the heart and found a clot in a vessel there too—and dissolved it.

The wagon covering moved behind her, but she couldn't spare a thought for who might be entering. Instead, she redoubled her efforts to patch up Beniel's damaged heart.

"Is he dead?" Vard Anton's harsh words made her jump.

She turned to him, unable to school her features to hide her dismay. The prayers of her maid continued, a somber symphony to the king's fight to live.

She drew a deep breath and met Anton's narrowed gaze.

"He still lives, but I don't know if he can win this fight."

"He had better win, or the kingdom suffers!"

Benae squared her shoulders and lifted her chin.

"His heart is almost worn out. I'm doing everything I can, but it may be too late." She turned to Beniel and placed her hand on his chest. *One last try!* She pushed more fluid from his lungs, and into the vessels that would drain it away, and saw the king's color improve.

A last check of his body showed she had done everything possible for now.

"We must get him to Brightcastle so he can rest. I think he's stable for the moment."

Benae turned and crawled toward Vard, and he helped her out. After so long crouched beside the king, her legs protested the climb from the wagon. Tyra stayed with Beniel and would do so until they reached Brightcastle.

Monive greeted her. "Well? How is he?"

"He's out of immediate danger. Please examine him again so you may confirm the king's condition for Lord Anton."

The doctor hurried into the wagon while Benae mounted Flaire. Anton ordered them to move out. He rode on one side of Benae while Delacost rode behind. They felt more like guards than escorts.

"What's the nature of your healing, Princess?" Anton asked.

She frowned. "It's herbal in nature. King Beniel has a serious heart condition, and there are certain herbs that help the organ pump more effectively. Others remove fluid from the chest. It all helps to improve quality of life and extend it."

Delacost trotted up on her other side. "I hear a 'but' coming."

"Of course, there's a limit to what herbs can do. I'm not a god to grant life when the body fails. Jiseve died of heart failure, and it seems Beniel will eventually succumb to the same illness. I just hope he can live long enough to defeat the *Sis Lenweri*."

Vard fixed her with his eagle eye. "You don't wish to ascend to the supreme controller of the kingdom, Princess?"

He didn't know her at all if he thought she wanted Beniel to die.

She would wish death on no one and certainly not on a man who had supported her when he had every reason not to.

"I didn't ask for this, Lord Anton. Though it's none of your concern, I had no desire to run the kingdom when I sought Jiseve's hand in marriage. My only hope is for peace in Thorius, and for my son to be safe and happy. Beniel can sit on his throne until he's an old man, and I'll rejoice." The fire in her voice died as she realized that was unlikely.

Anton nodded, his brows drawn. "Your words have the ring of sincerity, Princess. I'll try to protect you, but you must be careful. If the king dies, and you have tended him, suspicion may again fall on your shoulders. Have a care about how you conduct yourself."

"You've said enough, Lord Anton!" Benae struggled to reign in her anger, and Flaire tossed his head. "I'll do all I can, even unto drawing suspicion on myself. I can't stand by and watch while a man suffers." She wanted to rant and rave at the injustice of his words, but it was no use. She would keep her own counsel, and her actions would be blameless. Her hands shook on the reins, and Flaire danced to the side, bumping Anton's horse.

Beniel had indeed almost died during her healing, but she wouldn't make the same mistake again.

CHAPTER 21

V ARD stopped for the night in a large clearing just off the high road. The king had improved during the day, and was now conscious and complaining about the food. He grinned as he listened to the monarch's grumbling.

"Not long now, Your Majesty," he said. "We should be in Brightcastle by late morning tomorrow. Then you can rest easy and recover."

"Yes, Vard. Recover from the rugged healing at the hands of Monive and Princess Benae. I don't know what they did, but between them, my poor body is tender in places I didn't know I had. My insides feel like they have been pummeled."

"You seem better, if it's any consolation, Majesty," Vard said.

"I'm an ungrateful idiot. I am stronger and breathing easier. And I have my appetite back. My mind is clearer, too. And I have Monive and Benae to thank. Did you see anything of their healing, Vard?"

"It involved herbs, Your Majesty. The princess said they'd make your heart beat more efficiently and draw fluid off your chest. That would account for your improved breathing."

"Mosard gave me herbs which he said would do those same things and nothing ever changed." His eyes narrowed. "You don't think Princess Benae used magic, do you? I know it exists, and her healing of Ramón Zorba was nothing short of miraculous. She stayed with him night and day. That man should never have survived his chest injury." He grabbed Vard's hand. "I must know if Benae's treatment involved magic."

Vard relaxed the muscles of his face to hide his dismay. "I saw nothing that indicated magical powers, My Liege." He thought back to Benae and her hands on the king's chest yesterday. She might indeed have magic, though she hid it well with her herbs. Regardless, her secrets, if she had any, were safe with him. He could hardly accuse Benae when he held his own miraculous gifts.

The king relaxed against his pillows. "Good, that's good."

"I'm glad you're feeling better, My King," Vard said, handing Beniel the herb concoction Benae said he must drink. "When you've finished the medicine in this goblet, please get some rest. We start early in the morning."

Vard left the tent to be replaced by Benae's assistant, no doubt to make sure His Majesty imbibed the entire contents of the goblet. Vard had sniffed the liquid, finding nothing dangerous within. He approached Samael, who sat on a log before the fire, drinking ale.

Sam slapped Vard on the shoulder as he sat down. "How is the king tonight?"

Vard paused, startled at the familiar gesture from Sam, one which he'd seen many times between his men. It felt good to be on such terms with Sam.

"His Majesty is improved, but looking forward to reaching Brightcastle. He tires of the wagon." He lowered his voice. "I just hope we reach the city with no trouble. I have this itch at the base of my skull that warns of danger."

Sam sighed. "I have the same itch. I've posted a ring of rangers around the camp in addition to the soldiers. No one will approach without a warning. You can be sure of that."

"Thank you, Sam. I'm glad it's not just me being paranoid."

"It could be both of us being paranoid, but better to be safe than sorry. We have precious company with us, including Benae and Monive. I have no wish to lose any of them."

Vard's senses were on high alert as he circled the camp, speaking to those on sentry duty. He spoke to the soldiers and rangers who would take the second shift after midnight, and asked them to keep their weapons and horses close. Benae and Doctor Monive set up their beds below the wagon while the maid bedded down at the foot of the king's pallet. A double ring of soldiers took their rest around the conveyance.

He sent Sam to bed and stalked off into the surrounding forest to a position away from prying eyes. Vard morphed into the wolf and padded off into the forest, his enhanced senses on alert for anything which shouldn't be there. Danger screamed at him, but he found no sense or sight of elven or human foes. He shook his thick pelt and released a low, threatening growl. If there was something out there, it was well hidden. He stopped, his senses alert for the threat. Only his sixth sense was being triggered; a feeling of foreboding so strong he couldn't ignore it.

He must get to the camp and rouse the others. Vard returned to human form once close to the outer ring of sentries and warned them to be vigilant; that the threat may come from any quarter. Arriving in camp, he woke Sam and the others, telling those in and under the wagon to stay put. The king grumbled, but knew he wasn't in any shape for fighting.

They stoked the fire, the minutes ticking by like hours as they waited. Vard began to think he had imagined the threat, but a blood-curdling cry came from the woods to the north. A call from the east answered.

"Look to the north and east!" Vard cried, drawing his sword and slamming his body against the side of the wagon. "Take cover if you can!" The men in camp were exposed to arrows, but at least no one could drop from the trees. That was the favorite tactic of the *Sis Lenweri.*

The clash of swords came from the forest around them as their men battled the unseen attackers. Many of those in camp started to run toward the trees, but Vard called them back. They couldn't afford to leave the king vulnerable, or Princess Benae.

"Stay under the wagon, Princess," Vard said, pulling a knife from his boot and handing it to her. "Use this if anyone should approach you."

Her eyes were wide as she took the knife from him. He handed Monive a short sword. "Do you know how to use this, Doctor?"

"Enough to hold them off for a few moments, Anton."

Vard nodded. The doctor was made of stern stuff by the lack of fear in his voice. He stationed a ranger inside the wagon with the king, and pulled the maid out, ushering her under the vehicle. Surprisingly, she had her own knife already drawn.

"I won't let them get to the princess, My Lord. You can count on that."

Benae's lady guards made a ring of their own around the wagon. Vard had seen them fight, and they were well-trained, if unseasoned. It was one thing to train with a sword, and another to perform in battle. But they were as prepared as they could be.

And then he had no time to think or worry as dark elves invaded the camp. One minute they were on their own, and the next at least thirty elves stepped into the light of their fire.

"Prepare to die, human dogs!" their leader cried before leaping at Sam.

"Attack!" Vard shouted, trying to keep his eyes everywhere at once— on the ladies, on Sam, and on the wagon which held their precious king. But he couldn't fight like this; he *must* concentrate on what was before him. Cold, focused, and deadly, he fought his way to Sam, who was hard pressed by the excellence and reach of the elven leader.

Human and elven dead littered the camp by the time Vard joined the fight with the elven master. He elbowed his friend out of the way.

"Protect the ladies!" he said, deflecting a savage swipe aimed at his neck. The elf was good, but he was better. He dispatched the foe with a thrust through his gut. Vard swung his gaze across the camp site, dismayed by what he saw. They were losing this fight; his casualties outnumbered the elven dead and more enemy arrived in the clearing as he tried to regroup.

"To me!" Vard tried to gather his men close to the wagon. "To me!"

Sam fought off two elves trying to climb into the conveyance, and Vard leapt over the fire and crashed through a knot of fighters to get to him. He helped Sam disable three elves and found himself facing a fourth.

Sam left him to chase off an elf who was sneaking under the wagon. The *Sis Lenweri* screamed as Benae's knife flashed out. But Vard couldn't spare another thought for them as more *Sis Lenweri* closed in. They appeared to have decided the prize was there, and so it was. He gritted his teeth, determined the enemy would only get to the king over his dead body.

"To me! To me!" Vard cried as the fighting escalated. Benae's ladies joined him, along with the remaining kingdom men in camp. They formed a ring around the wagon, trying to give themselves room to move. But it was no good. The fire was dying, and the light was too poor to assess the threats coming at them. The elves had excellent night vision, and fought with leering grins that announced their upper hand in this fight. They were winning, and there was nothing Vard could do but stay alive as long as possible.

He couldn't risk changing form; he'd be too vulnerable. And so he fought as those beside him steadily fell. A growl started as he battled two elves at a time. He realized the animal sound was coming from him. No! He must control this.

And then the elf in front of him screamed and was pulled down from behind. A huge hound landed on the *Sis Lenweri's* chest and clamped its jaws around his throat. It was the size of a large wolf, but heavier set. The front feet were those of a dog, but the hind paws contained deadly claws. Red eyes fixed upon Vard as the creature turned to him. *Night hound!*

Just when he expected the beast to leap at him, it turned and attacked the nearest elf, dispatching the *Sis Lenweri* and letting out a blood-curdling howl. More hounds joined the fight, and, in minutes, their elven foes lay dead.

Vard hadn't needed to raise his sword since the first hound killed his opponent. A whistle sounded, and the hounds gathered on the far side of the camp. Sam appeared at Vard's side.

"Glad to see you in one piece, Anton," he said. "Do you think we're next?" He nodded his head toward the hounds. "If so, it's been good knowing you."

Vard grunted and turned his gaze to his fallen comrades. "Check on the king, and then collect the injured and see to their wounds. Get Princess Benae and the doctor to tend them." When he looked back at the hounds, they had turned and were melting into the forest. "I'm going to check on the sentries."

"Let me go with you," Sam said.

Vard shook his head. "You have plenty to do here. I'll be fine."

He stalked after the hounds, allowing a partial transformation into the wolf to take advantage of the enhanced night vision, something he hadn't been able to risk in the heat of battle for fear of losing control.

He moved carefully, senses alert to small noises, movements, and smells that might signal danger. Nothing presented, and the night hounds vanished as abruptly as they had arrived. Thank the Goddess for their help, but why had they come? If they had a new ally, he had to discover why and how.

He crept through the forest, ghosting from tree to tree, and shadow to shadow. He found the bodies of three sentries, but it was too late to help them.

Dread swept through him as he turned from checking the third sentry and his eyes met the menacing crimson orbs of a night hound. The beast was the largest he had yet seen, its muzzle streaked with gray. It growled and bared yellow fangs, crouched as if to leap.

Vard stayed in a squat and slowly slid his left hand to the knife in his boot. The hound growled again.

"Down, Fang," a cool female voice said.

The beast sat on its haunches, and Vard looked up into the sparkling blue gaze of a woman he had last seen almost six months before.

"Lady Aranati, we meet again." He rose slowly, hands away from his body, and bowed to the woman.

She hissed. "Well met indeed. I'd rather you didn't use my real name. Call me Lady Star."

"As you wish, My Lady. Are these hounds now under your control?"

"It is as it appears. They are mine to command. This is Truthfang, their leader," she said, placing her palm on the hound's head. The beast whined.

Vard bowed again to the hound, which settled into a drop.

"You are free to approach, Lord Anton." Lady Star said.

Vard did so, but kept his enhanced sight. "I have little time before they come looking for me. We were hard-pressed. But for your intervention, we would've been slaughtered. I owe you profound thanks."

"The hounds alerted me to danger several days ago, and we left immediately, hoping we were here in time. I only had a rough impression of the locale of the strife. I'm glad we could help."

"You have changed much, Lady Star. I'd like to hear the story of how you came to have charge of these hounds. You were enemies last time we met."

"That's a story for another day, Lord Anton. I'd appreciate it if you could keep my secret, both of my powers and my stewardship of the hounds. My brother-in-law is with your party, and he knows nothing of my other life. I want to keep it that way. The hounds allow me to hide my powers. They fight for me, so I don't have to."

"A formidable fighting squad. How many are there?"

"Twenty-one currently, but Dawngaze is pregnant with four pups. I hope this heralds a new era for the night hounds. You have nothing to fear from them as long as you and I are on the same side."

Vard raised his brows at this. "I can't imagine a time when we're not aligned."

"When wars and magic are involved, much can change, Lord Anton." Her eyes pinned him as the seconds ticked by. "There's something else." She paused again as if unsure. "The hounds also warned of a looming darkness. It seemed a separate threat, but possibly linked to the *Sis Lenweri*? I can't discern more than that."

"I'd appreciate anything you can do to enlighten us. Again, I thank you for your aid."

Lady Star took a step backward, and Fang bounded to her side. "I'll send word to Wildecoast Keep if I come across any new intelligence. Farewell."

She slipped into the trees and vanished. Vard took a deep breath and continued his patrol. He found only two sentries who had survived and helped them back to camp.

He arrived in a camp buzzing with activity and cries of pain. A ring of able-bodied soldiers and rangers stood guard, along with three of Benae's lady guards. A makeshift hospital had been set up on one side of the campfire, and Monive, Benae and her maid were tending to the injured. It looked like hell.

Sam pounced on him as soon as he appeared. "Thank the Goddess! You were gone for a long time. I was about to come looking." He helped Vard lower the two sentries to the ground.

"How goes it?" Vard asked, running a hand over his jaw.

"We lost thirty near as I can figure and another twenty injured. Some may not make it."

Thirty! They could ill afford to lose any, let alone that many. "And the king?"

"He's well. Those hell hounds came just in time. A few more minutes and we would've been overrun."

"Indeed. Someone was watching out for us."

"I'd like to know who," Sam said. "I heard a whistle when the dogs backed off. One particularly vicious bitch was staring me down at the time. I was assessing my options when she turned away. Do you have any light to shed on them?"

"They're night hounds, creatures of legend. There have been no sightings in the last fifty years, but now they've returned."

"I've heard of them. But why are they back now—and is it coincidence you seem to know more of them than most?"

There was a knowing light in his second's gaze. Was it possible Cosara had spilled Vard's secret? With no time to ponder this, Vard gave a cautious reply.

"I spoke with their mistress in the forest. She too I've met before. I vowed to keep her identity secret."

Sam's eyes widened. "A woman commands those creatures? Holy Goddess, she must be some lady."

Vard nodded. "She also mentioned another threat linked to the elves this night, but couldn't say what that was."

"Couldn't? Or wouldn't? Is she truly our ally? Would she withhold critical information?"

"I don't believe so." He looked at those caring for the injured. "How is morale?"

"As you'd expect. I've done what I can to bolster them…" He stepped closer and lowered his voice. "Princess Benae is shaken up. She's holding onto her composure, but only just. I thought she was made of sterner stuff."

Vard watched the lady, noted her pale complexion and trembling hands, saw the way her assistant kept watch over her mistress. "She and Zorba were once ambushed by *Sis Lenweri,* and were the only survivors. Her maid was murdered trying to defend her. I don't suppose you forget that in a hurry."

"Oh!" Sam frowned. "I understand. I'll keep an eye on her; make sure she gets support."

Vard clapped him on the shoulder. "Thanks. I better make the rounds. Can you see that the guards get a hot meal? Allow half of them to stand down for a couple of hours."

"Of course."

Vard moved among the injured, laying his hands on their shoulders, murmuring encouragement. He had an innate ability to assess health. There was no contamination of their wounds, but their spirits were at a low ebb.

"Princess Benae," he said, stopping before her as she finished stitching an arm wound. "Thank you for your devotion."

She looked exhausted, and her green eyes held shadows of despair.

"What else would I do but help, Lord Anton? These are my people, and they were injured defending me. I'll see that no more die in my name."

He guided her away from her patient and lowered his voice. "I meant no offence, Princess. I know this must have been a traumatic experience. I appreciate the help you're giving to the injured when you must be sorely taxed."

She straightened her shoulders. "I'm doing what any leader would. I'll help until I drop if necessary. Now, if you'll excuse me…" She returned to her patient and lay her hand on the man's brow, closing her eyes.

Princess Benae had a core of steel that he hadn't expected. Still, she was only human, and if she pushed herself too far she would be of no use to any of them. He sighed. He had to have faith that she knew her limits, or that her attendants did.

Vard continued his rounds, talking to the men and women who were conscious and saying a prayer over those who weren't. Several hovered between life and death. Then he spoke to those on sentry duty. They had moved further from camp and patrolled in pairs to enable them to support each other and stay awake. Some had slings and bandages, but all were alert.

He was more than a little tired by the time he returned to the fire to eat. The stew was only lukewarm, but nourishing. He sipped a cup of mulled wine Sam prepared for him.

"Perhaps you should get some rest, Vard," Sam said. "You look dead on your feet."

"So do you, but you're not hitting your bedroll."

"I need comradeship more than rest."

"I need to think and anticipate the next move by the enemy." His eyes found the pile of dead elves near the tree line. "Thanks for having them moved. How many?"

"Fifty-six, and many of them killed by the hounds. I don't think many escaped. But they would have won the day if not for the beasts. I hope the hounds dog our steps to Brightcastle."

"I have no such commitment from their leader. But I think we're safe for now. This was a mission to kill the king. Somehow, they knew His Majesty was in that wagon, and a small force got close to accomplishing their aim. If not for the intervention of the hounds…"

"We certainly would've perished," Sam said. "The king and Princess Benae, as well as the king's right-hand man, in one fell swoop." He shivered. "I don't like to think of it."

"But we won out," Vard said. "Our losses are great, but they could've been much worse. You take an hour to rest, then I'll take the same. It will be close to dawn by then, and we can carry on to Brightcastle."

The rest of their journey was uneventful, save for the difficulty of caring for so many injured. But Benae and Monive had done a marvelous job, and many of their patients could ride by the time of departure. Two of the most severely injured joined the king in his wagon amid protests from His Majesty that he was fit enough to ride. Even if that were so, Vard wouldn't allow his leader to expose himself in what was clearly hostile territory.

On arrival at the city gates, Vard sent a rider to fetch an escort while they continued through the streets. He kept his eye on the rooftops, watching for assassins, the curse of his life. He recalled the night that one had nearly ended his life in the palace garden in this very city—the night Alecia was betrothed to Lord Finus. That episode had changed their lives and spelled the end of Alecia's innocence. She was a different woman now. He only hoped she still needed him in her life. Excitement grew at the prospect of spending time with her and their daughter.

Benae rode in a crowd of guards, the hood of her cloak down and her eyes straight ahead. Occasionally she waved to the crowd and there were calls of "Princess!" from the townspeople who made way for them. But the mood sobered as eyes fell upon the cloaked forms laid upon horses—men and women who would never ride again, would never greet their loved ones, or share an ale with a friend. Benae's shoulders drooped as she heard the cries of pain at the losses.

Their escort arrived with Ramón Zorba himself. He rode straight to Benae and pulled her onto his horse, his arms around her and her face buried in his shoulder.

His eyes met Vard's. "I hear there was trouble on the road."

Vard nodded. "Almost more than we could handle. Someone had intelligence. I'll tell all when we're behind closed walls. Your lady is well, but her life was threatened."

Ramón nodded. "The king?" he asked quietly.

"Is much improved." Vard said. "I can't say the same for thirty of our guards and rangers who won't draw breath again."

"They'll have funerals befitting their sacrifice," Ramón said. "But it will be scant comfort for their families. We must make the elves pay."

"And they *will* pay. Ride ahead with the princess. I'll be along as soon as I get my men settled and the bodies of the dead stored. Perhaps Monive can help with that?"

"Still giving orders?" Ramón said. "Old habits die hard."

"I think you'll find I have the authority, Guardian," Vard said. "Take the wagon with you. I know you'll want to see that the king is cared for."

Zorba frowned at him. "Of course! I almost died for that man not so long ago. His health is paramount, and I'm overjoyed to hear he's on the improve. It would be unthinkable to be without him at this precarious time."

Vard gave Zorba a hard look, but turned away without further instructions. Alecia trusted the man, but as far as Vard was concerned, he got an itch every time he was around the Brightcastle Guardian. A sixth sense told him to be wary. And the man was far too close to Iona for comfort.

As he trotted for the castle, Vard ground his teeth at the thought that Zorba could see Iona whenever he wanted, while he, her father, had to console himself with brief visits. He had missed so much of her young life.

Vard checked the injured into the infirmary, then settled his rangers and soldiers into their accommodation. After seeing the dead to their place of rest, he visited Trax in the stable then trudged up the drive to the castle forecourt. The chief steward greeted him at the front steps.

"My Lord! Let me show you to your chambers where you can refresh and change your clothes before meeting the king and Lord Zorba."

Vard allowed the man to do just that, not surprised the king had insisted upon being involved. He changed clothes and washed his face and hands before wolfing down the food that lay on a tray on his breakfast table. He allowed himself the luxury of imbibing the red wine at full strength for a change. The attack of the previous night had left him bone weary. He wanted nothing more than to sleep, but there was no time.

He stepped outside his room, and a footman showed him to a small audience chamber. He hoped Alecia would be present, but only Zorba, King Beniel, and Captain Estevot awaited him.

Vard approached the king. "Your Majesty, are you sure you should be here? You need your rest."

"Pah!" Beniel said. "I can rest when I'm dead. This is the best I've felt for months. I'm still the king, and I'll go where I please."

"Of course, My Liege," Vard said, turning to Zorba. "I thought perhaps to speak with Alecia?"

Zorba huffed. "Not possible! She disappeared weeks ago, and it now appears she went to Amitania."

"What?! Why wasn't I informed?" Vard barely stopped himself from laying his hand on his sword. That wouldn't have gone down well. Zorba already had enough reasons to spit him like a pig.

Ramón drew his shoulders back. "Alecia is a free woman and doesn't answer to you. Besides, I have better things to do than sending messages to you whenever she goes tripping off."

"Did you search for her?"

"Of course I did! May I remind you I was the one who never gave up trying to find the princess when she vanished with you? She clearly didn't want to be found. I eventually learned she had arrived safely in Amitania with her ladies."

"Her ladies?" Vard asked, pushing his hands through his hair. Alecia would have some explaining to do when she returned. "And what about Iona? Where is she?"

Ramón scowled. "We have cared for Iona as the loved family member she is. As for the ladies, Alecia left with four female guards."

The king gave a great gasp. "My niece is absent with only four guards for protection? That is not acceptable." His face was red, and his breathing had taken an alarming hike in intensity.

Vard stepped close and took his elbow. "Please don't alarm yourself, Majesty. It's important you stay calm. Let me deal with this." He struggled with his own composure, but it would do no good to allow the king or Zorba to see it.

"Anton is right, Your Majesty," Zorba said. "Please take a seat and a sip of tea. Alecia is well. I've heard from Amitania as recently as two days ago. She arrived safely and will return soon, guarded by a contingent of soldiers from Amitania, human and elven."

Vard ground his teeth, both at the thought of what Alecia might be up to and at the tone of Zorba's voice. He was haughty when he had no cause to be. Vard desired to see that smug smile wiped from the man's face. But he must remain conciliatory when Zorba had such influence over his daughter.

"There, My Liege," Vard said, leading the king to a chair and helping him sit. He poured a cup of tea and added honey, as Beniel preferred. "I urge you to stay calm or all the good work of the doctor and Princess Benae, not to mention those who recently fought for you, will count for naught."

Beniel frowned and took a sip of his tea. "I know you are right, Anton, but Alecia is important to Thorius. She doesn't have the proper respect for her safety."

"She's safe for now, and I'll personally see she returns no worse for wear." Vard turned to Zorba, who scowled at him.

"Your interference isn't necessary, Anton," Zorba said. "The matter of Alecia is under control."

"Let's put this matter aside and discuss this recent attack by the *Sis Lenweri*," Vard said, sending Zorba a look that he hoped encouraged the man to change the subject.

"Indeed," Captain Estevot said, coming to stand beside Zorba. "As far as I can see, this was a deliberate attempt to kill the king. I'd like to know when we can expect the next attack, and what we can do to attain more intelligence."

Vard cleared his throat. "I fear our network of spies is compromised, Captain. This mission was undertaken with the greatest of secrecy, or so we thought. I believe there has been a leak in Wildecoast or in Brightcastle amongst those closest to the throne or in our intelligence system. Perhaps a new player has entered the field." He turned to the king. "Your Majesty, I think we should be alert to any unusual interest and movements amongst those we can supposedly trust. We need to play our cards close to our chests, only allowing those beyond reproach to be privy to our plans. If those plans are again exposed, it will be easier to judge who to suspect."

The king nodded. "A good strategy, Anton, but the captain is correct. In the meantime, we need to know when the major attack, or indeed the next attack, will occur. We are weakened. I can't help but think Faenwelar will move soon."

"I think it's time to speak with High Prince Kain Arenil," Vard said, knowing the declaration would be controversial. "We need his help and the help of his elven people. We need to gather all who would side with us, and wipe out Faenwelar once and for all."

"I'd rather not depend on a man who has lied to me in the past," Beniel said.

"My Liege," Vard said, "it's not his fault that he was born half elven. He was lied to for thirty years and would never have wanted to leave his adopted people. Not only that, but his half-sister, Gwaethe Arenil, is committed to peace between elves and man; even more so now that she has married Jacques Vorasava. Let's at least talk with the *Lenweri* leader and see what he has to say."

"Formosa will never agree," King Beniel said. "He hates all elves. I can only see trouble ahead if we accept Kain Arenil as an ally. He will never work with the man."

Then perhaps you need a new leader of the army!

Vard calmed himself to continue. "As to that, I fear you're right, Your Majesty. We need a general who has an open mind and a sharp wit for strategy. It may pay to think on that while I travel to Selinore to speak with Arenil."

The king's sharp eye snapped to Vard, and he feared he had said too much. However, he held the gaze of the king and eventually the monarch nodded. "Your words hold merit, Anton. I only wish I could speak with Arenil myself, but I fear this body is not yet sufficiently recovered. I shall stay here until you return. If only we had someone of the caliber of Kain Jazara to lead our army. Admiral Cosara will help keep the general on track, it is to be hoped."

Vard nodded, his mind working furiously. He couldn't take on the task, and the only person who sprang to mind was Sam. However, the nobles wouldn't be in favor of an ex-pirate leading the army, *and* the man had previous links with the *Sis Lenweri,* having used the elves for his pirate crews in the past. He discarded the notion, knowing Sam wasn't experienced enough for the position, even if his pedigree was more suitable.

His eye fell upon Estevot. Perhaps he could make Estevot second-in-command, and bring the Brightcastle and Wildecoast armies closer than they had been in the recent past. Or Nikolas Cosara could work closely with Formosa. He had the strength of character necessary to steer the general in the right direction.

"Your Majesty," Vard said, "I respectfully suggest you return to your chamber to rest. I'll organize support for the mission to Selinore and check on the injured. Lord Zorba has graciously offered a monument for the fallen, to be placed in the Queen's square. The Statue of Izebel will be removed to another location, and a new one of yourself erected to remember the fallen who died defending your life."

King Beniel stood, chin raised and chest puffed out. "It seems you have thought of everything, Lord Anton. I am pleased with the idea of the monument. It will be a fitting reminder of the sacrifice of Brightcastle and Wildecoast citizens alike."

The king held out his hand, and Vard bowed to kiss his ring. The other men farewelled their monarch similarly, and Vard helped King Beniel to the door where a footman would guide him to his rooms. When he returned to the others, they were speaking in hushed tones. Estevot turned to him.

"Lord Anton, I sense you're withholding information from us. Are you able to add anything to our discussion?"

His accusation startled Vard. True, he was hiding all sorts of information, but nothing he particularly wanted to impart to these men. Zorba he didn't trust and Estevot he didn't know well enough. But he must give them something.

He drew a deep breath. "The last two incidents involving the dark elves—the escape of Gorin and the attack on the king—I feel we are missing critical information. We still haven't been able to detect how Gorin escaped. It happened while I was away from the city, which was likely a strategic move by Faenwelar. The bars of his tower cell were pulled outward, straight through the stone of the walls."

Estevot sucked in a breath. "Could it have been explosive powder that was used?"

"I spoke to an alchemist who advised there would've been distinctive signs of an explosion, such as blackened stone, plus a loud noise. Nothing suggests an explosion." Vard walked across the room to give himself time to consider his other words.

"And the second incident?" Zorba asked, hands on hips.

"I had rangers stationed around the camp on the night of the attack. I had personally scouted most of the day. The elves are sneaky, but one of us should have seen signs of such a large group. I fear they had help that enabled them to approach us without raising an alarm."

"Magic? Perhaps tunnels?" Zorba asked, his brow furrowed. At least he was actively trying to help. Vard had expected not to be taken seriously by the man.

"Perhaps," he said, "or another device we have yet to think of. The elves have magic of their own that only they understand. That's another reason a trip to Selinore is vital."

CHAPTER 22

ALECIA rode at the head of her escort provided by Gwaethe and Jacques for her safe return to Brightcastle. She ground her teeth at the need for so many men and elves. The band was two hundred strong, answerable to Ruven Magbalar and one of Jacques's lieutenants, a man called Caspian. She suspected this was Gwaethe's punishment for Ruven's impoliteness to her that night at dinner. He'd not said two words to her since they left three days ago. A stiff bow or nod was all she could raise from the elf, who was supposedly loyal only to Gwaethe Arenil.

Alecia couldn't help but be suspicious in light of his recent *Sis Lenweri* affiliation. He *said* he had sworn to Gwaethe, that Faenwelar had imprisoned him and treated him worse than a dog. Gwaethe trusted Ruven, yet it was clear he didn't trust Alecia.

Couldn't someone who had fought for both sides easily change their loyalty as needed? How could they be sure this elf wasn't a *Sis Lenweri* spy? The elves were as slippery as eels and cunning as foxes. She had asked Lin and Kenna to monitor Ruven's movements.

More importantly, what Alecia had assumed was an escort part of the way to Brightcastle had evolved into her personal guard. They had been ordered to remain in Brightcastle under her direction. She should be glad. The Goddess only knew she needed a force of her own. But she wanted to be the one to inspire their loyalty. She didn't want anyone in her force because they had been ordered there, especially someone who harbored hostility toward her.

And if Ruven didn't respect her, then how could the elven soldiers under his command hold her in esteem? This wasn't working out how she had planned at all.

Lin rode up.

"What are you doing up here?" Alecia hissed. "Where is Ruven?"

"Calm yourself, Princess. Arelle has taken over from me. She has struck up a friendship of sorts with the elven commander. Thank the Goddess! It at least means I can have a break from him."

"You don't have to ride alongside him!" Alecia said. "Just keep him in your sights."

"But he was giving me strange looks. I swear he knows what we're doing."

Alecia blew a breath through her teeth. "I don't trust him! Damn Gwaethe for sending the only elven leader I can't abide."

"How many elves have you met?" Lin asked, smirking.

"You know very well I've met few. Stop being so sensible."

"I thought that was what you liked about me?"

"Horses approaching!" One of the forward scouts trotted back to them and saluted Lieutenant Caspian. "Looks like kingdom men, Sir."

Alecia took a deep breath to steady her heart. She didn't want more nasty surprises. Perhaps Ramón had sent his own escort. The timing would fit.

She kicked Silver forward. "Let us pick up the pace and see who it is." She urged her mount into a canter, and Lin came with her hand on her short sword.

"Princess, fall back," Lin said, her words just carrying to Alecia. "You're doing it again. There could be danger ahead."

Alecia reined in. When would she learn? "Lieutenant. Could you detail an advance party to intercept whoever it is approaching?"

The man bowed from his saddle. "Yes, Princess." He efficiently detailed twenty elves and men, and sent them south.

"Much better," Lin muttered. "You're learning."

"I know I can't do everything myself. It just grates that I have to consider all this so much more than if I was a man!"

"When you're queen, you can change some things, slowly," Lin whispered. "In the meantime, be patient and don't ruffle too many feathers."

"I knew I was wise to choose you as my second." Alecia cast her attention to those ahead. "I wonder who's approaching."

* * *

Vard shrugged off the itch between his shoulders. He had flown above those heading south from Amitania, and Alecia was present. Knowing she was safe had settled the fear he had harbored ever since learning of her escapade. The promise of her company caused the discomforting itch. He no longer had any way of anticipating her actions, except that her first words would likely be full of concern for Iona's wellbeing.

Their daughter was thriving. He had spent a few hours with her before departing. She appeared to know him. He may be deluding himself, but he had felt an answering awareness within her, an intelligence, a knowing in her gaze. He huffed out a breath, frustrated with his neediness. It seemed when you had more to lose, you *needed more*. And he required more than occasional visits with his daughter; more than sporadic and formal contact with Alecia.

He tried to distract himself by watching the country through which they rode. Their force was large, and he had rangers and scouts out in all directions. But what he wouldn't give for some elven help. Or perhaps another Defender. His thoughts turned to his father and the other man he had sent to Melandrach. They should be fully come into their gifts by now. Joy filled his heart at the thought of reuniting with his father.

"Vard!" Sam called from up ahead. He approached, his cream stallion prancing and snorting. Vard admired the beast. A part of him longed for a more worthy steed, but only a small part. Horses that would tolerate the wolf in him were few and Trax, despite his odd black and white patches, was yet to let him down.

"What news?"

"They've sent an advance party to make contact. Our scouts advise Princess Alecia and a large contingent of men and elves are coming this way. Shall we make camp and await their arrival?"

Vard shook his head. "I need to reach Selinore as soon as I can. Every minute could be vital. We continue. How long until we rendezvous?"

"Less than an hour." Sam wheeled his horse about and cantered forward to give the orders while Vard raised his arm and his command picked up the pace. As far as he was concerned, the sooner they met Alecia the better.

* * *

Alecia knew it was Vard before she could make out the man's features. He had always had a commanding presence, and now he had come fully into his gift, he was impossible to ignore. Men deferred to him, and women wanted him.

She took a moment to wonder how Vard was coping with Queen Adriana. He had drawn her since their first meeting. The fact that Vard and she shared a child wouldn't make him safe from Adriana. She was used to taking whatever she wanted.

Lin joined her. "Why have you stopped?"

It was only then that Alecia realized the sight of Vard had stopped her in her tracks. The rest of the group continued past, except for those detailed with her immediate protection. She could feel her face heating, but she wouldn't tell Lin her mind had been on Vard. Besides, she would work it out soon enough.

"I respectfully suggest you keep up, Your Highness," Lin said, in her court voice. She was culturing an elegant accent in order to present herself as a noble.

Alecia smiled. "Of course." She heeled Silver forward, eager to see Vard, but with a pit of squirming vipers in her stomach. She sighed. When would life ever settle into the simple pattern she longed for? Perhaps never if she succeeded in her goals. And would Vard be part of it?

She practiced deep breathing to control her nerves, and was pleased with the timbre of her voice when confronted with Vard.

"Lord Anton," she said. "Well met. I assume you've come from Brightcastle. How is Iona?"

He bowed from the saddle. "Iona is the picture of health, Your Highness. She becomes more delightful by the day. I bring mixed news, however."

"Perhaps we should dismount and speak somewhere with more privacy."

"Just what I was going to suggest." He dismounted and helped her down from Silver. They led their horses to a stand of trees. Vard paused, gazing into the forest on all sides. Finally, he turned to her.

"I detect no eavesdroppers."

She drew a deep breath and met his gaze. It would be all too easy to fall into those green orbs and be lost amongst the swirling golden glitter. She shook her head clear.

"What news? Is Iona really well?"

He gripped her hands. "Our daughter is perfect, Alecia. I spent time with her and can only say she is special; you and me in equal parts."

She released a trapped breath and fully relaxed. "Then what's the mixed news?"

"The king has fallen ill… his heart, we believe. We left immediately for Brightcastle to seek the help of Monive and Princess Benae. They met us just east of Brightcastle and stabilized King Beniel, but the *Sis Lenweri* attacked us that evening."

"The king? Benae?" Alecia found the thought of anything happening to Benae scared her more than she thought it would.

"They survived. Though the princess was deeply distressed by the event, she was able to help the injured. But we lost thirty men and women we can ill afford." He lowered his voice. "Night hounds aided us, otherwise we might all have perished. The elves ambushed us despite numerous guards and sentries being posted. I scouted the surrounds myself only an hour before the attack and detected no threat."

"What are you saying?"

"That there's a way the elves are covering their presence. Prince Gorin's escape was similar. There are questions we can't answer. I don't like not knowing."

"Some new magic?"

"I hate to say it, but it's possible. I travel to Selinore to speak with Kain Arenil. And I hope to see Melandrach too. And my father."

His words stopped her heart. "Your father? He's alive?"

Vard smiled. "Alive, and a Defender. He's studying under Melandrach and should be whole by now. I can't wait to see him again."

"Vard," she breathed, wrapping her arms around him. He stiffened, then drew her against his body. It felt wonderful to be in his embrace again. She wanted to stay there. Forever. "I'm so happy for you."

"One day I'll tell you about it. But today I need to proceed to Selinore."

"I'm going with you."

He set her at a distance and dropped his hands from her body. "That's not wise. It's not safe, and you must return to Iona."

"You said Iona was well, so I assume she's coping without me. Is that not true?"

Vard huffed. "Surely you don't wish to be apart from our daughter any longer than necessary? I'll handle this. It's my duty."

Anger stabbed at Alecia, but she kept a tight rein on it. "Of course, I want to see Iona, but I also have a duty to the kingdom."

A voice in the back of her mind suggested she had an ulterior motive for wanting to accompany Vard. She pushed the voice away and met his gaze. "I have my own security force. You won't even know I'm with you."

"Alecia!" Vard's jaw tensed and relaxed as his eyes bored into her. "You can't bring your entire force to Selinore. This mission is covert, meaning I'm taking the minimum people necessary. I can't guarantee your safety with the manpower I have."

"Allow me to take two of my female guards. They're competent, Vard. Please."

His forehead wrinkled, and he stepped closer, lowering his voice. "What's this really about? Do you still hold the desire to rule as queen in your own right? Is that what the trip to Amitania was about? And your request to journey to Selinore?"

She drew a deep breath. "You must keep this secret… promise."

"I work for the king. Before I promise anything, I must know. Are you plotting his downfall?"

"No! Of course not! I fully support my uncle. I have only ever strived to be named his heir. When he dies, I intend to replace him… I just don't know how I shall achieve it yet."

Vard placed his hands on her upper arms and squeezed gently. "I'm relieved to hear that. You have the good of Thorius at heart and would make a wonderful ruler. But I don't think it can happen, not now, perhaps never."

"Once there were queens who ruled. Look at my aunt. Tell me she doesn't rule in all but name. Well, I don't wish to be that sort of queen." She laid her palm on his cheek. "Vard, I know I can be the ruler Thorius needs. We can't have the situation where the king dies, and a babe is monarch. Ramón and Benae would have too much power. I'm the logical choice."

"A pity the king doesn't agree," Vard said. "I'll keep your secrets, and I truly wish you could be heir. But, Alecia, I think this road you've chosen can only lead to sorrow."

"That's my choice, isn't it? Those elves and men I ride with are under my control. Jacques and Princess Gwaethe have sent them as an escort, but they are to stay in Brightcastle. Ramón and Benae will be told their purpose is to reinforce Brightcastle's army, but they're mine. I'm building my force and have people loyal to me. If the king dies, I'll be ready to step into his shoes."

Vard drew himself up. "This is a dangerous game you play. They could proclaim you a traitor."

"I'll never declare while my uncle is alive. But I won't have Ramón and Benae rule this kingdom. And I *am* going to Selinore."

Vard sighed. "As you wish. We travel light. You may bring two of your lady guards and perhaps two elves would be helpful."

"So, now I can be of help?"

He cocked an eyebrow at her and motioned for them to return to the others.

Alecia headed straight for Lin. "I want you to choose one other to accompany me to Selinore."

"What?" Lin jumped down from her horse. "You can't go haring off on a wild goose chase to speak to Kain Arenil." She folded her arms and stood glaring at Alecia, her finger tapping on her elbow and foot doing the same. "I wish you'd consult me on these decisions."

"Just choose wisely. We travel lightly and leave as soon as we are ready." Alecia turned her back on her second and strode to Silver. She checked her gear and added extra warm clothes to her packs, mindful the mountains could be cool in autumn. The rest she would send to Brightcastle.

Then she went in search of Ruven. She found him leaning against a tree, speaking with another elf. He excused himself and bowed to her.

"How can I help, Princess Alecia?"

"There's been a change of plans. I'll travel to Selinore with Lord Anton and a small party. He has asked that I take two elven soldiers. I wish you to choose the two."

He showed no surprise. It was so damned hard to read these people. But she would learn… she must if she was to be the ruler she knew she could be.

Ruven considered for a moment and then spoke. "*I* will go with you and take one of the best trackers. Please excuse me." He bowed and turned to go.

"Ruven," Alecia called.

He turned back to her. "Yes, Princess."

"Why have you offered to go with me when it's clear you don't like me?"

"My feelings have nothing to do with my choice." His dark eyes held no emotion. "I have been charged with your safety and will stay with you until we reach Brightcastle." He bowed again and left her.

Somewhat satisfied with his answer, but not convinced the elven leader didn't have an agenda of his own, Alecia returned to Silver. She found Lin, who had chosen Arelle to accompany them. She smiled and nodded to Lin. It was a good choice. Arelle's fighting skills were impressive and continued to improve daily. Lin could help with the scouting, as would Ruven's comrade.

When all was in place, she said goodbye to her lieutenant, with instructions to return with all haste to Brightcastle and give her apologies to Lord Zorba and Princess Benae. Ramón would be furious with her, but he had no right. He had made himself *her* guardian, as well as Brightcastle's, and she hated it. But this wasn't about showing him that she could do as she wished. It was not!

No, it certainly wasn't. If she were to be queen, she couldn't lock herself safely in a castle and allow events to unfold around her. She must be an agent of change, and involve herself in the discussions that would mold their future. This meeting with Kain Arenil was one such negotiation, as was the one she had just undertaken with Gwaethe and Jacques.

Alecia smiled as she turned for the north with Vard. Finally, she could see how the future might change for the better.

* * *

Vard rode at the head of the group, Ruven Magbalar by his side. The elf admitted he had been one of the *Sis Lenweri* before the battle in Amitania. Gwaethe Arenil had freed him from the prison they had both been locked in. He had immediately sworn allegiance to her. It was to be hoped he would stay loyal. Vard didn't know the details of how Faenwelar of the *Sis Lenweri* had risen to power or when it had occurred. Therefore, he couldn't assess the risk.

The thought gnawed at him, just as having Alecia with him was distracting. He would have preferred it far better if she had continued on to Brightcastle. Their daughter needed her, but, he grudgingly admitted, so did the kingdom, in whatever capacity it would accept its princess. Could she succeed in her goal of leading Thorius in her own right? If she had set her heart on it, he believed she could make it happen.

But for all Vard's belief in Alecia's suitability for the throne, King Beniel also demanded his loyalty. It was the king who had bestowed upon him this lofty office. As King's Blade, he was now in a position to help the vulnerable citizens of Thorius. He'd always make his choices based on what was right for the populace. At the moment, that was a strong king. He straightened in his seat and allowed pride at his position to settle in his heart.

"What has brought that smile to your face, Lord Anton?" Magbalar asked, his shorter black elven mount prancing and shaking its head. The elf controlled the frisking with a tightening of his reins.

"If I told you, Commander, you'd think me full of pride, and that's not who I am. However, sometimes I reflect on my current circumstance and find it is rather to my liking."

The elven leader grinned. "Truly, it is pleasant to be riding through the beauty of this forest. Or is it the presence of a certain princess which has caused your pleasure?"

"Neither, though both are worthy. I'm at home in the forest and love nothing better than to smell the fresh tang of pine needles."

"I've heard you spent time with Princess Alecia during her year in exile. Is that the case?"

He didn't wish to discuss Alecia with this elf who saw more than most did. But he had to be polite all the same.

"We did. You must understand that I aided her escape from a difficult circumstance. We share many things… including a daughter."

"Children certainly bind two people. Is there a future for you and the princess? It seems to me she is making some difficult political alliances. The king may not appreciate this, and you work for him. How do you reconcile these two positions?"

Vard lowered his voice. "Alecia is King Beniel's niece and loves him. She supports his rule, I have no doubt."

"But what if the king should die? I hear his health isn't good."

"Let's not talk of this where all can hear. I want to concentrate on reaching Kain Arenil, and we can debate more there."

Ruven nodded and fell silent. When Vard looked behind, he saw Alecia frowning at him. He cast her a smile, which made her scowl even more. He turned to his companion.

"Tell me, Ruven, what elven magic does Faenwelar have at his disposal? Some of us wonder if he employed sorcery in the recent ambush and in Gorin's rescue. Do you have any ideas?"

"As to magic, only certain elves have access to it, and, sadly, I am not one. Best you ask Princess Gwaethe or one of the mages. It is possible, though."

Vard fell to explaining his theory in more detail as they passed through the thick forest south of the Usetar Mountain range.

* * *

Alecia glared at Vard's back. What was he discussing with Ruven? It made her itch to think of him striking up a friendship with the elf.

"Princess," Lin hissed, "if you don't smooth your frown lines, you'll soon look like an old hag. What's the matter?"

Alecia drew a breath and turned to her second. "I'd love to know what they discuss. I don't trust Ruven to show me in a favorable light. He doesn't respect me." She glared at the elven leader. "The feeling is mutual."

"It doesn't matter. Vard knows you and isn't likely to be swayed by a stranger. Besides, didn't you say he wasn't willing to support your campaign to become queen?"

"He won't while the king is alive, which is not an issue, as I would never want to upset the throne with Uncle Beniel on it. He's a good king, even if he doesn't support me and hates magic."

"Hush, Princess! You can't talk of magic like that! Any changes along those lines must occur over time. There are too many people who are afraid of what they don't understand. And I'm not sure they're wrong."

Alecia guided Silver closer to Lin's mount and lowered her voice. "We must stop outlawing it! It will only hold us back if we don't embrace it, especially healing magic. Think of the good it could do!"

"I find it odd that you would embrace it so fully, coming from the ruling class as you do. You do realize a powerful sorcerer could usurp your position with ease? Or do you have gifts you aren't telling us about?"

"I have no magic, or only the slightest gift of prophecy, which is useless in its current state. But I have friends who have gifts. I wouldn't be here if it weren't for their help. I won't stand by and have them persecuted for something they can't control."

"Just hasten slowly on the magic thing," Lin said. "Keep it quiet. Believe me, your support of the magical arts won't help you win the hearts of the people; not right now, anyway. First, we must defeat the *Sis Lenweri,* then we must ensure the stability of the kingdom. Nothing else will win you favor."

Alecia drew a deep breath and blew it out her nose, causing Silver to snort too. "I know your counsel is sound, but it doesn't feel right to hide things."

"Keep your cards close to your chest, Alecia. It's the only way you'll win."

Alecia disliked defying her natural urges. She wasn't patient, never had been. Was Lin correct? Must she hide so much of her true nature that she became just another princess, no different from the rest?

She watched Vard. He listened to Ruven and laughed. He had changed. She didn't remember him ever laughing in that light-hearted way. It seemed she wasn't the only one experiencing something new. Had he *ever* laughed like that with her?

"That man of yours is certainly something," Lin murmured beside her.

Alecia pulled her gaze from Vard and glared at her friend. "Eyes off.! I'm a jealous woman and don't like to share."

Lin's brows shot up. "If you decide you have no future, the man must move on with someone, surely."

She shook her head. "I can't even contemplate that. In my heart, I know that Vard and I will be together someday. I must trust it will be sooner rather than later."

Lin turned her gaze to Vard, and a predatory light entered her eyes. "Don't wait too long, Alecia. I won't step across your boundary, but others will."

Later that day, when they had finished dinner and Alecia sat with Lin and Arelle, a shiver rolled down her spine. She knew Vard approached long before her ladies fell silent.

"Ladies," he said, bowing. "Please excuse my intrusion." Alecia looked up into his sparkling green gaze. It seemed he only had eyes for her. "Can I have a word with you, Princess?"

Lin and Arelle stood and curtsied before hurrying off.

She cleared her throat and stood. "You have them well trained."

"I would say it's you who have them trained, Alecia."

Her name on his lips sent shivers up her spine. It was too long since she had known his love. She longed to have his hands on her body once again. But was it wise? Didn't she need to keep Vard at a distance?

She strived for cool and collected. "What did you wish to speak about?"

"Can we take a walk? You'll be safe, I promise."

Her skin tingled all over, and she swore it was a kind of magic cast by him. She drew a deep breath. *Pull yourself together, you ninny!*

He led the way along a game trail, grasping her hand to help her in the darkness. Above, in the trees, an owl hooted. A crescent moon glinted through the branches. The forest was hushed, and soon the voices of their comrades died away. Vard found a small clearing and threw his cloak over a log, then pulled her down beside him.

"I needed time alone with you," he said, his breath hot on her cheek. "Even if we just sit and listen to the night, that will be enough for me."

"Much water has passed under the bridge," she said. "I'm confused about what part you can play in my life."

"Like I said, I'm content to just sit, Alecia."

They did so for a time, Alecia slowing her breathing to Vard's. It calmed her more than she would've imagined. "I've missed you."

He sighed. "And I you. Now that I'm no longer a threat to you and Iona, life has complicated things."

"You're a Defender in the true sense of the word. Uncle Beniel has recognized you. I take pleasure in your success. You suffered for so long and now you seem almost happy."

His eyes glinted in the moonlight. He gripped her hand, then raised it to his lips. "I am, Alecia, more than I've ever been. Still, there's one thing I need." The way he said the word thrilled her to the core.

"You and Iona will complete me, and I must have you in my life." He turned her hand over and kissed the palm. "I've taken no woman since we parted. You've ruined me for all others."

Alecia caught her breath. She wanted him so much it hurt. She was drawn to him, to his heat, and his lips. He slid his other hand up to cup her skull and tilted her head, his gaze falling to her mouth.

"I love you," he said, and his lips crashed into hers, sending her thoughts into a spiral and her fists into his hair. She growled as his whiskers rubbed deliciously against her cheeks. They were soft, and she longed to feel them elsewhere as he loved her.

Emboldened by the dark, she pulled his shirt from his breeches and reached for the hard muscles of his abdomen, her fingers tracing the hills and valleys. She ran her hands up to tweak his nipples, and he gasped, his fingers cupping her breasts through her tunic. Her nipples peaked, and she pushed them into his palms. Her hands wandered to the ties of his breeches. She was wet, so wet, and all she could think of was Vard inside her. Damn the consequences! If a baby resulted, they'd welcome it. For the first time, she cursed her breeches. A dress would be much more accessible.

Vard's breath came hard and fast as he paused, his forehead on hers. "Are you sure this is what you want, love?"

"What? Yes!" She couldn't believe what he was asking. It took her back to that day in her room before her betrothal ball. The time they had almost made love, and he had called a halt at the last moment. Alecia had begged, but he had held firm. He'd been thinking of her honor. Well, her honor was long gone!

"I need you, Vard," she breathed, her lips finding his. She opened her mouth fully to him, and he plundered her. Caught up in a maelstrom, Alecia lost awareness of anything but this man she had chosen, the father of her daughter, her savior.

He pulled her to her feet and dragged his cloak from the log, laying it down in the clearing. Then he lifted her into his arms and gently placed her on the cloak. His movements might have been gentle, but he vibrated with a fine tension, and his breath came in ragged gasps.

Once again, his mouth claimed hers, his hands roving across her breasts and down the length of her thigh. His hand cupped her sex, and her hips bounced against him. She groaned, frustrated at the clothing that kept their skins apart. It had to end!

Alecia climbed to her knees and removed her clothes, delighting in Vard's ragged gasping breath, the intensity of his gaze as it followed her every move. When she had done with her garments, she removed his, kissing him lingeringly after she tossed aside each item. When they were both naked, she reclined before him, legs spread, weight on her palms, knees bent.

"Goddess, you're beautiful," he whispered, taking a long moment to drink in each line of her form. Despite the dark, she knew he had the vision to appreciate everything she offered. She gloried in the power she held over this potent man. That she could command his love and respect was one of the greatest joys in her life.

Vard crawled toward her and stopped, bending to lap her sex with his tongue. She thought she'd die of longing and was soon on the edge of her climax. He stopped, and she cried out, only half conscious, every thought driven by the animal need to mate. With one last sweep of his tongue, her belly clenched, and she came hard, a shudder wracking her body.

She clutched Vard's shoulders, and he thrust inside her, his rod triggering a second wave of pleasure.

He moved above her, thrusting deep then withdrawing before thrusting hard again. Alecia pushed back, lifting her hips and begging for more. Vard gave it to her, his hands on her hips, his teeth nipping her neck. Desire roared through Alecia, beyond her control. It had her in its grip and she could do nothing but submit.

"Come with me, love," he groaned.

Her orgasm crested, crashing down on her and sweeping her into oblivion. She was barely conscious of Vard as he reached his own climax.

Soon, their heavy breaths were all that could be heard in the clearing. She should've been cool, but the rapture was all-consuming. Her mind wouldn't register such basic feelings as temperature when she had so recently been transported to another plane entirely.

Alecia pushed herself up on her elbows and looked at Vard, who had rolled to the side of her. She wondered if he had felt it as intensely as she. It was too dark to read his expression. He reached for her and kissed her with great tenderness, his palm resting along her jaw.

"I'm yours, completely and utterly, Alecia. If you ever doubted, let this night put your fears to rest."

She was still without speech. Words could never express what she had just experienced.

At her silence, Vard turned her face to gaze into her eyes. "I need to know you too felt the intensity, my love."

She smiled. "I did. It was more than I could've imagined; more than we have ever had together. But I don't understand."

"What don't you understand?"

"Why now? Why does the Goddess choose this moment to give us this gift? Is it a sign that we should heed? Or did we merely get carried away after so long without?"

He frowned. "I'm yours and you're mine. Our bodies have long known it. Perhaps our hearts and minds are finally catching up?"

She laughed. "Or perhaps your Defender powers bind us. Whatever it is, I don't want it to end."

He drew her to him, kissed her soundly, and showed her how deep his love ran.

THE END

Glossary

Places

Kingdom of Thorius - (Thor – ee – us) the kingdom of men which encompasses the King's seat of Wildecoast and the Prince's seat of Brightcastle, along with many smaller towns

Wildecoast - (Will – dee – coast) city perched on the top of a cliff overlooking the sea on the east coast of Thorius; climate is mild but windy

Brightcastle - large inland town surrounded by forests and farms, three to four days ride west of Wildecoast

Amitania - (Am – it – ay – nia) or *Elvandang* (Elle – van – dang) in elvish- the deserted city north of the Usetar Mountain Range in northern Thorius; once a thriving city and now home to elves and humans under the leadership of Princess Gwaethe Arenil and Earl Jacques Vorasava

Usetar Range - (You – set – ar) the mountain range running across the northern parts of Thorius

Selinore - the forest home of the peaceful *Lenweri*, in the mountains north of Brightcastle

People

Lenweri - the elven people who are tall and elegant with black skin and pointed ears; live in mountainous forests north and west of Thorius, in places encroaching onto Kingdom lands; also known as dark elves; they welcome males and females in their fighting force

Sis Lenweri - the faction of dark elves that wishes to take the kingdom of Thorius back from men; only males are welcome in their fighting force

Defender - a race of shapeshifters who are created to defend those in danger; they sense those in need of their help; a Defender can shift into animal form and the ability is inherited through family lines; when they shift back into human form, they retain their clothes from before the shift; their gifts may include the ability to compel others to do their will

Guardian – a person or people appointed by the king to oversee a part of Thorius

Ranger – an elite force trained to fight and track to the highest proficiency; may include females

Characters

Princess Alecia Zialni (Ah-lee-sha Zee – al – nee) - the King's niece and daughter of Prince Jiseve Zialni who once ruled in Brightcastle and was next in line to the throne. Alecia's story began in **Princess Avenger** and continued in **Princess in Exile**.

Vard Anton - the love of Princess Alecia's life and a shapeshifting Defender; once army captain of Brightcastle in **Princess Avenger** and his story continued in **Princess in Exile**.

Iona Izebel Zialni (Eye-own-ah Is – zee – belle Zee – al – nee) – Alecia and Vard's daughter, born while Alecia was in exile; she has inherited her father's Defender gifts; she is five months old when The People's Princess begins.

Benae (Ben-nay) Zorba - Princess of Brightcastle and joint Guardian with her husband Ramón Zorba; she was once married to Prince Jiseve Zialni (now deceased) and has given birth to his child; Benae can heal with her mind and has a close relationship with her stallion, Flaire. Benae's story was told in **The Lady's Choice.**

Ramón Zorba - Lord of Wildecoast and once squire to Prince Jiseve Zialni; now joint Guardian of Brightcastle with his wife Benae; brother to Lady Alique Zorba. Ramón's story was told in **The Lady's Choice.**

Solomon Daire Zialni – son of Benae Zorba and Prince Jiseve Zialni (now deceased); an infant of three months when The People's Princess begins

Hetty – mysterious ancient woman with magical powers; once Alecia's governess and nanny; declared a witch by Prince Jiseve and sentenced to death but rescued by Alecia

King Beniel Zialni (Ben – ee – elle Zee – al – nee) - King of Thorius; lives in Wildecoast; older brother of Jiseve Zialni and uncle of Alecia Zialni; married to Adriana

Queen Adriana Zialni - wife of the King; lives in Wildecoast; Alecia's aunt

Piotr Zialni (Peter Zialni) – son of Beniel and Jiseve Zialni's younger brother; next in line to the throne of Thorius (his father is dead) after Solomon, unless King Beniel or Alecia have a son.

Izebel (Is – zee – belle) – a previous warrior Queen of Thorius from centuries ago, when females could rule; Alecia's idol; her daughter Daphini was the last queen of Thorius.

Gwaethe (Gway-eth-a) *Arenil - Lenweri* princess, daughter of King Orionkael Arenil, who was murdered by High Prince Faenwelar of the *Sis Lenweri*. She has a golden stallion with silver mane and tail called *Rassar* which means Sunbeam; her love story was told in **Elf Princess Warrior**

Jacques Vorasava - Captain in the Brightcastle army. Jacques is tall with dark hair, beard and moustache; he has an olive complexion; he is married to Gwaethe Arenil and is now an Earl, and their story was told in **Elf Princess Warrior**

Doctor Damald Monive – chief physician in Brightcastle Keep; presided over the inquiry into Alecia's father's sudden death when he was married to Benae

Millie – Alecia's maid who also helps out with Iona's care.

Melandrach (Mel-on-drac) Arenil - brother to King Orionkael and uncle to Gwaethe and Isiloe; a hermit who lives in isolation in the remote mountains above Selinore; he is also a Defender and becomes Vard's mentor

Lyam Anton (Lie-am) – Vard's father who has been missing for over fifteen years; he is now a Defender and can shift into hawk or bear

Katrine Aranati (Kat-reen Ar- an- arti) – sorceress and younger daughter of an impoverished farming estate south of Wildecoast; older sister is Esta Aranati; once a smuggler called Lady Star; heroine of **The Master and the Sorceress;** now mistress of the night hounds

James Tomel (James Tom-elle)– master jeweler and oldest son of a farming family; lives in Costa; hero of **The Master and the Sorceress;** spy master for King Beniel

Esta Aranati- Katrine Aranati's older sister; she is head of the Aranati estate and was once a smuggler known as Lady Moonlight; heroine of **The Lady and the Pirate;** married to Samael Delacost.

Samael Delacost - once a pirate, was captured by Nikolas Cosara, admiral of the King's Navy and is now sworn to obey the admiral or spend the rest of his life in prison; hero of **The Lady and the Pirate** and now married to Esta Aranati.

Merielle – mermaid who has become human; she has vibrant red hair and is not familiar with the ways of Thorian people; heroine of **The Lord and the Mermaid**; good friend of Esta Aranati.

Lord Nikolas Cosara (Nikolas Cos-arra) – Admiral in the King's Navy; he is cousin to Queen Adriana and the hero of **The Lord and the Mermaid;** he is married to Merielle

Alique (Ah-leek) Jazara nee Zorba - beautiful blonde healer, married to Kain and brother to Ramón; cousin to General Josef Formosa. Her story was told in **The Elf King's Lady**

Kain Jazara – once general of the Thorian army, he has discovered his father was Orionkael Arenil (past elven king); he has taken up leadership of the peaceful *Lenweri*; he is married to Alique Jazara and is hero of **The Elf King's Lady**; half-brother to Gwaethe Arenil; son of Orionkael Arenil, the murdered elven king; has a black horse called Snow

Josef Formosa – promoted to general of the Wildecoast army after Kain Jazara was forced to resign; he is cousin to Ramon and Alique Zorba.

Alecia Zialni's lady guards –

Linnet Perfore – Alecia's second-in-command; talented scout; tall redhead; gray eyes

Cretia – the planner of the group; blonde with baby blue eyes

Arelle – the peacekeeper; inspired by Alecia to learn weapons; black hair, blue eyes

Kenna – scout and fierce warrior; hyperactive; brown hair and eyes

Jules Estevot (Jewels Ess-tee-vow) – captain of the army in Brightcastle; has blond hair and ice-blue eyes.

Reid Vetta (Reed Vet-tah) – Master goldsmith in Wildecoast and Esta's betrothed for a short time

Doctor Achan Mosard – Physician to the king in Wildecoast

Master Dunnet – Vard's man servant

Elora Arenil (Elle-Aura Arenil) – King Orionkael's widow and Gwaethe's mother.

Isiloe (Iz-il-oe) - Gwaethe's cousin by Orionkael's sister- unlike most of her race, Isiloe is short with white hair and pale blue eyes. She is a captain (*Ramar*) in the elven army

Chandrelle (Shan-drel) – Isiloe's sister; tall, dark elven woman with long dark hair; warrior

Exmund - Jacques's aide and corporal in the Brightcastle army; youngest brother of James Tomel, hero of **The Master and the Sorceress**.

Elvor Faenwelar - High Prince of the *Sis Lenweri*; enemy of Gwaethe and the humans

Niel Gorin Faenwelar - of the *Sis Lenweri*; Elvor's son

Rasalar (Raz-a-lar) - Isiloe's mother- is sister to Orionkael and Melandrach- once a soldier and still trains recruits

Sergeant Dodlan - second in command to Jacques in his trek north and remains with him in Amitania

Master Jenkin - Brightcastle weapons master

Tyra - Benae's maid - stocky, blonde; helps with healing

Julli (Ju-lee) - Alique's maid; gifted helper and healer; not a great horsewoman; gentle and caring

Alia Kelsis - the elven woman who leads the female *Sis Lenweri* in Selinore

Ruven Magbalar - Sis Lenweri soldier rescued by Gwaethe and became a loyal supporter; he is now elven army commander in Amitania

Théoden Leovaris - Sis Lenweri soldier rescued by Gwaethe and became a loyal supporter

Night hounds - beasts the size of a wolf, with short grey, black or red hair, heavy snout, and stumpy ears; the eyes are red; there are six toes on each paw and the back feet have retractable cat-like claws, huge and razor sharp; have not been seen in Thorius for at least fifty years.

ABOUT THE AUTHOR

Bernadette Rowley is a lover of epic fantasy who is a veterinarian by day and an author by night. She is currently published in the genre of high fantasy romance with nine books and a box collection, all set in her fantasy world of Thorius.

When she was a young teenager, an aunt gave her a copy of The Sword of Shannara by Terry Brooks and Bernadette has lived in various fantasy worlds ever since. The author who has influenced her writing most is Robert Jordan (Wheel of Time series). It's no surprise that her chosen genre when writing romance is fantasy.

"I can see these settings so vibrantly in my mind and hope my readers can too."

But Bernadette has no desire to spoon-feed her readers by laboriously describing her fantasy settings. She would rather the reader use their own imagination.

Along with sword and sorcery, dashing heroes and stunning heroines, this author includes strong healing themes in many of her books- an element which is central to her everyday job.

"When I started writing the Queenmakers Saga, I never imagined my day job would force its way into my stories as it has."

And of course, there are animals, especially Bernadette's beloved horses.

Bernadette lives in Southeast Queensland, Australia, where she enjoys a great coffee, walks in nature and catching up family and friends.

Connect with the Author

Website: www.bernadetterowley.com
Subscribe to the Bernadette Rowley newsletter and
get a free map of the world of Thorius

Facebook: www.facebook.com/bernadetterowleyfantasy
Twitter: www.twitter.com/bt_rowley

www.ingramcontent.com/pod-product-compliance
Lightning Source LLC
Chambersburg PA
CBHW070116120726
47909CB00002B/621